Driven By Conscience

RACHEL GOSS

Driven by Conscience is a work of fiction. All characters, with the exception of some well-known historical figures, are imaginary and not to be construed as real. I wrote the story using real locations and historical events, interweaving fictional characters and plot because I thought it would be a good way to immerse myself into another world. The depiction of the story setting is homage to my hometown, but the incidents occurring there are not factual. Although I quoted from Werner Heisenberg's works and utilized historical documents relating to his life, his role in the development of the atomic bomb and of his arrest at the end of World War II in the story, his depiction is a product of my imagination. Likewise, the portrayals of Douglas MacArthur, Dwight Eisenhower and Robert Oppenheimer are fictional. Uwe Johannes and his adventures are made up, but the POW camps were real. During World War II, Camp Robinson became one of 700 prisoner of war camps operating throughout the United States. By 1945, Arkansas housed about 23,000 German and Italian prisoners. Four thousand German soldiers were at Camp Robinson. Ultimately the US held 425,000 prisoners of war.

ISBN-13: 978-0-578-47284-3

Published by Tarkus Imaging Inc.

This book is dedicated to Maysel, Wheat, Paul and Joe Goss

1 IS LOVE A ROSE?

1942. Wartime Berlin, Germany.

"Uwe, run away!" Ursula urged. "Do it today." They were standing in the foyer of their house. Ursula had slipped downstairs in the early morning to have a private word with her brother before he left for work. Ursula made no pretense at maintaining her game face. Tears rolled down her cheeks. "I am afraid," she confessed in a whisper.

Mid-way through the process of putting his papers in the bag that served as a briefcase, Uwe stopped to look at his sister. Thinking of her future made him sick. Uwe reached over and patted her shoulder. "Evade the draft?" he said. "I won't do that. It would reflect badly on you and Mother and Father. I can't be responsible for the consequences if I left now."

"Well, it's because of us that you have to go, isn't it? We've made ourselves unpopular, we've raised our heads above the hedge and attracted notice." Ursula wiped her eyes with the sleeve of her nightgown. "And you know what happens in that situation. The hedge gets trimmed. If it weren't for us, you would have gotten an exemption and continued with your research. I know it."

"Maybe it will work out for the best," he said, but his heart was not in his words. He didn't see how things could work out well for any of them. Their father refused to give up his humanitarian work, and Ursula and their mother supported him, even helped him. They would have to watch it play out.

"Why can't Heisenberg do something about it? He is the most powerful man at Kaiser Wilhelm and he likes you. He is a world famous scientist, responsible for major progress in physics, and highly respected by the military. He should be your champion."

Ursula repeated the argument from last night's family dinner conversation, although she did not expect a different answer. Everyone knew it would be difficult for a healthy young man like Uwe to avoid military service.

"Not even Heisenberg has that much influence, I'm afraid." Uwe shook his head as he buckled the clasp on his bag and slung it over his shoulder. "Cheer up," he said, hugging Ursula. "I'll be home late for dinner. Tell Mother not to wait for me."

"Just a minute," Ursula said as she selected the freshest rose from the vase on the entry room table. She thought the deep coral red was the color of the hottest part of a blazing fire.

Uwe looked at Ursula and looked at the rose and could tell why she had chosen it. It reminded him of her.

Ursula inhaled the fragrance, her favorite from all of their rose varieties, and handed it to Uwe. "For Florian," she said. "I think he would like this one."

"Do you really think this makes any difference?" Uwe asked as he took the flower.

"Please just do it, Uwe. You never know," she answered.

"For you? Anything," Uwe said. He slipped the flower inside his bag, trying not to damage it, as he went to face his day. Uwe walked a few streets away from his house to the nearby transit stop and boarded the bus. He rode as close as he could get to his work in the upscale suburb of Dahlem and then walked the rest of the way. As usual, he stopped by his favorite café for breakfast.

Sun glinted off the bakery window as Uwe looked inside, squinting against his reflection in the glass. The turnovers looked good; maybe he would go with cherry today instead of apple or apricot. But then the crème horns were always nice, and yesterday's almond strudel had been good. Maybe Frau Krueger would have a recommendation for him.

A bell rang when he opened the heavy wooden door and entered the shop. It took him only a few steps to walk from the door to the check out counter. Frau Krueger, the shop owner, wearing a baker's coat over her dress, scowled at Uwe from behind the display case of pastries.

Surprised by the hostile reception, Uwe smiled anyway. "Good morning, Frau Krueger," he said, "I would like a coffee and pastry today, please," as he pulled a ceramic cup from his bag and placed it on the counter.

Frau Krueger did not return the smile while she prepared his coffee. "You! What kind of person are you?" she hissed at Uwe when she shoved the full cup of coffee across the counter, causing the hot contents to slosh about. She smacked a plain roll, packaged to take away, on the counter top. "I hope they ship you off to the front," she told him.

Startled, Uwe was at a loss for words. He didn't know why Frau Krueger was angry. The day before he had overheard her refer to him as "The Viking" to another customer. Sometimes she even added a free sample to his order. He used to think the shop looked clean and inviting. Now the white floor and wall tiles made it feel harsh, almost like an interrogation room.

Uwe jumped when the customer in line behind him jabbed him hard in the back. "Really! What's going on at Kaiser Wilhelm that they won't shelter their own people?" the woman said. "Last night I stood outside the door with my little Gerda and Astrid, bombs from Herr Churchill falling around our ears, pounding on the door until my hands were bloody, screaming for someone to open the door, and for what? Nothing!"

"I'm sorry. I don't make the rules," Uwe murmured to the incensed women as he looked down.

"I know people were there working in the basement!" The woman continued as though she had not heard him.

Uwe paid for his coffee and roll, deciding not to eat his breakfast at one of the tables placed against the bakery walls. Instead, he sat outside on a bench a block down the road and gazed along the promenade leading to the Kaiser Wilhelm Institute for Physics while he ate.

Flags bearing black swastikas lining both sides of the walkway flapped in the morning breeze, accentuating his feeling of doom. Several bombs had penetrated the city's anti-aircraft defense system and given the residents a good scare even though the damage had been minimal.

Pits on the sidewalk and the smoking remnant of an incendiary bomb in the grass beside the walk were tangible reminders of last night's terror.

More flags draped the windows on the front of the building that formed the focal point of the promenade. The flags gave an oppressive military feeling to the building despite the sunny morning sky. Finishing the last of his coffee, Uwe wiped the cup and stowed it in his bag.

Uwe walked down the street to the Institute, stopping in front of the three-story brick building to compose his thoughts before entering. He sighed as he contemplated the circular Lightning Tower to his left. Uwe knew he would not be able to complete the next experiment in particle acceleration he had planned.

The paper that had arrived in yesterday's post was heavy in his pocket. He continued into the building and walked downstairs to the laboratories that had been relocated to the relative safety of the underground basement at the start of the war. Uwe presented his identification papers to the SS guard who waved him in after examining the documents and searching his bag.

Uwe traveled down the aisle between the lab bench in the middle of the room and the equipment cabinet against the wall. The laboratory was dim due to the basement location and relied on the globe light fixtures hanging from the ceiling to illuminate the work areas.

Midway down the room, seated on a stool in front of the slate bench, was a slim young woman. She was dwarfed by the precision instrumentation arranged before her. Inge, Uwe's best friend and confidant at the KWI, paused a moment in her experiment, already underway at seven forty-five, to flash her good-morning smile at him.

Inge was wearing an oversized but clean white lab coat. She had selected it from the rack of other men's coats in the metal cupboard standing in the green concrete block hallway. She had rolled the sleeves up to fit. The name of the original and much larger owner, Otto Wolfe, was embroidered in black thread with a flourish over the breast pocket. Graduate students would come and go, leaving behind their lab coats for employees like Inge, who didn't rate a personalized coat but who always would be running experiments. The coat, while too long for Inge, did show off her muscular calves and slim ankles.

Other days Uwe would have stopped to say hello and visit a few minutes and perhaps brought coffees and breakfast pastries from Frau Krueger's bakery for them to share while their experiments were running. He would have kidded her about the lab coat, would have called her "Otto." Today, however, he met her now questioning gaze. "Is Chief in?" he asked. Inge indicated with an incline of her shining, light brown hair towards the back of the room that Herr Professor was in his office.

Uwe moved on, leaving Inge to watch the retreating figure of her friend and wonder what was on his mind. He walked to the corridor at the back of the lab with offices off of each side and tapped on the open door. Werner Heisenberg looked up from the stack of papers on his desk and smiled at his protégé. "Uwe, good morning, please come in," he said, indicating the chair next to his desk. Uwe sank into the chair, pulled his draft notice from his pocket and placed it on the desk.

Professor Heisenberg smoothed the paper out and read the notice, his expression grave. "We should not be surprised, Uwe," he said. "All the young men and older ones now too are being called up. I thought there might be a chance you would be spared a bit longer. Some time ago Professor Hahn and I spoke with the administration and requested a special exemption for you on the grounds that your work here at Kaiser Wilhelm would be considered essential for the war effort. They denied the request."

Uwe leaned in towards his professor and spoke so as not to be overheard because he was suspicious that the laboratory was under surveillance. "It is punishment because of my parents' work. They are held in disregard."

Heisenberg's compassionate gaze met Uwe's and there was a pause as they exchanged a significant look. They were in a bind, no doubt about it. The Third Reich had people of honor in a corner, especially scientists, and it would take every last bit of their considerable creativity and cunning to figure a way out of their predicament.

Professor Heisenberg cleared his throat, seeming to have come to a decision of sorts. "Uwe, please come to my country cottage for a farewell house party. You have three weeks before your induction. I'm sure you will want to spend most of it with your family, but Frau Heisenberg and I and the children would enjoy having you visit us before you leave. If I start the boys on some experiments, I should be able to get away for a bit to see the family. We would have a nice time of it."

"Thank you, sir. I would enjoy that very much," Uwe said, flattered by the invitation at what he knew was a stressful time for Heisenberg.

"That's settled, then." Heisenberg said. "Meanwhile, let's see how far along you can get on your experiment."

Uwe nodded and stood up to begin work.

When Uwe left the lab late that afternoon, the bright flowers in the rotunda caught his eye. Feeling guilty that he had almost forgotten his early morning promise to Ursula, Uwe stopped and extracted the bruised rose from his bag. He placed it on top of the mound of flowers beneath the statue of St. Florian, patron saint of firefighters.

"He's been receiving an unusual volume of tributes lately, hasn't he?" Uwe jumped. He turned to see venerable Professor Mayer standing beside him. Uwe had hoped to deposit his anonymous contribution and escape without being detected, but he had been caught. As he mumbled that the rose was because of his sister, something in Professor's Mayer's expression stopped him and he trailed off. They looked at the marble statue of St. Florian pouring water from an urn onto the flames of a small fire.

"Uwe, this old atheist is hedging his bets." Professor Mayer shrugged his shoulders and produced a spray of delicate Cecile Brunner climbing roses from behind his back. "Some might say this is not a scientific thing to do," he said, his face blushing as pink as his flowers.

"Do you think St. Florian is paying any attention to what we are doing here? Uwe asked. "Sometimes I think he and God are on a beautiful beach enjoying a vacation, watching the dolphins play in the surf."

"Those two should leave the white sand and blue waters and get back to work," Professor Mayer said. "We must call them over." He added his flowers to the pile at St. Florian's feet. "Given the nature of the work being done here, this one's fire fighting skills are needed."

2 OF PINEAPPLES AND KINGS

1942. From Berlin to Bavaria.

The next week slipped away and then it was time for the weekend at the Heisenberg mountain cottage. The train carried Uwe beyond heavily populated areas, through neighborhoods smoldering from recent bombing raids. He passed buildings with gaping holes in the walls and roofs. Destruction was so extensive that in peacetime the buildings would have been deemed uninhabitable but today people remained in them, retreating to live in less damaged areas.

Uwe looked out of the train car window at a little girl and an old woman. They stared at him from beside a curtain hanging over the hole in a bombed building. The little girl's gaze met Uwe's. He thought he would never forget her haunted expression, and he felt sad for her and the other children growing up in wartime.

As Uwe's journey continued south into the rural areas, the scenery changed and a plain spread out before the approaching mountains. The war had not reached the remote areas surrounding Lake Walchensee. The mountainous region had such a storybook feel to it that the Brothers Grimm might have used the area as a setting for Snow White.

When the train pulled into the station at Urfeld, a six-hour journey from Berlin, Uwe straightened his tie, slung his knapsack over his shoulder and picked up his violin case. There weren't many other passengers exiting the car at the isolated Bavarian stop south of Munich. Uwe double checked his map and then strode out of the station yard on his way to the Heisenberg summer home.

Several hours later he turned onto the path leading up to the alpine cottage. Dense forest hid the house from view. The five year-old Heisenberg twins formed a greeting party from their watch at the top of the stone front steps. As soon as the twins saw him, they ran down the steps calling, "Uncle Uwe, Uncle Uwe!"

Uwe smiled and picked a twin up on each arm, lifting one and then the other to demonstrate his strength. They laughed. Uwe carried them up the steps and deposited them on the porch floor. He straightened up to shake hands with Herr und Frau Heisenberg, who stood smiling on the porch.

Time passed with excursions into the surrounding mountains. They hiked trails overlooking the unspoiled turquoise green lake with the Karwendel Alps providing a grand backdrop. One morning Uwe and the professor set out on an expedition around the perimeter of the lake, their walking sticks stirring up dirt as they made their way along and talked from time to time.

When they reached a point several hours away from the house and the sun was high in the sky, they shared a picnic lunch on the rocky shore beside the clear water. They rested there, soaking up the sunshine and enjoying being alive.

Heisenberg's mind turned to a subject that was a contrast to the scene before them. It was something on everyone's mind those days. "I never thought the war would last this long, Uwe," he said. "Germany is not a large country, well, not as large as America or the Soviet Union, anyway, and we do not have their resources. How much longer can we hold out?"

Uwe looked at Heisenberg, feeling less sleepy. The boss did not confide in him in that way often.

"As you surely know," Heisenberg continued, "I am under considerable pressure from the military to make our lab produce advanced weaponry. So far I have been able to present a convincing argument to the Military Institute that they should abandon hope for the timely development and delivery of a uranium bomb."

Uwe focused his attention on his mentor. As was his habit when interacting with Heisenberg, Uwe considered each word before speaking. The boss' agile mind moved to some distant but logical place and it was up to Uwe to join him there. But Heisenberg continued without waiting for Uwe to respond.

"The men in charge now? They're criminals, Uwe. Absolute criminals. They want me to twist wonderful discoveries about the basic nature of our world into villainous works. As modern scientists, we have the potential to inflict unknown horror on humankind."

"We are in a tough situation," Uwe interrupted. "Sir, do you know how far along the Americans are with the development of the uranium bomb?"

"No. I have been cut off from the international community for several years. I can only speculate, but with the means at their disposal it is possible they have made significant progress." As if to clear his thoughts, Heisenberg shook his head. "Uwe, let's go home. We aren't going to change the course of events today."

They gathered their picnic materials and walked back to the cottage. Anxiety from the discussion earlier in the day faded into the subconscious as the colors of the sunset were reflected on the lake. After dinner, logs were heaped on the fire and the family settled around it. Uwe removed his violin from its case while Heisenberg drew up to the piano. "How about Mozart tonight?" he suggested. Uwe nodded and they were off into the music.

That evening Uwe's thoughts turned to practical matters as he gazed out of the window at the stars from where he lay in his comfortable bed. The imminent issue was his future, his purpose. It seemed a waste for him to leave the lab empty handed. His thoughts raced back along experiments and discussions of the past few weeks, reexamining their design and direction in light of his conversation with Heisenberg.

The next day the pair went farther afield, this time hiking up a mountainside. Uwe's mind was never far from the matter of the bomb. It preyed upon him. "A uranium bomb the size of a pineapple could destroy a city, you say?" Uwe asked on the way down the slope.

"Yes, about that size." Heisenberg nodded.

Heisenberg stepped off the path and settled down onto a rock outcropping, motioning to Uwe to join him. He pulled several pages of folded blank paper and a pencil from his pocket. "Look, as you see here," he said while he wrote a series of equations and diagrams, "it can be done." He handed the paper to Uwe to study.

"But, given the degree with which the military scrutinizes our work," Heisenberg continued, "it is impossible for us to operate with the openness necessary for faster progress. The project is too complex. This sort of thing is best done in collaboration. It is almost impossible for me to muster the motivation necessary to do this kind of creative work in my current circumstances. Additionally, given the political state of affairs, many of our best minds have left the country to work."

Heisenberg took the paper back from Uwe, turned it over and continued to jot thoughts down. "Uwe, always check the calculations yourself. Some of the boys made this mistake here," he said, his hand moving over the pages, "which is why our development projections are based on the use of heavy water instead of carbon. If efforts were directed a bit differently, like this," Heisenberg continued, clarifying his thoughts on the paper, "things would go faster indeed." Heisenberg finished writing and gave the sheaf of notes to Uwe.

"Why the interest, Uwe?" The professor looked at his protégé.

"I'm worried the Americans are close to a final product, which is dangerous for us, but at the same time I'm worried they haven't, because somehow the madness here must be stopped. Chief, I know you could have gone to America. Why didn't you?"

Heisenberg gazed off into the canyon in front of them before answering. "If I had accepted the offer from Columbia in 1939, undoubtedly it would have been my destiny to work on the bomb. I am stuck. I will not develop a bomb for the Americans to be used against my own people, but neither will I build one for the Nazis."

"Sir, what if your help is needed to end the war?" Uwe ventured.

"The Americans have no need of my help to make their bomb. They have plenty of people to do that," Heisenberg answered.

Uwe thought a moment before speaking. "I think I should take this information out of Germany when I go. I could wait for an opportunity to slip away and work my way to America. Maybe I could find Teller in Berkeley or Fermi in Chicago, or Leo Szilard at Columbia in New York. This country is sealed tight except for soldiers leaving for battle. Maybe taking it out won't be of any use, but I want to try."

"That would be treason, which is a capitol offense," Heisenberg said. "Not even Himmler's mother would be able to help you if you were discovered with such information."

"Himmler's mother?"

"Uwe, I'm going to tell you a story," Heisenberg began. "After I was awarded the Nobel Prize in 1932, I was slandered most shamefully, called all manner of despicable names and threatened with deportation to a concentration camp. All of this was in my own country. It was because I collaborate with scholars whose work they hope to discredit based solely on race. I was denied the best students."

"Sabotage!" Uwe interjected.

Heisenberg nodded. "Yes, you more than anyone, would understand that taking away the quality students was a fatal blow to the progress of the work. At the time I was young and idealistic, just 31 years of age, but then, I am still idealistic in my work, as are you. Aren't all pure scientists?"

"Yes, of course, it goes with the territory, so to say."

"My critics are virulent racists. Surely you've heard what they call me. When it's all said and done, what is the purpose of our work? It is to improve our lives, not destroy civilization."

"Our goals as scientists are not in fashion," Uwe remarked, well aware of the political climate.

"My mother and Heinrich Himmler's mother knew each other from years ago," Heisenberg continued. "Frau Himmler intervened on my behalf with her son and delivered a letter from me to him requesting independence in my work. She was able to exert influence with him, even though he is the head of the powerful criminal organization, the SS."

"Sir, your story seems to me to support an argument in favor of my plan," Uwe interjected.

"This thing that you are proposing could easily result in your death, Uwe," Heisenberg said. "That is my point."

"I am aware of that, sir, but sometimes great risk is necessary to achieve change. We can't see into the future. What if Germany falls and this information is lost? What if the Soviets somehow come into power and have knowledge of this process and the Americans do not? We could have another reign of terror."

"So, what is your plan, Uwe?"

Uwe reached into his pocket and withdrew a small leather bag. He removed his father's War Merit Cross earned in 1914 and held it out to Heisenberg, who took it and held the cross with four equal arms in the palm of his hand. The metal glittered in the sunlight. Heisenberg's eyebrows lifted and Uwe started talking, too fast at first, and then he tried to slow down so that he didn't appear to be babbling.

"I'm quite good in the machine shop and the photography laboratory. I could fabricate a back identical to the original so good you couldn't tell the difference. I could photograph the formulas and plans, shrink them down, put them behind the medal and forge the new backside on, this time with some small bit of space to hold the data within. I carry this medal with me everywhere. The Institute guards never give it a second look. I could get it out of the country. I could keep it with me always by carrying it into battle as a talisman."

He looked at Heisenberg, wondering what his reaction to the audacious plan would be. He hoped Heisenberg would approve.

"Uwe, I don't know," Heisenberg responded.

"What if 'Aryan Physics' is remembered as Germany's contribution to science?"

A flush spread over Heisenberg's cheeks as he exhaled and looked at the sky. "That would be disaster. It is one of my reasons to stay. I can provide leadership in the field if I survive."

"Do you want the world to remember the cloudy thinking of your adversaries as the best German minds could produce?" Uwe probed.

The muscle under Heisenberg's left eye started to twitch, as Uwe knew it would.

"No, no, Uwe. It is not just cloudy thinking. It is incorrect thinking."

"They reject quantum theory," Heisenberg said after a moment.

Uwe nodded, and when the vein in Heisenberg's forehead started to pulse he said, "And they are so persistent. What about your life's work, your legacy?"

Heisenberg sighed. "When the war is over, and it cannot go on forever, I will be in place to continue our works. Germany will be defeated. Meantime, I will do what I can to keep this country from being forever remembered as the architect of nuclear holocaust. I must try to salvage something from the wreckage."

There was silence. Uwe thought he saw a glimmer of tears in his eyes as Heisenberg continued, "Uwe, this idea of yours is dangerous. You would need to have full confidence in the people you entrust the information to."

"Somehow I would find an avenue to use this information for the good or destroy it, if necessary. Sir, do I have your blessing?"

Heisenberg clasped his hand on Uwe's shoulder. "I have faith in your judgment," he said. "Perhaps it is best to speak no more of pineapples."

They descended the mountain, their conversation reverting to less consequential topics.

Uwe said an emotional good bye to the Heisenbergs the last morning, leaving on foot as he had arrived. He was off to spend a few days in the lab before reporting to duty. The house seemed quiet after Uwe left as the family resumed its regular routine.

Later that evening the bedside table lamps cast golden light on the Heisenbergs as they read, propped against pillows in soft cotton pillowcases. A white eiderdown quilt was warm in the chilly evening mountain air.

Elisabeth turned to Werner. "How is your wunderkind going to fare?" she asked.

Heisenberg put his book down. "I have prepared him as best I can. I think a seed is in the wind," he said.

3 DAK

May 12, 1943. 28 miles south of Tunis, St. Marie du Zit zone, Tunisia, North Africa.

Uwe stood at attention in a line of soldiers of the 5th Panzer Army that stretched down the side of the road as far as he could see. A fair blue African sky and the cool temperature of 62 degrees were typical of the month of May, but the scene being played out there was not.

A massive Steyr 1500 A Austrian made luxury command vehicle rolled down the road in front of them, stirring up a cloud of dust. The Steyr was a dull yellow sand color and carried the desert logo of a white intertwined palm tree and swastika on the fenders. Hans-Jurgen von Arnim, Colonel General of the *Deutsches Afrika Korps*, DAK, stood in the open car. Von Arnim held onto the front windscreen of the car with his left hand while his right hand saluted his fighters. In response, the soldiers saluted and cheered their respect for the man they had served and who had carried their fates in his hands. The Commander's destination? The British 1st Army Prisoner of War camp. The flags flapping on the car? They were white.

Uwe dropped his salute and looked down the road as the car disappeared in the distance. He knew he was fortunate to have survived the past year of fierce combat duty. He turned to the soldier next to him. "Kaspar, it's over for us now," he said.

"Yes, it's over," Kaspar responded. Kaspar Bauer, Uwe's friend through a year in the field, was a doctor serving with the German medical corps. Looking enough like Uwe to be his older brother, Kaspar was tall with lean muscles and light brown hair. His blue eyes were troubled. "What will become of us?" Kaspar said. "The English seem friendly enough. I don't know what to expect from the Americans, though, if somehow we fall into their hands."

That week British and American forces had formed two arms of a pincer that surrounded the Germans and Italians, resulting in their surrender. They were at the mercy of the two armies.

In the wake of von Arnim's Steyr, the road filled with vehicles carrying soldiers following the lead car. Uwe and Kaspar climbed into the nearest Jeep with enough space to hold them and the driver pulled out onto the road. Like their commander who had relinquished his revolver to the British command, all German and Italian soldiers in Tunisia were required to lay down their arms. They were en route to complete the terms of their surrender.

A breeze blew across Uwe's face as he gazed out at the African landscape, lost in thought. "What do you think happened to Walter Witte and Karl Becker and the flyer boys who escaped?" he asked Kaspar. "Do you think they made it to safety?"

"I dunno. The countryside is full of Berber camps," Kaspar answered. "It is possible they found safe harbor there since Hitler has paid them for their allegiance. Whether they were able to find any free German troops, though, well, that's another story. What hope could they have of mounting an offense? Germany has capitulated in North Africa at least."

Uwe considered himself lucky to have avoided being coerced into uniting with those soldiers. About 10,000 men had slipped away in the night to roam the countryside in search of Nazi troops resisting the call to surrender. "They were very enthusiastic, weren't they?" he remarked to Kaspar.

Kaspar nodded in agreement before changing the subject. "Do you think we'll be allowed to keep our personal belongings?"

"We will if the terms of the Geneva Convention for prisoners of war are honored," Uwe said.

A certain War Merit cross was on Uwe's mind, considering that it contained a key to devastation far in excess of the combined firepower of the surrendering army. Uwe had carried it a long way from those last days in Berlin when he modified it in the basement machine shop at the Kaiser Wilhelm Institute.

"Maybe the Americans will be all right, if it comes to that," Uwe added.

The scene before them was busy. The British had thrown together a containment zone from cyclone fencing with a barbed wire top. It enclosed a flat area of dirt behind the tented processing facility. A British battalion sorted through the soldiers of the Axis powers, transitioning them from fighting men to prisoners of war. Soon thousands of men would be crammed together into a muddy, lice infested waiting area.

Earlier that morning had found Uwe frantic to find a hiding place for his modified War Merit Cross. Given that privacy was scarce, he was pressed for time. At first he put it in his boot, but he worried, what if someone took his boots? There was no true ownership of footwear, or much else for that matter, in the army. It was easy to imagine a soldier rooting around for a pair close to his own boot size and grabbing Uwe's. Next Uwe moved the medal to the inside of his pants waistband, but that irritated his skin and he thought the friction from wear might cause it to fall off. Then he pinned it to the inside of his shirt pocket, his fingers fumbling in haste. He swore when he stabbed himself with the end of the pin, drawing blood. He stopped. It was the best he could do. Maybe it would not attract the notice of anyone and he could keep it with him.

A cadre of armed soldiers fingerprinted and assigned a serial number to each incoming member of the surrendering army. Uwe and Kaspar stood in a line of soldiers waiting to be processed. They made it through the first hurdle and were directed to the holding area. By the time it was all done there were close to 270,000 prisoners of war, a field of khaki waiting for the next step.

4 "IF YOU WOULD KEEP A SECRET FROM YOUR ENEMY, TELL IT NOT TO YOUR FRIEND." BENJAMIN FRANKLIN

Mid-August 1943. A POW camp on the outskirts of Tunis, North Africa.

"There you are!" Kaspar called out to Uwe, returning from his routine reconnaissance of the prison compound. "I have news." After weeks of idleness, things were hopping at the camp. "Queue up! Hurry!" German prisoners, tasked with organizing their own, marched through the POW camp issuing instructions.

"What's happening?" Uwe asked.

"Our futures have been determined. Well, our immediate futures, in any case," Kaspar explained as they joined the other soldiers forming a line. "Information is that the Brits are overloaded with prisoners of war and we are being handed off to the Americans. We sail as soon as passage can be arranged."

"Oh, and do you remember Walter Witte and Karl Becker?" Kaspar asked. "They were part of the group that escaped just before the surrender?" Uwe nodded. Kaspar continued, "They ended up turning themselves in to the British after wandering in the desert for weeks. They're all right, no harm done to them. They were trying to avoid the Americans, given that they are less of a known quantity than the British, but the Brits turned around and off loaded them to the Americans after all and," he nodded in the general direction of the tent serving as headquarters, "the conclusion is they will be joining us on our trip."

Uwe absorbed this information. America. He wondered what the state of scientific research was during the war in the US. Of course it would have a military focus. America was a huge country and the last he knew Heisenberg's colleagues were scattered across it. He would be a POW with limited rights and many restrictions. How could he contact his former coworkers? Should he get in touch with them if he could?

Their line was approaching the checkpoint. Apprehensive about the checkpoint's purpose, Uwe strained to see around the soldiers in front of him. He stumbled and then regained his footing when he realized the prisoners were being subjected to a new search. Unable to see any way to avoid what was coming, there being no avenue of escape, he remained in the line, waiting his turn.

Additional to a circle of armed guards on towers surrounding the detainment camp, a squad of American soldiers stood at the checkpoint. Every soldier passing through was searched before being directed into yet another containment area. When Uwe's turn came, he stood ramrod straight and stared ahead of him as Sergeant Jim Small patted him down.

"Hey, hey, hey," Sergeant Small said when he discovered the medal pinned on the inside of Uwe's pocket. He held out his hand. "Come on, give it up, Fritz," he demanded.

Uwe decided to try for the direct approach. "Sir," he said to the guard. "This medal, it is from not this war. It belonged to my father. Please to let me keep it." It was nothing doing. With two soldiers pointing their carbines at him, Uwe unpinned the medal and handed it over. It was Christmas come early for Small, who pocketed it. Uwe's medal was on its way to becoming a mantle ornament in the states.

Panicked at his loss, Uwe tried again to reason with his captor, beginning, "Please," but Sergeant Small motioned him forward. "Get movin,' fella," he ordered. Uwe lunged at the guard in an effort to retrieve the medal, his heart pounding at the thought of losing it. Kaspar grabbed him in a death grip around the shoulders and pulled him back. "Uwe, let it go," he said. "It's not worth your life."

While his comrade held a gun on the other prisoners, Small roughed Uwe up with his fists. "Take that," he snarled when he finished. "Next time you can expect worse." Small tossed Uwe on the other side of the search area. "You ought to get more than that for what you Krauts done to my buddies," he yelled after him.

Manfred von Hoffmann, a senior officer tasked with maintaining discipline within the captive German troops, stepped forward. "I will take this from here, Sergeant," he said in clipped English. The sergeant nodded his okay. "Keep your men under control," he snapped.

Von Hoffmann jerked his head to indicate that Uwe should follow him. Once they were away from the American guards, von Hoffmann let Uwe have it. "What were you thinking, Johannes? And you an officer!"

Uwe stood at attention. "I'm sorry, sir," he said. "That was a well, kind of a special edition medal, sir."

Von Hoffmann made a face of disbelief. "Where's your dignity, soldier?" he said. "Let them take their trinkets. They'll have a different attitude when we invade their country, which will happen. Then we will be on top and they will be at our mercy." There was more, with threat of punishment, which Uwe withstood.

When he was done with the dressing down, von Hoffmann pulled out a cigarette and stalked away to join the higher-ranking officers waiting in the new containment area. He lit the cigarette and rolled his eyes. "You won't believe what Johannes just told me," he snorted. "He says his War Merit Cross is a special edition. How absurd."

"Ah, so was mine!" his fellow officer laughed. "Aren't they all?"

"I could do with a beer right now," Von Hoffmann said.

"Me too, it's a long war," added the other.

Walter Witte, a pilot taken prisoner after the recent failed escape attempt, stood to one side observing the scene. When von Hoffmann left, he strode over to Uwe. Walter pulled a handkerchief out of his pocket and gave it to Uwe so he could wipe the blood trickling from his lip. "This is a great wrong," Walter growled. "It is a crime against the Fatherland, that's what it is. Somehow we will get the stolen honor back for you, eh? The soldier with the medal of a hero in his pocket, he is on borrowed time. Scum."

5 A FEW GOOD EGGS

Mid-August 1943. A dock on a coastal port of Tunisia, North Africa.

Uwe squinted out of his good eye at the departure preparations underway for their voyage to the New World. His discolored right eye was swollen shut, a gift to him from Sergeant Jim Small. Uwe's back ached where he had been beaten. He hoped he wasn't going to die on the ship from kidney failure or a busted spleen. The vision of his body being tossed overboard into the depths of the Atlantic Ocean, the thought of a dark and cold sea burial, made him shudder. He didn't fancy that at all.

From his position next to him, Walter perked up, "Hey, hey, hey." The three watched Jim Small, new owner of Uwe's medal, board the ship along with other Allied soldiers. "This is good news."

Realizing all was not lost, Uwe brightened. He was willing to fight for his medal, but it would have to be a smart fight this time.

Several thousand people were shipping out. The dock was divided into two areas, one for prisoners with their guards and one for soldiers with business in the US.

"Cigarette, please," the blonde said in a husky voice. Beverly Macon, situated on the dock area reserved for Allied personnel, made the request from her position flat on the stretcher. She was beautiful despite the effects of living in the wilds of Africa for months at a time. Bits of twig and sand lingered in her hair, but she had managed to freshen up with perfume and red lipstick. Her stretcher was parked under a tent in the waiting area. She looked at the young American soldier tasked with getting her on board the transport. He grinned and pulled a cigarette from his pocket. He lit the cigarette and handed it to Beverly. "Anything for you," he said. She took a thankful drag. "Thanks, Clint," she said as she exhaled.

"No problem," he answered.

"I wish I weren't getting sent home," Bev remarked. "The boys need nurses at the front."

"Don't let it get you down. You did your best. It isn't your fault you fell and hurt your back."

"I guess I can read the writing on the wall. I don't think the army docs will approve me as fit for field service even after I've recovered from this."

"That doesn't break my heart. It wouldn't be right for something to happen to you at the front. You being a woman and a volunteer and all. I'm not at all happy to see our ladies as close to the front as you were. It's not right."

Bev shrugged as best she could while coddling her back. "Our boys need somebody to help them. I guess it won't be me, though." She worried that living in tents, often with only her coat for a blanket and her helmet as a bathtub, moving from place to place as she had done for the past year, was out of the question for someone recovering from surgery for a ruptured disc. Anyway, she wanted to be a help to the company, not a dead weight.

Clint surveyed the crowd of German and Italian soldiers destined for POW camps established in remote locations across America's heartland. "Sorry about your low-end traveling companions," he said, frowning.

"I dunno, Clint. A lot of them look like lost boys to me."

Liz Lancaster bounded down the pier. She waved back at the merry Italian soldiers who didn't seem upset at having their time at the front curtailed. Liz was five foot four, weighed 115 pounds, and wore her dark honey brown hair in a braid around her head. Exuding self-confidence, Liz was looking forward to furlough back in the states and didn't mind sailing with a boatload of prisoners to get there.

Liz caught sight of Bev and Clint and maneuvered through the crowded dock to them. She smiled at Clint and stuck her hand out to Bev. "Liz Lancaster," she introduced herself. "You must be Bev Macon. I'm to be your special nurse on board ship, and I'll see you to the hospital once we're home."

"Thanks, Liz. Pleased to meet you." Bev returned the smile as they shook hands.

Liz scanned the soldiers waiting for transport. "What do you think we'll have smooth sailing with this many prisoners?" she said. "I bet Jerry has his sights on us and won't blow up a thousand Germans."

"That's looking on the bright side," Bev chuckled.

The ship's horn blasted and notice came for the sick to board first. Clint and another private carried Liz's stretcher to the makeshift sick bay. Liz shook hands with Clint. "Best of luck to you," she said. In response, he saluted and disappeared off the ship and out of her life. Liz thought that was the way of things in the service, sometimes. She felt sad for those types who cared about their friends as much as she did.

A day into the voyage found sickbay full of customers. Trent Norbert, the ship medical officer, was relieved to discover the two nurses on hand even if one of them had a bum back. Being prisoners didn't stop people from getting sick. They were busy with everything from toothaches to an emergency appendectomy. With adequate rest and stress relief, Bev was able to toddle around and help as best she could. Liz was happy to be useful even though she was off duty except for taking care of Bev.

Dr. Norbert palpated Uwe's back, trying to determine if there was internal organ damage. Although the soldier wasn't talking, his injuries seemed to be from a fistfight. His buddies had escorted him to sickbay shortly after the ship sailed. There was swelling, but whether the soldier had internal bleeding was the question he needed answered. The doctor stepped away as he thought about the best course of action for his patient.

"Let's admit this soldier to sick bay for observation. We'll keep an eye on him for a few days. It's too bad we don't have more diagnostic equipment handy," Dr. Norbert told Liz. "You nurses are life savers," he said before turning to the next patient. "I don't know what we would do without you on board. I know neither one of you signed up for this."

"Oh, nuts, it's good to be doing something, Doc," Liz replied.

It struck Liz that Uwe was not the typical soldier boy. More intelligent than most, maybe, she thought. No, it was that but more. Liz frowned as she thought ooh, it was a great wrong, Thor should always fight on the Allied side, and she said as much to him, "How come a nice boy like you is fighting for Hitler?"

Uwe didn't say anything beyond "Thank you," when she handed him his shirt.

"The doctor says you need to stay here with us tonight, Mr. Johannes," Liz told Uwe while he was buttoning his shirt. As she showed him to his cot and prepared a compress for his swollen eye, Liz asked, "How'd you get the shiner?" Uwe shrugged in response.

"Talking to him was like trying to extract information from the Sphinx," Liz told Bev over dinner at the officers' table. "He was completely non-communicative. Clearly he was in a fight about something."

"Maybe he doesn't speak English?"

"I don't think that's it. His language skills seem pretty good."

"You'd think the soldiers had gotten enough fighting in the war."

Jim Small, from the next table in the mess deck, piped up, "It's my handiwork. That guy thought he could keep this. Check it out." He extracted the trophy from his pocket and passed it over for the nurses' inspection.

"You took this from the soldier who is in my sick bay?" Bev asked.

Small nodded.

"This looks old," Liz remarked as she looked at the medal. "It sure is heavy. Is it from this war?"

"It is old. I think it's from the Great War," Small bragged. "The best I can make out it's the Kraut equivalent to our Medal of Honor."

"Geez, guys, haven't you fleeced those soldiers to the point where most of them barely have buttons left to hold their shirts closed? This medal isn't even from this war, how about let's give it some respect?" Liz said.

Small rolled his eyes. "Oh, please, let's talk respect," he said. "The Germans want to clean our clocks. No. Whatever we can, take it, however we can take it, is my rule. Do you think they are showing decency to our boys?"

Bev shifted in her chair, seeking in vain for a more comfortable position. "If you think the only difference between us and them is strength, why do we bother fighting?" she said. "We might win a few battles, but we'll lose the war. The only thing standing between us and them is honor."

Bev raised her brows at Liz, then reached out and grasped the medal. "Sorry, guys, I'm turning this one over to the Commanding Officer," she said.

The nurses left the now silent tables and walked away across the rolling floor of the ship, Liz slowing to accommodate Bev's shuffling steps.

Jim Small looked after them but made no move to stop their progress. He knew better than to challenge those two. Nurses? As far as the boys were concerned, army nurses serving on the front hung the moon and flew with the angels.

"I guess they told you," someone at the table remarked to Small.

"You win some and you lose some, I guess," he shrugged.

"Pass the salt, please," another said, and the table conversation reverted to normal.

"See that this is returned to its proper owner, please, Lieutenant Lancaster," the Commanding Officer told Liz after taking one look at the medal. "Geneva Convention allows such things to be kept and worn." Foregoing further comment, he returned to the more pressing business of getting his boatload of troublesome cargo delivered safely to New York harbor and out of his hair.

Upon discharge from sick bay the next day, his injuries deemed non-life threatening, Uwe opened the manila envelope handed to him by the medical technician. When the familiar medal slipped into his hand, he stared at it, impressed. After a moment's deliberation, Uwe pinned it once again on the inside of his shirt pocket. He would have to tell Walter and Kaspar that he got the medal back.

6 UNDER HER SPELL

Late-August 1943. New York City, New York.

Raucous cheers erupted from the Americans on board the troop ship when they sailed into New York harbor. Shouts of "Ain't she great!" "Home sure looks good!" and "We made it through!" rose up as the troops celebrated safe passage. They had eluded the German U-boats patrolling the open seas seeking to blow Allied ships to pieces. Everyone, well, the Americans, anyway, were relieved and happy with anticipation at being back in the USA. The prisoners were an uneasy bunch. They did not know what to expect.

The skyscrapers filling the borough of Manhattan provided a backdrop to the figure standing on the island in the harbor. What was her job? In this time of war was she guarding the city or welcoming strangers to the city and the nation? Whichever it was, and maybe it was a combination, she made a powerful statement.

When the ship carrying 1000 prisoners of war passed underneath the Statue of Liberty, all heads were uplifted as the passengers took in a close up view. Uwe felt a strange urge to protect her, The Mother of Exiles. How fitting, considering their circumstances. Berlin had nothing like it. Nowhere else in the world did, either. She was unique. The shadow from Lady Liberty's torch fell over Uwe as the ship sailed through the harbor. Say what? Uwe was shocked at the rush of emotion that washed over and through him. *What's going on? Am I the only one who felt that?* Uwe wondered, looking around him at the faces of his fellow prisoner soldiers, hunting for confirmation that he wasn't alone. After all, he was on the same trip as everyone else, wasn't he?

The experience was undeniable. Surely he hadn't been singled out, but then he sometimes intuited things that others did not. His life often was lonely because of how he was. It was hard to get a bead on what the others felt, so guarded were their expressions. Uwe turned to Kaspar, who was standing beside him. "Ironic, no, to be arriving on a prison ship?" he remarked. Kaspar nodded his head in agreement.

All was hustle when the ship turned up the Hudson River and the crew got busy with the practicalities of docking. When given the signal, Uwe queued up and filed off the ship under armed guard with the other prisoners. The line of soldiers snaked down the streets of wartime Manhattan.

Uwe craned his neck to look up. "These skyscrapers are incredible!" he said. "Did you know there isn't even a German word for skyscraper? It's an American invention. I wonder how these things are constructed. How interesting it would be to discuss the design of tall buildings with an engineer."

"Uwe, better watch where you're going, you'll fall flat if you aren't careful!" Kaspar interrupted him.

Ignoring the warning, Uwe continued walking, sky gazing and talking. "What I would not give for the chance to travel to the top of the Empire State Building! I read about an observation deck on top from which you can see great distances."

"Hi there, handsome! You, Bruiser Hans!" Uwe looked towards a young woman standing across the street. He thought she was talking to him. He stared at her, unable to fully understand her English but nevertheless getting the drift. "I like tough boys," she continued.

"Yeah, honey, I bet it's been awhile," her companion added with a wink. "Why don't you and your friend come over for a visit? I'll tutor you in American." She and her friend cackled.

Kaspar laughed and nudged Uwe, who smiled at the girls. His black eye seemed to attract a different kind of girl. The American soldier walking beside the line of prisoners motioned forward with his rifle. "Keep going, Krauts. If anybody's gettin' anything it'll be me, not you." He muttered to himself, "Sassy gals."

"Oh you're breakin' our hearts, boys!" the girls cried after them.

A woman walking down the sidewalk stopped, and with her arms on her hips, her face distorted with anger, she shouted at the two girls, "Shame! Shame on you!" Silenced, the young women watched the line of soldiers pass.

Uwe contented himself with a backward look at the girls. He wondered if they could have directed him to Columbia University. Could he somehow slip away from the company and find his way to Leo Szilard, Werner Heisenberg's former colleague? What would he do if he were able to escape and locate Dr. Szilard? Present himself with a bow around his neck as a present from Werner to Leo? It wouldn't be easy as the army had an iron grip on his movements. In any case, those girls probably couldn't locate Columbia University if it reached out and grabbed them. However, were he with those girls he wouldn't be worrying about Columbia University because they were ready for a party. He would have to go with the flow and see what happened.

The American soldiers double time marched the prisoners four blocks from the port to Pennsylvania Station. No one had time to make an escape. The company walked down the station's wide stairway flanked by enormous Corinthian columns into an ornate ticketing area. Light streamed through windows set high on the long sides of the room and into the arched windows at each end. In addition to the regular civilian traffic, the terminal teemed with uniformed military personnel traveling on war related business. The positive energy in the throng of people was tangible despite the wartime anxiety.

The subdued German soldiers stood in lines against the train station walls. They were small figures in relation to the vaulted ceiling. A war bond mural was draped on the wall above them. In the mural five enormous photographs of American soldiers serving different branches of the armed service flanked a gigantic flag. Many eyes were on the prisoners. The eyes of the soldiers in the pictures gazed down on the uncomfortable German POW's. Citizens in the station gave startled looks at the prisoners who were waiting under armed guard as they realized who they must be.

"I always wanted to travel, but I never thought the military would provide this unusual opportunity," a fellow POW remarked to Uwe.

"Really," Uwe said. He added after a moment, "I wonder how far we are from Columbia University." The soldier gave Uwe an odd look at his peculiar line of thought.

The trains everyone was waiting for pulled into the station. The army had commissioned regular passenger trains to transport the prisoners. Squads of American soldiers boarded them and began intense conversations with the crews. When the go ahead was given, the prisoners were checked off by name as they boarded.

Uwe stood in a column of soldiers waiting to board a train. The line stopped moving and he heard a commotion ahead of him in the train compartment. "I can't believe it. Is this for enlisted men too?" a soldier said. Uwe stood up tall to peer beyond the soldiers in front of him and his eyes too widened in surprise. No one he knew of, with the exception of senior officers, had ever been provided with seats during troop transport. When his battalion was transported, they went in cattle cars, and this Pullman coach was not a cattle car.

The prisoners, perplexed at their fine travel arrangements, sank down on the comfortable seats and waited for the next step. They were aliens to that country. They had no idea where they were going nor what would happen when they arrived. At last the train pulled out of Penn Station and headed out of town. The soldiers were more optimistic than before with the lifestyle improvement extended to all prisoners regardless of their rank.

With a cynical look around him, Manfred von Hoffmann, the ranking German officer, remarked to his fellow officers, "These Americans know they are going to lose this war. They hope we will go easy on them when we take over their country. That's why we have these nice accommodations."

"They are soft, treating their enemies so well," another added. "This is proof that they will be unable to fight to the end, when it becomes difficult."

Not all soldiers thought as some of the senior officers did. Walter Witte, sitting with Uwe and Kaspar, exclaimed, "If I were not here to see this, I would not believe it!" Stewards in gleaming white shirts, ties and black coats were pushing carts loaded with coffee and sandwiches down the aisle of the compartment. They stopped at each row and offered the refreshments to the prisoners.

"This is a problem," Uwe worried. "We have no money and no way to get any."

"What if we can't afford to eat?" Kaspar agreed, thinking not just for that moment but also for the future in general.

When a cart stopped beside them, the three shook their heads at the steward. They indicated that they could not pay. "No, sirs, go right ahead," the steward said. "It won't cost you anything." He passed full cups and plates to each.

"This is not what I expected, how about you, Kaspar?" Uwe said, sipping his coffee between bites.

"Not at all, Uwe. Not at all," Kaspar responded.

When they were fed and the dishes cleared, a spokesman who had been chosen from their ranks, their *Lagersprecher*, appeared in the front of the compartment to make an announcement. "The destination of this train is Camp Joseph T. Robinson Prisoner of War Camp, North Little Rock, Arkansas."

Uwe and Kaspar looked at each other and said one word, "Where?"

7 STRANGE BEDFELLOWS

Late-August 1943. America.

The train moved forward bound for Camp Robinson, its location a mystery to the passengers. Despite the posh accommodations, Uwe and his fellow soldiers nevertheless were prisoners. As the kilometers clicked by, Uwe felt himself slipping into a depression. Kaspar turned from the window. "I can't get over how big America is," he remarked.

"It is bigger than Europe," Uwe answered, his eyes on the scenery. He was starting to panic at the thought of life in a POW camp. They didn't seem to be traveling to a metropolitan area. "We are headed west," he added. The train had traveled mid-way across the continent, cutting up through the heart of the state of New York before skirting the Great Lakes. Syracuse, Rochester, Buffalo, Erie, Detroit and Chicago. That they were booming wartime cities was not lost on the prisoners. The train passed shopping plazas along the route. "I can't get over how many automobile factories this country has!" Kaspar said to Walter as he observed the customers' cars filling the parking lots.

"That's exactly what I was thinking!" Walter answered.

Uwe didn't know how to prepare himself for the next phase of his life, or if it even would be possible to do so. Before the war, he had focused all of his energy on his scientific studies to the exclusion of everything else. Berlin had been the epicenter of twentieth century scientific thought until it was submerged by virulent nationalism. With no control over his situation, he felt disconnected from reality.

The train turned south at Chicago, then several hours later the passengers were looking down through the steel supports at the great

Mississippi River as they crossed into Missouri at East Saint Louis. The train shed of St. Louis' Union Station, the busiest train station in the world, loomed around them. The prisoners stared through the windows at the American soldiers traveling through the station.

"Someone said 100,000 passengers travel through here every single day," Walter said. "I don't know if I believe it, do you?"

"I believe it," Uwe said. The pulsing, high energy atmosphere of wartime USA reminded him of Heisenberg's prediction on one of their walks, that America would prevail in the war.

The prisoners were the subjects of the galley workers' conversation. The wait staff was busy clearing the dinner dishes, and one remarked over the clink of plates and cups being scraped and stacked, "One of the guards told me about where they headed."

"Oh?"

"They goin' to be choppin' cotton down Arkansas way."

"No!"

"That's what he said."

"Field handin' hard work, I can tell you from my experience."

"Don't you know it!"

"These gentlemen sure are light for that kind of work, if you follow me."

"It's a concern, it is. They'll have to cover up good."

"They sure will. I tell you, I'm happy to be turning around and heading back home after we let them off."

"Ain't that the truth!"

"However, there are some things back home you can't get anywhere else. I'll be going out on break before the turn about. My Aunt Dolores, who lives in North Little Rock, is cooking for me tonight. I cabled her from St. Louis and she started cooking soon as she got the cable. Goin' to get food unlike anything available up North. You know, they think they know good food up North but they really don't. I think she's planning ice cream and peach cobbler."

"Uh, Bo?"

"Yeah?"

"I have a break tonight too, same time as yours."

After dinner the compartment lights were dimmed and passengers stretched out as best they could in their seats to settle down for the night. The temperature rose as they traveled south. Uwe had never been that hot in his life, including his African stint. He dozed off and was lulled to sleep by the train compartment's rhythmic rocking, and then he woke up because it was stifling hot. He turned from side to side trying to find a breath in the thick air until he faded off into a dream filled sleep.

In his dream a large man wearing a black suit made of an unusual woven cloth sat in the vacant seat opposite Uwe. His leather boots appeared to be handmade. He had high cheekbones and forehead, and his auburn hair was combed back from a receding hairline.

The man gazed at Uwe, who, in his dream, straightened up and returned the stare. "Jim Bowie. Welcome to Arkansas," the man said, reaching across the aisle to clamp Uwe's hand in his.

"Thank you," Uwe said. "My name is Uwe Johannes, Mr. Bowie. It is a pleasure to meet you."

Removing a flask from his hip pocket, Bowie offered Uwe a sip before taking a generous swallow himself.

Bowie pulled a wicked looking knife with a curved tip from his boot. He sharpened the blade using a cream-colored whetstone pulled from his coat pocket. "This is what's known as an Arkansas toothpick and I am sharpening it on an Arkansas stone," he remarked in a no-nonsense tone. "You are going to need a set like this. It has served me well. This knife was my best friend in a little business some years ago, back in 1827. We were on a sandbar on the Mississippi outside of Natchez, in the no man's land between Louisiana and Mississippi jurisdictions. There had been a disagreement with a sheriff down there and he almost got the better of me, but I made it out all right, thanks to this feller."

"Where can I procure such a knife, sir?" Uwe asked, appreciating the wisdom of arming himself. "I have no money."

Bowie raised the knife into Uwe's face, the blade flashing in the carriage's weak light. "That's on you," he said. "Be resourceful."

Well, that's not especially helpful to me, Uwe thought, but retained a respectful face. Despite his polite demeanor, there was a dark undercurrent of violence about Bowie, and the tale of his murderous duel rang true. Bowie was not someone to cross.

Relaxing back into the chair, Bowie waved his hand in the air. "I own prime Arkansas farmland," Bowie said in a conversational manner. "Valued at $30,000 in 1834. No telling what it's worth today." Uwe wondered how that could be true, but again retained an impassive expression. He was beginning to worry about how to get

Bowie to leave. Relief came when the first rays of daylight shone through the windows. With his body starting to fade, Bowie shook Uwe's hand in goodbye as he gave some parting advice, his gray eyes the last to go, "Fight the good fight, Mr. Johannes, no matter how quixotic it may seem. Remember the Alamo!"

Uwe woke up with a jolt. While he slept the train had crossed the Missouri state line and entered Arkansas. Uwe's dream left him with an uneasy feeling about the future. His favorite childhood reading material had been tales of the American frontier. He knew that Bowie, slave trader, land speculator, bigger than life personality, sometime hero, sometime villain, had died at the Alamo. Shot through the head numerous times, he had died alongside Davy Crockett. They lost the battle, outnumbered against Mexican troops in a desperate fight for Texas' independence. Uwe worried that he might face a similar fate in prison camp or perhaps in his own bid for freedom. He determined to find a knife for self-defense.

Farmland stretched in all directions as far as the eye could see from the train windows. Flat rows of crops flourished under the sweltering summer sky, broken by occasional clumps of shade trees growing on the periphery of the fields.

"Dirt rich and people poor," Walter said from his seat on the other side of Kaspar.

"It is rural," Uwe agreed. "I wonder if the people have telephone service or paved roads? I don't see anybody in the fields."

"That appears to be cotton," Walter remarked. "There's not much to be done now, since it doesn't look ready for harvest. The bolls are not mature yet, but it's a nice looking field." When Kaspar and Uwe looked at him in surprise at this informed comment, Walter shrugged. "In my former life I was an agriculturalist," he said.

Several hours later rumors flew through the compartment that they were nearing their destination. Uwe saw knobby-kneed cypress trees rising up in low, swampy places. Pine, scrub oak and hickory trees grew thick on the surrounding rolling hills of orange-red bedrock. He thought the countryside was pretty. Somebody said they were close to the capital city of the state.

Vast numbers of tracks extended on either side of theirs underneath a concrete automobile overpass as they passed through the North Little Rock train yard. There was not a fancy station house. This yard was industrial, home to shops and railroad operations office buildings. The train trundled through the town until, in the neighborhood of Levy, it turned and took off on a short spur. It was slow going due to the many street crossings. Thirty minutes later the train stopped at Camp Robinson. Their journey of 9496 miles had concluded.

8 THE BUCK STOPS HERE

Late-August 1943. Camp Robinson. NLR, Arkansas.

Lieutenant Colonel Bill Edmund rolled out of his military cot at Camp Robinson. He anticipated an unusual day. Bill had been tasked with filtering out political extremists from a new batch of POW's due in that morning by train. Over a thousand potential threats were incoming, including a large core group of the *Deutsches Afrika Korps*, the German military's select fighting company. He hoped he was up to doing the job right and would make no mistake of consequence. Or as his supervisor had put it, 'Sift out the nuts and crazies, Edmund. Don't make a mess of it.'

Bill had instructions to ship all zealots off to Alva, Oklahoma, where there was a special camp waiting for them. It was up to his team to ferret those characters out of the pack. He took comfort in the knowledge that at least there were two high, reinforced barbed wire fences surrounding the prison complex. Armed guards were at the ready, should any slip through his net and try to escape and wreck havoc in the countryside. An escapee would have a job in front of him to reach civilization because Camp Robinson itself was 42,000 acres of uninhabited forest, and then it was a hike to the nearest community.

Towns across America's heartland like North Little Rock had been tapped as sites for POW camps. They were hustling to absorb captured German and Italian prisoners after Allied wins in North Africa and Southern Europe. Bill Edmund felt his crew was more or less ready for the first batch of POW's. When he toured the hastily built prison complex, Bill thought the white insulite buildings looked better than the usual black tarpaper. He was glad the housing had electricity and indoor plumbing because it would get cold enough to snow by winter.

Camp Robinson, originally built for the National Guard's use, now had three compounds accommodating 3000 prisoners. The prison area was designed to house enlisted men with a separate area for a smaller number of noncommissioned officers. Bill's superior officer had another piece of advice for him. "Edmund." "Yeah?" "Remember, like my mother used to tell me, 'Idle hands are the devil's workshop.' Figure out something for those guys to do."

Easy for you to say, Bill thought, but he didn't say it out loud. He tried to keep a lid on smart aleck comments. But of course it was true, he was going to have to find some way to occupy the prison population that exceeded 1000 souls. At least enlisted men were allowed to work, unlike their officers.

Bill knew the top brass, the higher-ranking officers, had been put on a different train back east than those destined for central Arkansas, and to be honest, he wasn't sorry about it. Those fellows were slated to spend the remainder of the war under moss draped grand oak trees somewhere in the state of Mississippi. But the hot dogs were going to be as hot, maybe more so, than those at Camp Rob.

At his sink, Edmund coated a blunt brush with shaving cream. Slathering a layer of foam onto his whiskers, Edmond shaved himself as he turned his head from side to side to monitor his progress in the bathroom mirror. His olive skin was darkened from two summers in the intense Arkansas sunshine. His brown eyes were intelligent and his chestnut brown hair was sprinkled with gray. He patted his face dry and pulled on his khakis, ready for whatever came his way.

Edmund left his solitary officers' quarters at eight am sharp and walked across the black top parking lot to ease his long legs into the jeep where Pete Peters, his aide and driver, was waiting. "Good morning, Colonel," Pete said. He nodded in response to Pete's short salute.

Pete started the ignition, wheeled the jeep out of the officers' residence area and headed towards camp headquarters, the warm morning air blowing against their faces. Pete whipped into the boss' personal parking place, the hard stop causing gravel to fly. "Jeez-O-Pete! Are the hounds of the underworld in pursuit?" Edmund exclaimed. A cheerful grin and, "Sorry, sir," was Pete's response.

Colonel Edmund entered the white stucco building housing his office. Claudette Reynolds, his civilian secretary, already was working at her desk. She greeted the colonel with a "Good morning" and a pile of papers ready for his signature, which she thrust at him with one hand as she swiveled her chair away from her typewriter. Bill returned her good morning and took the papers with his left hand as he walked past her desk into his office.

Carrying a cup of hot coffee doctored with a little sugar and a little milk, Claudette followed the colonel, the heels of her spectator pumps clicking a rat-a-tat-tat on the concrete floor. She placed the cup on the desk next to the heavy black telephone. Pearl clip-on earrings peeped out from under Claudette's short, curly hair. The coordinating pearl necklace resting on her grey suit jacket gave Claudette a polished air. As she turned away, Bill cleared his throat, causing Claudette to pause and look at him with a quizzical expression.

"Thank you for the invitation to your cousin's house for Sunday dinner. It's nice of them to include me. Will you please give my acceptance to Mrs. Brentwood?"

"I'll let them know. We'll look forward to seeing you then." Claudette returned to her desk in the adjoining room, and a few minutes later buzzed Col. Edmund's phone.

"Yes?"

"The intake group is ready, sir."

"Okay, thanks," he said, and hung up.

Claudette placed another call. "Aunt Gladys?" she whispered when the line connected. "Claudette here. He's coming on Sunday."

"I'll tell Tina," a pleased voice said after a sharp intake of breath. "Let's see if Mamie and Colonel Edmund hit it off. I'll kill a chicken and fry it up and we can have that and vegetables from the yard!"

"I'm looking forward to it," Claudette smiled.

"Tell the colonel to come after church, around one o'clock."

"See you then, Aunt Gladys."

"Bye, honey."

As soon as Bill Edmund left for the recreation building where the prisoner interviews were being conducted, Claudette made another call. When she heard the brusque, "Hello," she said, "LaChar here. He's started the interviews," then hung up the phone.

9 UNMOORED

Late-August 1943. Arrival at Camp Robinson, North Little Rock, Arkansas.

Wilhelm Schmidt, a German spokesman, appeared at the head of the prison train car. "All soldiers will march to the intake processing center for interviews, medical examinations and instruction," he announced.

"Welcome home," Walter remarked to Kaspar and Uwe as they made preparations to leave the comparative safety and familiarity of the train. They noticed the stillness first. Although the small station was busy with the arrival of many, the area into which they stepped was quiet, and their noise could not dislodge the serenity of the place.

The hot and humid air felt like it could turn into rain later in the day. Against a pale blue sky pine and hardwood trees grew close together. Acres of rolling hills stretched in all directions. The ground underneath the trees was spongy with decayed leaves and pine needles, the result of years of accumulation. It made fertile plant mulch for those willing to dig for it, but gardening was not on too many people's minds. Nobody but Walter noticed the fine loam underfoot.

The soldiers fell into formation and marched away from the train depot to follow the Military Police across the compound. They were a hardy group, still sunburned from the African sun, many of them wearing the shorts uniforms designed for desert fighting. As they passed by a short wall, Uwe noticed the materials and make. The irregular slabs of quartz-speckled Arkansas fieldstone sparkled in the sun. Thick white mortar bonded the brown stones together. The curved wall enclosed a round fieldstone patio ringed with flagpoles flying the stars and stripes, the Arkansas state flag and the Arkansas National Guard flag.

After a three-mile hike away from post headquarters to the northwest corner of the reservation, a 300-acre temporary garrison built in a valley came into view. The soldiers saw what would be their home for the foreseeable future. Quadrangles of administrative offices, a mess hall, recreation areas, a chapel, a small clinic and rows of 16x48 foot barracks waited for them.

The soldiers arrived at the camp recreation center that also served as an intake office. Tables had been placed across one end of the room and American soldiers stood ready to transition the prisoners to their camp home.

"It is only a matter of time before Germany invades this country and liberates these camps," Walter remarked as they waited in the processing queue.

"The natives might put up more of a fight than you would think possible." Thinking of his previous night's curious dream, Uwe interjected a note of caution.

Kaspar and Walter looked at Uwe in surprise, but he shrugged his shoulders. "Just a thought," he said.

In an unconscious movement, Uwe's hand strayed to hover over his left shirt pocket. His medal was still there.

"Interview sounds ominous," Kaspar said with a serious expression.

"Will they search us again?" Uwe wondered.

"See here, Johannes. Hang onto your medal. We can't count on a goodhearted stranger to rescue it again," Walter said.

Shielded by the mass of prisoners around him, Uwe fumbled in his pocket until he released the clasp and slipped the medal out. Uncertain of the better hiding place, he reattached it inside his pants waistband and hoped for the best.

"Watch out," Kaspar warned. Karl Becker, Walter's compatriot of the unsuccessful escape into the North African countryside after the German surrender, was working his way through the soldiers.

"Heil Hitler," Becker said when he reached their area. "*Heil* Hitler," they murmured in response.

Becker glared at them. "Today we are prisoners but we will never surrender," he hissed. "Remember, our allegiance is to the

Fatherland. Tell these people nothing or risk punishment." Becker moved on to issue his warning to other soldiers.

Uwe had been in the army long enough to know to present an aloof face to Becker.

"Disappointing," Kaspar remarked to Uwe, whose acknowledgement was a flick of the head. The prison social order seemed to be firming up, and not in a positive way.

Meanwhile, the first order of business was in progress. When his turn came, Uwe presented his green cloth-bound *Soldbuch*, the sacrosanct document German soldiers were required to carry at all times and never to part with, to the American soldier seated in front of him. The booklet contained 15 pages of information about Uwe, including his education, special training, rank, and personal information such as height, weight and vaccination record.

After a cursory look, the intake officer moved to confiscate the *Soldbuch*. Uwe lurched forward to retrieve it, grabbing one end and pulling as the intake officer jerked on the other. As he did so, he was aware of a flurry of activity and distress up and down the line as other soldiers engaged in a similar tug of war.

The intake officer, with a final yank and glare, took Uwe's *Soldbuch*, tossed it into a bag and put it in a box destined for storage in the camp commander's office. "Don't worry, kid," the American said. "You'll get it back when it's all over." The atmosphere in the room was tense. The prisoners had lost their *Soldbuchs*.

Later, the soldier deposited the box of confiscated books in the Commander's office. "Those fellows didn't want to give up their little green books," he remarked to the Adjutant. "I thought there was going to be a massive group coronary when we took 'em."

"Well, their books have a lot more information in them than the dog tags," the Adjutant said, "but since there's hardly anybody here who can understand the German they don't have much to worry about. Besides, one of my uncles emigrated from Germany around the turn of the century, and let me tell you, he is quite the record keeper. Taking the books away probably violated their idea of propriety as regards records."

Meanwhile, Uwe filled out a three-page information form and discussed politics in a brief interview with an intake officer. Uwe wasn't sure how open to be with these Americans, so his talk was cagey. He would see how things went before deciding whether to tell them anything of consequence.

The soldier motioned to the table behind him, where Uwe's pack was opened and examined by another soldier, and then it was on to the medical section. Goodbye itchies, Uwe thought with relief as he emerged from the fumigation area. It was the second de-lousing they'd had since capture and maybe the last. Uwe tucked his shirttail into his pants, which still held the medal. He grabbed his pack and gave the thumbs up sign to his buddies when they came out of the processing center.

Afterwards they were directed to the mess hall, where the camp personnel had outdone themselves with a welcome meal. The soldiers were served meatloaf, rolls, carrots, sliced tomatoes, canned fruit and coffee.

"Maybe we will be all right," a prisoner said.

"This is better food and there is more of it than I had back home," another responded. "And the coffee is real."

There were nods of agreement from the men sitting at the table.

As soon as everyone had been fed, Bill Edmund, the Camp Commander, stepped forward to the microphone to address the mass of soldiers, many of whom were quite young. Listening to the babble of masculine German voices, he surveyed the faces in front of him, some hostile and closed, others open and good-natured. They had one thing in common, though, which was an uncertain future.

Edmund cleared his throat and spoke in a matter of fact tone. "Welcome to Camp Robinson." He introduced himself and his subordinates who would be working at the camp and went into detail about the daily schedule and his expectations. Prisoners would be issued clothing. Prisoners would be issued scrip in lieu of cash that would be accepted at the camp canteen and the PX. Prisoners would not have money.

Edmund spoke about security. "Stay clear of the fence. The guards have instructions to shoot anyone who gets too close to the perimeter fence. I repeat, stay clear of the fence. You can expect good treatment if you follow the rules. Your camp spokesmen have your barracks assignments." Edmund wished them a good night and left.

Uwe walked down the center aisle and found his assigned steel cot in the barracks he would share with seventeen other men. While the soldiers were getting situated, Ulrich Winkler made his way through the room. When he reached Uwe, he announced with the air of one who has accomplished a coup, "I am working to obtain the material needed for our survival."

"Oh?" Uwe asked, "Which is?"

"Balls," Ulrich said.

"You think there aren't enough balls here?" Uwe stared at Ulrich.

"No, I don't think so," Ulrich answered. "I've requested an adequate supply for our camp football teams. I believe the field here will work for games."

"Oh." Uwe's expression cleared.

"Like I was saying," Ulrich continued, "these Americans probably don't have near enough to accommodate the demand created by the influx of so many athletes. They have a supply of their American style footballs, but not enough of what they call soccer balls, which is what we need. I am sure there will be a shortage soon. What position do you play?" Ulrich figured it would be the rare soldier who did not play, and indeed when Uwe answered, "Defense," Ulrich nodded and made a note on his paper. "Right. Good fellow. Tryouts will be as soon as can be arranged, hopefully next week. No time to waste." He moved on to the next person.

After lights out Uwe lay in his cot and looked through the window at the stars. He remembered another night when he had gazed at the sky from Professor Heisenberg's mountain cottage and dreamed of his future. He had traveled many thousands of miles since then. Now he was in America, but it wasn't anything like he thought it would be. He was nowhere near a laboratory. His *Soldbuch* was gone and Nazis were infiltrating the *Wehrmacht* soldiers in the camp. There were no women anywhere. His family was far away. On the positive side, he had managed to hold onto his medal, he had his health, his brains and some friends. He had sports.

10 GOINGS ON ABOUT TOWN

September 8, 1943. North Little Rock, Arkansas.

North Little Rock Reporter

Jessica Byrd

Mr. and Mrs. Wallace Brentwood and their family entertained Sunday last at their spacious Park Hill home after church, where they welcomed newcomer Lieutenant colonel William "Bill" Edmund to our fair community. Colonel Edmund is Commander of the newly complete, high security prisoner of war camp right here in North Little Rock. "Overseeing thousands of Afrika Korps soldiers is no small job," said Mrs. Brentwood, "We wanted to extend Southern hospitality and a touch of home life to the colonel, who carries so much responsibility." Mrs. Brentwood served her family's favorite Sunday dinner of fried chicken and late summer homegrown vegetables to the party crowd. Colonel Edmund, a West Point graduate, who hails from Erie, Pennsylvania, told this reporter, "This is the best food I have ever eaten." Attending the gathering were the hostess' niece, Miss Claudette Reynolds, friends Mr. and Mrs. Jake Holt, Miss Beryl Barkley, and Miss Mamie Holt. Also attending was Mr. Brentwood's young cousin Miss Juanita Simmons of Beebe. Miss Claudette Reynolds dons many hats: during the week she works in the Commander's office as Colonel Edmund's private secretary, and she also organizes the local canteen for soldiers. Mr. and Mrs. Holt have two sons serving in the armed forces: Private Barkley Holt is fighting in the European Theatre, and Captain Tom Holt is in the Pacific. Son Luke Holt is a senior at the University of Arkansas Medical School in Little Rock, with plans to become a surgeon. It won't be long before Luke joins his brothers serving their country.

11 THE INTERVIEW

September 15, 1943. POW Camp Robinson. North Little Rock, Arkansas.

Reviewing the intake results from his first batch of prisoners, Bill Edmund scanned the sheet listing those destined for Camp Alva. A slew of ardent self declared Nazi party members had secured transfers westward to Oklahoma. Bill figured there were still Nazis lurking in the ranks of his prisoner soldiers, but for now all he could do was keep an eye on things.

Bill Edmund couldn't empty the camp of prisoners on political grounds and besides, many of his prisoners looked to be regular good soldiers. They were fighting on the wrong side, of course, but it was his job to get them through the war. Washington had decreed that the Geneva Convention statutes for treatment of prisoners of war be followed to the letter in hopes for equal treatment of captive American soldiers in Germany. Those instructions didn't bother Bill at all; they fit right in with his idea of how to operate his camp.

Edmund reexamined the remaining open file in front of him. Uwe Johannes. He couldn't put his finger on it, but while something about the kid gave him pause, he didn't think the boy should be sent to Alva.

Reading the comment about the fight, Edmund shrugged, thinking at least the boy didn't rat somebody out.

Wavering between recommending the soldier for additional screening and letting it slide, Edmund leaned towards the latter. He wondered about the physics business. It might bear further investigation. There was the question of the probable fight, but if he quibbled with every soldier who got into a fight the entire army would be at a standstill.

Edmond scrawled his signature on the line at the bottom of the file: **Approved for supervised off compound prisoner work program.**

PRISONER OF WAR REGISTRATION RECORD

1. NAME JOHANNES (LAST NAME) UWE (FIRST NAME)

2. SERIAL NUMBER	3. RANK	4. ARM OR SERVICE	5. PLACE OF BIRTH	6. DATE OF BIRTH	7. RACE
81G-8846	GEFREITER (CORPORAL)	DAK	BERLIN, GERMANY	20 SEPT. 1917	W

8. HEIGHT	9. WEIGHT	10. COLOR EYES	11. COLOR HAIR
6 FT. 1"	190 LBS.	BLUE	BLOND

12. CAPTURE INFORMATION		13. U.S. PORT OF ENTRY	
DATE	LOCATION	DATE	LOCATION
12 MAY 1943	TUNIS, TUNISIA, NORTH AFRICA	25 AUG. 1943	NYC, NEW YORK

14. INTERNMENT LOCATION

CAMP JOSEPH T. ROBINSON, PULASKI COUNTY, ARKANSAS

15. POLITICAL PARTY AFFILIATION	
NAZI	COMMUNIST
NO	NO

16. EDUCATION	17. LANGUAGES
PHYSICS	SOME ENGLISH

18. REMARKS

REC'D MEDICAL ATTN. ON BOARD TRANSIT FOR INJURIES SUSTAINED IN FIST FIGHT. SOLDIER DENIES FIGHTING. POSS. DISRUPTIVE ELEMENT.

19. INTERVIEW BY:

T. DICKENSON, 2ND LT. CE.

(PRINT PLAINLY OR TYPE) NAME, GRADE AND SERVICE OF INTERVIEWING OFFICER

T. Dickenson

SIGNATURE OF INTERVIEWING OFFICER

Uwe Johannes

SIGNATURE OF PRISONER

DATE

1 Sept. 1943

20. RIGHT THUMB PRINT

21. **Approved for supervised off compound work program**

William Edmund, Lt. Col.

(PRINT PLAINLY OR TYPE) NAME OF CAMP DIRECTOR

SIGNATURE OF CAMP DIRECTOR

DATE

15 Sept. 1943

12 A LADIES' LUNCH

September 1943. Little Rock, Arkansas.

Late Saturday morning Claudette Reynolds walked along the downtown Little Rock sidewalk. Perspiration dripping from her forehead, the seven-story building was in her sights. Her destination at Fourth and Main shimmered like a mirage in the September heat.

Sighing in relief, Claudette pushed the door open and entered Blass Department Store. She stood there a full minute enjoying the frigid air aimed at the entrance. Dabbing at the drying perspiration on her brow with a handkerchief, she steadied her hat and passed through the jewelry and perfume departments. She threw a longing look into the shoe department but continued on.

After riding the elevator up to the Mezzanine level, Claudette went to the tearoom. Standing in the entrance, she surveyed the available tables. "Could I have that table for two over yonder, please?" she asked the hostess, gesturing towards the window table on the left hand side, isolated by a cluster of potted plants.

"Yes, ma'am," the hostess said, and led the way through the tables occupied by a light early crowd, ladies with the occasional older gentleman sprinkled in, enjoying lunch.

Claudette pulled off her white gloves and waited. When Guinevere Weintraub appeared at her table, Claudette had to smile. Carrying several shopping bags from her morning trip through the store, Gwen looked the part of a local matron. Even though she was middle aged, Gwen's strawberry blonde hair was bright and a smooth strand was combed across her forehead and tucked behind her ear underneath her hat. Claudette stood up and gave Gwen a hug before they sat down. A casual observer would have thought they were a mother and daughter enjoying a morning on the town.

"Gwen," Claudette remarked as she read the menu, "this is a whole lot better than meeting under the 14th Street Bridge in North Little Rock."

"You've got that right," Gwen said, raising her eyebrows up. They laughed at the memory of the two of them huddled underneath the wooden bridge late on a rainy night.

"Worried the entire time we would be robbed," Claudette said.

"Or worse. And then the MoPac train came thundering through really close and almost scared us to death!" Gwen chuckled.

"So close the wind almost pushed us over." Claudette shuddered as she remembered. "We could have reached out and touched the train! I can still hear it."

"And this is less conspicuous too, don't you think, than sliding up and down that steep embankment?"

"Yes, this is better for us."

"Tell me, how are things going at work?" Gwen asked after they had placed their orders and the waitress had gone.

Claudette sipped her ice water. "Pretty good, I think," she answered in a voice calculated not to carry. "We've gotten a shipment of a thousand POW's who are settling in. The review committee identified forty-three Nazis to be relocated to Camp Alva, and they're gone now.

"What about Bill Edmund? What do you think of him?" Gwen asked.

Claudette didn't have to think long. "A straight arrow," she said, "and handsome, too. He's a good catch for somebody. I don't think he's married."

Gwen clicked her red painted fingernails. "I should be able to discreetly answer that question next week," she said, her matchmaking skills awakened.

"Thanks, Gwen. Let me know. I have a nice girl in mind for him and I don't want her to get hurt. How about you, how are things in your world?"

"Oh, Pierre is doing great, thanks."

When Gwen started talking about her miniature poodle, Claudette knew it was time to stop asking questions. Claudette wasn't briefed on her connections, but she knew that Gwen met with other women placed strategically in the city, perhaps even in the state. She would like to know more, but Gwen kept it all close to the chest, and for good reason.

"Of course, you know, it is a boy's club," Gwen said as she picked up her sandwich.

Claudette realized Gwen was stressed. Her boss might not have many people she could confide in. "You have a lot of responsibility but no recognition," she ventured, hoping to prime the pump.

"Oh, that's all right," Gwen said. "I just want to do my part, but it's not easy without enough support. You know, I hardly have a broom closet at Third and Spring, and they don't seem to appreciate the contribution women can make. Most of the fellows are nice, good people, but they think it is not a ladies' game." Claudette had never been invited, herself, to FBI headquarters on the top floor of the Rector Building.

Gathering her courage, Claudette placed her hand between them on the smooth white tablecloth. "Gwen," she said, "do you have a more active placement for me, somewhere I can make a difference? I'm only a secretary, and if my boss needs backup the army is right there. I was wondering," and here she took a shot in the dark, "don't you need somebody undercover with the Jehovah's Witnesses? I could add that to my activities."

Gwen shook her head as she poured cream into her coffee. "I already have a gal in place," she said, "but I plan to pull her because from what I've seen, going after the Jehovah's Witnesses is a w-a-s-t-e waste of time, the hole is dry. Those folks are not fifth columnists."

"No?"

"No. I'll say, since it's been published in the papers, which by the way, you should already know too," and Claudette flushed at Gwen's admonishing glance, meaning that she should stay up to date on current events, "J. Edgar Hoover himself weighed in on the court case down in Texarkana. He personally wrote the judge that the Jehovah's Witnesses have no connection to the Nazis. Not that the judge listened to him. A World War I veteran convert did jail time and paid a big fine for distributing their church literature. We've been monitoring them since they won't salute the flag or say the pledge, they won't fight, and they even refuse to serve in noncombatant roles like the Quakers do. They won't take a blood transfusion, of all things, but they are not going to destroy this country from within.

They are strict pacifists and adhere to Jesus' words directly as written in the Bible."

"Refusing to salute the flag is shocking," Claudette said. "What's with that? How does it hurt anybody? It's plain disrespectful. Where does the Bible say not to salute a flag?"

Gwen made circular motions with her hands, trying to make the point better. "Witnesses believe saluting the flag and saying the pledge is the same as worshipping a graven image, and they're not going to do it," she said. "They look at things differently than you do, or than I do, as a matter of fact."

"Well, I'm honored to salute the flag and believe you me, I'm not worshipping a graven image when I do it!" Claudette said, her heart beating faster with indignation at the thought. "It's showing respect for the ideals of this country, not the actual material of the flag, for heaven's sake!"

"That sort of stuff offends people," Gwen said, "especially when young men are dying on the battlefields. The JW are an international organization. The Nazis persecute them and they're outlawed in the Soviet Union." Gwen shrugged and continued, "Here it's a civil rights question, but it's not treason. The only fighting they'll do is at the end time, you know, Armageddon, which if you ask me, I think we are at the end times now. Sometimes I wonder how the Witnesses would identify the end times as such." Gwen frowned at the thought.

"I bet they would tell you if you asked," Claudette said, and Gwen chuckled. "They take punishment for their beliefs," Claudette added. "Their annual meeting at the service station last year on Asher Avenue was scary stuff, where some members were beat up, others shot by the neighbors who worked at the munitions plant. I don't think the men who attacked them were ever charged."

"And their lawyer was beaten up by vigilantes too," Gwen said.

"I knew a Witness once," Claudette said. "She was a girl I went to school with. She seemed nice but she didn't want to be friends with me. They're clannish."

"Claudette, besides overloading you with assignments, it would be difficult for you to fit in with them." Gwen laughed, "Honey, let's face it, your shoe collection alone would make you stand out, and it would be tragic to put those pretty things in the back of your closet. You're too sophisticated. I can't see you distributing pamphlets on the street corners and knocking on doors to proselytize." Claudette was flattered and wondered if Gwen had something bigger in mind for her.

"Anyway, I'm going to have to remove my gal soon. She's been so successful the church has got somebody picked out for her to marry. It'll look suspicious if she doesn't move forward. She's already making noises about it. We all have our limits, I guess." Gwen finished, disappointed by the idea of such boundaries, "I should extract her and transfer her to a higher need area anyway."

Claudette heard "transfer," and "higher need area" and wished Gwen was talking about her.

"Is Edmund an octopus? Gwen asked, noting Claudette's dissatisfied expression. "You know, all hands?"

"No, not at all. He's a gentleman," Claudette answered. "I just don't want to waste my efforts."

"What?" Gwen said. "I give you an important assignment with a combination Jimmy Stewart and Cary Grant for a boss, and you complain? Dozens of women would give their eyeteeth for such a post. No. Stay. I need you where you are. You're sitting on a powder keg with so many soldiers behind barbed wire. You would have a job on your hands to convince me there aren't some stray troublemakers left, and before we're done Bill Edmund might be very glad you are his secretary. No telling what might happen out there. I need a steady hand and a trustworthy, level head monitoring the fire."

"All right, Gwen, I guess I'll have to stay put and keep my eyes and ears open," Claudette conceded, placated for the moment.

"That's my girl." Gwen smiled as she placed three quarters on the table and stood up to leave. "Got your ration cards? If you do, let's see if we can't get some shopping in before we leave. How about we check out the shoe department? We should take advantage of this wonderful air conditioning."

13 LIFE OUT OF THE CAMP ROB BAG

October 1944. POW Camp Robinson. North Little Rock, Arkansas.

Uwe had been looking forward to this game all season, and if it weren't for Walter being alone in the stockade on bread and water it would have been a whole lot more fun. The camp championship was the culmination of a season of aggressive training and razor close games. After a year in the pen, sports had taken on new meaning in his life. Uwe thought Walter had been looking forward to the game too. He didn't understand why Walter did what he did and got himself put away at this critical time.

On duty men stationed at the guard towers overlooking the recreation area turned soccer field laid down their rifles and watched the soccer game, cheering or groaning depending on the performance of the players as the game progressed.

The makeshift spectator area around the perimeter of the field was full to capacity. People had come from as far away as Jacksonville and Cabot to see the game and to cheer on their favorite prisoners. Off duty guards and their wives and children had pulled folding chairs and coolers of food and drinks from the trunks of their cars and set themselves up game side, making a right party of it.

After the last goal was made, Uwe wiped the sweat pouring down his face. It was a hard won victory against the opposing team from the adjacent prison compound. Game over, Uwe ran onto the middle of the field to celebrate with his teammates. He joined the line of players, slapping hands with the opposing team and saying, "Good game," over and over.

Bill Edmund strode onto the field to enthusiastic applause from both prisoners and spectators. As the war continued, Bill's responsibilities had grown. Now he oversaw 10,000 prisoners of war and their guards and administrators at Camp Robinson and also in satellite camps throughout Arkansas. Bill thought it wise to keep his distance from the prison population. On the championship game day, though, he unbent and presented the trophy to the winning team, shook hands all around and said, "Well done."

After the game the team, their hair wet from showering, walked into the mess hall to cheers. Karl Becker pressed a cup of liquor from the clandestine still under the floorboards of his barracks into Uwe's hand.

"Congratulations, Uwe, good job on the field!" Karl's voice was slurred and his cup wavered.

"Thank you, Karl," Uwe said, thinking that Karl had started celebrating early.

Karl followed Uwe to the food line and then to the table. No sooner had Uwe taken his first bite than Karl started in on him, pressing Uwe for information about Walter. "Why didn't Walter take me with him? I would have ensured success."

"Karl, I don't know. Walter didn't confide in me." Uwe looked around for help, but an empty circle had formed around them.

"Comrades. That's what we were before," Karl said, his voice cracking as he struggled for composure before continuing. "We had a history of making our way across strange new territory. We did it in Africa, we could do it again here." Uwe remembered how poorly that had turned out. "I would have made it back to Germany and offered my services to the Fuehrer once again," Karl continued. "Walter could have been part of that great glory. A hero." He trailed off, and seeing that Uwe had no more to offer him, wandered away in search of companionship.

Uwe knew better than to discuss current events with Karl, who had gotten angry when he heard the reports from the latest influx of prisoners. Desperate for news, Uwe and the entire camp prison population had stood by the fence until three am to meet the incoming prison train. The soldiers captured at Normandy predicted a German defeat, as Professor Heisenberg had foreseen two years earlier. The prisoners said their country was in a tailspin, people were starving and their families were not safe. Uwe believed the latest reports, but Karl said they were propaganda and lies. Uwe watched Karl move on with relief.

Once the contraband booze took effect the mess hall atmosphere resembled a Bavarian brewpub. When the men were swaying to the music and into the second stanza of "Don't Fence Me In," the camp theme song, Uwe prepared a sandwich from the food available in the mess hall. He wrapped it and some cookies in a paper napkin and slipped them into his pocket. When darkness came, he left the mess hall and made his way to the stockade without being noticed.

In response to Uwe's soft whistle, Walter, from the other side of the wall, came over to where Uwe waited. "Who won?" Walter whispered. Uwe put the food into a scraped out depression under the wall. "We did, my friend," he answered. "We missed you out there today. We pulled it out, but it was difficult without your help." Uwe sat down with his back against one side of the wall next to a loose board. Walter sat on the other side and pushed the board out of the way so they could hear each other better. Walter unwrapped the food and started eating. "Thanks, Uwe," he mumbled through a full mouth.

"Why'd you do it, Walter?"

"I dunno. I was sick and tired of being a prisoner, I guess. I wanted freedom. And let me tell you, Uwe, I would do it again given the chance."

"Really, it was worth it?" Uwe asked. "Even with your current circumstances, fourteen days of solitary confinement and the diet of bread and water? Missing the championship game?"

Walter nodded his head even though Uwe couldn't see him.

"Yes. Definitely. It was beautiful, Uwe."

"How did you get away, what happened, how did you get back?"

Walter told his story.

"I rode with the work crew in the back of the truck to pick cotton. It was a typical day; clear with the oppressive heat gone and autumn weather beginning. I had picked close to my quota of cotton that morning, and when noontime came I asked the guard would he mind if I went for a little walk. The work crew does that kind of thing from time to time and the guards don't care. He said it was all right, so I left. I went a bit further than he meant for me to.

"That morning I had stashed a new shirt in the truck bed. The shirt didn't have the large PW letters on the back. I had bought it from one of the camp guards. I paid him for the shirt with my cigarette ration, it being nothing on me since I don't smoke. He asked no questions.

"When I got off the truck to start work, I brought the shirt with me. I hid it inside the sack I dragged behind me, where I put the cotton bolls. When the time came, I slipped that shirt underneath the one I was wearing, and when I got into the woods at the edge of the field I changed shirts. It felt good not to have a label on my back. Anyway, I soon came across a road and started walking. I picked a direction at random. I had some wild idea to hitch a ride to Canada or Mexico, someplace far away. Really I just wanted to be free.

"I was in the outskirts of a rural community called Greenbriar. There was a sign announcing this on the side of the road, that's how I know where I was. It was a deserted country road surrounded by cotton and sorghum fields. The sorghum was almost done. I walked about a half hour and then I came upon a field of sunflowers with five scantily clad voluptuous girls in it. They invited me over."

"No!" Uwe exclaimed.

"You're right. I only said that to entertain you, Uwe."

Both of them snorted with laughter. "Okay, tell me what really happened," Uwe said.

"I walked quite a way and around a bend in the road I met Becky."

"Of course. Now I see."

"She had had an accident with a two seated cart she was driving behind an enormous horse. The cart was upended in the roadside ditch and Becky had been thrown clear. I ran over and helped her up, dusted her off and made sure she wasn't hurt. She had a few bruises but nothing was broken. We introduced ourselves and discussed the situation. The cart seemed to have survived the wreck without damages.

"Becky was more worried about her horse than she was herself. The horse had gotten away from her, even though I could tell she was strong. She had a lot of courage to drive a cart behind such a big horse. Her horse was the Percheron breed, that's a French draft horse. His name was Thunder, and he was black as coal. I'm a strong farm boy and knew what to do. I was able to quiet Thunder down and check him out, he seemed to be fine, and I set the cart upright."

Walter paused as he pictured Becky. She was taller than average with a slim muscular build. Her amber eyes went with her copper colored hair. She was about eighteen years old. At first meeting, it struck Walter that she was a genuine, forthright person. He liked the fact that she was so concerned for her horse.

"We got the cart set up and the lines straight and she invited me to her house to thank me. She wanted to introduce me to her mother, who she said would want to thank me too, so I said all right. We rode in great style behind Thunder to Becky's home.

"Her house wasn't too far away. It was a white painted wooden house with a covered porch all the way around the front and sides. There were flowering vines growing on a trellis up to the roof. The house was not grand but it was inviting. We put the horse out to pasture and stowed the cart in the barn.

"I met Becky's mother and they invited me to sit down and visit. I couldn't think of a way to decline and get down the road away from the guards who were probably searching for me by then. I was uneasy about that. But I wanted to stay because I hadn't been in the company of a nice girl in years. I told them I was a laborer on a neighboring farm and they didn't say anything against it.

"Becky's mother was kind like her daughter. When Becky told her mother how I had helped her after the accident, her mother hugged me and said, 'Thank goodness you came along when you did! It's Providence. I worry every time Becky takes the cart out. Do you think Thunder is too much horse for her to handle?' Then Becky said, 'Now, Mama, please don't get started.'

"They brought out coffee and sandwiches and we had a tea party on the porch. Uwe, there was something different about those people that was refreshing. They said things and didn't worry about it, what people might think about them, about who heard them. They laughed easily. The conversation was quite open. I wasn't used to their level of communication. They weren't worried about my social class or theirs, how they meshed or if they were better than me, stuff like that.

"Oh, and Becky had the sweetest Beagle named Winnie. Winnie came up and put her nose under my hand for petting. As I sat there visiting with the dog, I realized something. I had been raised to believe that German culture was the best in the world, that we were better than other people, but actually I have found the world to be a big place with a lot of good people in it."

Listening to Walter, Uwe thought about Karl and what a contrast there was between the two who were once good friends.

Walter continued with his account. "Things went smoothly until Becky's father came home. He was cordial and we talked for some time about crops and harvest and so on, and then he asked me if I could call the hogs. I said I would be glad to, and where were they and so on, thinking he needed help with the stock. Father said, 'no, no, you know, call the hogs,' and he looked at me oddly, like I should understand what he meant, like it was some sort of inside joke. I had no idea what he was talking about.

"The next thing I knew they were speaking seriously and telling me I should give myself up. It turns out they had gotten suspicious of me. I guess my accent had given me away even though I had tried not to talk too much. The question about the hog call was a test. They wanted to see if I really was a local, somebody who would have known they meant they were cheering a sports team, not trying to round up their farm animals. I had never heard of razorback hogs. They knew I was an escaped prisoner. I was busted.

"Becky was sad and worried for me. She seemed genuinely concerned about my welfare. They explained how this is a big country, too big to be loose in without resources, and they would be in trouble and I would be in trouble if I didn't return to camp. Becky's father looked at me and said, 'Son, you need to go on back there.' I didn't want to make problems for them because they had been so nice to me. I gave it up and sat there while they called the camp. They brought me over in their truck. When we got here, Becky's father shook my hand. He looked sad. He said, 'I'm sorry about this, my farmhands have all gone to war and you know your way around a farm.' Walter laughed a little.

"I got what was coming to me here. Ken, the guard, was sorry about it, too. When he put me in the stockade, he said, 'Walter, why'd you do this to me?' He didn't want to have to put me in here alone without enough to eat. I guess I let some people down by trying to escape, but Uwe, let me tell you. I discovered something. This is a land of wonderful women. They're nice, healthy, and energetic. Intelligent too. I mean, even the mother was grand and she had to be forty years old."

14 LIFE IN THE CAMP ROB BAG

April 1945. POW Camp Robinson. North Little Rock, Arkansas.

"Hell, no." Bill Edmund tossed the paper onto his desk.

"Don't shoot the messenger." Claudette held her hands up to deflect attack.

"Incredible cheek," Bill said. "Tell the nervy SOB the answer is no, I'm not authorizing a happy birthday party for *der Fuhrer.*"

"You know, I've heard that other camps have said yes to this sort of thing."

"I don't care what other camps do, this is Arkansas, not the Third Reich. The man is a world class criminal and Camp Robinson will not sponsor a…a…a hootenanny for *Herr* Hitler. I can't stomach it. And the answer is still no to allowing prisoners to display swastikas and pictures of their military men. This deal," Edmond said, twirling his hand around in the air, referring to the war, "is about done over there and those hooligans will soon hang."

"Right-o, sir. I'll type up a response and send it over." Claudette retrieved the request from his desk.

Back in her office, Claudette gave the notice to Pete Peters for delivery to the prison spokesman. "Boss says –'H'-no to a happy hootenanny for *Herr* Hitler, a hooligan who will soon hang,' she said with suppressed laughter. "He really has a way with words."

"Consider the message delivered, Claudette," Pete grinned as he walked out.

The smell of grease and motor oil lingered in the air of the camp motor pool repair shop. Uwe had been working since right after breakfast, enjoying the morning chill in the metal hut. He grunted as he gave a strong push on the wrench and loosened the last bolt holding the wheel on the Jeep. He put the wrench down and slipped the wheel off. Uwe examined the exposed front right brake as he wiped the grease from his hand on the towel and concentrated on how to go about replacing the wheel bearing, and whether he should do two wheels or one. It was "Ask Uwe, can you fix this, Uwe, can you fix that?" when his mechanical ability became known. Before long he had a job as head of the motor pool repair shop. It was okay with him as a way to pass the time. He'd been in camp for two years and had to do something. It was better than picking cotton.

When Uwe took a break from repair work, he sat down at the table in the workroom that doubled as an office and sipped a cup of coffee. He pulled the stack of papers from the last physics test over and picked up his red pencil. In September he had started teaching basic classical mechanics to prisoners who were interested in taking classes. He would like to move on to thermodynamics and quantum physics, but not everyone was ready. The class was unaware their teacher was the famous Werner Heisenberg's protégée. Uwe thought there might have been consternation in the upper echelon of the American military had they known the situation, but so far no one seemed to know.

Kaspar, in his position as postal deliveryman, appeared in the door and handed Uwe a tattered communication from Berlin addressed to him in his official capacity: *Gefreiter* Uwe Johannes, Camp Robinson University. Uwe recognized the return address as the Prisoner of War Academic Records Office. He stared at a stain on the back of the envelope and wondered, is that blood? He slit the envelope and read the request for his students' semester grades.

Kaspar frowned and shook his head. He pulled yesterday's newspaper from his pocket and unfolded it. "Uwe, I don't need to be fluent in English to read this map. Do you think this is real or propaganda? "

The two spread the article out before them on the desk. Uwe's cheerful expression faded. "I believe it to be true, Kaspar, and it doesn't look good, does it?" he said.

The Allies were closing in on Berlin. The white area of the map, all that remained of the German controlled area, was narrowing. Arrows pointed at recent Allied gains into Axis territory. It was only a matter of time before Germany fell.

"I will enter the grades now, and then we can get them into the afternoon post back to the records office in Berlin," Uwe said.

"Right," Kaspar replied. "Time is critical."

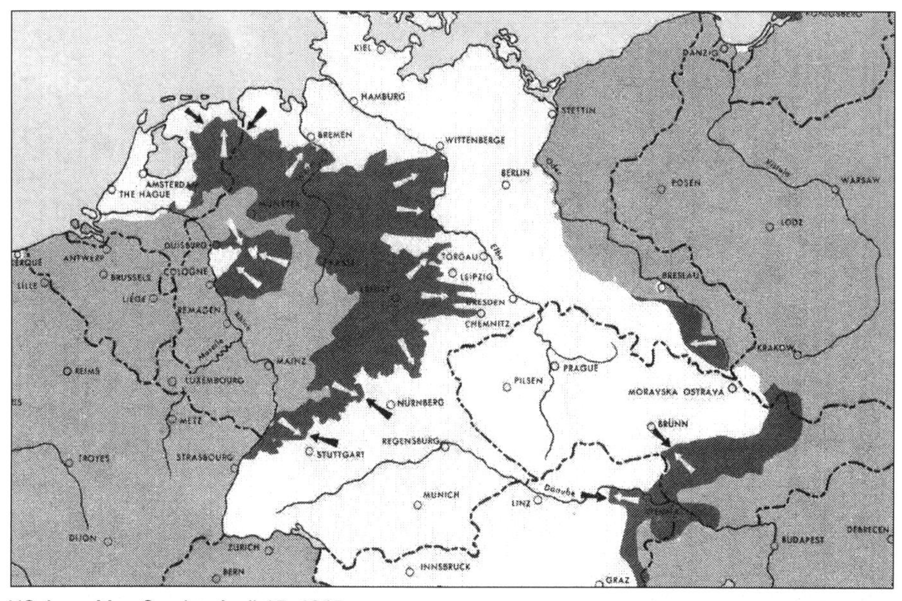

US Army Map Service April 15, 1945

15 THE LAST STRAW

April 1945. POW Camp Robinson. North Little Rock, Arkansas.

"It is raining cats and dogs," Walter remarked from his seat at the mess hall table. Observing the rain pouring down the windows and the trees bending in the wind, he continued, "No strawberry picking for us, boys, which is too bad because we would have gotten some for ourselves." The scary greenish yellow and gray cloud lurking on the horizon was gone. Now it was wet and windy with the occasional lightning bolt and rumbles of thunder as the spring storm rolled through. What a good day to stay inside.

"Well, Walter," someone down the table remarked, "at least we won't be thinking about running scared from the funnel cloud today to jump into the ditch and lie flat like pancakes as we did last week."

"Yes, listening for freight trains approaching when there aren't any trains, instead there is the tornado coming," another said.

Uwe saw Karl Becker making the rounds of the tables and wondered what he was up to. Probably no good, he thought. When Karl reached Uwe's table, he handed a paper to the closest person. "Circulate this but solely amongst us," he said before moving on to talk with people sitting at other tables.

"Oh, look what we have," the soldier receiving the paper said. "An invitation to Adolf Hitler's birthday party on April 20," as he passed it on to the person next to him, who read it and commented, "You Will Attend! is more like it."

A collective sigh rose from the group, and the opinions were of a mind.

"I had hoped we would be spared the celebration this year."

"The Third Reich is dead."

"When I came to America, I looked forward to experiencing political freedom even though we arrived in the proverbial chains, but thanks to the work of our Karl and his friends we are more repressed in camp than we were in the *Wehrmacht*!"

Several tables over, Karl, his Hitleresque moustache a stern line over his upper lip, delivered an invitation. "There will be birthday cake," he said.

"He must have gone underground with the party plans," someone at Uwe's table remarked. "I know for a fact that Colonel Edmund refused to authorize an official event."

Scanning the paper, Uwe frowned as he read. A problem loomed at the bottom of the page: "Uniform recommended." Uwe exhaled as he thought about why he no longer had a uniform.

Earlier in the week the entire camp population had attended a mandatory viewing of an American documentary film. Uwe watched as Allied troops liberated Auschwitz concentration camp on January 27. Uwe wanted to look away when the camera continued to record the horrors within the camp, but he forced himself to watch.

A period of uncomfortable silence followed the spluttering at the end of the reel. Several men jumped up and ripped their uniform shirts off their backs in revulsion. The idea spread and others did the same. They threw them into a heap on the ground of the outdoor theatre in renunciation of National Socialism and their association with it. A match was put to the pile and a blaze roared to the sky.

Uwe undid the clasp on the medal that rode inside his shirt pocket. He removed it and stowed it in his pants pocket. He unbuttoned his uniform shirt, slipped out of it, and in a fit of passion tossed it onto the bonfire. Uwe stood watching the shirt burn, the heat of the fire warming his face and the light illuminating deep anger, betrayal and growing resolve in his eyes.

So he no longer had a uniform to wear to the party he did not want to attend. Karl Becker knew about it too, because Becker and his friends had witnessed the ceremonial uniform burning. The invitation contained a veiled warning against collusion with the enemy.

"Most of our uniforms are ashes," Uwe remarked as he looked at the men seated around the table.

"There will be repercussions for us if we do not attend, and in uniform," Kaspar said. "I heard of someone in another camp who was tried for treason in a secret night court. It was called a Holy Ghost trial. He was found guilty and the members of the jury murdered him, dismembered his body," and after a dramatic pause, Kaspar finished, "and flushed the pieces down the toilet, a hand here, a foot there." He shuddered. "No one heard from him again."

"I heard of someone in a camp who died," a soldier nodded in agreement. "Suicide was the official cause of death, but everyone knew he was murdered by the Nazis in his camp who then staged the body to appear as a suicide."

"*Ordo Virtutum*!" Uwe exclaimed.

"You know, Hildegard of Bingen," Uwe said in response to the puzzled looks directed at him. "She predates *Herr* Hitler by more than 800 years. We will honor Hildegard with a presentation of her famous morality play *Ordo Virtutum*, which fortunately for us requires many voices. Some will have to play the female chorus, but that's okay, it's been done before."

"It is the struggle for a human soul between the virtues and the devil. It will be the perfect antidote to Hitler's birthday," Uwe tried to explain as the uncomprehending looks persisted. "I'm certain Mother Hildegard would agree," he added.

"Maybe Karl would consider auditioning for the role of the devil," someone offered.

"But can he sing?" Another put in.

"Actually, that would not matter because the devil's part is only grunts since he is unable to contribute to heavenly harmonies," Uwe answered.

"Type casting!"

"We will all have to be at the performance instead of the unapproved birthday party," Uwe continued, warming to the idea. "I have the materials for *OV*. I obtained them months ago. I was going to suggest it anyway, but now I will put in a rush request to the camp commander."

"Karl won't like having his party preempted," Walter warned.

"We must find the feminine side, fellows. Let us honor our German heritage with a worthy production. We've been in here too long. I'm going to see about getting this approved quickly."

Uwe hopped up and went out into the storm.

16 THE FATHER AND THE SON AND…

April 1945. POW Camp Robinson. North Little Rock, Arkansas.

Yes! It was Bill Edmund's first thought when the request for a prisoner performance of *Ordo Virtutum* crossed his desk. No matter that he had never heard of *Ordo Virtutum* or Hildegard of Bingen until then, that he had had to consult the *Encyclopedia Britannica* to learn more.

On paper it sounded encouraging. Now Bill knew it translated to *Order of Virtues* (educational), it was the first liturgical drama (there must be morals in there somewhere) and the first for over one hundred years (ground breaking). *Ordo Virtutum* was written and composed by a German (culturally sensitive) woman (feminine touch needed in prison camp) nun (virtuous) in the Middle Ages (enduring).

There were many things to recommend *Ordo Virtutum.* Given to the Church at the age of eight, Hildegard lived her entire life within cloister walls. Maybe her words would resonate with the prison audience even though their captivity was involuntary and hers was not. At the least, producing a play about honor must be a more wholesome use of time than celebrating a despot's birthday. The world was desperate for a hefty dose of wholesome.

Bill signed the authorization form and dispatched it for announcement to the prison population. So what if Pete Peters' first response was a furrowed brow and, "But sir, isn't this awfully high tone? Why don't we have swing music like a Count Basie or Artie Shaw band?

"This is not a dance party thing," Bill snapped back.

"A lot of the fellows in the audience will have worked in the fields all day." Irrepressible, Pete continued to push for a lighter evening. "They'll be tired and ready to kick off into a snooze. Wouldn't something, you know, more modern, be better received instead of making everybody go to church?"

"I don't care if it is a little dry," Bill said. "Send it out. I might even invite some of the locals and notify the press."

"Yes, sir." Put in his place for the time being, Pete took the notice out to the community.

Two days before opening night Uwe paused in his radiator repair to indulge in a rare spot of daydreaming. He stared unseeing at the olive drab paint of the interior of the Jeep hood in front of him. His mind was deep into details of *Ordo Virtutum*. In his most secret inner self, not to be shared with anyone, he imagined a standing ovation at the conclusion of the performance with tears of happiness streaming down the audience's faces.

Although Uwe had launched the project to avoid the party, it was something he hoped would turn out to be wonderful. He wanted to expose the devil for everyone to see. He wanted to make the audience feel satisfaction and elation when the virtues defeated the devil. He wanted to experience harmony on earth and to share it with others, to prove that it was possible. He wanted to take the leap from their reality of the rough prison camp and what had brought them there to a better world.

A knock on the repair bay door interrupted Uwe's thoughts. He looked up and squinted his eyes against the bright sunshine streaming into the room. He recognized the backlit figure of Alfred Bonner, the private who delivered messages for the camp prisoner spokesman.

"Sir, there is an organizing meeting for some of the Inmate Activity Committee Chairmen tonight at 8 pm in the chapel. Your presence is requested."

"All right. Thank you, I will be there," Uwe responded, absorbed in his inner world.

Alfred nodded and left.

"My infirmary job seems a good bit easier than getting twenty soldiers to make heavenly harmonies," Kaspar remarked to Uwe that night over dinner at the mess hall. "I don't envy you, Uwe."

"We shall see, Kaspar," Uwe chuckled.

After dinner Kaspar left to catch up on some work in the infirmary laboratory while Uwe went to rehearsal. Uwe walked outside into the spring evening and paused on the path to enjoy his favorite Arkansas phenomenon. The first lightning bugs of the year had emerged. There must have been hundreds of bright greenish yellow lights flashing on and off in the gloom around him, not too high in the air.

Uwe was reminded of summer evenings from his boyhood excursions to Bavaria. It was a beautiful sight and Uwe stood still as he scanned his surroundings, trying to determine where the next flicker would come from. It was as though the sparkles were engaged in a conversation. He thought about the flickers and how their timing could be explained by an interesting mathematical formula. Uwe could have reached out and grabbed a firefly and held it between his cupped hands or put it in a jar, but he didn't do it. The image of any captive, even a bug, shining its beautiful light in prison held no appeal for him. He walked on to rehearsal through the flickering lights.

"Good job!" Uwe said after the first run through and hoped he sounded sincere. No doubt the men had given it their all, and it was no wonder the performance was rough given there weren't enough days to practice. The members of the chorus looked as though they didn't have any worries and were enjoying their time singing. *Hildegard, help us*, Uwe thought.

Uwe glanced at his watch mid-way through the rehearsal. He needed to go to the meeting. He motioned at Hans, his second in command, to take over conducting, and stepped outside to walk across the compound. As he listened to the conversation between the grunts of the devil and the beautiful notes of the chorus, he nodded his head in appreciation. It was improving.

"Hello? Anybody there?" Uwe called as his footsteps sounded in the chapel's dark foyer. He wondered, was there a scheduling mix-up? His next thought, though, was that there was a more sinister explanation for the silent room, as in there was no meeting and he had stepped into a trap. Sensing trouble, Uwe turned to leave.

A match flared, a candle lit and Uwe's worst fear was realized. It was an ambush. When his eyes focused in the darkness, he saw five silent men standing in the room. He recognized one of them as Alfred Bonner, the chap who had invited him to the meeting. Each held a knife. Two men stepped to block his exit from the room while

Alfred grabbed him from behind and gagged him so he could not scream.

"Nice you could make it to the meeting, Johannes," Karl Becker spoke, his voice hostile with sarcasm.

"It's your Holy Ghost trial, *Gefreiter* Johannes." A man pulled out a chair and pushed Uwe onto it. He produced a length of rope and bound Uwe to the chair arms and legs. Stricken, Uwe thought of Kaspar's warning that this had happened at another camp. He concentrated, trying to devise of a way out of his predicament.

"The charge is treason," Karl said as he sat down in a chair in front of Uwe. "The penalty is death." The others seated themselves in a semi-circle on either side of Karl.

The mock court reached the unanimous guilty verdict without deliberation. Uwe had limited opportunity to present a defense, with a knife to his throat when the gag was removed to allow him to testify. It didn't matter anyway, since the court was a farce. The entire thing was orchestrated. A violent faction of the prison population disliked him. They felt that the Nazi soldiers must keep control of the prisoners, and they believed Uwe obstructed that progress.

The judges discussed Uwe's fate.

"How will we do it?"

"Let's slit his throat."

"Where will we do it?"

"Not here. Too bloody."

"If we kill him near the outhouse by the football field we can cut him up and throw away the parts right there."

"Good idea. It would be a convenient place to drain the blood too."

Listening to the grisly plans, Uwe decided he would not allow others to steal his life without a fight. The thought of having made it through a war zone only to meet his end at the hand of the lowest level of his fellow soldiers in an American prison camp made him furious.

The rehearsal music flowing through the open windows of the recreation hall hid the sounds of the ensuing fight. Uwe struggled as he was transported to his doom bound hand and foot and gagged. Large, fit and young, he didn't make it easy for the men carrying him. It took all five to get him out of the chapel and on the way to the outhouse area. They had to stop mid-way and beat him. Once on the ground Uwe managed to pull away and was in the process of dragging himself off the path and into some brush when the men regained control and reasserted their progress towards the execution spot.

The guttural pig-like sounds from the devil in the rehearsal hall accentuated those of his captors as they struggled to carry him, and the angelic chorus obliterated Uwe's muffled screams. Frustrated, Uwe tried to make a noise loud enough to be heard over *Ordo Virtutum*. He had chosen the piece in part because the twenty-voice chorus would allow more men to participate in the production, but now it worked against him. The chorus was so loud no one could hear his calls for help. Fearing the end of his life was near, he began preparing himself for the next world.

A small, dark clothed figure wearing a hood darted out from the shadows. Wielding a tire iron, the person commenced whacking in the general direction of the knees of the men struggling to maintain a hold on Uwe. In the confusion resulting from the surprise attack, Uwe was dumped on the ground as the men yelled and tried to catch their assailant.

Unable to move due to his injuries, which he feared were mortal, Uwe looked up and his eyes grew wide when he caught the barest glimpse of his savior. "Hildegard?" he mumbled through the gag, groggy from his head wound, as her hood slipped and a lock of bright blonde hair slipped out. The young woman turned to face him, not understanding what he said but smiling in relief to see him alive before she dashed away.

"Stop or I will shoot!" At last the tower guard had heard the commotion. He illuminated the shocking scene below with the searchlight. The participants froze in fear. The guard discharged his rifle in the air three times, the warning signal to the prisoners and the camp emergency alert.

17 VICTORY GIRL

April 1945. POW Camp Robinson. North Little Rock, Arkansas.

It was late to be working in the medical clinic, but Kaspar Bauer liked the quietness of the infirmary after hours. He sometimes spent time there alone in the evenings preparing for the following day. As he gathered the hypodermic needles and turned the sterilizer on, he heard a noise in one of the darkened exam rooms. Leaving the sterilizer, Kaspar went to investigate. He flicked on the light and pushed aside the curtain.

He saw a small figure dressed in black crouched against the far wall. Kaspar walked over and knelt down to see who was hiding in his clinic. When he pushed the hood aside, he sat back on his heels in surprise. "Who are you?" he asked the teenaged girl who stared back at him. A tire iron lay beside her.

"Juaniter," she said, standing up and holding the tire iron in front of her.

"Juanita?" he repeated, trying to be sure he understood as he too stood up.

She nodded. Kaspar looked at her, thinking, and then cleared his throat. "*Como llegaste a la enfermeria*?" he said, his Spanish being rusty with disuse.

"Huh? What'd you say?"

"You don't speak Spanish?" he asked.

"Why would I speak Spanish?" she answered, puzzled at the unexpected line of questioning.

Abandoning his first impression, that somehow a Spanish native had appeared in his clinic; Kaspar reverted to English and tried again, "How did you get to the infirmary?"

"Followed you," she said.

He stared at her, trying to understand how she had managed to accomplish that, being the only female besides the daytime office staff in a high security camp of 3000 men. "Why?" he asked.

"One of the guards told me I should find you," she answered. "He says you can take care of all kinds of problems. He says you're good at figuring out what is wrong with people. I thought maybe you would be able to doctor me and not tell anybody that you had." The girl finished with a question in her voice. Kaspar could tell she was hoping she had found a sympathetic ear. He was getting the impression that this girl was confident in her ability to get him to do what she wanted.

Kaspar frowned at his unusual patient. Back home in Germany he had been a full-fledged physician in charge of his own patients, but here he was an assistant to the regular doctor who commuted between camp and Fort Roots, the local military hospital.

Meeting her eyes and reading the desperation in them, Kaspar weakened and pointed to the exam table. Juanita hopped up, the clean paper cover of the table making a loud crackling sound as she settled onto it. Kaspar didn't say anything about the tire iron that she dragged with her.

Kaspar wasn't surprised at the diagnosis. Juanita had contracted a disease of the ages. He sighed and fixed her with a look. Juanita frowned back at him. "I don't need a lecture," she said, "but can you please fix me up?"

"Tell me why you are here in camp," he forged on.

"Some of my friends are camp guards and they need me to cheer them up."

"Oh, really?"

"Yup. I'm a Victory Girl."

"What's that?" he asked.

"Girls like me who help soldiers want to fight better," she responded. "It's good money. Well, here at this location it's the guards who I comfort and encourage."

"You are a lucky girl because we have a small amount of a new medicine that will help you," he said with a worried frown. "It is special and expensive and I am going to give you some, but it won't work unless you give up this sort of activity. I'll give you a shot of it tonight, but you'll have to promise me not to cheer any soldier up until you are completely cured," and he drew out the last words hoping she would understand the need to follow his instructions. "Do you understand me?"

"Okay, Doc, I promise."

Kaspar measured out the correct dosage of the new, precious antibiotic and gave Juanita the injection.

She flinched but made no other protest.

"Where are your parents? Don't they worry about you?"

"They're busy," she said in a tone meant to deflect further inquiry.

Kaspar knew he should report Juanita to Colonel Edmund's office. He could get into trouble for not telling, and Juanita already had big trouble of her own. What if Juanita had friends acting in a similar capacity? The probability was high. He decided to delay saying anything to the prison authorities.

"You will need to come back for another shot in a week, or you can find a doctor in town," he told her. "It would be better if you did that. It is dangerous for you to be in this camp with many strange men. Some of the people here would hurt you if given half a chance and no one would ever know."

"Naw. I've got my bar. I'll find you this time next week. Thank you, sir, for fixing me up." She grabbed the tire iron and went to the door, where she paused and looked back at Kaspar. With a provocative smile, Juanita lifted one shoulder. "I don't normally offer my, uh, assistance to enemy soldiers, but how about a rain check in a few weeks?" she said. "You know, like as a special thankee for helping me out?"

While Kaspar wasn't sure what a "rain check" was, he got the gist of it and threw up his hands at the type of offer she was making. "Go!" he exclaimed before adding the syringe he had used to treat Juanita into the sterilizer.

Considering her medical account balanced, Juanita slipped out of the clinic. She made her way towards the exit where her accommodating guard was stationed, the one who let her in and out and who had recommended Kaspar Bauer. As was her habit, she kept off the pathways and stayed close to the darkest shadows next to the buildings. Along the way she stopped to admire the lightning bugs sparkling around her, and then she heard Uwe's choir rehearsing through the open windows of the recreation hall.

Although Juanita didn't recognize *Ordo Virtutum*, she thought it was beautiful yet strange and she sank down against the outer wall of the recreation building to enjoy the free concert. Relieved to have gotten treatment for her problem, she guessed she would have to lay off her Victory work for a while like the doc said. Maybe she should give it up entirely. She didn't think he would tell on her, he seemed a good sort, and her problems receded as she relaxed.

While she listened to the music and watched the lightning bug show, Juanita heard odd muffled sounds. She crept forward from her place next to the building. What she saw caused her eyes to pop open. A man, bound hand and foot, was fighting against a bunch of men who were attempting to carry him somewhere he didn't want to go.

Juanita grabbed her tire iron and ran to help the underdog. She had never used her iron before and this was not the situation she had envisioned needing it for, but that didn't matter. She made the weapon work for her. Capitalizing on the element of surprise, Juanita flitted from one man to the other and hit wherever she could get a wallop in, aiming her shots to inflict the most injury while maintaining her freedom as they broke away and tried to grab her. In her innermost dreams she called herself the Wolverine, and now with the chance to live her fantasy she gave it her all.

Panting, she saw she had been successful. The bound man was on the ground and his attackers had scattered. He called something odd to her, something she didn't understand. Knowing the guards would be alerted soon, Juanita took a few seconds to lean down and listen to the man, although what he said sounded like gibberish to her. She was glad he was alive and gave him a sweet smile before disappearing into the shadows.

18 "THE BLOODY DOG IS DEAD"

Early May 1945. Fort Roots Military Hospital, North Little Rock, Arkansas.

"The day is ours, the bloody dog is dead." The BBC radio newscaster quoted lines from the final scene of Shakespeare's Richard III. On May 1 the words traveled over the ocean to cities and towns across the United States. They reached Fort Roots Military Hospital where Uwe lay recovering from his brutal attack. He thought it was a fitting first comment following the announcement of Hitler's death. The British had a way with words; there was no denying it.

Like everyone else, Uwe craved news and stayed close to a radio, but as a prisoner of the victors his was a solitary vigil in the American hospital. The end must be soon for Germany.

What would become of his people, what of the prisoners of war? Would they be shipped back to a country in ruins? He worried about Professor Heisenberg. Was he alive? The absence of a nuclear blast delivered from Germany suggested that Heisenberg had been successful in diverting the research away from development of a uranium bomb. Or maybe the Third Reich had by its oppressive nature failed to support the intellectual excellence necessary for an undertaking of that magnitude. Uwe's thoughts kept returning to the bomb.

It had been a solitary time in the hospital. Uwe's transfer to Fort Roots occurred after the camp doctor deemed his injuries too serious for the infirmary. The hospital was in a beautiful location on top of a high rocky bluff overlooking the Arkansas River, a view from which at first he had been too sick to appreciate. Due to the ambush at the camp and his being a prisoner from a hostile country, Uwe occupied a private room.

The military police had interviewed him as soon as he was able to communicate, but that had been his only interaction with anyone except the medical staff. Uwe gave the police a straightforward account of the Holy Ghost business except he left out the part about Hildegard, for obvious reasons. With the surrender imminent, no one paid much attention to him beyond seeing to his medical needs. Uwe fell asleep thinking about the young woman who had saved his life. That was more comforting than his depressing war related thoughts.

The next afternoon Angie Brewer, his day nurse, entered the room, her white rubber soled shoes making a squishy sound on the polished floor tiles. "An important visitor is coming to see you," Angie told him as she tidied up the area around his bed, smoothing the bedcovers and twitching the furniture.

Angie scrutinized Uwe before reaching for his comb and running it through his hair with a no-nonsense manner. He winced and pulled away when she got close to the bandage. "I'm not going to hurt you, but my patients must look their best, Mr. Uwe," she said while she continued combing, which he endured without further complaint. "Like Mama says, we must suffer for beauty." Uwe presumed he had passed muster when, without further comment, she swished from the room.

Uwe looked at the door as he wondered who would be visiting him.

Certainly he recognized Bill Edmund when he entered the hospital room. Uwe stared, startled, at the colonel. He wondered why Colonel Edmund was taking time from his busy schedule to visit him of all people. They had never had a personal conversation before. Edmund must have better ways to spend his time, what with the news of the day.

Edmund tossed the May 2 edition of The New York Times onto the bedcovers. The large font, bold face type headline announced Hitler's death.

"Well, young man, there you have it," he said to Uwe. "*Der Fuehrer* is dead. No more birthday parties to concern us. What do you think about that?"

Uwe stared at the headline. "Do you think it is true?" he asked Colonel Edmund, who had seated himself in the green vinyl upholstered visitor's chair. Edmund pulled a cigar from his pocket and lit it.

"I do," Edmund replied as he puffed on his cigar. The pungent smoke spiraled upwards and competed with the antiseptic smell permeating the hospital. "Of course, it wasn't the hero's death Hitler's successor Doenitz wants us to believe but yes, he's done for. No body found yet, but the Red Army is giving it a thorough look-see. The Third Reich is about done for, too." Bill pierced a sharp look at Uwe's bandaged head, trying to gauge his response. "The men who attacked you were charged with attempted murder," Edmund said. "They were transferred to an out of state federal prison yesterday to face trial in a military court. The penalty is death by hanging if they get a conviction."

"All the News That's Fit to Print"

The New York Times.

LATE CITY EDITION

HITLER DEAD IN CHANCELLERY, NAZIS SAY; DOENITZ, SUCCESSOR, ORDERS WAR TO GO ON; BERLIN ALMOST WON; U. S. ARMIES ADVANCE

MOLOTOFF EASES PARLEY TENSION; NEW MOVES BEGUN

Allies Invade North Borneo; Fighting Fierce, Tokyo Says

REDOUBTS ASSAILED

U. S. 3d, 7th and French 1st Armies Charging Into Alpine Hideout

NEAR BRENNER PASS

British in North Close About Hamburg—Poles Gain in Emden Area

NAZI CORE STORMED

Russians Drive Toward Chancellery Fortress, Narrowing Noose

BRANDENBURG TAKEN

Stralsund Port Swept Up in New Baltic Gains—Vah Valley Cleared

ADMIRAL IN CHARGE

Proclaims Designation to Rule—Appeals to People and Army

RAISES 'RED MENACE'

Britain to Insist Germans Show Hitler's Body When War Ends

Clark's Troops Meet Tito's In General Advance in Italy

NEW CIGARETTES FACE PRICE INQUIRY

HARD COAL 'HOLIDAY' BRINGS WLB BAN

Uwe absorbed the information.

"We're trying to figure out who it was who saved you," Edmund continued. "None of the prisoners we interviewed have been of much help. They're all mum. Can you shine some light on that?"

Remembering his confusion at the time, Uwe was embarrassed that he had thought Hildegard was his rescuer. After all, she had been dead for 800 years. "No, sir," he replied.

"Was it someone from within the camp? Edmund pressed further.

Uwe shrugged his shoulders as best he could while not causing additional pain from the movement, but he did not speak.

"And you didn't answer my question about how you feel about the end of the Third Reich."

"Sir, is there some way I can help you? If there is, my talent is in your hands." Uwe didn't understand the reason for Edmund's visit or his questions.

Edmund smoked his cigar before responding.

"The war in Europe may be winding down, but we've got a humdinger going on in the Pacific. We can't let up yet. I need someone who excels at math to work on a top-secret project. I'm looking for a bright, motivated person to do calculations at an off site location. I need someone trustworthy who can function semi-independently. You will be working under the supervision of a remote office."

"What is the project?"

"Son, that is beyond your security clearance, and some of it is beyond mine. We may never know how the work fits into the bigger picture. You will have to proceed with some level of trust. About all I can tell you is that your effort will help to end the war."

"What is the plan to return the German soldiers home after the surrender?"

"It's early stages, of course, we don't have a cease fire yet, but getting involved in this project might delay your return home, that's true." Bill answered. "On the other hand, it will take some time to repatriate the soldiers. No orders or plans have come my way yet. Military red tape of that magnitude will slow the process down. Do you have family you need to see to, maybe a sweetheart back home?" Edmund asked.

Uwe shook his head, unable to articulate the devastating news delivered by the International Red Cross last month. Both of his parents and his younger sister Ursula had been deported to Ravensbruck Concentration Camp. Classified as political dissidents, they were missing, presumed dead. He no longer had close ties in

Germany. Unbeknownst to Uwe, Colonel Edmund knew this already. Edmund held the reins tight on his camp.

"Sir, why do you think I am qualified for this job?" Uwe asked.

"I've observed you teaching the soldiers. You have the right background in physics and math. You've done an excellent job running the camp motor pool repair shop. I like to think I'm a good judge of character, and I think you will do fine."

Uwe thought a moment and then reached out and offered his hand to Colonel Edmund, who leaned over and grasped it.

"All right, then," he said, "I haven't established a location yet, but as soon as I do and you are well enough, we'll get you moved."

Edmund left the room, leaving Uwe to appreciate the view from his window in a happier frame of mind.

19 THE END IN EUROPE

From December 17, 1944. The Battle of the Bulge. Somewhere near St. Vith, Belgium.

Hell on earth. Barkley Holt could think of no other description for the scene before him. It wasn't new, either. Everyday it was the same but in a different location. The extreme cold numbed everything except his feelings, but the continual combat had deadened those. The dreaded screaming meemies had done their killing job and it was up to him to pull the wounded to safer positions and the dead to be buried. He climbed out of his foxhole and crept forward beside the medic. They approached his friend who was screaming in agony, his severed leg artery spurting bright red blood onto dirty snow.

When the medic had finished his fieldwork by stabilizing the wound and administering a hefty shot of morphine, Barkley pulled the soldier away from the battlefield while dodging enemy shrapnel. Because he wanted to survive, Barkley concentrated on the task at hand. He wanted to live to see his wife and boy again. Adrenaline surged through his system. He moved on to the next horror that a moment ago had been a young, healthy man with his life ahead of him. When the shelling lightened and the front line moved, he would remove the dead. There was no let-up in sight. Such was the lot of the combat infantryman on the frontline.

A realization had hit Barkley early on. In the eyes of the army he was a dispensable battlefield casualty statistic. The irony was that he hadn't had to go into the service at all because he had a wife and young child. He could have left the fight for his younger brothers and others. The powers that be had put him in the line of fire and seemed to want to keep him there. It was too late to turn back now, though, and he knew his fellow soldiers did not view him as expendable. He kept going because he couldn't let his buddies down.

May 1945. A Field Hospital in France.

Barkley's heart pounded, his body was coated with cold sweat, and he was panting as though he had run a foot race. He blinked his eyes as the wall across from his bed came into focus. He couldn't seem to shake those god-awful memories. They replayed over and over in his head as though it were happening in real time. The memories stole his mind and body away from reality. Barkley laid his head back against the clean pillowcase and struggled to compose himself.

A young nurse wearing men's army fatigues and muddy combat boots walked down the aisle between the beds in her ward of the repurposed schoolhouse. She dispensed medicine to the soldiers in her care according to the doctor's instructions on her clipboard. Something propelled Meg to check on the patient in the third bed from the door. Her nursing instructor would have called it her professional nurse's instinct.

Barkley's hepatitis was easier to manage than his other injury. Meg had a special spot in her heart for the boys who suffered from shell shock. They were battlefield casualties the same as if they had flesh wounds. The mental injuries were as difficult to treat, sometimes more so, than the ones you could see.

Meg caught Barkley's eye as she stopped by his bed with a smile. "How's it going, soldier?" she asked in her Louisiana drawl.

Barkley took in Meg's hazel eyes, brown curls and oval face. "Ma'am, you sure are a sight for sore eyes, is all I can say," he answered. "Just looking at you makes me feel better. You're good medicine."

"Well, sir, that's what I like to hear," Meg laughed. "Can I get you anything?"

"No, thank you, ma'am. I can't think of anything I need, no ma'am."

The nurse picked up the pencil that had rolled onto the floor and handed it to Barkley. "Looks like you were in the middle of a letter home?"

"Yes, I guess I was."

"Where's home?"

"I'm from North Little Rock, Arkansas," he told her as he took the pencil and picked up where he had left off before the bad memories hijacked his brain.

Meg continued down the ward. She hoped the scuttlebutt wasn't true. She had heard that plans were afoot to transfer Barkley Holt and his entire outfit to serve in combat in the Pacific. Germany had surrendered five days ago, but there was still a war on and Uncle Sam needed soldiers. She wondered if Barkley had heard the rumor too, and wondered what he thought about it if he had.

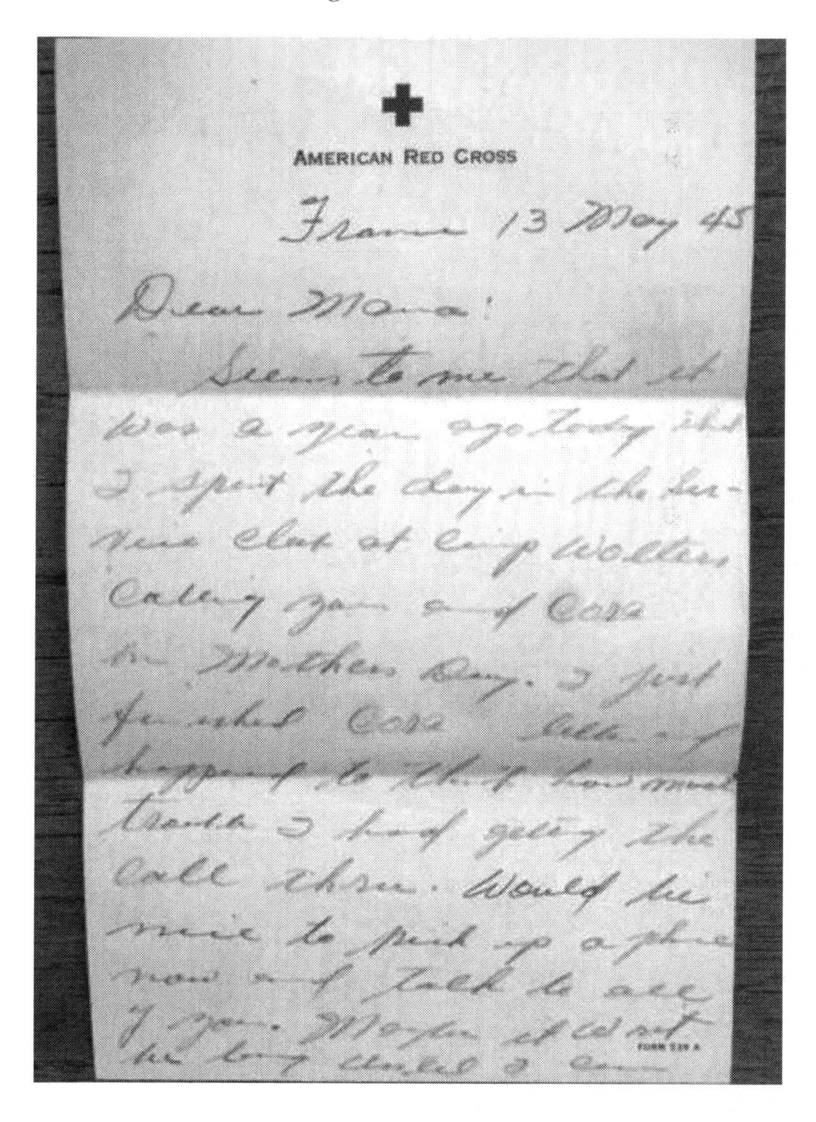

AMERICAN RED CROSS

France 13 May 45

Dear Mama!

Seems to me that it was a year ago today that I spent the day in the service club at Camp Wolters calling you and Cora for Mothers Day. I just finished [illegible] Cora [illegible] happened to [illegible] two months [illegible] I [illegible] getting the call there. Would like mine to pick up a phone now and talk to all of you. Maybe it will not be long until I am

FORM 539 A

20 RIVER VIEW

May 1945. Little Rock, Arkansas.

"Luke, show me where you live again," Imogene demanded with the intent to charm, which it did. The golden and pink sunset cast a glow around her as she looked up at Luke Holt, the youngest of the Holt brothers. Home on leave from his station at a military hospital in Columbus, Georgia, Imogene thought Luke was the epitome of sophistication. The consensus of Imogene's friends at the country and saddle clubs, after much discussion, was that Luke was, how best to put it into words, dashing, that was it. She should cultivate Luke post haste since his furlough was almost over.

With most of the local boys gone to war, the pickings were slim for girls like Imogene who were looking for excitement. Little Rock girls had their eyes on Luke, but he only had eyes for Imogene. Imogene had much to offer, and she was in despair that she was going to seed at eighteen. Her anxiety translated into an edginess that captivated Luke. Her gold lame off the shoulders evening gown reflected the light and she shimmered. Imogene's figure could stop men in their tracks, and her dressmaker had made the gown to show it off, clinging in all the right places, plus a side slit in the skirt up to there.

"Okay," Luke said, and he rotated Imogene around until she was looking over the wall surrounding the patio. Standing close behind Imogene, Luke gazed down the cliff overlooking the bend of the Arkansas River at Little Rock's River View Saddle Club. "Over there, across the river," Luke said, pointing north. "There's Fort Roots Hospital. My house is in a neighborhood that used to be called Argenta, off Maple Street sort of near the river, to the right of where we're looking. I warn you, the house isn't fancy. It's only a one-story rock house." He laughed and added, "But the people who live there are nice."

"How cute!" Imogene smiled. "Can you take me there sometime?" she asked. "I would love to meet your family." Imogene thought Luke her perfect foil. His tall, dark good looks enhanced by his officer's dress khakis were a contrast to her blonde beauty. And Luke was a surgeon to boot. Imogene's skin was flawless and her golden hair cascaded down her back in waves. Her hair sparkled in the day's last rays of sunshine. Luke took it all in. "Sometime," he said.

The opening notes of "The Carousel Waltz," from Rodgers and Hammerstein's new Broadway show, carried out onto the patio from the band inside the clubhouse. Imogene pulled away from Luke and grabbed his hand. "I love this song," she said. "Come on, let's dance." Imogene led the way into the ballroom, marching with her high-heeled sandals across the pink granite patio and pulling Luke along behind her.

Luke chuckled and allowed Imogene to lead him. They joined the other dancers waltzing around the parquet floor of the room. Waiters in formalwear had opened the French doors to allow in the evening spring breeze. Crystal chandeliers hanging from the ceiling cast a golden radiance on the ballroom.

Imogene's mother, Carole, sat on a damask upholstered loveseat, enjoying the music and watching her daughter dance and chatter with Luke. Carole was swaying along with the music when Byron, her husband, joined her. "Did you make her dress?" he whispered in her ear. "It's too mature for a young girl." Carole frowned. "No, Byron," she said. "I did not make it myself. We can afford a dressmaker."

"Well," he replied, "You must have approved it. It's inappropriate."

"Oh Byron, she's stunning in it. Don't be a spoil sport."

"She's stunning all right. At least I know where to find him," Byron said, meaning that as director of surgical residents he could track Captain Holt, a year out of his program, across the US and the globe if need be.

"Really, Byron," Carole shook her head.

"Yes really," he said, not to allow Carole the last word. "That boy can run but he can't hide," he said, scowling at Luke from across the room. "He's a marked man."

Hector, the maitre d', was a regal presence in the River View dining room and a conduit to the netherworld of the kitchen. He had seen to it that the buffet table was laden with delicacies absent from any overseas mess kits or, for that matter, most local kitchens. There were shrimp and oysters trucked up from Biloxi, Mississippi that day, fillet of beef, plus various desserts containing unspecified amounts of sugar and butter, and that was the tip of the food iceberg. There was grumbling in the lower echelon of the kitchen help about it.

"My boy in the Pacific been eatin' K rations for three years, lucky to get C rations." Aaron muttered to Kenny while clearing plates.

"Mmmhmm, some gots it and some don't." Kenny rumbled in agreement.

Knowing he had violated rationing rules and regulations a dozen ways from Sunday, Hector shrouded his acquisition methods in secrecy. That morning he had called a special staff meeting. "Say nothin' to nobody 'bout where we gettin' our food. Unnerstand?" Hector growled, glowering at each person in turn gathered in a semi-circle in front of him. "I better not get word one of anyone of you talkin', you hear me? Do I, you know where the door at. Got it?" A chorus of "Yes, Boss, we hear you," responded.

As the clatter of silverware on bone china died down, the party's host called for a toast. Henry Talbot, the portly middle-aged banker who was a society mainstay, raised his champagne glass high. "To our soldiers on their victory in Europe!" he shouted.

"Hear, hear!" The crowd roared their approval.

Later, Bill Edmund and his club host, DL Crowley, a wealthy cotton and rice farmer, sat on the patio with their after dinner brandy and cigars. Enjoying the evening, DL took a sip of brandy and flicked the ash from his cigar into an ashtray. "Colonel, does this mean my prison labor force will be drying up?" he asked Edmund. "Do you have a date when your Fritz Ritz is being dismantled and my German laborers are getting shipped back home?"

"DL, while I don't have any dates, I think you're probably safe for this year's cotton harvest, but after Christmas, I can't say," Bill replied.

From her position at the other end of the dining room, chosen for its distance from the older generation, Imogene put her hand on Luke's thigh. "So when do I get to meet your folks?" she pressed, tipsy from too much champagne.

"How about Sunday dinner?" Luke said. "But I'll tell you, Imogene, it might not be the happiest dinner. I'm waiting for orders any day now to be shipped overseas."

21 FRIDAY NIGHT IN MANILA

May 1945. Manila, Philippines.

"Come at once. BYOW." Private Derrick Monihan read out loud the scrawled note he had picked up from Captain Graves' desk in the Manila headquarters of the US Army Corps of Engineers.

"Hmm, that's Bring Your Own something…is that Bring Your Own Whiskey or possibly even better but trickier to pull off, Bring Your Own Women? Whatever it means, can I go along with you guys? Your plans sound a whole lot more interesting than what I've got going on here."

Captains Mark Graves and Tom Holt each carried a bottle of whiskey. The brief note had arrived that afternoon in response to their message to Colonel Moore suggesting a visit. They were on their way into the humid equatorial afternoon, responding to their summons from the colonel.

"Whiskey noted," Derrick observed. "You boys will be praying to the porcelain goddess before the night is out."

"In this case I think you mean the wooden goddess," Graves responded.

"You need me to take care of you. I would make sure you get back in one piece," Derrick offered.

"I don't think it will come to that. We can hold our liquor, can't we, Graves?" Tom remarked.

Graves nodded.

"The colonel's note is open to interpretation. Take some women too!" Derrick called as they left the room.

Ignoring Derrick, the pair ambled into the streets of wartime Manila.

"Long Island is a lot nicer than this in summertime," Graves remarked.

"Except for the afternoon showers this weather's not too different from an Arkansas summer," Holt said as he wiped his face.

The usual pack of ragged street children converged on them before they could make it two steps outside the door. Graves placated the children with chocolate bars he pulled from his pockets. The piece de resistance came when Tom extracted a packet of laundry soap from his coat and handed it to the nearest boy. A happy shout arose. Laughing but empty handed, Tom and Graves piled into the army Jeep waiting for them in the alley. They signaled to the driver and the Jeep roared out onto the main thoroughfare.

Tom's thoughts moved to springtime weather in Arkansas. Spring, unlike summer, was cooler than in Manila. He carried a recent picture of the home folks in their Easter best posing in front of the rock house after church. Something was wrong with the picture, though. The military age young men were absent.

He had been fighting the Japanese for 32 months, his brother Barkley had cycled in and out of European combat trenches and field hospitals since before the Battle of the Bulge, and his brother Luke's medical school course was on an accelerated track to prepare him for overseas duty. The new normal was surreal.

"The colonel hasn't been on the island long. I heard he's up for a promotion. He's got an important new job," Graves noted to Tom.

"I guess we'll find out more. He's probably glad to be back in civilization after what happened on Samar." Tom didn't want to say more in the presence of the driver. You never knew how far your words might travel and kick up trouble.

"We're all better off here than where we were before."

"Yeah, hopping from one miserable enemy infested island to another."

A few minutes later the Jeep pulled into MacArthur's headquarters and discharged its passengers. Graves looked at Holt, worried. "You don't think we misread the invite and he meant for us to bring company, do you?" he asked.

"Nah. The colonel sure is one for the cup that cheers," Holt said with a laugh.

22 FRIDAY NIGHT WARM UP

May 1945. Allied Command Headquarters. Manila, Philippines.

"Holt, Graves. Glad you boys could make it. Nice to see you again." Colonel Moore stood up from his desk to greet the junior officers and shake hands all around. "Did y'all run into any trouble getting up here?" he asked in his mild east Texas accent.

"No, sir, not much, just one little skirmish. Nothing like at the Solomons or New Guinea," Tom answered.

"That's good." Colonel Moore ushered his friends to the grubby backroom.

The soldiers spotted an olive drab wool army blanket folded once and spread out on the floor. On impulse, Tom went over and crouched beside it and the others followed along. Tom picked two dice from the bowl resting on the blanket. He blew hard on the dice as he rolled them between his hands. "Let's have fours! Little Joe from Kokomo!" he called. "That'll bring a Quota set at 90 points that gets us outta here and back home!" He tossed the dice onto the blanket.

When the dice rolled nine, the colonel scooped up the dice to return them to the bowl. "Maybe we'd do better with a card game," he chuckled. "I will say, though, boys, there's talk here about starting the quotas at 103 points for officers and 97 or 98 for enlisted men."

"I hope it won't take too long to get down to 91," Tom remarked.

"I wrote my wife to expect me back home in September, Tom. I've got 96 points," Graves commented.

"I don't know, Graves, you tend to be optimistic," Tom said.

"It feels like a long time for those of us who have been over here 24 months and more, although the war is anything but over and it doesn't look like it's going to wrap up soon," the colonel said.

"Yeah, I've got a numbness of the brain that I can't shake," Tom said. "I'm ready to take Temporary Duty home if I can't do any better. I'll take anything, Colonel. After two and a half years I'm pretty tired and worn out. I'm worried about my older brother, Barkley. I'm beside myself at the thought of him being transferred here to invade Japan. He's an enlisted man, barely survived the frontline in Belgium and now this. I don't think he'll last through another go round."

"They need to get some recruits from home to relieve these people who have been doing their duty," the colonel said as they moved to the battered wooden table.

"I don't like to see my younger brother, Luke, have to come out, but I think he will," Tom said, "and it is probably right that he should. In order for some of these people who have been out here 30 to 40 months to get home, somebody is going to have to come out and take their places. They should be getting them out here pretty quick like too."

The colonel plunked glasses on the table and sloshed some bourbon into them. "Thanks for the spirits, fellas."

"Colonel, do we have a fourth joining us?" Graves asked as he looked around the room.

"As a matter of fact, yes." Colonel Moore indicated the corncob pipe resting on a side table. Tom and Graves realized that their card game had gotten serious.

23 FIVE CARD DRAW

May 1945. A back room at Allied Headquarters. Manila, Philippines.

Colonel Moore pulled a fourth wooden folding chair from the office into the back room and plunked it down next to him with an almost comic apologetic expression. "Boys," he said in a low voice, "I'm afraid the evening might not be as relaxing as advertised. I'm sorry to spring this on you at the last minute, but Big Chief is exhausted and in need of a diversion." As though he needed to explain, Colonel Moore added, "Too many casualties."

In response to the stricken look on his friends' faces as they realized who would be joining their party, Moore waved his hands. "Just a friendly game or two, that's all," he said, adding as an aside, "Of course, he has a dim view of gambling, says it's degrading to the service, but I think I've convinced him to make an exception tonight."

"Is Big Chief who I think it is? Colonel, are you pulling my leg?" Tom's eyebrows were into his hairline in shock, which was saying something, since his hairline was beginning to recede. "Are you telling me you want us to play poker with the general even though he disapproves of it?" Tom said when he realized from Colonel Moore's expression that it was no joke. "What can you be thinking? This is a terrible idea, it'll be a disaster, and I'm calling the whole thing off. Come on, Graves, let's get out of here while the getting's good."

Needing no encouragement, Graves was beating his way to the door. "On it, Tom," he called.

"Stay. That's an order." Colonel Moore pulled rank on Tom and Graves with a fierce expression. As they stopped mid track in their departure preparations, obedient to a superior officer, the colonel continued, "He's on board with it, I guarantee you he is. The boss used to enjoy a good game. This is all I could think of that might get his mind off things. It's been grim too long. Even Mrs. MacArthur agreed this would be worth a try, and anything with the Missus' approval is A-okay."

A tall shadow fell into the open doorway, putting an end to further discussion. They were in for it now. The three officers jumped to attention when Douglas MacArthur, Supreme Commander of the Allied Powers Southwest Pacific Area, aka Big Chief, entered the room, followed by his young Filipino valet, Esteban.

"At ease," MacArthur murmured. Colonel Moore made introductions and they seated themselves around the table. The young officers, their game now fraught with challenge by the injection of MacArthur into the mix, took baby sips of bourbon.

MacArthur's reputation as a tyrant and egomaniac was well known, but that day he was at his most congenial. Lighting his trademark pipe, MacArthur puffed on it as he visited with his junior officers as would a favorite uncle.

The evening wore on and the whiskey flowed as they played hand after hand of poker. By the wee hours of the morning only Tom and MacArthur remained in the game, playing underneath a thick haze of tobacco smoke.

"Tom, where are you from?" MacArthur asked, fixing his sharp eyes on him.

"A town on the north side of the Arkansas River across from Little Rock."

"Of course," MacArthur said as though something clicked. "I've been trying to place your accent. You may not know it, but I was born at the Little Rock Arsenal."

"Oh yes, sir. You're famous in Arkansas. Everyone there is proud to claim you."

"Arkansas is a beautiful place. It is a bit off the beaten track. Of course I was military from the get go. Grew up more in New Mexico and San Antonio than Little Rock, though."

"I miss it," Tom confessed.

"What do you think of the Philippines?" MacArthur asked Tom over his hand of cards.

Tom sipped his drink and considered the question. "The people here are remarkable," he said. "Hard working. Clean even when they don't have soap to wash with. I've never seen such an interest in education. I mean, it seems like every third person I run into is a schoolteacher. I admire that. Their country certainly is devastated." Tom discarded a card and MacArthur dealt him another as he nodded in agreement.

Around three am Tom surreptitiously checked his watch. He had a fabulous hand that he hoped would put the game to bed. He had four kings. MacArthur could not compete with that. He laid his cards on the table and looked at the general.

MacArthur's eyebrows rose and he countered with four aces.

When he saw MacArthur's cards and realized he had lost, Tom's first thought was, *what are the chances*. The boys at home would have had some choice comments for him in such a situation. He groaned and then reached out to shake hands in defeat. He reflected that maybe it was best if he didn't come up the winner. MacArthur looked happy enough as he collected the money in the winner's pot and scooted his chair back. He motioned to Tom to step out into his office. Puzzled, Tom followed him. An hour later Tom emerged, his face impassive and his mind on his conversation with MacArthur. He nudged Graves to get up and head home.

As he and Graves walked out to the Jeep in the early dawn, Tom worried about the pig in a poke that he had just bought. He had authorized something MacArthur called a pillar of Project Stonehenge to operate out of his family's home. None of them, including himself, was to know the particulars of the project, other than that it was top secret and would benefit the war effort. MacArthur told him allowing the work to be done at his home would provide security for the future. Tom wondered what that meant, but nobody questioned MacArthur.

The deal he made had the potential to reach around and bite his family hard. Desperate to save his brother Barkley, Tom didn't see any other options. He had made the arrangement with the knowledge that his family's safety might fall to the wayside in the face of ruthless ambition to win at all cost, but a soldier could be on the frontline only so long before his number came up. The math wasn't hard to understand.

Meanwhile, back in his office, MacArthur motioned to Esteban, who was in constant attendance, waiting for the evening to conclude so he could go to bed. He jumped up to see what the chief wanted. Esteban was in complete awe of MacArthur. His boss was a hero and the savior of the Filipino people and he could do no wrong.

Esteban stood listening to the brief instructions before disappearing down the hall. A few moments later he reappeared in the doorway and indicated he was ready. He had initiated a transoceanic call to MacArthur's counterpart, General Dwight Eisenhower, Supreme Commander of Allied forces Europe.

MacArthur picked up his phone. "Ike? Can you do a little something for me? There's a soldier over there by name of Barkley Holt. I want immediate discharge papers drawn up for him. Honorable. A little pension. Yeah, yeah, he's in a hospital in France. Let's get him out of there as soon as you can. Hell, can you send the entire unit home? They've done their part and then some. I'll get replacement soldiers out here somehow or other." There was a pause as he listened to the response. "OK," he said. "Thanks. Bye."

Next MacArthur dictated a message to be translated into code before being dispatched. The recipient was Bill Edmund, Camp Robinson, Arkansas.

When the message was out, MacArthur's vision fell on Esteban. "Esteban!" he roared, "What are you doing up this late? Do you have any idea what time it is? Get yourself off to bed. How are we going to win this war IF NOBODY GETS ANY SLEEP?"

With that final bellow MacArthur stood up and patted his pockets. He withdrew his poker winnings and thrust them at Esteban. "Here, son, give these to your mother," he said before striding out.

Delighted, Esteban transferred the money to his own pocket. He lingered a few minutes to tidy up the desk before turning out the light and heading off to bed for a few hours.

24 DOT TO DOT

May 1945.

Moscow

Staff at the GRU in Moscow, the Soviet intelligence gathering organization, worked around the clock as the war in Europe ground to a stop. While preparing to accept surrender from Germany, their focus was shifting to their allies. They did not trust the Americans, even though they were at that moment fighting on the same side. Their urgent agenda was to discover what kind of secrets America was keeping from them.

The night shift had been slow until now. *Babi's got to see this!* Igor thought when he had deciphered the wire as best he could. He jumped up from his post and announced, "Sir, we intercepted this wire out of MacArthur's headquarters in Manila early Saturday," as he handed the latest piece of information to his boss.

Intrigued, Sergei Babikov stared at the message. Although only a few words were legible, since the Americans' code was incompletely deciphered, one curious word stood out: "Granite." Sergei knew they must learn more about "Granite."

"Find out who received this wire and pinpoint the location," Babikov ordered.

"Yes, sir," Igor responded, and hustled off to see what he could turn up. Given the breadth of their information cache about the American war operation, it should not take long to discover where the wire was received. Locating the intended recipient was trickier and would take some time.

Babikov knew the Americans would substitute code names for code names, so this "Granite" was probably not the real name for whatever it was and "Jeffrey" was not the recipient's actual name, but he was somebody and they would identify him.

Later that afternoon Igor told Babikov, "Sir, the wire sent from MacArthur's headquarters was delivered to a prisoner of war camp near somewhere called North Little Rock, Arkansas."

"Where?" Babikov frowned. He had never heard of Arkansas, but then America was a big country.

"It is a mid-sized southern state with a large rural population," Igor answered.

"Ah," Babikov nodded. It made perfect sense to him for the Americans to put their prisoners in a remote location. The Russians had been doing that for years in Siberia.

Berlin

Berlin was a mass of confusion. Soviet armored cars and tanks converged on the vanquished city in the wake of Hitler's suicide and the German surrender. Bristling with armed soldiers who had instructions to shoot to kill, the vehicles rolled through the streets. Fearing retaliation, Berlin's starving citizens watched the victors from barricaded basement windows.

British troops under Field Marshall Bernard Montgomery and American soldiers under Dwight Eisenhower, Supreme Commander of the Allied forces, joined the Soviets in the conquered city. A Soviet squadron erected an enormous portrait of a regal looking Josef Stalin, replacing the one of Hitler lying face down in rubble. Monty and Ike's soldiers watched, sensing impending conflict between the victors.

Ike had held his Allied troops back in order to allow the Soviets to reach Berlin first, honoring the Yalta agreement between the big three powers. If he'd disregarded the agreement, he could have claimed Berlin first and given the democratic governments a stronger negotiating position postwar, but he hadn't, and he'd been criticized for it. The Soviets had taken Berlin at great cost, losing one hundred thousand soldiers in the effort.

The more of Germany the Soviets saw they were perplexed, and then they got mad. Most of the rank and file soldiers had never been out of the Soviet Union before.

"I don't understand," one soldier remarked to another after invading a town. "Why did they make war on us? They are rich, much richer than we are."

"Never have I seen so many people living so well," his friend agreed. "I did not know it was possible."

A countrywide manhunt was on to find Werner Heisenberg, Nobel Laureate in Physics and director of the Kaiser Wilhelm Institute. Once discovered Heisenberg was to be detained and interrogated by special operations forces. Both the Americans and the Russians had an imperative to find Heisenberg first and discover what he had been up to since the war started. The burning questions needing answers were how far along was Germany in the development of the uranium bomb, and where was the research facility?

Soviet soldiers raided German state offices not destroyed by bombs or torched by the Germans themselves before their capitulation. The Soviets searched through government documents confiscated in hopes of finding useful information.

Midway through the third day of occupation a detachment of Soviet soldiers inspected the vacant Department of Education's offices on the fourth floor. The building was intact except for the bombed off exterior wall. Abandoned in anticipation of the invading armies, the office was open to the outdoors with a sheer drop of four stories down.

Natasha Hesse and Alisa Volkov, two young soldiers, wandered around the open-air office. They opened file cabinets containing meticulous records and flicked through the contents. They looked at each other, puzzled, wondering how to determine what was worth sending back home.

The unopened mail sitting on the counter caught Natasha's eye. She noticed several envelopes bearing American stamps. Pushing her rifle to one side in order to use both hands, she flipped through the mail. "How about mail from imperialist America?" she said, holding up the envelopes.

Alisa shrugged and tucked the envelopes into her bag. "Let's send it to Moscow," she said, "who knows, maybe it will be of value somehow."

Moscow

At the GRU, Babikov studied the intelligence gathered from his agents across the world. He had a list of the Kaiser Wilhelm Institute employees and all known current and former students of Werner Heisenberg as well as his scientific collaborators from the past ten years. The list included the current location, as best known, of each person. It was a vast yet incomplete list, and he was working to fix that.

A stack of papers referenced key information about the Manhattan Project, the secret atomic bomb development program underway in a remote part of New Mexico, as reported by Soviet agents in New Mexico and New York.

A wall map of the United States held pins for Chicago, Oakridge, Tennessee and Los Alamos, New Mexico. Babikov took a new pin and stuck it into the map in the approximate location of North Little Rock, Arkansas.

"Do we have someone in place here?" Babikov asked Igor.

"No, sir. We have a sleeper cell nearby and an informant at the Pine Bluff Arsenal, about fifty miles away."

"Activate the sleeper."

"Yes sir."

Urfeld

The American forces' Jeep jerked up the slopes of the Walchensee Alps outside the German town of Urfeld, the motor straining with the steep incline. The Jeep took the same route that Uwe Johannes had hiked three years before. Even though fighting in most of Germany had been subdued, this area was hot. The alpine region swarmed with dangerous soldiers of a wide range of nationalities and allegiances, SS groups poised to string a stray soldier up as a deserter and roving bands of starving people ready to steal or kill for food.

Riding in the front of the Jeep was Colonel Boris Pash, leader of the Alsos Commission, his expression reflecting the importance and extreme urgency of his trip. Pash had a direct line of communication to the Manhattan Project. He was in Germany to discover the progress of their atomic bomb program and destroy it and the countryside around it if need be.

Pash was determined to capture Heisenberg and take him to a secret location in Great Britain for interrogation. The son of White Russian-American immigrant parents, Pash maintained a healthy distrust of the Soviets. If he were to be successful, the Soviets and Werner Heisenberg would never see each other.

Pash's intelligence said Heisenberg had a home somewhere nearby. Midway through the afternoon the Jeep stopped at the base of a footpath leading to Heisenberg's remote mountain cottage. Frau

Heisenberg, alone with her small children, watched six armed soldiers walk up the mountainside and surround her home. Panic rising within her, she stood in the door with the knowledge that she and her children were cornered.

When Colonel Pash reached the house, he addressed her in fluent German. "Frau Heisenberg, my name is Colonel Pash, and I am with the American army. Is your husband home?"

"Heisenberg is not here," she replied, leaning against the door in relief with the news that the Americans had reached them before the Soviets.

"Place a telephone call to your husband and tell him to come home immediately," Pash instructed her.

At the same time that Colonel Pash and his soldiers were approaching his home, Werner Heisenberg was in a nearby village visiting his elderly mother. He heard the grinding gears of a Jeep negotiating the steep road and looked out of the window to see who it was. When he saw the Jeep full of soldiers drive by, he knew why they were there; they were looking for him. He told his mother goodbye and rode his bicycle home. He pedaled faster and faster as he thought about the implications of the soldiers reaching his home before he did. They would be expecting to discover his progress on making the uranium bomb, and he feared they would not be nice about it.

When Heisenberg appeared on the path leading to his house, Colonel Pash approached him with his orders, "Werner Heisenberg, you are under arrest."

Pash interrogated Heisenberg all night, mining him for information on the status of German weaponry research and all of Heisenberg's communications with scientists outside of the country. The following morning Heisenberg left the cottage amid an entourage of armored tanks and Jeeps that arrived in the night. A contingent of the Alsos Commission took Heisenberg to Heidelberg, Paris, Belgium and then to Farm Hill near Cambridge University in England.

Moscow

Word filtered through the Soviet intelligence community that Werner Heisenberg had been captured by the Americans and transferred out of Germany to an unknown location.

Sergei Babikov sifted through his information, trying to find a string to pull on the atomic bomb project going on in the states. The loss of Heisenberg was a disappointment but perhaps not fatal to their goal of learning how to produce and deliver an atomic bomb.

The Fuchs-Greenglass-Gold-Rosenberg Soviet spy pipeline was funneling useful information out of New Mexico. With receipt of his newest intelligence, Babikov suspected that the Allies had diversified and were supporting atomic weaponry research locations operating as satellites to Los Alamos. Igor had cracked part of the American code. Babikov wanted to learn more about Stonehenge.

"Igor!" Babikov called.

"Sir?"

"Call Colonel Osokin in for a planning session. Ask him who we have currently in the area. We will need one person to serve as liaison with our agents there and to create a team to ingratiate itself with the people at this house, such that they don't know what's happening. I know a young woman agent who speaks fluent American English and who is good at accents who might be perfect."

"Right away, sir."

25 A PILLAR OF STONEHENGE

May 1945. #800 West 8th Street, North Little Rock, Arkansas.

It was Saturday morning and Pete Peters and Bill Edmund had finished eating a counter breakfast at Argenta Drug Store on Main Street. "All right then, it's time for you to meet the family now that the house is ready, before we install our engineer," Edmund said, putting on his hat and walking out the door.

"I guess they've got a spare bedroom available for a foreign boarder since Luke Holt's been deployed," Pete remarked as they walked down 8th Street from Main where they had left their car.

Pete was fishing for information, something he had to do since his security clearance apparently did not place him in a need to know category. That irked him, given his suspicion that his new assignment was going to be security for the Arkansas arm of Project Stonehenge. He didn't even have a clear understanding of what the project was since it was buttoned up tighter than anything he had seen yet.

"It was going to happen eventually," Edmund said as he took in their surroundings.

Pete thought, so it was true, Luke Holt was on shipboard headed to a medical unit somewhere in the South Pacific, probably unaware of the reason for his abrupt departure.

Bill had had to take action. As he answered Pete's question, Bill thought that if the project had any hope of maintaining secrecy, Luke had better become scarce. He attracted security risk hangers on such as Imogene Park.

It was like Luke had told Imogene; the neighborhood they walked through wasn't fancy. The houses were built in a flat area close to the river. The houses were not large although there was space between them. Oak, magnolia and hickory trees thrived in the topsoil from the ancient flood plain. Frequent blasts of train whistles and clangs and thumps sounded from the rail yard to their right.

"Wow, that's really loud," Pete said.

"That's the city's night music," Bill laughed. "A lot of the people in this neighborhood make their livings working at the yard."

"My uncle is a railroad man and he wants to be buried next to the train tracks so's he can hear the trains running even after he's dead," Pete said.

As they continued on their way, a middle aged, heavy-set woman approached them. She wore her hair in a bandana tied in two places on the front of her head near her temples, and grizzled strands of hair peeked around the edges; the effect gave her face the appearance of a round flower. Her worn shirt and skirt were nondescript. She seemed to have come from the vicinity of the train yard.

"Suh's, I wonder, could you spare a nickel?" she spoke in a soft voice. "I need to make a phone call and oh my, I'm in a sorry way today. I need to call my son to come get me and help me home. I don't got no way to get there my ownself."

Edmund fished inside his pocket and pulled out a hand full of coins, which he gave to the woman.

"Oh, I do thank you, sir. God bless you, sir," she said as she faded away.

"I was going to say this seems like a nice neighborhood, but now I'm wondering," Pete said as they continued towards the house. "Do you think we'll have to worry about break-in's?"

"I give you, it is a little troubling," Edmund answered, "but while parts of this town are depressed, and a good sized portion of the population is poor or at least not well off, I think our house is as secure as an individual home can be. Just because somebody is poor doesn't make 'em a thief."

Well, I know that, but still…, Pete thought.

"This house has so many people living in it plus a housekeeper it is never vacant for long," Edmund said, "so there won't be much opportunity for someone to break in. That works in our favor. There will be stretches of time where only Mrs. Holt or Mrs. Lane will be home, though, so our engineer, which is what we're supposed to call him, will be able to get work done. Peters, I'm counting on you to make this a secure project."

Hah, I knew it, Pete thought.

"Fortunately, the house has a basement for our fellow to work in, and we've managed to make renovations without arousing neighbors' suspicions," Edmund continued. "We've put in a special telephone line. The alley behind the house will come in handy because it is shielded from the surrounding homes. This is war work after all, and I'm not too keen about mixing it up with civilians any more than necessary. I guess it takes a whole lot of different kinds of people, though, to win a war."

Pete scrutinized the house and yard. There was a wide strip of lawn in front, and the house had exits in front and back. The house was one story and made of native brown fieldstone. The porch screen obscured the front door. Windows faced the street, side and back yards. The backyard was hidden from view by shrubbery growing against the fence, and the gate across the driveway would allow for private access.

"The house is all right, the question is the people. I hope they can keep a big secret," Pete remarked.

"They've all, including the housekeeper, been cleared," Edmund said. "They've also been briefed as much as is allowed about the project. With three sons on active duty, they're motivated to do whatever they can to help the war effort."

The gravel driveway crunched underfoot as they walked beside the house. A screen door slammed to. "Shoo, bird, get on with yourself, you don't belong inside!" a cheerful voice called.

When Edmund and Peters rounded the corner, the speaker came into view. "That is the housekeeper, Mrs. Cristobel Lane," Edmund told Pete. "She's an important part of this project since she is home during the day. She's also a bit of a concern from a security standpoint. She's got eight children to keep this secret from, but everybody tells me she's all right."

Cristobel was standing on the landing of the short concrete stairway leading from the house. She was a woman in her late-thirties of medium height and a wiry build. Her shoulder length black hair was kept in a smooth roll in the back with a hair net. But it was her sharp, good-humored wit that hit hard at first meeting and eclipsed thoughts about her appearance.

"Are you kiddin? Eight kids and a job?" Pete said, too low for anyone except Colonel Edmund to hear. "She probably can't stay awake long enough to tell tales."

"Chicken," Cristobel said as she flapped her apron at the chicken that stood looking at her through the screen door, "move along!" She chuckled, her laugh resonating deep inside her throat as she looked at the bird's bright eyes, her own eyes sparkling. Because Cristobel had clipped the chicken's wings, both she and the bird knew it could not go far, and indeed it only hopped down the back concrete steps leading to the kitchen and began pecking for worms in the backyard.

"Hello there." Cristobel had caught sight of Pete and Colonel Edmund and held the door open for them.

"Good morning, Mrs. Lane." Bill Edmund shook her hand.

"'Mornin,' sir."

"This is my assistant, Sergeant Peters. Pete, this is Mrs. Cristobel Lane."

"Pleased to meet you." Pete stuck out his hand.

"Pleasure to meet you," she said, shaking his hand. "And both of you's, you can call me Cristobel." She ushered them through the kitchen to the front of the house.

They followed Cristobel across the alternating black and white linoleum floor tiles, past the sink on the left and the white enamel gas stove on the right and through a wooden swinging door into the front of the house. She walked with a slight shuffle because she had pushed the backs of her shoes down to make them slip-ons.

"Come right on in, they's waiting in the living room." Cristobel shot a calculating look at the pair as they moved through the house. While Pete and Colonel Edmund were evaluating the house and its occupants, they were unaware that as far as Cristobel was concerned they too were on probation.

The window on the left hand wall allowed filtered light into the room through Venetian blinds and tied back floor length floral drapes. In front of them, on the left hand side of the large open space connecting the dining and living rooms, was a china cabinet. The glassware was pretty in the dim light. The restful atmosphere of the house reminded Bill Edmund of home, and he thought how nice it would be to linger there. It was a contrast to the rough prisoner of war camp, even if he was the captor and not the captive.

A walnut dining room table on the right hand side and the coordinating buffet against the wall behind it took up most of the remaining space in the dining room. Pete noticed the student Bible with a battered black cover and gild edged pages lying on the buffet. An intruder, that's what he was, Pete thought. He knew he was carrying violence into somebody's house because while he didn't know the particulars of Project Stonehenge, he knew it wasn't knitting.

A mirror on the wall above the buffet reflected the light and images from outside the living room windows opposite and made the rooms appear larger than they were. The old trees lining the street were full of new leaves and cast a green light into the house. Pete was reminded of the tree house he'd had when he was a kid.

Pete and Colonel Edmund stood in the arched entry between the dining and living rooms. The living room had a sofa against one wall and two armchairs flanking a small fireplace opposite. Four people sat on this furniture waiting for their meeting. Coffee cake fresh from the oven, little napkins, and steaming pots of coffee and tea waited on a coffee table in front of the sofa.

Jake Holt, tall and thin, with receding gray hair, stood up to shake their hands. He wore a starched white button down long sleeved shirt, grey trousers, and a narrow striped tie. "Let me introduce my wife, Tina Holt, my sister-in-law, Miss Beryl Barkley, and my daughter, Miss Mamie Holt," Jake said with the measured and courteous manner characteristic of an older Southern gentleman.

Earlier, in preparation for the inspection, Colonel Edmund had given Pete the dossier on the Holts, and now Pete matched faces with the names on the paperwork. Jake, age 69, was an established insurance agent with a firm in Little Rock.

Tina, age 60, Jake's wife and the mother of their four children, was a housewife. She suffered from debilitating bouts of nerves, which had lead to the hiring of Cristobel to help her. When he read that part, Pete had stopped. "Nerves?" he said. "What does that mean? Is that going to give us a problem?"

"What do you expect, anyways, for Christ sakes?" Bill Edmund had snapped back. "Just because she gets down in the dumps sometimes doesn't mean she's a security risk. God knows if we eliminated everybody who got down from time to time in this world our ranks would be too thin to fight the fight. The lady's under a lot of stress."

Touchy, touchy, Pete thought, but held his tongue. Pete had to agree, though, after he met her, that Tina would be all right. She didn't look to be on the verge of collapse or worse.

Pete had read on. The daughter, Mamie, age 35, had not married, and lived with her family. She had a degree from Draughton's Business School in Little Rock and worked as a secretary and bookkeeper for the Office of Price Administration. Pete noted that it was Mamie who had contracted the building of the rock house nine years earlier, and the house title was in her name.

Pete and Mamie smiled at each other and shook hands. His first thought was why hadn't some great guy scooped her up and married her before now. She was real pretty and she seemed smart and nice too. A bit old for him, maybe, but somebody was missing a good deal. And, unless he was mistaken, Pete thought it didn't hurt Mamie's feelings to host a foreign engineer who was working on a clandestine war project in her basement. She looked like she didn't mind having her cage rattled.

Tina's sister Beryl taught 10th grade at the local high school. She was unmarried and had a permanent home with her sister's family. Despite her fashionable dress and hairdo, Miss Beryl bore an uncanny resemblance to Sister Mary Emmanuel, Pete's fourth grade teacher at Holy Wounds School back home in Eau Claire. Miss Beryl was in fact giving him a sharp eye, and he flinched just from memory. She looked to be cut from a similar cloth as Sister. Pete thought if Sister Mary Emmanuel had had his number, which she did, and Miss Beryl Barkley took after Sister Mary Emmanuel, then he should sit as far away from Miss Beryl as possible, and when the time came that's what he did.

"This is our final meeting before the project gets going," Edmund said after the initial pleasantries were over.

"Cristobel, please join us," Jake Holt said to Cristobel, who was standing in the dining room.

"Oh yes, yes, this should include everyone," Edmund said.

Pete reached around and brought in another chair from the dining room.

After everybody was seated and the coffee and tea were poured, the cake cut and passed around, Bill Edmund spoke. "We have selected an engineer to work here, and he should be ready to begin next week. There has been a hitch in the plans, uh," and he cleared his throat before continuing, "and we hope you will be able to help us with a protracted adjustment period for the fellow who has experienced an unfortunate problem." The group answered with questioning looks and raised eyebrows to Colonel Edmund, who responded with a condensed version of the circumstances leading up to Uwe's injuries.

The meeting was short, the details having been worked out before. "That went well, I thought," Bill remarked after they had said their good-byes and the door closed behind them.

"Yeah, they took it pretty good that their new boarder is going to be arriving in pieces because his brethren deemed him unpatriotic," Pete answered.

They walked down the porch steps on their way back to the car and Camp Robinson and the prisoner of war world. Pete motioned to the colonel to slow down when something a few houses down caught his eye. He couldn't say if it was a movement or something else that wasn't right.

A man sat in the shade on a porch swing facing the street. He wore an undershirt, work pants, house slippers and, despite the warm day, a knit cap. Pete walked over to the house to investigate. When he got closer, he froze. Bill Edmund saw it the same time Pete did and they crouched down in the camellias planted beside the porch.

The man was staring straight in front of him. A rifle was balanced across his lap. It was difficult to read his expression. Pete's hand went to the pistol that he wore inside his jacket. Edmund shook his head and Pete dropped his hand to his side but stayed alert. There wasn't much time to wonder what would happen next because the man set his rifle down before he stepped off the porch and walked out to the yard.

Edmund and Pete stood up when the man came over to them. When he stuck out his hand to shake, they relaxed. "Hobart Harrison, pleased to meet you," he said.

On closer inspection they could see that the man was old, and when he spoke it was with a lisp because most of his teeth were missing. Pete knew he was not much of a threat when unarmed. Pete and Edmund shook hands with him.

"I was born in 1862," Hobart informed Pete.

"Is that right?" Pete said, lacking a better response.

"How old am I?" Hobart asked.

"Well, Mister, I guess you're 83 years old."

"Oh thank you," Hobart said before returning to his porch swing and placing his rifle back on his lap.

Pete and Edmund resumed their walk to the car, by unspoken agreement deciding not to pursue the matter further.

"You know the house across the street?" Edmund said.

"The red brick one?"

"Yes. I've rented it for you, and you are going to sleep there and keep an eye on things."

"Boss, why don't we give this guy an office at Camp Rob?"

"No can do. Orders are for an off site location. I'll tell you this much, the orders are from on high."

"Well, I see lots of problems with this situation," Pete said. "There are all sorts of odd people around. I'm being charitable when I say that; you can bet there will be vagrants from the rail yard or wandering in from the riverboats. Gun toting nuts."

Pete also was seeing potential problems with an adventure and thrill-seeking secretary. And what about the housekeeper? She might be all right, but how about those eight children? How about an insurance agent? How about the lady with bad nerves? It could bring trouble crashing down on their heads, well probably the insurance agent was okay, but he couldn't say the same for the others. He thought it would be far more sensible to have all this at a military facility. What had the colonel said, something about it taking all kinds of people to win a war? They would get to see how that worked out.

"I'm counting on you, Pete. Try to keep Mr. Harrison from blowing up the neighborhood," Edmund said.

What had appeared on paper as a stable, even keeled environment was anything but. Pete now was thinking kind thoughts about Miss Beryl Barkley. She might be his salvation. He might need her to keep the neighborhood in line.

26 TEA AND SYMPATHY

May 1945. #800 West 8th Street, North Little Rock, Arkansas.

When Tina Holt looked at Uwe tucked up in her son's bed it was as though he was any soldier, not a German prisoner of war who had fought against her own. Mental pictures of boys across the globe who were maimed for life, held captive in prison camps or dead flitted through Tina's mind, and she cried for everybody.

"Lord have mercy!" she murmured. "Poor boy, poor boy."

Uwe smiled at her to show he would be all right. She seemed to be a few years older than his mother. Tina's dark brown hair was captured in a tight bun at the nape of her neck, but that was the only severe thing about her.

"You're like one of my own boys," she said. She removed her wire frame glasses and mopped her eyes with a handkerchief and turned to look at her younger sister.

"Beryl, don't you think this could be Barkley," Tina said, her voice quavering as she fought for composure while thinking of her oldest son who had been in and out of European field hospitals for months, "or Tom or someday soon Luke, hurt and away from home in a foreign country?"

"He could be, Sister, he surely could." Beryl nodded her head of wavy light brown hair. She pulled a handkerchief from her pocket to dab at her own eyes and reached out to pat Tina.

The rock house was seven miles away from camp in distance but it was worlds apart in other ways. Uwe was installed in the Holt's home, his head in a clean white bandage and his ribs bound in place with tape. He had arrived by private car earlier in the morning and gone straight to bed.

"Lawsy, Lawsy!" Cristobel exclaimed in shock as she came into the room and stood at the foot of Uwe's bed. "This is the boy what got put up in bed in sorry shape because he didn't want to go to a birthday party? What kind of world are we livin' in?"

"And put there by his own people too," Beryl added.

"This is somethin' else," Cristobel said. "If I were managin' things at that camp wouldn't I see to it that somebody got their comeuppance."

"Isn't that the truth," Beryl said. "Cristobel, you would have the whole camp marching straight before dinnertime."

"Yes, indeed," Tina contributed. "If the ladies were to wield more influence wouldn't the world be in a better place?"

Uwe looked at the tenderhearted faces clustered around him, two sets of worried blue eyes and one of brown, and knew he had reached safe haven.

"Mercy me, young man," Tina said once she had regained her self control, "you must think of me as your adoptive mother and my house your home as long as you remain in this country.

This declaration brought earnest nods from the other two women.

Beryl, always the schoolteacher, addressed the business at hand, "And this young man is supposed to solve engineering related problems here?"

Tina straightened up. "Yes, it is private work," she said, "and as Jake and Colonel Edmund explained, his presence here is to be kept discreet, as unobtrusive as possible. Mr. Uwe will work downstairs in the storm cellar as soon as he is able. Tom asked us to do this. He said it is very important." Beryl and Cristobel nodded.

Noting the pencil, slide rule and pad of paper on the bedside table, Tina said to her patient, "But no working on problems taxing to your brain, sir, until you're good and able."

"You listen to her, young man," Cristobel said as she turned to go. "I'll step out now, but I'll be back soon with lunch."

In the kitchen Cristobel prepared a lunch suitable for an invalid. That morning she had made a vat of vegetable soup from tomatoes, bell peppers, corn and green beans. Cristobel tossed in a handful of spaghetti noodles and seasoned the soup with salt and pepper. When the noodles were cooked, she ladled the soup into a bowl and put it on a tray. She added a side plate with a hot buttered biscuit on it. Lunch was ready.

"Now you eat everything, young feller. Build your strength back," Cristobel instructed as she placed the tray on Uwe's lap so as to not hurt his ribs.

27 CHECKING IN

May 1945. #602 West 8th Street, North Little Rock, Arkansas.

It was almost dark when Pete got off the bus and walked to his billet on 8th Street after a meeting with Colonel Edmund. The red brick house had a bull's eye view of the rock house across the street. Days he spent close by so that he could keep an eye on things. Early evenings found Pete on the front porch with the newspaper after a walk around the block. Late evenings he sat in the darkened front room looking out the window, shielded by the drapes. So far 8th Street had been boring and normal, which was what they wanted, but he was an unhappy soldier.

Pete turned the key in the lock and swung the front door open to the still house. It was hard to say what tipped him off, maybe it was the faint familiar scent he couldn't place, but he suspected the house was not empty. Pulling his revolver from the holster strapped under his jacket, Pete walked inside, his footsteps echoing in the bare house.

He stopped and lowered his gun when he entered the kitchen. "What are you doing here?" Pete asked.

Claudette Reynolds sat on a folding chair facing the door in the darkening house. It was the only chair in the house. She wore her work clothes and was sipping a beer she had pulled from Pete's refrigerator.

"Hello, Pete."

"Claudette, you almost got yourself killed and gave me a heart attack in the bargain." Pete reached over and flicked the overhead light on.

"Flat feet, Pete? Really? And a heart murmur? Since when? What's going on?"

"Claudette, I can't talk about it," Pete said, realizing it was useless to pretend. "Anyway, how did you find out?"

"I typed up the paperwork."

"Mother asked you to do that?"

"Yes. He tried to disguise it, but I figured it out. Edmund tried to do it himself but he ended up having to ask me for help. He acted like it was run of the mill paperwork for a 4-F assignment, but then you disappeared and I put things together. Plus, he's bad at subterfuge. You know how straightforward he is."

Pete went to the refrigerator and got a beer for himself. He popped the cap off using the bottle opener screwed to the kitchen cabinet next to the sink. Leaning against the wall, he sipped his beer to give himself time to think.

Pete gave Claudette a searching look. "While I understand about the 4-F paperwork, that doesn't explain how you tracked me here."

"Pete," Claudette said, "I'm a local. I know almost everybody in town."

"I guess you do. Does anyone else know?" This last he said with a worry.

"No, don't fret about that, but don't you want to tell me what's going on? I could walk across the street, poke my head in the back door and ask my cousins for the time of day, but I'll tell you, they have become close lipped. I no longer feel as welcome as I once did."

"Claudette, I can't tell you, and please don't ask me." He sighed. "Everybody in this town seems related, or at least to know each other really well."

Claudette changed tactics, hoping to extract information with a new approach. "How's it going, living in this neighborhood?"

"I'm not having trouble maintaining a low-profile, seeing as how nobody wants to associate with a young guy who's not in uniform." Pete took a swallow of beer. "The nice girls don't want to have anything to do with me, so I couldn't get a date even if Mother allowed it."

Claudette tried to appear sympathetic, hoping Pete would confide in her.

"The mailman is the most popular guy on the street," Pete continued, it making him feel better to share his misery with someone else. "It's embarrassing to watch the mothers waiting for mail from their boys at the front while I'm sitting on the porch, so when I see him coming I slip inside. I can't hold my head up. People cross the street when they see me. Give me the stink eye. Melrose Grocery wants me to come to the back door for my groceries." Pete broke off, unable to continue.

"Can you slip away for dinner? My treat at the White Pig Inn."

"Oh, Claudette, that would be nice, but no way can you treat."

"How about we not bother Mother with this?" Claudette said on their way to the White Pig.

"I dunno, Claudette, he might should know."

"Let's not add to his stress," she answered.

28 THE HIDING PLACE

May 1945. #800 West 8th Street, North Little Rock, Arkansas.

Uwe had given considerable thought to the storage of his medal. He didn't want to keep it on his person any longer. Wearing the medal was keeping him from concentrating fully on his work, and he needed to find a safe place to store it. The data was old now, but it was Heisenberg's work and he wanted to save it. He had nixed all outdoor hiding places because the seal on the medal probably was not watertight enough to survive a thorough soaking. Tom's bedroom didn't have any suitable nooks or crannies, the basement workroom held possibilities, but Uwe worried about getting cut off from the basement in case of an emergency. Colonel Edmund had issued instructions for the immediate take down of the basement workroom if they were betrayed. No, he couldn't risk getting cut off from the medal.

Uwe emerged from the middle bedroom into the short hallway of the darkened house. Careful, be careful. Don't wake anybody up. The thoughts ran through his head as he edged down the hall. The other two bedrooms were in close quarters. He looked to either side, hoping that Tina and Jake were asleep on the left and Beryl and Mamie in the room on the right, at opposite ends of the hall. After checking to confirm that all doors were closed, Uwe eased down the hallway to his right, avoiding the middle of the oak floorboards lest they creak, and turned left at the end of the hall.

Given the few opportunities for privacy in his new home, Uwe had decided to make his move the evening of the full moon. The moonlight shining through the living room windows provided enough light for him to find his way without bumping into things and waking anybody up, eliminating the need for a flashlight.

Entering the living room, Uwe made his way across it to investigate a box that he had noticed on his first day in the house. The rectangular shaped box had been sent from the Holt's son Tom who was fighting in the Philippines. The sides were carved with scenes of Filipino life, and it occupied a place of honor on the table beside the sofa.

Uwe picked the box up, sat down onto the sofa and slid the top off. A shaft of moonlight coming in through the window shone on the contents. He removed a cylindrical metal tin from the box. Unscrewing the top, he ground his teeth when hundreds of cowry shells from a far away seashore spilled out and clattered from the container as they scattered around the room. Frozen least he create further noise, he silently cursed seashell collectors the world over.

Uwe waited to see if Beryl and Mamie, asleep in the room on the other side of the wall, were disturbed. He took deep breaths and willed his hands to stop shaking. Why was he sneaking around a strange house in which he was a guest, in Arkansas, in the nighttime, looking for a safe place to stow his medal? And his hosts were nice people. One day in the house and that was clear. What if they turned on the lights and discovered their houseguest sitting in the dark with war hero Tom's box open on his lap? He cringed at the picture of him trying to explain himself in such a situation. It would be an awful scene with serious consequences.

After a few minutes and the house remained quiet, Uwe scooped the scattered shells up and returned them to the canister, sliding them in and trying to minimize the clink-clink sounds. He ran his hands over the rough upholstery of the couch to ensure he hadn't missed any, because how would stray cowry shells be explained in the daylight? Next he went down on his hands and knees and felt the entire floor of the room in search of shells. He discovered that the floor was clean, but he did find the odd shell in a remote corner. Hoping he had located them all, he screwed the lid back on the container.

Considering the risk already undertaken, Uwe decided he might as well finish the venture, and he continued exploring the box's contents. He picked up a velvet pouch measuring about six inches long by three inches wide. Loosening the drawstring closure, Uwe reached in and found a thick roll of paper money. A handful of silver coins weighed down the bottom. Squinting at the bills, Uwe could see they were foreign. Tom must have collected them on his travels through the South Pacific. Uwe put the pouch beside him. As his fingers searched further through the nooks and crannies of the box, his heart rate quickened when a hidden compartment sprang open.

Inside the secret compartment was a medal so similar to Uwe's, minus his adaptation, of course, that the two could be confused at first glance. Tom must have earned a special battle commendation and sent his medal home hidden in the box for safekeeping. Uwe held Tom's medal near to his eyes for inspection in the moonlight. Except for the eagle on the center of Tom's there wasn't much difference between the two medals. The colors on the ribbons were different, but the patterns of the stripes were similar. Both medals were crosses with four short, equidistant arms. Uwe doubted, however, that Tom's medal was as loaded as his.

Deciding that Tom wouldn't be home to claim the box anytime soon, since he probably was stuck in the Pacific for the duration of the war, Uwe slipped his medal in beside Tom's and closed the secret compartment. He replaced the box's contents as close as possible to how he had found them, slid the top on and put the box back on the side table. He adjusted the tilt to the same angle as it had been before he picked it up.

Uwe made his way back to his bedroom and closed the door, satisfied with his night's work. He thought about fate, and how strange it was for him to be sleeping in Tom's bed and working in his house while Tom was slogging it out in an equatorial jungle. He would have to make good use of his time while he was in the rock house to make it worth Tom's sacrifice. The box was as good a hiding place as he was going to get. The medal was out of sight yet within reach. Uwe climbed in between the cotton sheets on his bed and slept sounder than he had in years.

Meanwhile, someone else had been robbed of the luxury of sleep. Mamie closed the door leading from her bedroom into the hall and leaned her head against the frame. She wanted to know what Uwe was doing in the living room with the lights out in the middle of the night.

29 PROJECT STONEHENGE

May 1945. #800 West 8th Street, North Little Rock, Arkansas.

Since recovering from the injuries sustained after his Holy Ghost trial, Uwe had immersed himself further into his project. Most days found him deep in thought by five am. It was then that he was reminded most of Heisenberg's observation, "Not only is the universe stranger than we think, it is stranger than we can think[1]."
The morning smells of bacon frying in the iron skillet and coffee percolating wafted downstairs from the kitchen into the storm cellar. Despite the windowless space of the basement workroom, life had taken a positive turn. Uwe inhaled and hurried through the calculation.

Living with the family had had a remarkable effect on his mental capability, and Uwe's creativity was greater than it had been in years. The longer he worked on the project, however, the more he realized that Heisenberg had been correct; working in a vacuum was an inefficient way to solve a complex problem. He suspected his work was part of the design of a missile delivery system; and further, that the latest exchange of material carried characteristics of the work of some of Heisenberg's colleagues from Berlin's pre-war days. He wondered if they would remember him.

Staring at the recent communication in front of him and tapping his pencil on the table, Uwe decided to send a message to Camp Robinson. He needed to speak with Colonel Edmund about linking

[1] Heisenberg, Werner, Across the Frontiers

up with scientists from the other lab or labs he knew must be somewhere in the Allied countries, perhaps not too far from him. He supposed he had not received security clearance to allow him to meet with the scientists at their labs. Maybe he could convince Colonel Edmund to approve his travel to other locations. He would try to get his clearance upgraded.

Upstairs, the kitchen was bright from the early sun shining in the windows over the sink and through the panes in the back door. The attic fan thrummed and pulled in the outdoor May air, causing the yellow curtains to billow in the breeze. Cristobel was ironing a shirt. The iron made thumping sounds as she worked, and the smells of starch and steam mingled with those generated by Tina's cooking and distilled into the kitchen air with pleasing effect.

The women chatted while they worked. Cristobel was midway through telling the latest goings on of one of her boys to Tina.

"My Jimmy. He had brought home a spelling test with a "D" on it. Jimmy! I said. Jimmy, you march right out in the yard and pull a good switch off that tree yonder. O'course, he unnerstood, you know, what I was about, but he said, 'Yes, ma'am, Mama,' and he brought it to me. Ooo, I whooped him good." With a laugh approaching a cackle at the end, Cristobel finished in triumph, "And do you know what? The next test that came home? It carried an "A!"

Cristobel, pleased with her success using the gold standard of motivational methods, put the ironed shirt on a hanger and did up the buttons. "He had the ability, he needed to find the enthusiasm, if you know what I mean," she said.

"Oh, my! That's wonderful, Cristobel! He'll grow into a good man. I know he will. Children need encouragement," Tina said.

"Education is the key to advancement," Cristobel said with conviction.

"It certainly is!" Tina agreed as she pulled white bread slices browned from the toaster and then buttered and cut them on the diagonal. She cracked two eggs and poured them onto the hot bacon fat in the fry pan. While the eggs were cooking, she spooned a serving of grits from the saucepan where they were keeping warm on the back of the stove. She shook the white corn grits onto a plate and added a dollop of butter to them. When the eggs were done, Tina added those to the plate, dabbed away the excess grease, then stepped into the bedroom adjoining the kitchen.

Midway across the bedroom she shared with Jake, Tina took a left hand turn into the cedar walk in closet, the smell of mothballs strong in the confined space. Blankets, jigsaw puzzles and office supplies were stacked on the shelves above the clothes racks. Tina walked a few steps across the closet and pushed aside the coats hanging against the far wall. She opened a door so well camouflaged within the panels as to be indistinguishable from its surroundings and called down the steep staircase leading to the basement, "Uwe, dear! Come get your breakfast while it's hot!"

Uwe bounded up the stairs and entered the kitchen. "Thank you and good morning!" he said.

Tina smiled at Uwe and patted his cheek as he took his place at the chrome-trimmed kitchen table. The table was on the opposite side of the room from where Tina and Cristobel worked.

The Holt family sacred breakfast ritual was in flower. Coffee flowed and having divided the newspaper into sections, Jake, Mamie, Beryl and Uwe shared it. They exchanged sections, murmuring as they did so, "If you're done."

Mamie took a sip of coffee and scrutinized Uwe from over the Lifestyle section of the *Gazette*. He was eating his bacon and eggs, the B section of the paper propped against the water glass in front of him. While Uwe seemed innocent enough, Mamie thought it was peculiar for him to have been in the living room at night with the lights off. When you got down to it, he was an unknown, a foreigner who had fought for an enemy nation. She wished she could talk to Tom; however, that was out of the question since he was out of pocket somewhere in the Pacific. Maybe she should try to find a private word with Colonel Edmund even though she knew the family was not supposed to interfere with the special project.

They heard light footsteps outside approaching the kitchen door, the door most often used by everybody. Because Uwe's presence and purpose were secrets, everyone in the kitchen looked alarmed. Uwe put his fork down and stood up.

"What can Freddie want?" Cristobel wondered out loud as she peered out of the kitchen window overlooking the driveway.

Uwe was partway across the kitchen on his way to disappearing into the bedroom when the door opened after one tap. He stood trapped in the middle of the room.

"Good morning, everybody." Fredericka Lane walked into the back entry and smiled her mother's smile.

As usual she was well turned out, today in a blue shirtwaist dress that complimented her curvaceous figure. The black leather belt showed off her waistline and coordinated with her patent leather slippers. The hair wrap around her ponytail matched the dress, as it should since she had made them both herself. Her cheery expression at the early hour was remarkable, and everyone in the room except Uwe smiled back and answered, "Good morning, Fredericka."

"Excuse me for interrupting breakfast," she said. They smiled and responded, "Oh not at all, Fredericka." A visit from one of Cristobel's children was always welcome and often entertaining, but with Stonehenge established in the basement things were different.

Fredericka glanced at the stranger, wondering who he was, and paused as she sensed the awkward atmosphere in the room.

Cristobel turned from draping a shirt on the ironing board. "Baby," she started, "meet Mr. U-," and she paused an imperceptible fraction before continuing, "-lysses," then finished with a surname pulled out of the air "… Jones," and concluded with a further invention, "Ulysses Jones is Mr. Jake and Miz. Tina's nephew from Vilonia. Ulysses, this is my daughter Fredericka."

As soon as the words left her mouth, Cristobel regretted them. What had she been thinking? Who in Vilonia would name a child after a Union general? It was a Yankee name, no way otherwise to see it. But Fredericka was in a hurry, maybe she didn't notice. Least said soonest mended, she figured. She had done as best she could under pressure like she was to protect Uwe's identity. Anyways, he had a peculiar name nobody could pronounce and something needed to be done about it.

From their positions at the table and Tina's in front of the stove, the Holts accepted the new name with poker faces. In truth, they should already have had a plan for this contingency. Ulysses Jones was odd but it would have to do. Suspicion would float around such a name with such a face, but there it was, out.

Uwe didn't miss a beat in accepting his new identity. He thought it was fitting for him to adopt a famous mythical traveler's name. He stepped forward to shake Fredericka's hand, lingering a second before releasing it.

"It is very nice to meet you, Miss Fredericka," he said, trying his best to speak without an accent.

"It's nice to meet you, Mr. Ulysses," Fredericka replied with a merry smile, her dimples deepening as they did when she felt happy.

Funny, she thought, Ulysses Jones didn't seem to resemble the Holt people. He was much blonder, for one thing. Maybe he took after Miss Beryl Barkley's side of the family. Something in his manner and expression caught Fredericka's attention. Altogether he was quite an interesting package. Her gaze dropped in confusion when she realized she was staring at the stranger in the kitchen and he was staring back.

Fredericka diverted her attention to her mother as she remembered the time. She would have to move fast to catch the bus in order to make her first class across the river at Philander Smith College. "Mama," she said, "do you mind if I stay late after class tonight, and Marcel is planning to work at the store today, he asks do you need any groceries?"

"OK, baby, you can stay late, but be sure you back home by nine o'clock. And let Marcel know we could use some laundry powder," Cristobel said.

"Yes, ma'am, Mama!" Fredericka said, with one last look at Uwe, who was staring at her, "I'm getting going now! Bye, everybody!"

30 THEY BELIEVE IN MIRACLES

May 1945. North Little Rock, Arkansas.

Tina stopped in the doorway, dazzled by the light in the room. It looked like an aurora borealis had come to town to celebrate with her. Streams of sunlight shone through the chapel's stained glass windows and rays of brilliant red, yellow and blue fell over the wooden folding chairs arranged in a circle in the room at First Methodist Church.

Tina's arms were filled with early summer flowers of various colors and types. She had carried them the few blocks from her house to the church at Third and Maple, it being Thelma Owens' and her day to set up for Circle meeting. Thelma looked up from arranging the chairs when she saw Tina standing in the doorway.

"Your flowers! They're beautiful!" Thelma exclaimed. "Tina, I swanny, there can't be a bloom left in your yard because you're holding them all." Thelma looked closer at her friend and said, "Something's happened. What is it?"

"There's been a miracle! Thelma, Barkley's coming home!" Tina said, smiling bigger than she had in years.

Thelma shoved a chair in place and ran over to hug Tina hard. Neither of them cared that the magnolia and rose blossoms got squashed.

"How wonderful! When is he coming?"

"We don't have a date yet. His telegram said his discharge is pending release from the hospital. He will be put on a boat home! I'm so grateful. He's not going to the Pacific. He won't be part of the invasion of Japan."

"I see the hand of God at work," Thelma declared, lifting her head back and laughing a happy laugh.

"So do I!" Tina exclaimed.

Later, during refreshments, the newcomer maneuvered through the crowd of chatting ladies to claim the empty seat on Tina's right. She balanced a dessert plate of chocolate cake and salted nuts on her lap with a napkin underneath it. Her coffee cup she put on the floor under her chair.

"I'm Jean Manning," she said, extending her hand to Tina.

"I'm pleased to meet you, Mrs. Manning," Tina said, wiping her fingers on her napkin before shaking Jean's hand. "I'm Tina Holt. Welcome to Circle meeting."

"Thank you, Mrs. Holt."

"Where are you from, Mrs. Manning?" Tina asked, detecting a slight Northern accent.

"I'm from Delaware." I'm in town visiting my son who is a patient at Fort Roots Hospital."

"Oh, my goodness. How did he end up here?"

"He was on a troop train passing through and got sick, so when he was admitted to the hospital I came down to see what I could do to help him," Jean said. "I thought I would stop by here today for fellowship."

"Well, I hope your son recovers quickly! You must come as often as you can to church. Let me introduce you to the other Circle members."

"Thank you, I would love to meet the other ladies. But first tell me about yourself. Do you have children, Mrs. Holt?"

At the end of the meeting the organist asked, "What'll it be, ladies?" as she was poised to play the concluding song.

"Oh, I feel so happy today, how about "Bringing in the Sheaves"?" Tina said. There was a murmur of approval from the group, several quiet "Amen's," and they sang the old hymn together.

Afterwards, since Jean didn't think the Circle ladies would be suspicious enough to follow her and discover her lies, she took the direct route home. She drove across the river to the house on Addison Street she shared with her husband, Maxwell.

Their frame house was on a short but steep hill on a side street in Little Rock. It was across Markham from the schools for the deaf and blind. The location was convenient for developing their business associates at the state capitol. They could almost see the capitol building from their yard.

Max was in his favorite chair reading the evening paper when Jean walked in. She dropped her purse on the entry table and picked up the mail. "How'd it go?" he asked.

"Tedious, as you might expect," Jean said while she looked through the mail, "but Tina Holt was there and I made friends with her. I think one or two more meetings and I'll be invited for a visit at her house."

"You're so clever," Max said as he leaned over to kiss her.

"Tina Holt is so easy," Jean smiled as she flopped down on the couch.

"Don't make plans for tomorrow," Max said. "We've got a meeting with Vivian to see how she is progressing with developing Imogene Park."

"We don't have time to waste, I warn you," Jean said. "The Professor needs the information sooner rather than later."

"I know," Max said. "Vivian knows too, but these things are an art form. You can't push it too hard without arousing suspicion."

"Believe me, I'm aware," Jean said. "I'm trying my best to work that Circle group."

"What on earth are you thinking about with that expression on your face, Maxwell?" Jean asked as he sat down beside her.

"I was wondering, what about trying to get one of those young Victory Girls on our side? From what I read about them in the paper, I bet that wouldn't be too difficult to do. I'm sure they're easily manipulated. Of course, I wouldn't let a child of mine, if I had one, get into that kind of thing, but it might be useful to us."

"Give it up, Max. Absolutely not. Church people across the state are up in arms about Victory Girls. It would be disastrous if somehow we became associated with sin. Remember, I just spent half of my day 'in prayer' with a bunch of them," and she made quotation marks with her hands as she spoke. "I can manage Tina Holt, but I'm worried we're going to have trouble with the likes of Imogene Park, who is a heartbeat away from being a Victory Girl herself. And while I agree that we're going to need her, it will require a fine touch." Seeking a diversion, she said, "Come on, let's go out for dinner." She tapped Max's shoulder. "I could do with a drink."

Later in the evening, while sipping martinis in the bar of the Marion Hotel, Max returned to their earlier topic of conversation. "I wonder if there isn't money to be made in organizing those Victory Girls."

Jean crossed her legs as she admired her new skirt and again dismissed the idea. "Max, the Victory Girl thing is a distraction. We should stick with our assignment and get the Professor his information."

Desperate to banish further thoughts of Victory Girls from Max's mind, Jean decided a preemptive strike was in order. She needed a Victory Girl in her life like she needed a hole in the head. Ever since she had visited the woman with dubious credentials to take care of a problem fifteen years ago, there even had not been any children to interfere with her giving Max one hundred percent of her attentions. Now she wasn't as young as she used to be and this competition, although unsophisticated, should not be dismissed. It was a threat. Turning on her charm, Jean ran her fingers up Max's arm and indicated to the waiter to refill their drinks. Jean noted in relief that Max looked distracted. Victory Girls, indeed. Jean believed in making her own miracles.

Meanwhile, back at the rock house, Tina put dinner on the table. Cristobel had gone home for the day and it was family and Uwe for dinner. Tina hummed as she set the baked spaghetti casserole and green beans down.

Over dinner they couldn't stop talking about the news of Barkley's homecoming. The ladies carried on, making plans for a party celebrating his return, while Jake said nothing but looked pleased.

When Tina had filled everyone's cups with hot coffee, Aunt Beryl asked, "How was Circle today?"

"Oh, it was nice to see everybody," Tina answered. "I'll say this, the war has brought some new people into town."

31 MEET VIVIAN TAYLOR

May 1945. Little Rock, Arkansas.

The water was so clear that Imogene thought she could reach her hand out and touch bottom. The thought was scary because she was looking down from the eight-meter diving platform into Fair Park swimming pool. It was the first week the pool was open for summer, but Imogene's chill was more from her fear of heights than the air temperature. She stood as high as the American flags waving from each side of the platform, and they were visible for miles.

There was a line of people waiting for her to dive. The wavering black lines painted on the pool bottom fifteen feet below the surface looked too close, but she knew it was an optical illusion and there was plenty of water for diving. Either dive off or back down the ladder. That was the deal. Refusing to admit defeat with an ignominious retreat, Imogene looked beyond the diving, shallow and baby pool complex below. The sounds of feet hitting springboards and the corresponding splashes, the shouts of children playing in the water and the summer smell of chlorine faded as Imogene gathered her courage and focused on the task at hand.

Taking two purposeful steps and a hop to the platform edge, Imogene linked her hands over her head, tucked her chin, grabbed a lungful of air and jumped up and over, keeping her legs and feet together, knees straight and pointing her toes. Seconds later she was kicking up to the surface of the deep water under the diving platform.

Imogene swam to the side of the pool. She dipped underwater and surfaced with her head tilted backwards to let the water pull her hair out of her face, enjoying the relief from having made the dive wash over her. Then she did it again because it felt good.

"Nice dive."

Imogene looked around, wondering if somebody was talking to her.

A dark haired girl who looked older, but not by much, than Imogene, had sat down on the pool deck and put her feet in the water. Her painted toenails shone ruby-red. The girl was smiling at Imogene. It was she who had spoken. "I'm Vivian Taylor," she said.

"Imogene Park," Imogene said, smiling back.

"Do you swim here often? You must since you dive so well."

"This is my favorite pool, but I'm more of a swimmer than a diver," Imogene said. "Honestly, I'm trying to cure myself of my fear of heights, that's why I was diving. I don't really dive well, at least not consistently."

Looking around at the clean water, Imogene thought she couldn't have designed a nicer pool. There were six diving boards in addition to the platforms, and the deep-water pool was big enough for the Fair Park Seals swim team to hold work outs in. The shallow water was below waist high on her and the area was larger than the diving pool, with a platform in the middle. Imogene thought the platform was an interesting touch of pool architecture. She liked to swim to it and pretend she was on an island.

Imogene idled next to the side, sculling the water with her hands to stay in place while she talked. She got a kick knowing how deep the water was underneath her. The water was colder around her feet than at the surface, like at a lake. She considered diving down to see how long it took to touch bottom, but didn't because that was something a kid would do and she was about grown.

"Wow. You must have a lot of courage to be able to dive that well even though you're afraid. I'm not sure I believe you when you say that!" Vivian said.

"Oh, I am afraid, believe me," Imogene laughed, "but I can't think of any other way to get over my fear of heights except to dive off the platform over and over, if you know what I mean."

"I guess so."

"I want to give kids swimming lessons this summer and I have to be able to demonstrate a dive to qualify as a teacher, so I'm working on it. Plus I'd rather not look incompetent in front of my students."

"I can understand that!" Vivian said.

"I mean it's like show no fear!" Imogene laughed.

Vivian chuckled as she slipped into the pool next to Imogene and treaded water, being careful not to get her hair wet. She thought that Imogene was quite spectacular, as athletic as Esther Williams but with a figure like Mae West. That, combined with her innocence and touch of naughtiness, could make her a valuable asset. If only Max could keep his hands off her.

Imogene swam to the ladder and got out, followed by Vivian. Imogene grabbed her towel and fluffed her hair up. Imogene felt self-conscious about her wet hair that got plastered to her head like a chicken. She knew it wasn't her best look, but she could never resist getting her hair wet once she was in the water. She hated sitting on a towel to sun instead of swimming.

Imogene sat down on her beach towel and Vivian spread her towel out next to her.

"You know, you look familiar to me," Vivian said.

"Really? I'm sorry, but I don't think we've met before."

"Were you at the River View dance last week?"

"Yes, I sure was." Imogene said.

"Were you were dancing with a tall, good looking officer?" Vivian asked, smiling at Imogene, a calculated touch of admiration in her eyes.

"That was Luke Holt." Imogene chuckled. "I guess I didn't see you there. Luke's leave is over, though. He had to report back to duty."

"Oh, that's too bad."

"Really. It's been boring with Luke gone." Imogene commented.

"Have y'all been dating long?"

"Off and on. Since he's been in the service he's been out of town a lot. That kind of changes things, if you know what I mean."

"Do you stay in touch with his mother, to see how she's doing? She must be worried about him."

"I haven't seen her since Sunday dinner. To tell the truth, dinner was kind of gloomy. Luke's her third son to go."

"Wow. She has three sons in the service? That must be so hard."

"Well, she has a lot of family to help her."

"I'm sure a visit from you would perk her up, though. Maybe it would take her mind off things," Vivian pressed. Imogene had a puzzled look as though it had never occurred to her to visit Luke's mother.

Dark clouds had been rolling in while Imogene and Vivian were talking, and a sudden lightning flash crackled across the sky. The lifeguard sounded the whistle signaling a quick pool evacuation. Imogene started counting, and when a loud rumble of thunder sounded at four seconds she figured the storm was not far away.

Imogene and Vivian stood up and started folding their towels when it began to sprinkle, then when the rain drops got bigger and closer together they grabbed their things and ran with the other swimmers to the shelter of the stone bathhouse.

"Say," Vivian said as the rain poured down and thunder and lightning crashed around them, "If you're free this afternoon, how about we go to the movies, since who knows when the pool will be open again?"

"Sounds good. Let's see what's playing at the Majestic," Imogene said, flattered that a sophisticated girl like Vivian wanted to spend time with her.

"Then afterwards, if you'd like, I thought maybe we could go over to my friend's house who is having a little party. Just a few friends," Vivian added.

"Tell me more," Imogene said, smiling at Vivian.

32 UNDER SIEGE

May 1945. #800 West 8th Street. North Little Rock, Arkansas.

"It's the end of the world!" Mamie yelled and ran full out, gasping for breath as her feet pounded down the street. Her eyes looked upwards in terror as she held her arms in front of her head to shield herself from impending blows. She was part of a mass of people running in panic, and they were screaming it too, "It's the end of the world! It's the end of the world!"

Aunt Beryl woke up when she heard Mamie thrashing about. She got out of her bed that was against the wall across the room from Mamie's and slipped into her robe and house shoes. She padded over to check on Mamie, who was wide-awake and shaking. Aunt Beryl leaned over the bed, her hair encased in a hairnet and her face smelling like almond scented cold cream. It was a comforting smell and Aunt Beryl was a comforting presence.

"Mamie honey, it's that same old bad nightmare, I can tell," Aunt Beryl said as she pulled the cool beaded chain on the bedside table lamp. The light shining through the pink dotted Swiss lampshade cast the room in rose-colored light and made everything better.

"Mercy, Aunt Beryl, it always seems so real. Every time I have that dream it's terrifying. I'm sorry I woke you up," Mamie said. She sat up and pushed her pillow against the spindle headboard. She leaned back and tried to collect her thoughts. The dial on the bedside clock read two am.

"It's all right." Aunt Beryl smiled and patted Mamie's shoulder. Aunt Beryl didn't have children of her own and she had never had a husband, had never seen the point of wanting a husband. She did love her sister Tina's children as if they were hers, though.

"It's no wonder you have nightmares, Mamie, what with a world war going on for years and worrying about Barkley, Tom and Luke. And now we have a foreigner living in the boys' room and working on a secret project in our basement."

Mamie reached for Beryl's hand and held it. "Aunt Beryl, I'm not used to keeping secrets like this," she said.

"I know what you mean," Beryl whispered as she sank down on the big stuffed chair next to Mamie's bed.

"I always try to put the best foot forward, don't you know, but that's about keeping family business private," Mamie said. "This is different, much different, from giving a smiling face to outsiders."

"You're right, it's not the same," Beryl said. "This is dangerous war work and it is our patriotic duty to deal with it as best we can, Mamie."

Beryl stood up and handed Mamie a copy of the latest edition of the slim paperback devotional, *The Upper Room*, from the bedside table. "Why don't you read this to help you relax and then maybe you'll be able to get back to sleep. The stories in here always make me feel better," she said. "I'll get us each a glass of hot milk. That should do the trick." She slipped out of their bedroom and went into the kitchen to prepare the time-honored remedy for chasing away night terrors and insomnia.

When they were sipping the milk, Mamie looked at Aunt Beryl and remarked aloud as though saying it would make it so, "It was just a dream. It wasn't real." Beryl nodded and patted Mamie's hand again.

The next morning was Saturday, which meant no work for Mamie because the Office of Price Administration was closed and Aunt Beryl didn't have school. After breakfast Mamie sat at her desk under the front corner bedroom window. She pushed her hair back as she concentrated on what to say in her letter. If only Tom were there to talk to. He had the best judgment of anybody she knew. He always gave good advice and not much of it. Funny how those two things always seemed to go hand in hand, she thought.

Mamie typed her letter with the rapid fire of a professional typist. Now and then her hands slowed and her eyes left the page in front of her as she stared out the window at the concrete carriage block that stood next to the street, a throwback to an older era, as she considered what to say.

There were all sorts of things she would like to include in her letter but couldn't due to the wartime mail censoring. She didn't want Tom to get a nonsensical letter he couldn't read because most of it was redacted. Mamie pursed her lips as she thought about Ulysses and Imogene and wondered whether to bother Tom with her worries.

She thought Tom would warn her from getting close to Ulysses, even though he was an interesting fellow. She did like him. Papa said to let Colonel Edmund handle Ulysses. As for Imogene, maybe the ladies should deal with her. Anyway, there was nothing Tom could do about home troubles since he was so far away. They would have to take care of their business as best they could. She finished the letter and freed the paper with a few quick turns of the roller and read it through.

Mamie was readying the letter for mailing when Aunt Beryl entered their bedroom and closed the door behind her. She sat down on the chair next to the desk. "She's here already," she said.

"Petit Jean Mountain?" Mamie sighed.

"That's as good as any," Beryl said, and she picked up some papers to grade.

Mamie's steps were softened as she walked across the area rug decorated with pink cabbage roses that covered most of the living room hardwood floor. She stepped out onto the screened in front porch and dropped the letter in the outgoing mailbox, then went back inside.

Mamie entered the kitchen through the swinging door from the dining room and smiled at Imogene. "Good morning, Imogene. You're out and about early."

"Oh, good morning, Mamie." Imogene looked up from eyeing the pile of fresh green peas waiting to be shelled. She had arrived at nine o'clock and was wearing a black rayon dress with a red geometric pattern on it. Mamie thought it looked new and the stockings black market.

"Imogene, you must protect this beautiful dress," Tina said while tying the strings of one of her aprons at Imogene's neck. "Thank you so much for wanting to help." She sat down and put a sheet of newspaper in her lap and handed one to Imogene.

May 15, 1945

Dear Tom,

We are beside ourselves with happiness that Barkley is coming home. We are so relieved and grateful. How it happened we don't know. The news of the surrender in Germany is all people talk about here. I only wish it were done out where you are. One thing is for certain; there will be a whole lot less people getting hurt in Europe.

We are glad that you have permission to tell us your location now. Aunt Beryl has put pins in her wall map of the world. Yours is blue, Barkley's is red, Luke's is white and Floyd's is silver. We weren't sure exactly where to put your pin and now we know. We read your last letter out loud after dinner. Everyone is interested to know about life in the Philippines. Of course we have our subscription to The Stars and Stripes for war news, and the Gazette and Democrat too, but it is better to hear the news from you boys.

We saw Richard Jennings the other day. He was home on leave and stopped by for coffee. Mama put together a nice little tea party for him and we had a good visit. He delivered your mahogany wood box with the carved sides. Richard told us about how you bought it in the open air market in Manila. Mama put it in a place of honor in the living room. The Japanese money in the burgundy velvet sack is something.

Papa took Richard out to the garage for some Old Crow before he went home. Mama didn't know.

Luke's friend Imogene has been spending a lot of time here at the house, even though he left for Fort Benning. Do you think he is serious about her? He brought her to Sunday dinner just before he left, and we've gone to the movies a few times since. She seems lonely for company. I guess you heard that Luke is being shipped somewhere out your way.

The azaleas put on a good show this year. Wish you could have seen them.

Love,

Mamie

Picking up a pea pod, Tina pulled the string down the long end of the pod, squeezed the ends until it popped open and then pushed the peas into a bowl. She dropped the empty pod onto the newspaper on her lap. "There you are, that's how it's done, but honey, you don't need to work so hard."

"But I want to, Mrs. Holt," Imogene said and smiled at Tina. "I've learned a lot from you about keeping house." Imogene picked up a pea pod and started shelling. "After this could you give me a tour of the house? Would I be putting you out to ask? My goodness, I've been here how many times and all I've seen are this room and the living and dining rooms!"

Tina looked an appeal at Mamie. Mamie knew her mother hoped someone would take Imogene off her hands for a while. Earlier, over breakfast, she had confided to Mamie, "I'm on pins and needles trying to keep Imogene from discovering our boarder. My goodness, until we took that young man in I never realized how much traffic there is through this house. It used to be like a tomb during the day with just me and Cristobel rattling around."

Luke was Mamie's youngest brother, and Imogene younger than Luke, which put Mamie almost old enough to be Imogene's mother. She would have been in big trouble had that been the case, but it was possible. She couldn't imagine any good reason for Imogene to cultivate a friendship with her. Dating Mamie's little brother didn't seem like a strong enough reason for the attention.

"Oh Imogene, you've seen all there is to see around here," Mamie said. "Since this is my day off work, how about we pack up a picnic lunch and take a day trip to Petit Jean? We can see Petit Jean's grave and hike around the trails. I have saved enough gas coupons to get us there and back." Mamie knew, however, that she could have a special fill up at Camp Robinson because of Project Stonehenge, and gas rationing would not keep them stuck at home.

"But what about the peas?" Imogene looked surprised.

"Don't give them a second thought," Tina said. "An outing to Petit Jean is a wonderful suggestion! You young people should not be housebound on such a beautiful day."

"I have an idea." From her place at the kitchen table where she was grading papers, Aunt Beryl made a suggestion. "Why don't you include that nice Colonel Edmund from Camp Robinson? I bump into him from time to time around town. Last week I saw him at the USO canteen. He is such a nice man. He might never have been to Petit Jean. You know how ordinary citizens are encouraged to support the soldiers." Beryl added that last, trying not to sound sanctimonious when she said it.

"Beryl, you are inspired!" Tina said, cottoning on to her sister's intent. "I'll call the Brentwoods and ask if they can get in touch with the colonel to invite him. I know they're friends. It's last minute notice, of course, but maybe he can go," she added in an optimistic voice on her way into the hall to where the telephone was installed in a wall alcove.

Mamie thought the day was looking up. She wouldn't mind spending more time with Colonel Edmund herself. She looked forward to when he dropped by to check on the project. Thirty-five and unmarried didn't mean her heart was dead.

"How about it, Imogene?" Mamie asked.

"Oh, well sure," she said. "I should call my mother and ask her if it's all right. I don't know, Mamie, I'm not wearing the right clothes. Maybe we should stay here and your mama could teach me how to sew?"

A chorus of light-hearted but emphatic opposition shouted Imogene down.

"Imogene, you'll have to let me loan you some trousers and a top," Mamie said. "I bet between Mama, Aunt Beryl and me we can get you some shoes that fit. We'll have fun."

33 IMOGENE'S DAY TRIP

May 1945. North Little Rock, Arkansas.

As Imogene swung into the saddle, she thought, not for the first time, how the smells of saddle leather and horse sweat made the nicest perfume. Maybe she would bottle it for sale in stores, call it something like "Saturday at the Stable" and retire a millionaire at twenty. Not that she had money worries. Her pressing concern had been capping parental suspicions of her motivation for switching stables.

Dr. and Mrs. Park had exchanged a look when Imogene advocated for their support of her plan to move Snip, her American Saddlebred mare, from River View across the river. There was an available stall in a small barn off Remount Road in North Little Rock. Imogene caught the look and thought, *Not!* Her parents thought they knew so much. With Luke Holt unavailable she had made new friends.

Mama's response was typical. "Why don't you want the nicer facility, Imogene? The new place is just a stall on somebody's farm. I bet those people are so country they drink buttermilk with dinner. We'll have to pay more for the River View clubhouse membership if we don't stable Snip there. Plus, you won't have anyone to muck out the stall for you at the new barn. Are you sure you want to do all that work? You'll get tired of it, mark my words," she finished.

"There's Ray," Imogene countered, referring to the boy who helped out on the farm. She figured it wouldn't be difficult to pull Ray into her orbit. A fourteen-year old boy? A piece of cake.

"Imogene, I can see advantages to this move," Dr. Park said after giving it some thought. "Doc and Bea run a nice farm, and it should be a wholesome place for you to spend time."

Yes, Daddy was moving in the right direction, Imogene thought.

"The new stall is near trails you've never ridden down that are inaccessible from this side of the river," he continued. "You could ride all the way from Remount Road to Crystal Hill and back, explore the north side of the riverbank, or turn the other way and ride for miles. It will be pretty in the spring and then again in the fall when the weather is cool and the trees turn beautiful colors."

"Imogene, I'll put Chief there and we can ride together on Sunday mornings," he said, having talked himself into the idea. "I bet there are country stores where we could stop on our rides and get soft drinks for refreshment."

"Oh Daddy, that would be great fun! We'll have father daughter time," Imogene said, hoping she sounded enthusiastic enough.

Her father smiled at her. She could tell she had pleased him. After a pause Dr. Park added, "Speaking of buttermilk, it has been years since I've had a fresh, cold glass with dinner. I think I'd like to try some today."

"Oh, really, Byron," Carole shook her head.

"I mean it, let's get some, Carole," Dr. Park responded. "Come on, you grew up liking it, I know you did. Doesn't it remind you of your childhood?"

Now that they were arguing about food, Imogene figured the stable change question had been decided to her satisfaction, and she ran over and hugged her father. He smiled at Imogene and returned the hug.

"Do you think we're too easy on her? Did we spoil her, Byron?" Carole asked with a touch of worry in her voice after Imogene disappeared into her room. "You know, as an only child she hasn't even had to share so much as the cake batter left in the bowl with another soul, and she always gets the beater too. She's never had to nudge a sister back onto her side of the bed at night."

"She might be a tad spoiled, but her heart is good," he conceded. "Taking over more of Snip's daily care will be good for her. It will teach her responsibility."

"I wish she had more friends," Carole worried out loud. "Do you think she has any real girl friends, Byron?"

"Oh it'll be all right, honey. She always has her daddy."

Saturday morning, with clearance from her family to be gone on an all day trail ride, Imogene had packed for the outing. She put two full canteens and a massive lunch, big enough for two, into the saddlebag. She wore a cowboy hat for protection against the sun. Her horse Snip was a beautiful five-gated chestnut mare with two white stockings. Imogene had named her for the flash of white on her cute, soft nose. It was a fine May morning, not too hot or cold. What more could anybody want?

Imogene picked up the reins and nudged Snip out of the gate. "Thank you, Ray," she said when he handed her Chief's reins with an admiring smile. The big Palomino gelding was saddled and ready to go, but he would be traveling without a rider for a while.

Ray hadn't questioned Imogene's story about why she was leading a saddled horse out of the barn. She had told him she was taking Chief to a girlfriend's house and they would ride out from there. Leading Chief while riding Snip was tricky, but Imogene pulled it off fine.

The sound of hoof beats on hard packed dirt sent a tingle of happiness up Imogene's spine as her little train started out. Half an hour later she left the trail and struck across the vacant field behind the older residential section a few blocks west of Main Street.

Her destination was on the edge of town, which meant that she wouldn't attract too much attention riding one horse and leading another on a Saturday morning. Besides, maybe people would think she was being patriotic by saving gasoline. Imogene pulled Snip and Chief to a walk and took a left hand turn to disappear into the rundown asphalt alleyway behind West 8th Street.

Earlier that week she had gone to the Holts' to visit, and finding no one home decided to investigate the back yard. That's where she met the intriguing Ulysses Jones. He was someone she wanted to get to know better. He had been working in the garden and they had struck up a nice conversation; a huge oak tree shielded the garden from view. They had talked about a lot of things, like horses. Trying to guess where number 800 was, Imogene walked Snip since she wasn't used to arriving from the back. She stopped when she saw the spreading branches of the oak.

Imogene dismounted and tied both sets of reins to the back fence. The horses leaned down to graze on the weeds growing beside the street, pulling dry yellow grass out of the earth with strong tugs. Imogene walked along the galvanized steel cyclone fence that enclosed the Holt's backyard. Red tipped photinia bushes planted inside the fence provided a privacy screen for the backyard and kept anyone from seeing inside.

"Hello. Ulysses? Are you here?"

When there was no answer, Imogene opened the back gate and let herself in. The Holts had planted a big victory garden that spring. Young bell pepper and tomato plants set out a month ago stood in neat rows. Cucumbers, pole beans, yellow crookneck squash, okra, corn and Crowder pea seeds had germinated and were starting to grow.

Imogene did not stop to admire any of this as she picked her way in the troughs between the neat rows, her riding boots sinking down in the deep loam. She was focused on meeting her new friend. It was a triumph to have arrived there with food, on horseback and with a spare saddled horse by nine am.

"Ulysses?" she called as she walked around the yard. The detached garage stood in the back corner of the yard. It was at the end of the driveway running the length of the lot beside the house. She peered into the shadows in the narrow place between the garage and the fence. It was a scary place where frogs or worse might live.

She didn't see Ulysses anywhere, and she wondered if maybe he was waiting for her inside the garage. Maybe he'd had that fun idea. She tapped on the side door, which was ajar. When there was no answer, she pushed it open into a cool, dark and vacant cavernous space. The dirt floor emitted a moist smell reminiscent of dank, spidery basements.

As Imogene's eyes were adjusting to the dim light, she heard the distinctive rattle that signaled danger. Imogene froze, as she knew to do when hearing that sound. Then she saw a long, thin rattlesnake dangling head down right in front of her, its body hanging from the top door hinge.

She stared in horror at the up-close view of the diamond pattern on the back of the body. It could have been in a color plate on a textbook page about identifying characteristics of rattlesnakes. She felt as if a heavy weight had crashed through her stomach, straight down to the ground. The snake was at least two feet long and swayed in the open doorway, the pit viper triangle shaped face close to Imogene, its mouth open and fangs exposed.

Imogene leapt away so fast that the surprised snake failed to strike her, though it wasn't for lack of effort on its part. She shrieked and her heart pounded harder than it ever had. She walked around and around the yard far away from the garage, trying to get her breath. Meantime, she kept a weather eye on the snake that seemed to have lost interest in her.

Jake Holt was relaxing in the living room listening to the radio when he heard Imogene's terrified scream coming from the yard. He jumped up and came running, the screen door slamming behind him. When he saw who was in the yard, he stopped in surprise. "My goodness, it's Imogene!" he said. "What's happened? What's wrong?"

"I, I, I, there's a rattlesnake in your garage, Mr. Holt!" Imogene said, searching for composure. She pointed a shaky finger at the open door.

"Why, look at that!" Jake exclaimed as he reached for the garden hoe that was propped against the side of the house. With several quick strokes he cut off the snake's head. It was trickier to kill because it was swinging in the doorway instead of lying on the ground, but Jake took care of it.

"Oh my goodness, oh my goodness," Imogene repeated as she sank down on the back door steps. She removed her hat and fanned her sweaty, hot face with it. "Thank you, Mr. Holt."

"Imogene, are you hurt?" Jake asked, reaching her in a few strides of his long legs and crouching in front of her, a concerned look on his face.

"No, sir, Mr. Holt," Imogene shook her head. "I'm fine, or I will be in a little while. Thank you, sir, for killing the snake!"

"Imagine a snake hanging there! What a scare it must have given you!"

Imogene nodded her head as she tried to calm down.

"Were you looking for Mamie?" Jake asked. "I'm sorry, but she and Mrs. Holt and Miss Beryl went to pick strawberries this morning up in Bald Knob, if that's who you were here for. Can I get you a glass of water?"

"Oh, no sir, I'm fine, I'll be all right," Imogene said, her mind racing in search of a plausible explanation for her unannounced presence in his backyard. "I was just stopping by to say hello, Mr.

Holt. I'll, uh, be heading out." Imogene stood up and clamped her hat on her head as she started walking through the garden to the horses. "Please tell everybody hello. Sorry to have missed Miss Mamie. Please have a wonderful day. I'll let myself out back. I uh, rode my horse over and uh, thought Miss Mamie might like to ride Daddy's horse."

"Are you sure you're all right?" Jake said as he followed Imogene out. "Won't you take a minute to rest?"

"Oh, no sir, I really should get going," she said.

"Imogene, is this your horse?" Jake stroked Snip's neck. She nodded.

"I didn't realize you kept horses near here. This is a beautiful animal. And this Palomino belongs to your daddy? He sure is fine. I'm sorry you came all the way over and missed the ladies. Mamie has a soft spot for horses. She would have enjoyed a ride."

With hands shaking from her shocking encounter with the rattler, Imogene untied the horses, mounted Snip and told Mr. Holt good-bye.

She was upset, disappointed and put out. Where on earth was Ulysses? He had told her he would be working in the garden that morning. She had gone to a lot of trouble to share her favorite thing in life with somebody who she thought was special. She had been under the impression that he thought she was special too. Guessed she had been wrong. Maybe Vivian would be available for girlfriend time.

Imogene turned Snip in the direction of Remount Road and the barn and pasture. The ride had turned into a dud. She guessed she might as well take Daddy up on his offer for a Sunday morning ride. Chief had Tennessee Walking horse blood in him somewhere, and they could have fun seeing if Chief and Snip would give them a racking gait. Maybe they would stop at a cute country store for a soft drink like Daddy suggested.

The morning's clear sky was gone and it started to rain. Imogene pulled the brim of her hat down and then sighed in frustration. She had forgotten something important. She should have cut the rattle off of that snake and kept it for a good luck charm.

34 HERDING CATS

May 1945. North Little Rock, Arkansas.

"By all that is holy, I did not put it there," Pete repeated himself. It was true, it never would have occurred to him to use a rattlesnake as a weapon, and never at a house full of people. "That's not how I run security." Maybe Colonel Edmund looked unconvinced because Pete couldn't help but think the snake had done them all a favor. Fate, divine intervention, call it what you will, it had shooed Imogene away from the rock house better than anything he could have devised.

"Rattlesnakes are not known for climbing," Edmund said as he appraised Pete.

Colonel Edmund, Uwe and Pete sat around the battered table in the basement workroom discussing the day's events. Edmund had returned Uwe to the rock house from their off site meeting place where he had gone to submit his weekly report and found Jake waiting for them with the news of Imogene's visit and the snake. The atmosphere in the room was tense.

"Boss, being a city boy, I am unfamiliar with the habits of rattlesnakes," Pete shrugged. "I'd get myself killed setting a trap like that."

"How can this project continue with every young girl in the city bringing refreshments and saddled horses to you, ready to ride away, when you're supposed to be working in secret?" Colonel Edmund frowned at Uwe. "We're under the gun, and I mean it. What do you have to say for yourself?"

"I met Imogene last week when I was outside planting vegetable seeds in the garden for recreation," Uwe said. "She surprised me by appearing in the yard. I told her I was a hired man. We talked about gardening and horses, not much more than that. Imogene is a friendly girl. I tried to discourage her overtures but not so much as to make her suspicious. "

"Did you know she was going to stop by today?" Colonel Edmund pressed.

"I thought she might, but I also thought it better if I were to be away at that time."

"Is that so. Tell me, Johannes, is there anyone else we should be expecting to stop by here?"

"No, sir."

Colonel Edmund wished the war were over and this boy was on his way home to Germany. He was too smart for his own good. But he had no indication the project was wrapping up; in fact, it was doing the opposite.

Edmund had news. "Just telling you two, I received an order expanding this facility to include two more engineers."

Uwe and Pete absorbed this surprising, no, shocking announcement.

"Here, sir? They will live here?" Uwe looked around the cramped room.

"We'll be responsible for the security of three engineers here? Exactly how will that work?" Pete sputtered.

"We will do what we have to do, put cots down here or something, and Peters, we'll have to beef up the security even though it will be hard to spare the manpower." Edmund glared at Uwe as though he were to blame, which in a way he was. "Johannes," Edmund said, "your work has been well received, which is why we are expanding. I don't know when the new men will arrive and I have not spoken with the family yet, so keep it under your hats for awhile."

Pete walked Colonel Edmund back to the car they had left parked on Main Street.

"Do you think he was telling us the truth?" Edmund asked Pete.

"Probably mostly."

"That's about what I thought," Edmund said. "What about his name change? Ulysses Jones? Give me a break. Did you see the look he gave me when I called him Johannes?"

"Don't you think it's reasonable for him to take an American name?" Pete said.

"Ulysses Jones is not a run of the mill name. It stands out and he doesn't have a clue about it. Not a clue. We've got to keep a handle on him and hope this entire project doesn't explode before its time." They had reached the car. "I'm looking forward to two more "engineers" working there as much as I would enjoy a double root canal," Edmund said as they got in.

"Ain't it the truth," Pete said.

In the basement Uwe worked on his calculations. He didn't understand why everyone was so concerned about Imogene. He was glad she hadn't gotten snake bit.

35 XOXO MAX AND JEAN

May 1945. North Little Rock, Arkansas.

The man in an ill-fitting suit walked down Hickory Street searching for an address. Dark Hollow was near the railroad tracks and the rail yard, built in a swampy place that flooded when it rained. The mix of ramshackle houses and well-kept homes were built close together and not all of them had house numbers visible. On one corner was the Visit-Us-Now Liquor Store and New Hope Church was on another. The man stopped in front of one of the nicer houses. He walked up the brick step onto the short covered porch and rang the bell.

"Are you Marilyn Kenner?" he asked the woman who answered the door.

Studying the stranger standing on her front porch, Marilyn wondered what kind of trouble had come home to roost. She nodded.

"I bring you greetings from Max and Jean," he said.

Marilyn stared at him.

"Aren't you going to invite me in, Marilyn?" he asked.

Impertinent, him calling her by her first name, Marilyn thought. She should be "Mrs. Kenner" to this stranger, but she let the familiarity slide. Marilyn was worried. "I don't know any Max or Jean," she whispered.

"Now, Marilyn, it has been awhile, but don't let's talk business here on the porch," he said.

She opened the door wide enough for the man to slip inside the house.

Marilyn closed the door and turned to face her visitor.

"Who are you? What do you want?" she asked him.

"Call me Daryl," the man said. "Aren't you going to invite me to sit down?" he asked.

"Whatever you sellin' I ain't buyin'. I want you to leave," she said, her hand on the doorknob.

"Marilyn, Marilyn, I'm here on behalf of oppressed people everywhere. I want to enlist you to fight fascism."

"Fight fascism, huh," she said. "I do that everyday. My friends and me knit sweaters, we sew bandages for our soldiers. We fightn' it."

"I remember you were secretary of the Arkansas Delta Tenant Farmer's Union in 1930," he said to her.

"Maybe I was. That was fifteen years and a whole lot of miles ago and I don't remember you," she responded.

Marilyn could not remember this man but she did remember Max and Jean from when she lived in Scott. They were people from out of the area who attended tenant farmer union meetings off and on during the early '30's. They were different from the sharecroppers she grew up around and went to church and school with, old friends whom she still loved. She had been uncomfortable around Max and Jean; she'd had trouble relating to them. They didn't seem straightforward like the others. At the time, she had thought it was because they were outsiders, she'd assumed they were civil rights activists from up North, but in hindsight they seemed sinister, subversive even.

"I've got a favor to ask of you," he said.

"What kind of favor?" she asked.

"Marilyn, we should sit down. This might take a few minutes." Daryl made himself comfortable on the protective plastic covering of her living room couch. Marilyn perched on the edge of the chair across from him and waited.

"Some of our mutual friends have a job we need done, and preferably by someone local," he said.

"Job? What kind of job?"

"We need information from inside a house in an adjacent neighborhood." When Daryl said that she glared at him, and when he told her it was 800 West 8th Street, Marilyn's jaw dropped. Then she let him have it. "No! Get out of here! I'm going to call the police if you don't leave," and she rose to go to the door and the nearest telephone, which was at the liquor store.

"I wouldn't do that, Marilyn," Daryl said, staying put, unperturbed. "Hear me out. I suggest you enlist Abe's help."

Marilyn stared at him in shock.

"Why on God's green earth would I drag my boy into this kind of big, big trouble?" she said. "How do you know my son's name? Let me tell you something, Mister. First, you and me, we're not friends. Second, it is not now or ever was illegal to belong to a union. We was just trying to make life better, and that is no crime. So get out of here."

"I'm sorry to hear you have lost the fervor, Marilyn. I hoped not to have to do this," Daryl said. He handed her an envelope from his pocket.

She opened the flap, and when she saw the contents inside she screamed and fell to the ground as though someone had hit her hard. "Lord Jesus, Lord Jesus, please, no," she wailed. "I thought he had quit that. He promised."

Fifteen minutes later Daryl left the house after telling a subdued Marilyn, "You have two weeks. When the job is done, take that flowerpot off your front porch. Someone will check your house regularly. One day later take the information, put it in a sealed envelope and place it under the second seat from the right facing the screen, front row of the Gem Theatre, 9th Street in Little Rock, Matinee showing." He laid fifty dollars on the coffee table on his way out.

Daryl walked back the way he had come and headed for the train depot. He was off to check in with his contact at the Pine Bluff Arsenal. Confident he had shaken his tail before Memphis, he took the direct route, chuckling at the thought of the FBI man chasing no one on a New Orleans bound train.

Later, but before Al got home from work, Marilyn had a private conversation sequestered in her bedroom with their sixteen year-old son.

"Abe, honey, Daddy's back doing the thing he swore off of," Marilyn said in a dead voice. "He's dating men again," Marilyn continued, describing as delicately as possible what she had seen in the photographs, "and a bad man name of Daryl has found out, and if we don't do what Daryl wants he will report Daddy for being different. Daryl knows too much about us. I got the impression there are powerful, bad people behind him."

Marilyn pointed to the fifty dollars on her dresser. "There's the blood money. I don't want nothin' to do with it, and I don't want you to, neither."

"Oh Mama, this is bad trouble. I'm so sorry," Abe said. "Daddy will lose his good teaching job. We'll lose the house." He patted his mother on the shoulder, wishing he could make her feel better.

"It was next door to impossible for him to get a nice job."

"What does he want done?"

"He wants someone to break into a house on 8th Street, where Mrs. Cristobel Lane works," Marilyn said, her voice clogged with tears.

"What could he possibly want there?" Abe asked in surprise.

"Information. I didn't really understand it. Daryl wants to find out if scientific papers are stored there. He wants me to work on Cristobel, try to get her to tell tales about her family and their friends, but of course he doesn't know how loyal she is." Marilyn paused and then said, "Cristobel and me 've been in prayer group together for years."

"So, look for signs of unusual type of work?"

"Yes. He wants me to make a report about it. I have instructions on how to get it to him. It's all strange and no good."

Abe picked up the money. "Don't worry about this, Mama," he said. "I'll talk to some fellas who are probably up to this type of work and who know how to keep their mouths shut. I'll pay them with this money, then you can give Daryl what he wants and hope he goes away."

Marilyn kissed Abe. They didn't talk anymore. Marilyn lay down on the bed and pulled the blue seersucker bedspread over her head to shut out the mean, lying, betraying world.

36 JAKE LANDS A WHOPPER

May 20, 1945. North Little Rock, Arkansas.

Jake Holt leaned back until he was reclining on the blanket Mamie had provided and crossed his feet. He watched the cumulus clouds make fanciful shapes above the narrow arm of the lake. "It's a strange thing, Ulysses," he remarked. "I have a strong sense that my father is here with us right now. It's odd to feel his presence this close because he's been gone since 1906. That's pushing 40 years ago."

"Did he like to fish?" Uwe asked.

"Yes, he did," Jake answered. He watched Uwe cast fishing line out from his position on the end of the stone dock jutting into the lake. The red and white striped float bobbed up and down in the water. Tadpoles swam in the shallow water near the bank and water bugs skidded across the lake's surface.

Jake sat up and glanced at Uwe's newspaper that lay folded on the blanket. "What's this?" he asked, and then his eyes widened when he looked closer at the print. Jake glanced around the deserted lakefront before he opened the paper up. "Ulysses, am I going to get in trouble for bringing you out of the house today, if you carry this kind of thing out into the open?" he exclaimed.

"Makes no difference, Mr. Jake," Uwe replied, "we can put it in the food basket if you wish, but I hope to assure you it is a publication approved by the United States government. This is *Der Ruf*. It is a paper published in the state of Rhode Island by German prisoners of war. In English translation it means *The Call*."

"Ulysses, I confess, I'm curious," Jake said. "What is the purpose of the publication?"

"It's a German language paper written for soldiers, with essays and news. Some of the men at Camp Robinson don't like it. They say it's American propaganda and that it's not to be trusted as a news source. I wish it carried more items about current events in Germany, but it's something at least."

"Ulysses, while I believe you," Jake said after double-checking to ensure that they were indeed alone, "I bet we wouldn't be given a chance to explain if someone with a vigilante bent were to notice, but nobody's nearby. Can you read me something from your paper? I'll hold the fishing pole."

"Sure. What do you wish to hear?" Uwe asked.

"Anything."

Uwe transferred the pole to Jake and read an article aloud from the front page of the paper, translating from German to English. The piece was about the state of affairs in Germany following the recent surrender.

Jake nodded his head from time to time. "Oh, that's like after the War Between the States over here," he said. "Parts of the South, like Arkansas, never fully recovered from it. It's important to help a defeated country to rebuild."

"I wish there never had been a war." Uwe said.

"Ignorance played a big part in the War Between the States," Jake said. "Too much of the population here was illiterate. When people are short changed on education they have to rely on blind trust instead of making their own informed judgment. An undereducated public is at a grave disadvantage."

"I would say too many of my people believed in an illusion that was not supported by logical thought," Uwe said. "That, combined with a need not to be wrong, is a dangerous combination. If you deluge such people with hate and false information for years the result is a train wreck. People must learn to distinguish truth from lies, and also to act with kindness." He paused, looking out at the water. "There's something more, though," he said. "There is a sickness in the society reaching back centuries." He sighed, "I don't understand it."

"There's always somebody to beat the battle drum and manipulate people into doing poorly," Jake agreed, warming to the subject. "Before you know it, there go the regular people to the frontline, pointing loaded rifles and cannons at each other."

"I've read that your Civil War was a terrible thing with many casualties," Uwe said.

"Yes it was," Jake said, then after a moment's hesitation he took the plunge. "I have the strongest urge to tell you about a difficult time in my grandfather's life."

"I am interested to learn more about your family," Uwe responded. "Maybe there is a lesson in it for us today."

Jake composed his thoughts. "Well, in 1863 my grandfather was, oh, let me see, about 34 years old, with a wife and two little children. They had a family farm in White County, which is not too far from here in today's world. I wasn't born until 1876, so this happened earlier than that, of course. My brothers and I moved to North Little Rock for the railroad jobs around the turn of the twentieth century, but before that all of our people were farmers, like so many others in the country.

"But to get back to my story. My grandfather was a soldier with the 36th Arkansas Infantry. That was part of the Confederate Army. He was at the Battle of Helena in July 1863. It was a turning point in the war and a turning point for Papa. Helena is a Mississippi River port on the Arkansas side, about eighty miles south of Memphis."

"There are cotton farms there," Uwe interjected.

"Yes that's right," Jake said. "The Confederates had lost, badly, and Vicksburg had fallen too. That gave the Union control of the Mississippi River. It was only a matter of time before the entire Confederacy collapsed. Grandpa surveyed the situation and decided he'd had enough. After all, he was a farmer first and a soldier by command."

"But Mr. Jake, your grandfather could walk away? I did not have that option," Uwe commented.

"It was a different world 80 years ago, in some ways at least," Jake conceded. "Yes, Grandpa was able to go home to his farm. He wasn't alone. About 150 soldiers left around the same time. As you can imagine, the higher ups didn't much like that. The army brought court martial charges against the commanding officer but then reconsidered and dropped them. They thought he had encouraged the soldiers to leave. In actuality, it was just a bad situation, and his commanding officer knew it.

"Pay? Not for months, and you can bet the soldiers were hungry. And then his family was back home with nobody to help them. Word came to Grandpa that they were starving. Who was going to do the plowing but Grandpa?" Jake asked, not anticipating a response. "Grandma wasn't strong enough to keep the heavy farm work up and the children were too young to do much. Besides, they did not own slaves. They didn't believe in it. Slavery was as wrong in 1863 as it is today. Defending state's rights can only carry you so far, if you know what I mean. I guess you could say Grandpa's heart wasn't in the fight."

Jake's gaze returned to the cloud patterns in the sky, the edge of the decorative concrete bridge in the Old Mill Park visible to his left, as he thought about the past. There was something calming about clouds.

"But what about you?" Jake asked Uwe with a concerned expression. "What's on your mind on such a beautiful day?"

Uwe watched the water rippling in circles away from the bobbing float, thinking that the last few years in camp had a dream-like quality about them. He had tried to use the time constructively by working on cars and teaching classes to other prisoners, but life in camp hadn't seemed real until his Holy Ghost trial.

"I'm thinking of how grateful I feel for all the friendly acts of the people here," Uwe said. "I remember a day two years ago when the prison train stopped at a station on our way to Camp Robinson. Local people approached the train and offered us ice water through the windows because we were so very hot. We had been fed surprisingly well on the train, but nevertheless the water was most welcome. I am ashamed to tell you that some of the soldiers said it was propaganda, but I don't think any government could control its people in that way. The act of strangers giving their enemies water made a deep impression on me. You and your family, Cristobel and all the Americans I have met have been so kind to me. It was most unexpected."

"Ulysses, I'm glad for you as well as us that the war, in Europe at least, is over," Jake said.

"Thank you, sir," he said. "You Southerners have a very good way of treating your enemies." Uwe started struggled for composure. "I can't stop thinking about my family that is gone," he said, "and so many of my friends I will never see again. The many millions of dead on both sides are such a terrible waste."

"You and my boys, those of us who are left, must work to build a new world," Jake said.

"The fears, prayers and tears of the past years have been for nothing," Uwe continued, his words pouring out after holding them in for a long time. "My entire generation has been betrayed and misused by the Nazi criminals. I am ashamed of my country. Why didn't the good people make more effort to change the course of events? We will never be able to remove the stain from this history we have written, not for a thousand years. It is just too much. How could this happen in the twentieth century?"

"What a world we are in!" Jake agreed.

Uwe was thinking about the new world his work would create. The implications of Project Stonehenge had been weighing on him, and now those worries bubbled up. "When I was in Germany," he began, "I worked for an important scientist whose name is Dr. Heisenberg. He is the director of the Kaiser Wilhelm Institute." Jake's eyebrows rose when he heard that. "His work was applicable to the development of a powerful new weapon," Uwe continued, thinking of the pineapple. "I feel certain that the project I've been working on at your house is the same subject as the one we worked on in Germany. A full out war using this weapon could destroy the world. Once it is made it will be impossible to return to how things used to be. Dr. Heisenberg understood this. It's difficult to say how important it is that only the right people, honorable people, know how to make this weapon, and even then maybe the whole thing is a bad idea. My conscience is not clear about this work."

"Ulysses, the Japanese government refuses to surrender," Jake said. "Think of all the young men who are going to have to invade the mainland, Tom and Luke among them. If we can stop that, well then, more power to us."

"When Colonel Edmund invited me to work on Project Stonehenge, I gave it thought," Uwe said. He was remembering the promise he made to Heisenberg when they were hiking in the Alps, that he would entrust his knowledge only to those he thought were worthy.

"What made up your mind?" Jake asked.

"I thought about the cups of ice water thrust through the train windows that hot day in 1943," Uwe said. "That's why I said yes."

"I'm glad you did," Jake said, paying close attention to Uwe.

"When I received my conscription notice and was sent to North Africa," Uwe said, "I brought technical information from Dr. Heisenberg about this weapon with me. I hid it on a military medal and wore it all the way here."

"Why did you do that?" Jake asked.

"Because I didn't know what would happen," Uwe said. "Due to the work we had done in Berlin, and the notable scientists who had left Europe for the US, I knew they would be working on that project but I did not know how the war would go, who would succeed and who would fail. I thought totalitarian governments like Russia would compete for the information needed to build this weapon. I believed it would be important to make sure the better people had the lever to use this powerful bomb instead of the other way around."

"You said the information is on a medal?" Jake asked. Uwe nodded.

"Where is it now?" Jake asked.

"The wooden box that Tom sent, the one on the table in your living room, has a secret compartment in it. I put it there." Uwe answered.

Jake let the fishing pole slide into the lake. "Are you telling me the key to ending this war is in a box in my house?" he said.

"After a fashion," Uwe answered.

"What does that mean, 'after a fashion'?" Jake asked.

Jake insisted on leaving the lake after Uwe confided his secret to him. They packed up their fishing gear and drove home. Jake had known the project operating out of his house was classified and high priority, but Uwe's clearing of conscience had caused him to panic and he had no thought other than to get home and protect the house and contents.

37 SCHOOL'S OUT

May 20, 1945. North Little Rock, Arkansas.

Pete ambled down the sidewalk on his daily walk. Taken to carrying a cane and cultivating a limp, he leaned to his right as though favoring one foot over the other. He shuffled around Melrose Circle and stopped when he saw George and his dog, Porter, delivering papers. "Hello, George," he called.

George coasted to a stop. "Hi, Mr. Peters," he said. Pete bent down to rub between Porter's ears. Pete chuckled because while polite, Porter kept looking around him, uninterested in socializing when he was busy. "I know, boy, you're just putting up with this. You want to get back to work." Pete stood up. "Have a nice afternoon, George," he said. George waved and then stood up on the bike pedals to get moving. Porter fell in beside him.

Ever since the embarrassing security lapse when Imogene Park had brought two saddled horses through the alleyway ready to ride away with his engineer, Pete had increased surveillance of the back. That afternoon it was quiet on the rare day when the house was empty. Pete paused when he rounded the corner onto 8th Street.

He didn't like how close the boys were to the house. They looked high school aged. One was looking in the front window and the other was walking around the side of the house like he had tried to go into the backyard. Now they were joining two others who were waiting on the walk.

The boys turned south on 7th Street and started up Main. Pete followed from a distance, curious to see where they were going. They turned right at the foot of the Main Street overpass and walked towards the rundown warehouses lining the rail yard. Pete was thinking about returning to the house, since he was getting too far afield, when the boys disappeared. Curious, he walked down the decayed asphalt road running between two of the warehouses in the direction the boys had gone.

"Y'all go wait over there. Thompson and I'll stay here," Price, one of the boys, told his friends as he glanced behind him at Pete. The boy's eyes were hard and he stood with his head tilted back and his chin jutting out. "He shouldn't be following us." North Little Rock High School had let out earlier and the boys were spoiling for a fight. Their math test results were back. None of them had scraped by with better than a "D," and there was discussion about parent teacher conferences. Now it was time to move on to other more important things, such as learning about the man at #800 and the loser following them.

Midway down the narrow road, Pete saw them. Thompson stepped out from one side and Price from the other. Pete's eyes darted around him as he tried to find a way out. He couldn't look too fit without blowing his cover, but he would do what he must. So far the boys were only flexing their muscles, but Pete had been around long enough to know what was coming.

Pete stepped back, which was a mistake. Before he knew it, all four of them had grabbed him and pushed him to the ground. Price's angry face was right in front of Pete's. "We don't believe you have any problem that would keep you from serving," he breathed.

Pete struggled but was held down by Price's friends.

"A real hero, who is not you, is the guy livin' across the street from you," Price said. "The one who is recuperating from war wounds." Price talked like he thought it was Pete's fault.

Pete listened to the garbled neighborhood report as he stared at the sky and wondered who was responsible for the decision to place a top-secret project in that neighborhood.

"He could teach you a lesson in patriotism," Price said. "I've seen you going over there to visit. Haven't you learned anything?"

Miss Beryl Barkley rounded the corner. She had gotten off the bus at the foot of the overpass on her way home from teaching at the high school and seen Pete Peters walking into what looked like trouble. She detoured to investigate. What she saw made her heart pound hard and her face flush. A lifetime of school teaching came to her aid and she strode forth. "Price! Thompson! Marshall and

Howell," she exclaimed, "what are you boys doing? Stop it right now! Break it up!"

Miss Beryl pulled the umbrella out from under her arm and poked at the boys with it. "For shame, Mr. Thompson, for shame!"

Miss Beryl could have given Pete's combat instructor tips. She was good. Pete watched with admiration as Miss Beryl improvised with the materials at hand. Gone was Price's swagger and bravado. Doughty Miss Beryl pushed and prodded with her umbrella. She weaponized her navy blue purse and flung it about with precision, fighting with the intent to subdue rather than maim. Her mouth was a determined line and her wire framed glasses flashed in the afternoon light as she manipulated the boys into a line against the fence.

The boys fell into place since they knew better than to give Miss Beryl Barkley attitude. She had taught them all, as well as their sisters and brothers, even some of their parents.

"WHAT do you boys have to say for yourselves?" she demanded.

They scuffed their feet in the dirt and looked down. "Miss Barkley, ma'am, we're thinkin' this man is no patriot," Price said.

"Who asked you?" Miss Beryl demanded. "Did someone ask you?" They looked at the ground or up at a distant point in the sky in answer. "Hmmph, as I thought," she said. "Have you boys done your homework?" she asked after a long minute.

"Listen here, young men," she said when no one answered, fixing each boy in the eye. "Don't make me have to speak to your mamas about you. Go on home, all of you, and get started on it." They mumbled something. "What do you say to me?" Miss Beryl demanded.

"Yes, ma'am," they said in unison.

"I wonder if Miss Barkley might be off her game," Price remarked to John Howell as they ambled away. "You would think she could see right through that Mr. Pete Peters." But he said it out of Miss Barkley's earshot. He looked behind him to see her returning Pete's cane to him and brushing the dirt off his back.

"Maybe she should be thinking about taking retirement," Howell said.

"This is the longest the house has been unattended since I've been on duty," Pete whispered to Miss Beryl when they were out of earshot of the boys. "We had better get over there. I've been gone at least thirty minutes, it might be closer to forty-five."

38 CUT AND RUN

May 20, 1945. North Little Rock, Arkansas.

Fifteen minutes after entering the house, Gabriel Walker emerged from the front door. He tried to be inconspicuous. His brother Lazarus, serving as lookout, jumped up to join Gabriel on the walkway leading from the screened in porch. He had been keeping watch from a hiding place behind the azalea bushes planted against the foundation of the house. It was a sleepy afternoon, and they were counting on that to allow them to get in and out without the neighbors noticing.

"We didn't get much, and I don't know if I got what Abe wanted or not," Gabriel whispered to Lazarus. Gabriel had taken the difficult part of the job because he considered he had more expertise with breaking and entering than his twin did.

"Are those cake crumbs on your chin?" Lazarus asked, surprised. "Were you eating in there?" When Gabriel didn't deny it, Lazarus said, "You were! Isn't that unprofessional, Gabriel?"

Gabriel wiped his face with his sleeve and gestured towards Maple Street, their escape route out of the neighborhood, as he continued walking away from Number 800. "Cookie," he mumbled while pulling a deteriorating chocolate chip cookie wrapped in a napkin out of his pocket. He handed it to Lazarus, who unwrapped it and said between bites, "Wasn't it kind of risky, taking time for a cookie during a job?" He added after a moment, "We got the right house for sure. This is Mrs. Cristobel Lane's recipe."

The twins looked guilty because Mrs. Lane always made those cookies for church functions. They were locally famous. She kept a full cookie jar at her house, less often in recent years, given the sugar and butter rationing imposed by the Office of Price Administration. The Walker boys were nervous around Mrs. Cristobel Lane. She was a warm and generous lady but not somebody to cross. They avoided her whenever possible. She could tell by looking at them when they were up to no good and needed no encouragement to whip them into shape.

It had taken almost a week of surveillance before a brief window of time opened up when the rock house was empty of its many occupants. As they watched the taillights of Jake's car disappear down the street, they were ready to go. "Finally," Gabriel said to Lazarus, and they got to work. Ordinarily they never would have spent so much time in that neighborhood, would not have dawdled around waiting for an opening, but Abe's promise of payment was a great motivator. As it was, they were pushing Abe's deadline.

"I didn't find much," Gabriel said, "and it wasn't an easy job either, considering how long we had to wait until nobody was home, considering how many people are crammed in there…I mean, this is about like robbing our own house."

The brothers shot puzzled looks behind them down the street's glorious tunnel of green leafy trees as they hurried away. Quartz crystals in the surface of the unassuming brown fieldstone house sparkled in the late afternoon sunshine, and the house radiated a slight golden glow that had nothing to do with money. The thought crossed Lazarus' mind that the house looked relieved, but then that was a fanciful idea because stone and mortar could not think or feel.

Gabriel was unaccustomed to feeling qualms of conscience from his work. Pleasant jolts of adrenalin ran through him when he was somewhere he shouldn't be, and he didn't worry overmuch about what he took from others. That day he had liberated a burgundy velvet sack from a box in the living room and used it to carry the stolen goods. Gabriel couldn't brush off an uneasy feeling that he was carrying a bag of trouble from the house. He shook the meager proceeds into his hand on his way down the cracked sidewalk. When he opened the sack, stray cowry shells spilled out and bounced on the sidewalk.

Given the vagueness of Abe's instructions, Gabriel had figured the entire house was fair game. The man's gold wedding band, worn from years of wear, with the faint inscription TE to JH, which he had found in the master bedroom, was marketable at least, and he pocketed it for himself and Lazarus. The bag held some odd items. "I don't think these silver coins are even American money," Gabriel said. His forehead was furrowed in concentration as he examined the loot while they strode forward.

The tap, tap tapping coming towards them on the sidewalk interrupted their discussion and caused Lazarus and Gabriel to jump off the walkway and onto the grass beside the First Christian Church on Maple Street. The blind broom salesman, his brooms across one shoulder and the leather strap of his satchel across the other, walked down the street on his way to sell door to door. Swinging his cane from side to side on the sidewalk, he nodded in the direction of Gabriel and Lazarus. "Good afternoon, and excuse me," he said.

"Afternoon, no problem, brother," Gabriel mumbled as he and Lazarus continued on their way. "Let's wait a minute and think," Lazarus said, motioning a block away towards the shelter of an alleyway between the red brick buildings off Main Street. They stopped there to rest, catch their breath and review the take.

Gabriel pulled a roll of paper money from the velvet bag. He was optimistic about the weight of rolled bills, and had waited until they were in a private place to check it out. "What is this?" he said as he unrolled the currency and saw the Japanese one peso bill on top. He thumbed through the wad of money. "Fiji! Indochine!" he exclaimed. "Who's that lady on money? We want green money! There's no American bills here! This stuff is worthless." In disgust, he let the peso drop into the trash at the alley edge. He felt like crying.

Taking a steadying breath, Gabriel sorted through the goods hoping to find something of value. "And what do you think about these two funny looking crosses? They don't look like anything I've ever seen." He held the two similar well-traveled gold medals, the ones Uwe and Tom, on different days and different continents, had hidden in the box.

Lazarus examined the crosses. "What you got here are somebody's battle medals," he snorted, "and nobody will want to buy these. Does Abe want us to fence this stuff for him? This is hardly worth carrying to a pawn shop."

"Well, they sure enough were hid in a secret place. I bet even Miz. Holt don't know they there."

The medallions fastened to their colorful blue, red and gold striped ribbons lay in the palm of Gabriel's hand, mute testimony to someone else's trials far from home. He shook his head in disappointment and stuffed them into his pocket.

"What do we do with this stupid money?" Gabriel wondered aloud. He removed the Fiji bill and tucked it into his pocket because he thought it was pretty. He had never seen pink money before. He shoved the roll of folding money back into the velvet bag. Maybe, after he'd had time to think about it, there would be a way to use the money.

"Abe was not clear about what he wanted," Gabriel told Lazarus. "He didn't say anything about having us sell the stuff. He was more interested in the goings on in the house. I would guess that Mist' Tom Holt sent these home for safekeeping. I don't know why Abe would find them interesting. He didn't say anything specific about medals, maybe we could try to sell them and the coins and Abe wouldn't care. If we did they would be gone and the po-lice wouldn't be able to connect us with the job."

"There's something more," Gabriel continued as he pulled a rolled up newspaper from his back pocket. The front page of last week's *Der Ruf* came into view when he smoothed it out, frowning as he did so, worried about what he had uncovered. "Somebody stayin' in the middle bedroom what prob'ly belong to Mist' Tom and Mist' Luke, since they've gone to war. It didn't appear to be a lady. That's where I found this. I don't know what it means."

The brothers stared at the German language newspaper, unable to understand it, as they considered what to do next. They knew they should report everything to Abe because he had commissioned the job. The paper might be what Abe wanted. The job would be done and they would get paid. It would be over.

"What has Abe got into, I wonder?" Lazarus asked.

"What has Abe got us into?" Gabriel countered.

They knew Mama would disapprove. And she would insist on reviewing the take, they could never hide things from her for long. She knew them too well. As soon as they walked in the door she would sense something and wheedle it out of them. Mama would be unhappy when she found out whose house they had been in. She would say it was too dangerous and bad for business.

Mama's eyes first would open wide in surprise, then narrow down, and her lips would purse in an expression of disapproval when she saw the goods. The wedding ring was pushing it, but war medals were over the top. She wouldn't know where to begin worrying about a foreign language newspaper.

Of course, the fifty-dollar payment would give Mama pause, but then she would thunder on. She would say 'Dum-dums signing up for God only knows what with some terrible kind of payback! Who would hire the two of you kids and pay you big money? You should know better!'

"She'll carry on about a curse." Gabriel said.

"Ummhmm. She'll say, who know what kind of catastrophe headed our way now."

"Yeah. She'll say fast moving cancer coming to somebody, or if not that, then a stroke that don't kill quick enough."

"And finish up with how this will attract bad women."

"You got that right, that where it always ends up. Bad women. I don't know why she worries so much about bad women."

The happy anticipation of fifteen minute's work for fifty dollars had not panned out. The cookies were turning out to be the best thing about the entire adventure.

"Fat Moo L'Foo." Lazarus stated.

"Yes. You're right! What if he finds out? What if he already knows?" Gabriel said in an ominous tone, his eyes focused ahead of him on something he could see but no one else could except for Lazarus because he was his twin.

"It's a trap!" Lazarus exclaimed. "Fat Moo L'Foo'll burn our house down!" he moaned.

Gabriel shuddered as he considered the problem in front of them. What if by their brazen actions they goaded the local enforcer of the law of the street and resident arsonist to take drastic steps to keep them in line?

"Let's get out of here, baby brother," Gabriel said. He headed south down Main Street, followed by Lazarus.

Gabriel paused at the corner of Broadway and Maple. "Lazarus, I been thinking," he said as he pulled the battle medals from his pocket. "Let's not even go home tonight. Let's take the ring and this other stuff and go over the river and find a pawnshop 'way on the other side of town. Maybe we can find somebody who'll give us something for the metal."

Lazarus wiped the cold sweat from his brow while considering the suggestion. He made up his mind. Having already sinned big by stealing crosses, he didn't want to further mess with fate by trying to sell them at a pawnshop. They would have to jettison them.

Scooping the medals from Gabriel's hand, Lazarus scanned the street to make sure nobody was looking, and with one decisive gesture tossed them into the gutter. "There's too much risk involved here," he said. "We'd best make ourselves scarce."

Lazarus crossed Broadway and headed towards the river and the railroad bridge, Gabriel dogging him.

"Let's see if Diamond State Pawn on Main over the river will give us something for the ring and the foreign money," Lazarus said.

"Lazarus Arimathea Walker, I cannot believe you threw crosses in the gutter," Gabriel sputtered in horror as he followed his brother. "Sacrilegious, it's what it is for sure! Risk. You're somebody to talk about risk! Throwing 'em away is worse, worse, worse than stealing and selling. There's goin' to be a storm outta this. We've disrespected Jesus, there's no other way to see it," Gabriel continued, crying now. "Brother, we're lost!"

A whistle sounded behind them as a train pulled away from the yard a few blocks away and approached a crossing, the blast echoing throughout the town and emphasizing Gabriel's despairing howl. The pair hustled as they headed towards the train tracks with the unspoken understanding that they would be jumping onto the first southbound train.

The conversation continued, disjointed now, as they panted, trying to make the Rock Island train before it started over the bridge.

"What about Abe? Shouldn't we have saved the medals for him? Do you think that's what he wanted?"

"Forget about Abe!"

"Shouldn't we go back for the medals?"

"No! Leave 'em."

The single sheet of newsprint that was all that remained of *Der Ruf* fluttered like a kite in the wind when Gabriel let it fly.

"Fat Moo L'Foo!"

"Oh no!"

"After… the pawn shop… let's go to…Pine Bluff and hide…outside of there for… awhile."

"O...kay… Corn…bread."

39 GWEN GETS ON BOARD

May 20, 1945. Rector Building, Little Rock, Arkansas.

"Federal Bureau of Investigation. Gwen Weintraub speaking."

"Hey Gwen."

"Gil?"

"Yeah."

Gil could hear the office chair creaking as Gwen leaned back, curling the cord with manicured hands. "Gil Henderson, how are things in the pawnshop world?" Gil could hear the smile in her voice too. He enjoyed a mental picture of Gwen, her jacket and skirt tailored over her curves.

"Not bad, not bad," he answered.

"Something going on?"

"Maybe. I had a couple 'a fellas in here this afternoon. It wasn't so much what they were selling as how rattled they were."

"Oh? How so?"

"They sure were jumpy and in a big hurry to get going. They were trying to exchange money from places in the Orient like Indochina, some small Pacific islands, both silver and folding. The town's floatin' in foreign money the boys collect as souvenirs, there's no value in it, so I turned it away. Also, and this is going into my daily police report, they brought in a wedding ring. It's most likely hot. There's an inscription on the inside that says TE to JH."

"Hmm. Did you recognize them?"

"No. They were just kids. I can give you their description. I would say they were local. Like I said before, it was their attitude more than their business that has me calling you."

"We'll send someone out there, Gil. Maybe my boss will let me go."

"That would be great, but if he doesn't, are we still on for dinner at Bruno's Saturday night?"

"You bet."

Her detective instincts on high alert, Gwen's first action after disconnecting was to beg the assignment from her boss.

Agent Mitchell Jennings looked up from the stack of paperwork generated by his massive case backlog. He didn't think much of the tip. "A stolen wedding ring? Happens all the time. Foreign money? Everywhere."

"Then you don't mind if I take the assignment?"

Swamped with work, Agent Jennings thought the trip sounded routine and nonthreatening. "Well, if we don't call it an assignment you can go. Take some notes for me and bring them back here. It'll save me time."

Back at her desk, Gwen made a call, her voice quivering with anticipation. "Claudette? I've got a case."

"I'm off work in five."

"Want to tag along?"

"Let me get my hat."

40 OUT OF THE FRYING PAN

May 20, 1945. North Little Rock, Arkansas.

Gone. Heisenberg's information was gone. Uwe pawed through the contents of the box, sifting through spilled cowry shells, but it was a futile search. He stood in the living room with the secret compartment open and empty of any medals. A true scientist's primal instinct being to save the data, Uwe was devastated by the loss. Further, the implications of his failure to save the medal and the loss of the information on it were chilling. Who could have known about his medal, and how did they trace it to 8th Street?

Uwe and Jake had arrived home from the curtailed fishing trip to find the front door ajar and Tom's box open with the contents strewn on the sofa. They ran outside looking for anyone suspicious, but the street was quiet. Whoever had been there was gone.

"Where is Pete?" Jake panted as they ran onto the porch of Pete's lookout house across the street, their footsteps loud on the wooden floor, and tried the door. No one was home. Seconds later they returned home and checked the rock house.

"They don't seem to have discovered the basement work room at least, but they got my wedding ring," Jake said. "Well, somebody did. I guess we don't know if it was one person or more. So, was it a plain burglary or something else?"

"I don't know, but Mr. Jake," Uwe said, "I need to find my medal, and I should go now."

Jake thought a moment and then removed his worn billfold from his back pocket. He handed some bills and silver to Uwe. "You'd better get moving," he said. "I'll stay here and contact Camp

Robinson and tell them what happened. I'm worried about Pete. Good luck, Ulysses."

Shoving the money into his pocket, Uwe shook Jake's hand and started for the door, then turned around and ran to the kitchen for insurance. He fumbled in the drawer next to the sink. His hand closed on a short, sharp knife that he stowed in a special pocket on his pant leg. He breathed a silent thank you to Cristobel for having sewn the pocket there at his request. "You're right, Ulysses, you never know what's comin' your way, it's best to take precautions like this when you have the time," she had said.

Realizing he might not see the Holts again, Uwe shook Jake's hand a second time. "Thank you for everything, sir," he said before darting out the door.

Uwe paused on the sidewalk to get his bearings. He had no idea where to start looking. The train yard was to his left, the river to his right, a vacant field behind him, residential homes around him and the downtown ahead. The thief could be anywhere, could have gone any direction. He could even be holed up in a neighborhood house. This last thought caused him to look around suspiciously, but he only saw silent houses in the quiet afternoon.

Uwe noticed crumbs scattered on the ground, and he walked along 8th Street wondering if they were from the thieves. It crossed his mind that it was like the fairy tale about Hansel and Gretel, who left a trail of breadcrumbs to mark their way home. Uwe thought of the fate awaiting Hansel in the story, held captive in a cell, being fattened up by a witch so that he would be good eating. Here he couldn't see much of a trail, though, besides the few crumbs outside the house.

Uwe tried to devise a plan to retrieve the medal but came up empty. His anxiety wound up as tight as a top the more he thought about the magnitude of the problem in front of him. A flood of depression overcame him. He was a stranger there and didn't know where to begin his search.

That he had been a fool to stop wearing the medal was the lesson of the day, the week, the month, the eon. The possessor of the information carried within it was in a powerful position and could unleash violence unimagined on the world. And it was his fault. It was he who had cajoled the information out of Heisenberg, who had gone to the lab where he modified his father's medal, encrypted the information on it and then carried it into and out of a prison halfway across the world, only for it to be stolen in a smallish town in the middle of America by God knew who. His plan all along, which was to bring Heisenberg's work out to the free world, could result in a disaster unless he made a miracle happen and soon.

"Hello, hello! Ulysses?" He was drawn back to the present by a familiar voice. When he looked up, he saw Fredericka Lane standing in front of him smiling. "What are you doing?" she asked.

"Fredericka!" He was happy to see her. Her nearness caused his anxiety to dissipate like lightning to ground and his thoughts cleared. "Where did you come from?"

"I babysit for a family who lives around the corner on Orange," she said cheerfully.

When Fredericka saw Uwe's expression, she stopped smiling. "Ulysses, what's wrong?"

"I, I, I've lost something very important and have to get it back."

"Oh really? You look like you've lost something important, Ulysses."

The desperation in his eyes cut to Fredericka's heart and made her say the fateful words, "Can I help you?"

"Would you?" The appeal in his voice broke any vestige of reserve Fredericka had and she was in.

"Tell me about it. What are you missing?"

"The Holts have been robbed," he started, and Fredericka exclaimed, "No!"

"Mr. Jake Holt's wedding ring was stolen, and some international currency belonging to Mr. Tom Holt and a few other small items."

Fredericka exclaimed at each revelation.

"Have the police been called?"

"Mr. Holt is dealing with that. I want to start searching before more time elapses."

Uwe scanned the horizon for trouble, hoping he was ahead of the military policemen he feared would be after him since he wasn't supposed to be out loose. He retained the hope that he could retrieve his medal himself. As far as Uwe was aware, only Mr. Holt knew both the nature of his work and the significance of the medal due to his full disclosure at the fishing lake. However, if no one else knew what was on the medal, why had it been stolen from its hiding place?

He leaned down and picked up a stray cowry shell, marveling again at the parallels between his reality and the fairy tale. Hansel and Gretel also had marked a trail with pebbles. "The thief dropped these shells," he said, but didn't offer an explanation to Fredericka as to why he knew that and she didn't ask.

"Oh ho, like Hansel and Gretel, huh?" She laughed again. "I've been reading that story to the kids I babysit." Listening to Fredericka, Uwe thought, she thinks like I do. It pleased him to no end, and as if to underscore their connection, Fredericka added, "Let's hope you and I don't end up in a cage somewhere, Ulysses!"

Uwe's conscience told him he should disclose everything to Fredericka, but Stonehenge was a classified project. Fredericka might be better off if she did not know everything. He resolved to slip away from her and go it alone if the search turned dangerous.

He looked around and decided that, given the way the shells were scattered, the thieves might not have made their escape to the train yard, rather had gone ahead of them to the downtown area or maybe the river. Taking a gamble, he walked towards downtown and kept an eye out for more shells.

"I'll send word to Mama that I'll be late coming home tonight," Fredericka said, ducking into a phone booth on Main Street. "Now where do you think we should start looking for your things?" she asked when she emerged.

"Where would someone exchange a ring for money?" he asked.

"A pawnshop, of course!" Fredericka answered with raised eyebrows, surprised by the question.

"Can you take us to the closest pawnshop so we can verify whether the thieves tried to sell it there?"

"Where have you been livin,' Ulysses?" For the second time Fredericka's brows went up. "What planet did you land from? You and me, we can't go shopping together. It's not done."

"Oh," he said.

"There's more than one way to skin a cat," Fredericka said. "Why don't you go to the Washington Avenue pawnshop down by the river while I go visiting?"

"Who do you know to visit?"

"This is my hometown, Ulysses. I'll ask around and see if I can come up with some information. I'll meet you on the corner of Broadway and Washington." Fredericka pulled a pencil and paper from her purse and drew a rough map for Uwe. "This is us here, the pawnshop is over there. Let's meet in forty-five minutes. We'll have to hustle." Uwe nodded and strode off to the pawnshop.

Fredericka scanned the horizon as she tried to get an idea of where to start looking. Several of her mother's friends worked nearby. She could start knocking on doors and asking around.

An hour later Uwe was pacing up and down at their meeting place. What if Fredericka didn't show? He had come up empty at the pawnshop, but he supposed there were other pawnshops to visit, and he was ready to get moving. He considered returning to the Holts, but what if Colonel Edmund arrested him?

He had almost decided that Fredericka wasn't coming and he would have to devise a new plan on his own when in the distance he saw something straw colored bobbing up and down. As it neared, he saw that it was Fredericka carrying a pile of brooms over her shoulder. When she got closer, he could see she was pleased.

"The cost of doing business," she sighed in relief when she dropped the brooms to the ground. Uwe looked a question at her. "I had a useful conversation with a broom salesman. O' course, since he's blind his information was limited," she said. Uwe wilted with disappointment.

"Now, Ulysses, don't look like that, " she said. "He could see shadows, and his hearing is very good."

Not wanting to hurt Fredericka's feelings, Uwe refrained from saying what he thought about her informant, and he tried to make his expression receptive, as though he was looking forward to what she had to tell him.

"I caught up with him under the viaduct," she said. "He had information about the robbery."

"Really?"

"Yes. Now hear me out. I can tell by lookin' at you that you don't think Mr. King, that's my broom salesman, had anything to offer. But, you know, people discount handicapped individuals to the point that they're invisible, I've noticed that, and people will do and say things as though no one is there, which is what happened today."

"What did he say?" Uwe asked, still pessimistic on the strength of a blind witness.

"He passed two men when he was out sellin', he guesses they were young, more boys than men, from the way they talked," Fredericka said. "He thought they were of similar height, not too tall, maybe five foot nine or so, and slim."

"Could he tell if they were local?" Uwe asked. This last was an important piece of information, but Uwe wondered whether Mr. King would be able to tell that.

"From what he said, I would say yes, they were. Mr. King caught something else. Their paths crossed twice. He said he stopped to take a rest on the riverbank and overheard them talking, and this is where it got a little strange. Mr. King swore they say they were goin' to Pine Bluff for cornbread."

"Cornbread?" Uwe shook his head. "Were they going to eat some or make some or maybe they had business and were going to sell some? Why would somebody who just robbed a house be interested in cornbread?"

"I don't know, but that's what Mr. King said he heard. He was very clear about it."

"Where is Pine Bluff?"

"It's about 40-50 miles south of here on the river."

Fredericka wondered, why didn't Ulysses know where Pine Bluff was? Anybody should know that, well, a nephew of Miss Beryl Barkley's from Vilonia, anyway, should know that. His speech was odd too. Mr. King had cautioned her that she was asking about trouble but she hadn't paid much attention to that part of what he said, she thought he was being dramatic.

He'd sat in the cool shade of the concrete viaduct, his brooms beside him, and shaken his head. His eyes conveyed no expression because they were hidden behind dark glasses, but his tone was serious. "Mmmm, I dunno," he said, "but those boys seemed to be deep in something they din' know how to get out of. They were tryin' to run away from it. I'd watch out if I were you, Miss. Steer clear. It sounded like bad business to me, jus' the little I overheard."

Focused as he was on making a plan to regain his medal, Uwe did not see the questions in Fredericka's eyes. She comforted herself with the thought that her mother, who was the most remarkable woman she knew, and who worked in the same house as Ulysses, had never said anything alarming about him. Come to think of it, though, her mother had not said much of anything at all, which was unusual since her mother was so gregarious. She did trust Ulysses, and she was only helping him out for an afternoon. Surely that would not be dangerous.

While Fredericka's information from Mr. King was sketchy, it was all they had. "I should go to Pine Bluff," Uwe said. "Can I get there by rail?" he asked, looking at the train tracks.

"Mr. King thought the thieves rode the rail," she said.

"Then I will too. But do you know which line leads to Pine Bluff?" he asked.

"I believe we need to get over to the tracks beyond Washington Avenue," Fredericka answered.

Uwe thought it best not to alert the authorities by purchasing a ticket in a station house and decided to hop the next freight train going his way.

"Maybe you shouldn't go with me, Fredericka, it might be too rough," he said.

"Something tells me you are going to need my help." Fredericka meant what she said, but did not add, that she was mighty curious about this man. There was more to him than met the eye.

"Have you ridden the rails before, Fredericka?"

"You mean hobo'n?"

"I mean riding secretly."

"You mean hobo'n, and no, sir, I have not, I always buy my ticket and sit in a seat, but I have brothers who have traveled that way. I think I can figure it out."

Ten minutes later Uwe and Fredericka were rocking along in an empty boxcar of the Cotton Belt Line with the rails rumbling beneath them. They sat against the far side of the door on the dusty floor. It had taken some effort to get themselves onto the moving train, but once they were on board they exchanged a look and laughed, glad to be alive. The breeze blowing in from the open door felt good.

Fredericka cleared her throat and turned to Uwe. "I've got to ask you, Ulysses, what's really going on?" she asked.

Startled not so much by the question itself but because he was on the spot, Uwe looked at her, uncertain where to begin and how much to say.

"Now, Ulysses, you can't possibly believe I haven't noticed your accent," Fredericka said. "You don't speak as though you were from Vilonia. Where are you from? Besides, why isn't a young, healthy, bright guy such as yourself in uniform?"

"Fredericka, I am a German prisoner of war on furlough from Camp Robinson," Uwe said, thinking as he said it that he wasn't sure if he used the correct wording, but continued, for lack of a better way to explain it, "at the Holt's house."

"A German soldier on furlough?" Startled, Fredericka watched out the open door as the train left North Little Rock and the cotton fields of the old plantations of Scott spread out from each side of the train. She had family in England, the stop after Keo. Maybe she should throw herself off the train and hope she didn't break anything. Could German prisoners of war even have furloughs? Probably not, but then what was Ulysses doing at the Holt's house anyway? The United States and Germany were no longer at war with each other. That was a fact, but still....

"Do you know who Werner Heisenberg is?"

"Who?" She stared at him.

"Never mind. I, he's a, he's somebody I used to work with back home," he said. Uwe took the plunge. "Fredericka, something important to do with the war effort was stolen from me at the Holt's house and that's what I need to get back. The other stolen items the police can find, but this thing I must retrieve. I don't know who stole it and finding it might be dangerous. If you want to leave now I won't hold you back, maybe it even would be a good thing for you to do." As he spoke the words, he hoped she would exclaim, "No! I must stay with you and provide all of my help and support."

"Does my mother know about this?" she asked.

"Yes. She is the one who gave me my American name." Uwe said, hoping Fredericka would find it reassuring.

Fredericka wavered, wondering what her mother of all people had gotten involved with. She knew her mother would want her to stay out of it, but on the other hand, her mother's active participation made it seem more acceptable, whatever it was, which she did not know. Her gaze caught the curving track ahead and she thought there might be an adventure in the making down in Pine Bluff. She was thinking about Pine Bluff in a new light.

Fredericka decided to draw a line in the sand. "Ulysses, you are going to have to be honest with me from now on out or I'm leaving, got that?"

"Yes."

"All right, then, tell me about the thing we're searching for."

"It is about the size of a locket or a pendant you might wear. It contains important technical information hidden inside."

"Oh really?" Her eyes widened. "Well, let's go over what we know and see if we can figure out what we should do next."

Uwe and Fredericka launched into a discussion whereby they examined the various facets of the problem. The train picked up speed and trundled through the countryside as they talked and talked. When they reached Altheimer, the train turned west, and when they crossed the Rob Roy truss bridge, the next stop being Pine Bluff, they didn't have much of a plan.

41 INTO THE FIRE

May 20, 1945. Little Rock and Pine Bluff, Arkansas.

"Man, I sure thought we would have done better," Gabriel said for what seemed to Lazarus like the hundredth time. "Don't say it again, I'm tired of hearing it," Lazarus snapped. Their business trip had taken them to Little Rock, and they walked down 12th Street away from Diamond State Pawn with a few dollars from the sale of the wedding ring and nothing else.

"Gabriel, we got to get back on the train," Lazarus said. He was worried about more than their disappointing earnings. "Did you see how that man looked hard at us? He suspects we stole the ring."

"And he didn't care to get involved with the foreign money, did he?" Gabriel said.

"No," Lazarus answered. "I even got the impression he might be going to make a phone call because of us."

Gabriel had taken to looking from side to side, and once he said, "Do you think somebody is following us?" They turned off the main road, intending to lose themselves in the back alleyways of neighborhoods where nobody knew them, in case somebody was after them.

In fact, Daryl Green, who had commissioned Abe to do the investigative work on the rock house, was on their trail. He kept a string of informants posted around the area pawnshops, and he had gotten a call about two suspicious characters turned away at Diamond State. Daryl's out of state handlers had increased their interest in his business and sent new people to town. Unused to such scrutiny, Daryl had had to step up his game, which resulted in his following Gabriel and Lazarus that afternoon.

Sweat pouring from his body, all Daryl could think as he tried to keep up with the Walker boys and remain out of sight was that he was too old and fat for that kind of work. He gave it his best, though, as he moved along, an odd stout figure in a gray striped suit and a hat pulled down over his brow. Part of his white shirttail had worked its way out of his cinched pants and waved behind him. His fat gut hung over his belt and bounced with each step, causing him to wince, as he trotted after the younger, fitter boys.

Lazarus looked behind him and walked faster. "Let's get a move on," he said.

They moved further away from town, no longer keeping track of their location, in an effort to shake the tail they worried was following them. They crisscrossed Bayou Fourche, clambering up one creek bank and down the other, getting drenched in the process.

Daryl managed to keep up, cursing in dread when he saw them crossing the bayou as he prepared to follow. He slid down the muddy embankment and tried to cross the water by teetering on rocks poking up from the surface, none of them flat enough to stand on. His socks got soaked and his wet pant legs flapped around his ankles.

When the Walkers reached the cemetery, Daryl groaned. The serenity of the manicured grounds failed to please him. Cemeteries gave him the creeps. There were dead people, for one thing, and then he got reminded of things he didn't want to think about. He maintained a nagging worry in the back of his mind about which way he was going once his time came, concerned it would be down instead of up, but he didn't have time to make any adjustments to the trajectory now, and he forged forth. Given the choice between pleasing an unseen God and his boss, he chose the latter. Live for today was his motto.

Lazarus and Gabriel walked across rows of silent graves. No one, no one alive anyway, was in the cemetery, and there were plenty of oak trees with expansive trunks suitable for hiding behind. Daryl jumped from tree to tree as he managed to keep up with the boys.

The boys headed downhill, and when they passed Babyland, the burial area reserved for babies, Gabriel brushed a tear from his eye. "Oh, brother," he said, " look here at the dead babies, don't it make you sad?" Lazarus stopped a moment to look at the sparkling pinwheels spinning in the sunshine that mourners had placed on the short graves. "Yes it does," he said. "So many little ones who didn't get a fair shake at life. Remember Veronica who Mama lost at only a day old?" And they stood there thinking about their baby sister who had gone to heaven early.

The sound of an approaching train brought their attention to their current predicament. Lazarus looked around and got his bearings. "Gabe!" he exclaimed. "I'm pretty sure we're off course. I think this track goes to Texarkana!" They ran across the tracks in front of the train that was bearing down on them, causing the conductor to sound the horn and throw on the brakes to avoid hitting them.

They powered up the slope away from the track, cutting through dense undergrowth, surfacing beside Asher Avenue, oblivious to how close they had come to being smashed flat. "We're going to be covered in chiggers from this tall grass," Lazarus moaned.

"No, it's ticks!" Gabriel shouted.

The grass was crawling with the tiny, hard bodied bugs, ready to hitch a ride on the next convenient host, which happened to be Lazarus and Gabriel. The ticks were questing, holding onto the grass tips with their third or fourth legs and reaching for the boys with their first legs. The ticks acted like they had never eaten before, which may have been the case. They took advantage of their new dining opportunity and transitioned from the grass to the boys, scampering up their clothes in search of a place to dig in.

The boys ran out of the grass and brushed the ticks from each other, shouting, "Get my back!" and "Get them out of my hair! Blood suckers, oohee, Jehosephat!" When they had gotten rid of those ticks they could see, they resumed their course, relieved to be getting out of tick territory.

Gabriel stuck out his thumb and a battered pickup truck stopped. They piled into the truck bed beside a dog lunging against a chain attached to the back of the cab, trying to keep a safe distance from his snapping teeth. They shouted through the open window to the driver that they wanted to pick up the track leading to Pine Bluff. He nodded and drove to a highway lined with pine trees. Soon he pulled off the road and motioned towards the train tracks paralleling the highway. They climbed over the tailgate and waved their thanks to the driver, who waved back as he drove off.

Daryl managed, by the hardest, to keep up with the boys. He panicked when they darted in front of the train, believing he had lost them. After standing awhile waiting for the train to amble by, Daryl realized there was an overpass a few hundred yards away. He hustled away to his left and surfaced on the road leading out of the cemetery.

The tick incident worked in Daryl's favor, slowing the twins down so that when he emerged from the cemetery they had not gone too far. Daryl spotted them jumping into the back of a pick-up truck down the road. He threw money at a boy with a car to drive him, and before long he was behind the truck carrying his quarry.

When Gabriel and Lazarus heard a train whistle, they ran with relief towards the sound. Being young and adept at rail travel, it wasn't difficult for them to swing up onto a line of cars gathering speed after a crossing. They started to relax after they had climbed to the top of a boxcar and lay back flat.

"Do you think Dwight is still sharecropping?" Lazarus said, watching afternoon cloud patterns in the sky.

Pulling a stray tick from where it had installed itself behind his ear, Gabriel shuddered as he wiped a trickle of blood from the attachment point. "I imagine so," he said, flicking the tick overboard. "What else would he be doing?"

"I don't know. Let's hope we can get there before dark. They's no lights on the farm and I'm not entirely certain where the turn-off is."

While the brothers were enjoying the view from the top of a boxcar, Daryl clambered sweating and muddy but triumphant onto the last car of the same train. Lying on his back and feeling like a beached whale, Daryl pulled out his hip flask and raised his head enough to take a restorative sip.

When the train stopped at the Pine Bluff yard next to a waiting train, Lazarus and Gabriel, shielded from view by the two trains, slipped down from their perch on the boxcar top. They crossed the open space surrounding the tracks and disappeared into town.

Trailing behind the Walker boys, Daryl felt a sense of relief to be on terra firma, his home territory of Pine Bluff. He watched with interest to see where the boys were going.

Thirty minutes later Lazarus and Gabriel turned left onto an unmarked dirt road in a cotton field. The road ended in the middle of the field at a sharecropper's cabin. To somebody else heading to such a destination it might have triggered a depression, but not Lazarus and Gabriel. To them it was a sanctuary at the end of a long and trying day. It looked good, like home.

"I can't wait to spend time with Dwight," Lazarus said.

"Me too, and I bet he has dinner cooking," Gabriel said as he walked faster. "I see smoke coming from the chimney."

"Hey, Dwight! Hey, Dwight!" the boys called when they got closer.

The door creaked open and a little boy dressed in ragged clothes poked his head out. "They's nobody named Dwight here," he said.

A tired woman appeared behind the boy. "May I help you?"

"Mama, they's looking for somebody by name of Dwight," the boy said.

"Oh," she said. "Dwight has moved. He took a job over to the Pine Bluff Arsenal. He's earning good money cooking for the munitions factory workers."

"Do you have any idea where he might be living?" Lazarus said.

"I think he's on the quarter-boats," she said.

The boys stared at her. "You know, over on the river. The floating barge hotels," she added.

With Daryl trailing far behind, they trudged back the way they had come, hoping to hitch a ride to the river and try to find a quarter-boat.

"I thought we'd get dinner with Dwight. I'm so hungry," Lazarus said in disappointment.

"Me too," Gabriel agreed.

42 THE TWELFTH MAN

May 20, 1945. North Little Rock, Arkansas.

"Woof!" It came from deep inside Porter's throat as he surveyed the world from the window. Soon George would be home and the meaning of life would be realized once more. Porter was caught up in the moment, as all superior dogs like him in the security, herding and nursing professions were, dogs at the peak of life as he was. His attention was one hundred percent on alert in the event of any possible threat or interesting activity, in this case the imminent arrival of George.

Porter's plumed black tail with the white tip was held high. His black ears stood up straight, and one short and stubby white front paw was bent back at the elbow in a slight pointer position when he thought he saw George. Yes, there he was, George was almost home. The blond, lanky twelve year-old walked down Willow Street and turned onto the concrete walkway leading to his house. He dropped his book bag on the floor inside the door and accepted his tribute.

The rocket of Welsh Cardigan Corgi that was Porter, ears now rotated backwards flat against his head, hurled himself around the corner and flung himself at his master, jumping four feet and higher into the air, leaping towards George's mouth and barking. Porter stopped, made an about face and ran the length of the downstairs, turning tighter than a prize winning Quarter Horse in a barrel race to return to George. He swiveled to repeat the process two and three times before the finale, a triple doughnut, as he chased his tail, snapping at it repeatedly before flinging himself down to the ground, which was not too far, and panting.

"Hey there, boy, hey there," George said, smiling and patting Porter on each side of his sturdy body. He called, "Hi Mom," in response to his mother's hello, on his way to the carport to sort through the copies of the *Arkansas Democrat* waiting for the evening delivery. Porter bustled after him and watched as the newspapers were placed in the saddlebags hanging on each side of the back wheel of the bicycle.

When the papers were loaded to balance the heavy weight, George rode down Willow Street to begin his delivery route. At the foot of the railroad overpass, George waved to Mr. Cartwright, the legless man who sat sentinel to the town. The man was in his usual afternoon spot greeting passersby. He was bald and his upper body was muscular from pushing himself in his wheelchair. Although George rode by the same corner everyday on his delivery route, all he knew about the man was his name. Both of his pant legs were knotted where the knees should have been, the bottom parts flapping empty. George had no idea how he had gotten to be without legs, whether he had been born in that condition or if it had come about some other way. The man returned George's wave. "Happy day, George, happy day, Porter," he said.

"Hello there, Mr. Cartwright," George responded.

Porter ran alongside in the slipstream between the bike and the curb, unencumbered by a leash, his fur sweeping the curb. As they glided past the house where Romo lived, Porter lifted his nose to the wind hoping to detect the Doberman's presence. He was too busy guarding his master and delivering papers to issue a bigger challenge to his stern neighbor other than sending a flying salute into Romo's territory.

When George finished his deliveries, he turned left onto Broadway, off of Maple, ready to head homeward. Porter, as always, was by George's side. George did not have any customers on Broadway, it being home to the Cotton Belt train station and small businesses. The late afternoon sunlight flashing on something in the street caught his attention. He and Porter paused to take a closer look.

They saw what looked like coins attached to short, wide ribbons lying in a puddle of water in the gutter next to a storm drain. George glanced around to see if anyone to claim ownership was nearby. The street was deserted except for the occasional car.

"Come on, boy," he said to Porter, and they left, taking a circle of the block, riding up town and looping through Melrose Circle. They stopped for a visit with Mr. Peters, but George kept it short because Porter wanted to get moving. It being a warm day, housewives were outside sweeping their walks or removing dry laundry from the lines in their backyards. "Hi there, George, hi there, Porter," they called. George and Porter were familiar neighborhood fixtures.

George stopped at Melrose Grocery and bought a cold drink as a delaying tactic while Porter waited outside by the bike. When George came out, he and Porter cruised back down to Broadway. George scanned the streets for unusual activity, which he did not see. On the second pass, the items were still there and no one was around, so they stopped.

On closer inspection, the objects were intriguing. Porter pushed his nose close in to record the smells. The ribbons in particular held interesting information. Porter inhaled the scents, storing the data in his remarkable filing system. He would remember those smells for a long time. "These aren't coins, boy," George said to Porter. "They're crosses, but I've never seen any like 'em at St. Patrick's. "What do you make of this stuff?" he asked.

Porter looked at George but did not say anything. He didn't know what they were either. The two items were similar when inspected side by side but not identical. "Porter, finders keepers, losers weepers," George said.

George rotated Porter's collar around to the back of his neck. He ran the metal loop attached to Porter's collar through the rings welded to the medal tops. When he rotated the collar, the crosses hung down pendant style in front and became hidden in the white triangle of thick chest fur. He patted Porter's head and rubbed around the base of his ears. George couldn't think of anybody with a bigger heart than Porter.

Satisfied with the notable find, they headed home. With the papers delivered and his load lightened, George lifted Porter and inserted him into one of the saddlebags where he rode shotgun. Porter rested and enjoyed the scenery while the wind rustled through his fur and he surveyed his territory with bright brown eyes and a panting grin.

Standing up in the saddle and leaning from side to side, George pushed hard to peddle the bike. His leg muscles strained under the effort required carrying his friend.

"Porter, I'm going to put you on a diet!" George panted. "You're going to have to… cut… back… on the tacos and barbeque. I'm sorry, I know you love 'em."

"No, Porter, it's okay, you don't have to get out and run even though you've put on weight," George continued, as though Porter had spoken. "I know you would if I asked you to. Being heavy runs in your family, I guess. Your mother ran to plump." Porter rolled his eyes at George in an endearing way. Porter had happy memories of his soft and furry mother.

"Your new crosses sure are fine," George said, changing the subject because he thought Porter might be sensitive about his weight.

"But I warn you," George continued, his voice coming in short jerks while pedaling, "Porter, don't expect Romo to share his girlfriends with you. Being decorated won't change how he feels about you. He wants to beat you to a pulp."

Porter looked like he didn't have a care in the world. George worried about him.

"Romo should worry you because he's three times your size and you don't seem to understand that significance."

George panted as he pedaled, thinking of what total strangers said about Porter and right in front of him too, things that might have destroyed a lesser dog. Stuff like, "That dog don't got no legs!" or, more refined but also ridiculous, "Excuse me, is your dog a German Shepherd and Dachshund mix?" It was like water off a duck's back to Porter.

Reaching around, George rubbed Porter's ears. "Of course, we would both like to meet some girls, wouldn't we, boy?" George thought Porter nodded when he said that.

"Do you remember the time the beautiful girl ran out of the restaurant where she was eating lunch when she saw you outside? It was when you were just a pup. She was a complete stranger and she held you and snuggled you so nicely."

George's memory of that day was a star-spangled get to meet a Martian kind of wonderful. The girl was drop dead, heart stopping gorgeous and nice too. If he could have, George would have married her right there, but he had been a kid and she wasn't paying attention to him, it was all about Porter.

While he thought about the subject, George pedaled in silence. "Of course, you aren't a pup any more, Porter, but maybe we could retool," he finally said. "I could pick a girl out and then let you loose and you could go over to her and I could run up all worried because you were lost. I could gain entrée that way. A little deceptive, true, but we'd know she was a dog lover. It could be a test of sorts."

As he and Porter approached a commotion ahead, George faded off.

George coasted by a group of soldiers who had surrounded a man and were talking to him. Someone was relaying information through a portable radio dispatch machine. George tried to stop but was waved on by a gruff soldier. He was shocked to see that his friend Mr. King, the broom salesman, was the center of attention. He overheard Mr. King say, "Of course, I couldn't see them, you unnerstand, bein' blind. I've tole you about all I know."

"I wonder what that was about?" George said as they rode by.

Porter had slunk down into the safety of the empty saddlebag, his nose and eyes peeking up over the edge. He looked backwards as George pedaled the bike away and was reminded of a beehive he had once seen at George's uncle's house in the country.

43 ROAD FOOD

May 20, 1945. The outskirts of Pine Bluff, Arkansas.

"Food!" Uwe announced with a happy smile in what he hoped was a confident tone. He held out the limp body of a squirrel for Fredericka's inspection. The grey tree squirrel had fallen down dead following a fatal encounter with a high voltage power line.

Uwe had been tramping through swampy thick underbrush in the delta outside of Pine Bluff for an hour searching for something edible when the squirrel landed at his feet. He must have wandered near to civilization, although all he could see for miles were curving rice paddies and straight rows of cotton fields extending to the horizon. He had carried his bounty back to where Fredericka was waiting.

Fredericka stared at the rodent's white underside as a thought dawned on her. "Ulysses, do you expect me to cook this up for our supper?" she said in an incredulous voice, her lips pursed in a pout, as she looked sideways at Uwe.

"Yes, thank you!" he nodded. "A great idea isn't it? This is like camping out and living off of the land. Self sufficient we are today." Ever since he had come clean to Fredericka about Stonehenge and his true identity, it was nice not to have to evaluate every word before speaking.

Fredericka shook her head, but she did not have anything to counter with in the way of food. Plus, she hated to be a wet blanket since Ulysses was so pleased with himself. Anyway, they both were famished. "All right, I guess we can give this a try," she acquiesced. "How bouts you skin this guy and I'll build a fire and we'll roast him up? We had best cook this fellow good and done. God knows what kind of disease he or she might be carrying. We'll have to cook the living daylights out of it."

"You know, you are one lucky boy you got squirrel and not cane snake!" Fredericka remarked while she arranged wood and kindling within a circle of stones and Uwe got busy with his knife.

"Oh yes, Fredericka! I know about it, they were in the cotton fields we worked in Conway. I several times had to kill a snake with the shovel. Don't worry, I can protect you."

"Well, then, Ulysses, I do feel better!" Fredericka chuckled.

Thirty minutes later the cooked squirrel lay before them.

"After you, my dear. Ladies first." Uwe looked expectantly at Fredericka.

"Oh no you don't, buddy! We in this together," she responded.

"All right then," he said. "On the count of three." They each picked up a piece of hot squirrel meat and dropped it into their mouths in unison.

A moment later they looked at each other, gagging, and burst out laughing. "This is terrible!" "Oh, this is the worst!"

When their laughter died down, Fredericka wiped tears from her eyes. "We shouldn't disrespect the squirrel," she said. "While that may have been awful, I bet when my mama and daddy were babies they would have gobbled Mist' Squirrel up and been glad about it."

Fredericka thought and then inspiration hit. "Ulysses, I have a plan for you and me to get some good, hot, healthy food that is not electrocuted squirrel. Are you in?"

"Sure, yes ma'am. I am listening," he said.

"Okay. Lucky for us today is a Wednesday. You and me, we're going to have to split up for a little bit. You will have to clean up and spiff up. I will do the same. We need to look as nice as possible. Not dirty like we've been riding the rails without tickets and on the run in the wilderness like good-for-nothin' people."

"But how will this get us supper?" Uwe shot a puzzled look at Fredericka. "Are we going to visit somebody? Do you know somebody to visit? Why do we have to split up?"

"Trust me on this. You go over to that side of the creek and clean up and I'll go down this way. I'll explain more when we get going."

"Watch out for water moccasins over there," Fredericka called out as they moved off to make their preparations. "That's a kind of snake, not a type of shoe, just to tell you."

"My friend Imogene had a scary encounter with a rattlesnake right in the Holt's backyard."

"I heard about that. Do you see any turtles over there?"

"Yes, two."

"Well, leave 'em alone 'cause they bite."

"Oh, all right."

"And don't put any creek water in your mouth during your clean up. This creek is almost a bayou and the water isn't any too clean. We got enough troubles without the typhoid jumping down our throats with all four feet. Typhoid is mean business."

"There are many hazards here in this one place, Fredericka."

"You gotta watch out, Ulysses. I'd keep an eye out for alligators too."

"I'm clean," Uwe said as he jumped back from the creek.

As the pair continued on their way, the conversation returned to the squirrel.

"Do you think the electrocution could have negatively impacted the flavor?"

"I don't know, Ulysses, maybe, but I wouldn't want to make book on it."

They were glad for the protection of the evening darkness as they approached the outskirts of town and Fredericka fleshed out her plan.

"Ulysses, up ahead is a Baptist church. You should be able to get dinner there. Go on in and locate their Fellowship Hall. If they have a basement that's where you'll find it. Or just follow your nose. If they're in the sanctuary finishing up having church when you get there, slip in and then go with the crowd down to dinner. Should anybody ask, tell them you are a soldier home from the war. Don't talk too much. Try to blend in. They'll take good care of you."

"But Fredericka, where are you going? Uwe stopped in concern. "Why can't you come with me?"

"It isn't done," she said. "Let me tell you, I'd be shuttled back to work in the kitchen if I showed up there. Today we have a different kettle of fish to fry than that one. I'm going over to my people at the AME. I saw it on our way into town. And no, you can't go there with me. We'd draw way too much attention to ourselves doing that. It would be suspicious."

"How do you know there will be food? You should get fed too. Can I bring you something?"

"It's Wednesday night," Fredericka said. "There'll be food. You'll get fed. I'll get fed. Let's meet up here as soon as we can slip away. Eat efficiently but don't appear to rush."

At the juncture to the walkway leading to Christ the Redeemer Baptist, Fredericka nodded in the direction of the church. Uwe's mind was whirling away. Although expanding, his cultural immersion in rural Arkansas ways had been minimal, and this was a nerve-wracking situation, a real test of his ability to fit in. Uwe tarried. "But I'm a Roman Catholic." He blurted out the confession in case it was a deal breaker.

"No siree, not today." Fredericka shook her head at Uwe as she propelled him forward with a nudge in the small of his back and said in a tone that brooked no argument. "Today you are a happy Baptist."

As Uwe headed off in the right direction, Fredericka hissed another instruction after him as a worrisome possibility occurred to her, thinking there was no telling what somebody from the other side of the world might do. "Don't do anything to draw attention to yourself."

"If I did, would they try to hurt me?" Uwe stopped and turned around.

"Prob'ly not, but they might take you aside and witness to you and want to know all about why you are there." Fredericka flapped her hands at him to move on. "That would be the best outcome. On the other hand, somebody might call the FBI. That is dangerous territory not to mention something we don't have time for. So keep it on the down low."

44 PARTNERS

May 20, 1945. #804 East 8th Street. North Little Rock, Arkansas.

Mamie ran two doors down the street to the buff brick duplex and up the steps leading onto the covered porch. She tapped on the door of the unit on the right hand side loud enough for Mrs. Jones, who was hard of hearing, to notice. After a wait, the door creaked open and a short old lady stood there leaning on a cane. She was Mamie's widowed Great Aunt Iva Lynn Jones. Aunt Iva Lynn had a car.

Mamie, who was not tall, nevertheless stood a full head taller than Iva Lynn, and she looked down on her great aunt. Her hair's slight blue tinge and tight curls were new as of that morning's trip to Estelle, her hairdresser. "Why, hello, Mamie, how nice to see you!" Iva Lynn smiled. "Honey, its been too long since you've stopped by!"

"Say what?" Iva Lynn stared at Mamie, her brows knitting together. "Did I hear that right? Did you just tell me that one of Cristobel's girls has run off with a boarder? She drew the word boarder out to be long. "What kind of boarder do you all have? I didn't know anything about a boarder."

They were seated in Iva Lynn's small, neat parlor. Mamie decided for the direct approach. Time was precious, and knowing it would be best to tell Iva Lynn as much of the truth as she could, she answered, "His name is Ulysses Jones." Mamie winced and hoped Iva Lynn would never know they had named Uwe after her. "Ulysses is a German prisoner of war from Camp Robinson, and he was assigned to our house on temporary duty." Hoping to make the situation sound more conventional, Mamie added, "He was waiting for repatriation."

"Well, what on earth is he doing at your house?" Iva Lynn demanded. "Why wasn't he at the camp with the rest of them? What kind of name is that? It doesn't sound German to me."

"He was doing odd jobs for Mama and Papa, and we Americanized his name to make it easier to pronounce. But ma'am, what I was wondering was, could I borrow your car to search for Fredericka and bring her home?"

"Alone, Mamie?" Iva Lynn exclaimed, aghast at the idea. "Where's your daddy?"

"Papa is minding the fort and needs our car. There are a lot of people looking for Ulysses, but I think someone should search specifically for Fredericka."

Iva Lynn stood up. "You may use my car but only if I go with you."

Unprepared for this wrinkle, Mamie hesitated, and in the moment of indecision won a traveling companion.

Leaning on her cane, Iva Lynn walked around the room closing the curtains. "I do what I can to keep the riffraff out," she asserted as she yanked on the pulls.

Iva Lynn continued to her bedroom and reemerged wearing her hat, sturdy brogans and a light raincoat to protect her from the warm May air. She had freshened her lipstick and carried her purse over her arm.

"Let's get going, Mamie." Iva Lynn walked up the hall connecting her room to the rest of the house, swaying from side to side. "Do you have any idea where they are?"

Mamie stood in the middle of the living room trying to decide what to do. "We don't know for sure, but we think they went to Pine Bluff. I'm afraid this is too dangerous for you." Mamie thought, but did not add her other worry, which was that Iva Lynn would slow her down.

"Mamie, I didn't get to be ninety by being stupid!" Iva Lynn announced with the assurance borne from years of living. "We'll solve this problem and come out alive and get that sweet girl back home. Come on, let's go out by way of the kitchen." Unable to think of a way to dissuade her aunt from wanting to go along, Mamie decided to make the best of the situation.

Iva Lynn teetered on the edge of the back door landing as she locked the deadbolt. She leaned on Mamie's arm as they walked across the yard to the car.

Mamie helped Iva Lynn into the front passenger seat of the seldom-used Chevrolet and then got behind the steering wheel herself. "Mamie, honey, would it kill you to put a smidgen of lipstick on?" Iva Lynn asked.

"It won't be noticed where we're going," Mamie answered.

"How could she begin to think this would end well for her?" Iva Lynn asked. It was a rhetorical question requiring no answer from Mamie because they both knew the answer. Fredericka was in grave danger. Iva Lynn sighed, clutching her purse in her lap. "I sure am tired," she said. She fixed her warrior eyes straight ahead as she steeled herself for what was to come.

It was late afternoon but not dark when Mamie backed out of Iva Lynn's driveway. When she had shifted into first gear and started to accelerate, they were startled to hear urgent tapping on the car.

"Mamie, what's that?"

"Oh, my goodness, it's Marcel Lane!" Mamie said as they peered out of the car.

Mamie rolled her window down. "Marcel, we're heading out to look for your sister!"

"Afternoon, Miss Mamie, Miss Iva Lynn. Mama asks will you take me along?" Marcel asked.

"Climb in!" Mamie said.

Marcel jumped in the back seat and Mamie pulled out onto 8th Street. She had not gone far before pulling over to the curb when she saw a teenaged boy with a determined expression hurrying down the street. "Roland, are you looking for Fredericka?" she called.

The boy broke into a run, his expression relieved, "Yes'm, I am." He peered into the back seat and saw Marcel.

"Come on, get in, because that's what we're doing too," Mamie said.

Roland climbed in beside his brother and Mamie took off.

Iva Lynn and Mamie dominated the conversation in the car. Fredericka's brothers presented a silent, unified force sitting shoulder to shoulder on the backseat of the car. They were intent on reaching Pine Bluff and retrieving their sister from whatever kind of trouble she was in. Their mother's instructions had been clear, but they didn't need them because they knew their job.

"I don't know where to start looking once we get to Pine Bluff," Mamie confessed.

Iva Lynn surprised everyone in the car by piping up. "I know some people down there in the area from when Harold," she referred to her dead husband, "worked on the railroad and we lived in Redfield. I stay in touch with my old friends. They may be able to help."

45 FREDERICKA'S PINE BLUFF DINNER

May 20, 1945. Mount Zion African Methodist Episcopal Church, Pine Bluff, Arkansas.

Fredericka pulled the spiced crawfish meat from their shells and enjoyed the rich flavor of the combination of meat, sauce and rice. The hot, buttered French bread torn from the loaf was a perfect accompaniment to the dish. The etouffee hit the spot in a way that electrocuted squirrel did not.

She hoped Ulysses had fared as well as she. Her arrival had coincided with the break between church and dinner and she had been able to slip into the chattering crowd making its way to the dining room. Fredericka thought no one noticed that she had not attended services.

Wiping her mouth with her napkin, Fredericka turned to the lady seated next to her on the rough plank picnic table. "Somebody went out of his way today to trap crawfish over at the river," she remarked. "I can tell it is fresh."

The lady nodded her head with such vigor that the plume of her hat waved back and forth. She leaned in to Fredericka. "That was my husband. He has a cousin who works in the kitchen at Tujague's, don't you know," she said. That's where he learned to cook. This is how it is done down in N'Awlens."

"Oh that explains it, then," Fredericka said. "The etouffee tastes like a professional chef made it."

"Mrs. Pearl Jackson." The lady smiled and offered her hand to Fredericka.

"Fredericka Lane. I'm pleased to meet you, ma'am," Fredericka smiled and shook Mrs. Jackson's hand.

From her seat, which was close to the kitchen, Fredericka could overhear the ladies talking while they worked. They were shouting to be heard over the running water in the sink and the clanking of pots and pans.

"I miss your boy Dwight, Alma!"

"Hmmhmm, I love his cookin'! When I see Mr. Dwight in the kitchen, I feel optimistic!"

"He don't have time to help out here on Wednesdays, he's too busy cookin' for the munitions workers."

"I miss him. We don't call him Cornbread for nothin'!"

"Ha! Yes, he knows his way around a kitchen and he enjoys eating too!"

"Of course he does, that's what makes a good cook, 'n it?"

Fredericka sat up straighter as the good-natured laughter of the cooks faded away while she thought. She felt like she was searching for the proverbial needle in the haystack, and now it seemed that she had a lead from a most unexpected place. Anyway, it was all she had to go on. She would investigate.

Turning to Mrs. Jackson, who seemed to know the congregation, Fredericka tried to keep her voice steady. "Where is Dwight living now, do you know?"

"Oh, honey, he's moved off to the quarter-boats."

"The quarter-boats?"

"You know, the Corps of Engineers brought them up river from Memphis and docked them here to relieve the housing pressure brought on by the new munitions factory."

"On the river, you say?"

"Yes. He's a friend of yours?" asked Mrs. Jackson.

"Yes, ma'am," Fredericka answered, hoping the penalty for telling a bald faced lie on holy ground was not too steep. "I wonder, do you know which boat he is assigned to?" She hoped she sounded casual.

"He's on the third one from the right as you face the boats from dock," Mrs. Jackson said. "Of course, you won't be able to visit him there, though. Men only."

"No, ma'am, I guess not!" Fredericka answered.

Fredericka wrapped up dinner, trying not to attract attention. When Mrs. Jackson was immersed in a conversation with her neighbor on the other side of her, Fredericka took the opportunity to slip away.

Fortified with good food and the unexpected information, Fredericka shook hands with the Reverend Ernest Smith and thanked him for dinner. She stopped by the kitchen to say thank you to the cooks and then left, trying to contain her excitement at making sense about cornbread or, as she now thought, Cornbread with a capital "C." She wanted to get to Ulysses as soon as possible to give him an update.

She was partway down the darkened sidewalk outside the church building when she froze, caught between disappearing into the shrubbery and dashing away. Somebody was following her.

A tall, heavyset man emerged from the shadows. He wore a three-piece suit and the chain of a pocket watch glittered in the moonlight. The moonlight also illuminated part of his face but left the rest in darkness. Fredericka couldn't read his expression. Was he friend or foe? She decided not to wait to find out and turned to go, but it was too late. A large hand grabbed her by her upper arm and held her fast.

"Young lady. Young lady." His gentle voice restrained her and she stopped struggling to free her arm. When the man released his grip, he stepped closer and Fredericka got a better look at him.

"Maybe I shouldn't speak, but I feel called to tell you something," he said. "When I was trapping crawfish over at the river today, I saw you and a young fella cuttin' 'cross a cotton field. I don't know what you are thinking, but young lady, that can't go nowhere good for you."

Vigorous protest bubbled to Fredericka's lips, but the older man waved her to silence and continued, "The only place where I can think you all might be headed is Mississippi." Fredericka stared at him, thinking that going to Mississippi was not in her plans at all. He continued, "Is that where y'all are going? I feel called to caution you. I don't know, is there even still a community at Free Woods? Surely it has died out."

"What's that you're sayin', sir?" Fredericka asked in confusion.

"Back in slave time, in the deep thicket, the dark part of the woods, that's where the white men sent chillen they had with slave women to live free," he continued. "They didn't want their chillen to live as slaves, don't you know, and so they went into Free Woods, on the far side of the Homochitto River."

With a furrowed brow of concentration, Fredericka listened to the man drone on, wondering what he thought this ancient history had to do with her.

"Is that where you and that boy want to go? Because you know, young lady, white people and people of color can't marry even today. And the two of you's, you don't look like the type to bury yourselves deep like that. There's more the world has to offer young people, isn't there? Please, don't throw yourself away. I can tell you are a nice girl."

Fredericka opened her mouth again, and again he waved her down. She thought, ooh that fella had it all wrong. He thought she and Ulysses were fooling around.

"What would your mama say about you running 'round with that fella?" He fixed her with a firm eye. "Why don't you let somebody here take you home?"

Fredericka was silent at this, as of course her insides were shaky and her heart thumping fast and hard like a captured wild thing at the thought of what her mother would have to say on the subject. Mama would not like it. She was batten down the hatches, hide in a corner under cover scared when imagining Mama's reaction to her current predicament.

She worried her wily mother already had dispatched an elite posse after her with instructions for her discovery and return. In fact, Fredericka had taken to peering over her shoulders during the past few hours. She hadn't expected to be gone as long as she had been. She had had no plans to go to Pine Bluff that afternoon, and here it had moved into night. The question was when, not if, someone from home would surface looking for her.

"All right, then. I can tell it is no use trying to talk sense to you," the man continued, misreading the fear in her face for stubbornness. "I can tell you ready to fly right outta this place." The man withdrew a brown paper sack from his shoulder bag. "Here's some food to keep you on your journey. The church ladies packed it up for you even if all of them," and he placed the food in Fredericka's hands, emphasizing with its weight the end of his sentence, "disapprove."

"Thank you, Mister, and thank you to the kind ladies!" Fredericka exclaimed. She took off down the path on her way to meet Uwe and devise a plan to visit the quarter-boats.

The big man shook his head in worry as Fredericka ran down the path. He crossed the street to speak to the teenaged boy behind the wheel of a parked sedan. "Guthrie, follow her and keep an eye on her. Take care of your mother. And watch that you take good care of Reverend Smith's car."

"Right, Daddy," Guthrie whispered. Just then the door of the house across the street opened and closed. The brief shaft of light threw the plume of Mrs. Pearl Jackson's hat into silhouette from where she sat in the front passenger seat next to her son.

"See if you can get away without using the headlights. There's not any traffic on the street," instructed his mother.

"Okay." Guthrie followed Fredericka, and then pulled over when she stopped at the corner. He and his mother peered out of the windshield at Fredericka.

46 SINGING FOR HIS SUPPER

May 20, 1945. Christ the Redeemer Baptist Church, Pine Bluff, Arkansas.

Fredericka was right, Uwe thought as he worked on his plate of food provided by the nice ladies. The Baptists knew how to cook. The chicken and dumplings tasted wonderful. Their flaky crust covered chicken in broth seasoned by an expert cook. A meatball in tomato sauce followed. The tangy sauce was made from homegrown, home canned tomatoes that retained their summertime goodness. Last year's fresh frozen purple hull peas in spicy chow-chow, cream style corn, he thought they were delicious.

An attractive, middle-aged lady offered him a choice between homemade yeast rolls with insides dripping with butter or a slice of crusty golden cornbread. As Uwe wavered, the lady plunked one of each on his side plate. "Thank you so much, ma'am," he smiled in gratitude. She beamed at him in reply and ruffled his hair on her way back to the kitchen. She reminded him of his mother.

Mrs. Ava Gilcrest watched Uwe with narrowed brown eyes from her position at the window between Fellowship Hall and the kitchen. She was about forty years old and carried an air of command. Her blue apron protected her dress from spills. She had changed from her heels into comfortable canvas slip on shoes. When her business of dishing up food died down, she moved away from her post. Ava picked up a full coffee cup with one hand and a brown paper grocery sack with the other.

Pushing backwards through the swinging door connecting the rooms, Ava walked into Fellowship Hall while balancing the two items in her hands. She placed the coffee cup and paper bag down before pulling out a chair across from Uwe. "Is this seat taken?" she asked.

Uwe, who had moved on to coconut cream meringue pie by then, rose partway from his chair. "No, ma'am, please join me," he said.

She offered her hand to Uwe. "Ava Gilcrest."

"My name is Ulysses Jones," he said as he shook her hand. "Mrs. Gilcrest, I am pleased to meet you." He sank back into his chair as she sat down.

"Ulysses, hmmm? What, are you Greek?" Mrs. Gilcrest fixed a level eye on him with raised brows.

Mumbling a polite response, Uwe took a bite of pie.

Ava Gilcrest sipped her coffee and decided to get down to it. "Honey, I spotted you and a young lady walking out of the woods onto the highway over near the cutoff to White Hall this afternoon as I drove into town." Straight talk was second nature to her, accustomed as she was to dealing with boys. She'd successfully raised six to adulthood.

Uwe swallowed. Why hadn't he gotten out of there when the getting was good? Staying for dessert had pushed his luck too far. He had been hungry and the food was good.

Ava put her hand on the table between them and leaned towards Uwe. "Young man, I have a son about your age. I believe you have some kind of problem. Is there anything I can do to help you?"

Uwe remained silent, but his thoughts whirred and he squirmed in his chair while he considered bolting. He had chosen a seat close to an exit in case he needed a quick get away. He put his fork down. "Oh no, ma'am. I'm doing fine. Thank you ma'am for dinner. I should say excuse me and go."

"You have a beautiful singing voice." Ava continued to appraise her dinner guest. "Everyone noticed it." When she said that, Uwe flinched as he pictured himself carried away in the moment and singing louder than anyone in the room. "I can't believe that somebody who sings church music with as much heart as you did this evening could be trouble," Mrs. Gilcrest continued. "In trouble, maybe. That I would believe."

Uwe could imagine what Fredericka would say. "Hmmph. I'm put out with you, Ulysses. Did I not tell you to keep a low profile? You didn't hide your light under a barrel, did you? Plus, my feelings are hurt. Singing for strangers but not to me?" He thought it prudent to leave ASAP, as it was getting too hot for him there.

"Clyde Moore, our choir director, is planning to sign you up with our choir," Mrs. Gilcrest continued. "He'll be stopping by here soon. I warn you, with all the young men off to war he is desperate for choir members." She pierced Uwe with a sharp look to see what his reaction would be to that piece of information.

Uwe watched a clean-cut, middle-aged man wearing a suit and tie working his way across the room towards him. Now and then he stopped to exchange pleasantries with various members of the congregation. Finishing his last conversation, he turned and plowed his way down the aisle between tables en route to Uwe, a pleased, expectant expression on his face. Anticipating a difficult conversation with a determined man, Uwe knew it was time to leave. As he pushed his chair back, Mrs. Gilcrest nudged the paper bag towards him. "If you won't let me help you, at least let me feed you. I made something for you and your friend for the road."

Uwe jumped up from his chair and pumped her hand before grabbing the bag and beating a hasty exit from the room.

Ava Gilcrest stacked the coffee cups and dessert plates as she watched Uwe leave the room. She was worried about him and hoped he would be all right.

Tucking the bag of food into the leather bag slung over his shoulder, Uwe walked down the sidewalk outside of the church into the evening on his way to meet Fredericka.

A turquoise blue sedan cruising down the street pulled over next to Uwe and the driver honked.

Uwe looked up.

"Hello, hello! Ulysses!"

He walked over to the car and peered inside. Imogene Park was waving at him from behind the wheel.

"Hello, Imogene. What are you doing in Pine Bluff?" Uwe was uneasy about Imogene's sudden appearance.

"Looking for you!" she exclaimed. "Climb in!"

Imogene wouldn't have known it by his expression but Uwe was nervous as he opened the passenger side door and slid in.

"Imogene, what are you doing in Pine Bluff?" he repeated.

"That's kind of a long story, Ulysses. Where are you headed?"

Uwe worried about exposing his project to yet another person, and he wondered if Mrs. Gilcrest had her eye on him. He thought she might disapprove of Imogene.

In fact, Mrs. Gilcrest was watching from the window set high in the basement kitchen wall, level with the street. Sitting in her car parked on the street next to the church, Imogene was illuminated by the streetlight. Mrs. Gilcrest got a clear if tangential view of the flashy car and the flashy girl driving it. She shook her head as she frowned, thinking, *it is always thus.* She wavered between letting the boy with a voice like Ezio Pinza run away with a Jezebel and calling for help. Reflecting on her sterling reputation for spotting trouble, as in she was seldom wrong; Ava stepped away from the window, went out to the hall telephone and dialed. She drummed her fingers against the wall while she waited for the connection. "Jefferson County Sheriff's Department," the operator announced.

"This is Ava Gilcrest. Is Sheriff Lemoyne in?" Ava hoped her brother was working that night.

Luck was with her. "Bubba, this is Ava," she said when Alvin came on the line. "There's a situation you might ought to keep an eye on." She gave her brother the lowdown.

"Ava, you've got the knack for sleuthing. I just now got a call from North Little Rock to look out for that very thing. I sent Donny out."

In the dark of the car interior, Uwe turned to Imogene. "Could you take me to pick up my friend Fredericka?"

"Which way?" she said as she put the car into drive.

47 KILLING TIME

May 20, 1945. Pine Bluff, Arkansas.

"Turn to the right at the next street." Uwe observed Imogene from the corner of his eye as they drove the short distance to his meeting place with Fredericka.

Imogene pulled hard on the big steering wheel in the turn, downshifting as she slowed for the corner and maneuvered the car in the narrow street.

Fog had rolled into town and obscured Fredericka, who was a solitary figure waiting on the corner clutching her bag of food. She was impatient to tell Ulysses about Cornbread. She stared at the unfamiliar shiny turquoise car that appeared out of the fog, and when it pulled over to the curb she stood poised, ready to run away. When she saw Uwe in the car with the striking blonde girl, she did a double take.

Uwe got out and walked over to Fredericka, calling on approach to keep her from blurting out anything damaging, "Guess what. My friend has offered us a ride."

Imogene smiled at Fredericka from the car. Fredericka moved out of Imogene's range of vision and made a frowning face at Uwe. "Who is that?" she demanded in a whisper.

"She is Imogene Park, an acquaintance of mine from town. Imogene wants to help us locate the thieves who broke into the Holt's house and stole Mr. Holt's ring."

Stunned, Fredericka hissed, "This is a bad idea, Ulysses. I know who she is."

"You do? How do you know her?"

"I do not actually know, know her, I know of her. She has a reputation."

"Let's take the ride but not discuss the details of our project," he whispered back. "She says she wants to help and we don't have a car."

"Bad, bad, bad idea." It was all Fredericka could get out, as she was unable to articulate her consuming worry about the dangers involved in accepting help from Imogene Park. Imogene's appearance in such an out of the way place was ominous, Fredericka could not think of another way to see it.

Uwe was uneasy too, but he was trying to maintain an open mind. "She was Captain Luke Holt's friend before I ever came to the house," he countered.

"Big surprise there." Fredericka rolled her eyes. You are incredibly naïve, and the same goes for Luke Holt."

"I will admit I don't trust her completely."

"Do you still have your knife?"

"Yes, but Fredericka, I could easily overpower Imogene if it came to it, even though I admit she is a strong person for her size."

"All right, see'ns how I can't figure a way out of this...but I am not sitting in the back seat by myself. I'm not going to do it. I'll find my way home first." She would do it, too. The church people had offered. It probably wasn't too late to go back there.

"Right."

By now they had reached the car. Fredericka whispered to Uwe before getting in, "We are going to draw the wrong kind of attention to ourselves driving around in this car together." Uwe got in first and then Fredericka sat next to him and closed the door.

"Let me introduce you. Imogene Park, this is Fredericka Lane. Fredericka, this is Imogene," Uwe said.

Imogene looked across Uwe at Fredericka. "I'm pleased to meet you, Fredericka. I believe I know your mother."

"It's nice to meet you, Imogene. Yes, my mother works for the Holts."

"So you two almost know each other already," Uwe said.

"We're trying to find the thieves who stole from Mr. Holt?" Imogene asked.

"Yes that's right," Uwe said. "We think they came to Pine Bluff, and Fredericka and I have tracked them here, but we don't know where to find them."

"We'd better get moving then," Imogene said. "Where should we start looking?"

"Why don't we drive around awhile and see if we find them?" Fredericka said, caught between the urgency of finding Dwight on the quarter-boats, yet unwilling to give away her lead to Imogene, of whom she had heard her mother speak.

Imogene, Uwe and Fredericka, riding three abreast on the bench seat, pulled away into the night.

"Imogene, how did you happen to find Ulysses all the way down here? Fredericka asked. "That's quite a drive for you to make alone."

"I'll confess," Imogene laughed. "I was lonely this afternoon and drove over to North Little Rock looking for company. I was hoping to catch a few minutes with this guy," she said, giving Uwe a nudge with her elbow. "Ordinarily it's so quiet over there, but today there was quite the ruckus."

"How's that?" Fredericka slid a look at Uwe.

"Let me tell you, right on the street close to the Holt's there were a lot of cars parked and military people everywhere. It looked like somebody had kicked over an anthill there were so many uniformed men running around, you know what I mean? I pulled over and got out and went as close as I could, curious about what was going on. Somebody waved me away so I couldn't tell much. There was an old blind man surrounded by military police, not regular police, and they were really going hard at him."

Fredericka nudged Uwe. "Oh, no! Did they hurt him?" she exclaimed.

"I don't think so," Imogene said. "They were just talking to him, but like I said, they looked serious. I overheard him talking about some boys going to Pine Bluff, and then I'll confess," she laughed. "I had seen you two jumping on a freight train and I put two and two together." Imogene finished up, "I probably got here before you did. I stopped at a diner for a bite to eat, and I've been cruising around looking for you ever since. Thought you might like some help. It would have been fun riding the rails with y'all, I've never done that before, but I like having my car."

Twenty minutes later, after an uneventful drive around the area, Imogene turned off Dollarway Road at Connie's Diner, the retired Pullman car that had been converted to a roadside diner. Imogene drove onto a gravel parking lot on the side away from the windows.

"Gee, it's really tough looking for people when we don't know what they look like!" Imogene said as she opened the car door. "I need to make a quick phone call to let my parents know I'm okay. There's a pay phone inside the building. I know that 'cause this is where I stopped to eat earlier. Y'all can stay here. I'll be right back. This won't take long." Imogene disappeared around the corner.

"It's suspicious that she wasn't concerned about driving me around in her fancy car." Fredericka told Uwe.

"You stay here. I will see if she is really making a phone call," Uwe said.

Fredericka and Uwe got out of the car. Uwe walked around the building. Through the front window he saw Imogene standing by a booth talking to a young, dark haired woman and a man who appeared to be a little older, about thirty.

Uwe spun around and returned to Fredericka. "She isn't making a phone call," he whispered. "She's meeting some people inside. They looked excited about something."

"Let's go." Fredericka took off at a run, Uwe keeping pace beside her. Panting, she added, "At least after all that driving around I have my bearings. We got to make it to the river."

"Why the river?" Uwe asked, stowing Fredericka's sack of donated food into his bag along with Mrs. Gilcrest's contribution.

"Ulysses, follow me. I know about Cornbread."

"Really! How?"

"Yes. Cornbread is a person. He works… down… on the river. That's where we'll find our boys who stole your information. I learned about Cornbread at church."

Uwe looked behind him as they ran, wondering what would happen when Imogene and her friends discovered they were gone. When they were out of sight of the diner, they slowed down to a rapid walking pace.

"I don't know who Imogene was meeting, but Colonel Edmund may think I am a traitor and put the US Army on our trail," he said.

"All the more reason to find Dwight," Fredericka said.

"Who?"

"Dwight is Cornbread. Same person. I think Dwight is hiding the people who stole your medal."

"I don't know Imogene's affiliation," Uve said. "I think she and her friends will try to follow us."

"Yes. I'm pretty sure somebody's following me, too."

"Let's go find Dwight!"

48 THE QUARTER-BOATS

May 20, 1945. Pine Bluff, Arkansas.

Gabriel and Lazarus looked at the row of boats, counting seven quarter-boats plus four loaded barges. The two-story, floating rooming houses were moored in the mild current outside of the main river channel. Only the tops of the huge boats were visible through the heavy fog and light mist. They had arrived at dusk, and the enormity of trying to locate Dwight amongst all the possible options seemed as big as the boats before them.

"There must be 1000 men living on each boat." Lazarus observed.

"Let's get started." Gabriel walked down the gangplank of the barge on the far right and was swallowed up by the fog.

"Let's look for the kitchen first," Lazarus said from right behind his brother. "If Dwight's cookin', that would be the logical place to locate him even if it is past suppertime."

"Surely there are showers somewhere for the munitions workers. We should take advantage of that," Gabriel said as he peered around, trying to see where he was going in the dense fog.

"We need to wash off the ticks," Lazarus agreed.

"Maybe when we find Dwight he can spare some fresh clothes," Gabriel said.

Never too far behind, Daryl watched the boys board the boat before stepping to the telephone booth on the dock to report in. He planned to request removal from the case. Pursuing the boys further did not seem likely to yield useful information because they appeared to be ready to wind down for the night.

"No. Stay with it. Give me your exact location. I'm sending reinforcements," his contact barked at him. Irritated, Daryl got off the phone with his instructions. He'd been looking forward to meeting up with Lorraine at the bar after his hard day at work. She might get tired of waiting if he took too long. He didn't see what those two had to offer anyway.

Daryl sat on the grassy bank and pulled a half smoked stogie from his pocket. He lit it with a match struck on the sole of his shoe and then tossed the burnt match to one side. He inhaled a far-reaching drag of smoke deep down into the most remote lobes of his lungs, thinking it was lucky that he'd found the cigar on the boxcar floor. Daryl's grey suit and hat faded into the fog. The end of the burning cigar that glowed brighter orange with each inhale and then faded with each exhale was about the only thing visible on the riverbank.

Gabriel and Lazarus walked all over the first quarter-boat searching for Dwight. "This feels sturdy, like a ferry boat," Lazarus remarked, jumping up and down on the steel floor.

"Yes, it does," Gabriel agreed.

Twenty minutes later, Gabriel and Lazarus stood in the doorway of the mess hall of the third boat from the right.

Dwight was the last man in the room, dinnertime over and dishes done. He was finishing cleanup by wiping the tables with a wet cloth. When he looked up, he blinked in surprise at seeing his cousins appear in front of him without warning, then he grinned. "Look here. Oh, my goodness, what are you fellas doing way down here?" he said.

It was the reception Gabriel and Lazarus wanted in the worst way, and they spun a tale of their day, skimming over the part about robbing the Holt's house, which took some ingenuity. Dwight, being a close companion since childhood, however, was astute enough to fill in the blanks. He sized up the situation and took his cousins out of sight into the back of the kitchen and reheated plates of leftover food.

"Dwight, can we stay with you for awhile, until things calm down back home?" Lazarus asked between bites.

"You know, of course you fellas are welcome here, but it's not like over to the cabin, where nobody ever goes, if you follow me," Dwight answered. "I have a roommate here. He's a shift cook like me so we have the same schedule, don't you know."

Gabriel nodded, his mouth full, but he looked so pitiful that Dwight was moved to say, "Maybe I can find a cabin assigned to one of the night shift workers for awhile, but then you'd have to move on in the daytime. That would be risky, though. I'll see if I can find a place in a storage container on one of the barges. They aren't being used like they used to, not since the Arsenal got established."

49 OH, BROTHERS!

May 20, 1945. Pine Bluff, Arkansas.

"I know I'm repeating myself, but that is a very unusual group of people," Guthrie said, squinting his eyes and pursing his lips in an attempt to see through the dim light. "And such a beautiful car." He fell silent when his mother frowned at that and said, "Hmm!"

They had followed the turquoise car, making a right hand turn from Dollarway Road at Connie's Diner, the diner's pink neon sign reflecting on the car as it drove onto the parking lot. Guthrie turned the car around and backed into a space on the rear perimeter of the parking lot. They were on the same side as the turquoise car so they could see what was going on. He was ready for an easy exit, and the line of trees at the back of the lot provided natural camouflage. "I don't think we've been made," Guthrie remarked to his mother.

"We got away without using headlights," Pearl said. "That's what did it."

They watched the driver leave the car and go inside the diner. Guthrie and Pearl tried to discern what was going on inside the other car but couldn't see much. "Do you think she's being held against her will? She got in the car without a struggle." Guthrie said, speaking of Fredericka.

"I don't know, she seemed cheerful enough at dinner," Pearl said. "Of course, those three can't go into the diner together. This whole thing is very odd. Whatever is going on?" She trailed off as they watched a sheriff's car pull into the parking lot.

"Surely the law isn't here to monitor who eats where and who goes in what door? She's still sitting in the car! That can't be it," Guthrie exclaimed.

"Oh, oh, trouble, trouble, big trouble. What has our girl gotten herself caught up in?" Pearl breathed, wringing her hands, apprehensive about the police interest.

"Stay here, Mama. I'm going to investigate." Easing out of the car, Guthrie walked around the edge of the parking lot to get a view inside the diner's front windows. He saw the deputy doing the same thing from his patrol car. From their vantage points outside the diner, Guthrie and the deputy watched the driver of the turquoise car chat with a man and a woman in a booth.

To his right Guthrie saw Fredericka and the young man exit the car. The man left Fredericka and walked alone around to the front of the diner and glanced in the window. Guthrie moved to try to speak to Fredericka alone, but the man wasn't away long enough, he turned away and returned to Fredericka. They began an intense discussion. Worried that he best be getting back undercover, Guthrie returned to his car. Guthrie and his mother watched Fredericka and the young man leave the diner parking lot and start running down the dirt shoulder of Dollarway Road.

The radio squawked. Donny Watkins, in the sheriff's car, picked up. There was a robbery in progress across town. Donny shrugged his shoulders. "Tell the sheriff that car he's interested in is at Connie's Diner," he said. "The girl driver went inside and is talking to some people, but I'm leaving to see to this robbery now." He started the engine and drove away.

Pearl and Guthrie breathed a sigh of relief when the deputy's car left, and then turned their attention back to watching Fredericka.

"Mama, what should we do?"

"Follow them and try to pick them up," she said. "They can't run forever."

Guthrie pulled the car out onto the highway. He didn't put on the headlights, and he drove along the edge of the road. He rolled the window down. "Hey, there, hey there," he called.

No sooner had Pearl said, "Oh, I hope we don't scare them off," than the two young people looked behind them and ran into a clump of trees beside the road.

Guthrie shook his head in defeat. He pulled over. "Where to now, Mama?"

"Turn around and go back to the church," his mother ordered. "We can round up some help. I think I know where she's headed."

Guthrie switched on the car headlights and turned back the way they had come. "The police seem to have left for good," he said, his eyes sweeping the surroundings.

"Maybe," Mrs. Jackson said.

An Esso gas station outside of Pine Bluff

Mamie whistled tunelessly as she walked away from the telephone booth beside the filling station. She slid behind the wheel of Iva Lynn's Chevy and turned to the boys in the backseat. "I got through to a friend of the family in North Little Rock," she said. "Your sister and Ulysses were spotted in the parking lot of a place called Connie's Diner."

"Connie's?" Iva Lynn said. "Why, I know where that is, Mamie. I can take you right to it. It's on the old Dollarway Road. It's been there for ages." She added in a disapproving tone, "It's more of a bar, really, than a nice place to go. They serve alcohol."

Marcel leaned forward to speak into the front seat. "Ma'am, if you could drop us off there we would appreciate it. We won't trouble you more." His brother's nod of agreement was almost imperceptible in the dark interior of the car.

"Oh, no, we'll give you all a ride back home once we find her," Mamie said. She pushed away the recent memory of Bill Edmund's order to stop and return home in light of new, classified intelligence. Colonel Edmund's harsh words crept back into her mind. "Mamie. Stand down. That is an order. Fredericka Lane is a person of interest in an international case of espionage. Go home." Mamie's belief that only those people in Iva Lynn's car were looking out for Fredericka's best interests gave her the courage to keep going despite her instructions to quit.

Her check-in call hadn't been all one-sided, though. Mamie had provided some information of her own. "Light bluish green car?" she'd said. "That sounds like what Imogene Park drives."

Mamie focused on the task at hand. With Iva Lynn, her right hand man, and two of Cristobel's boys with her, she felt confident that she could retrieve Fredericka and Ulysses too. She consoled herself with the thought that she was not herself in the military, and so not under Bill Edmund's authority.

"Whoever is driving without headlights at night?" Iva Lynn said as they approached the diner, her eyes and the top of her curly hair peeking over the dashboard. "That doesn't look right." A slow moving car was driving down the opposite side of the road on the shoulder.

"Over there! Do you see? Roland exclaimed, staring out of the window into the fog. "Please stop, Miss Holt! I think I see her!"

Mamie responded, pulling over to the side of the road and skidding to a stop with a spray of gravel.

"Thank you for the ride!" Marcel whispered behind him as he and his brother piled out of the car and disappeared into the stand of pine trees in pursuit of the glimmer of skirts they hoped belonged to their sister.

"I'll wait right here," Mamie called out the door before it closed behind them.

"In case it's not her, let's don't call out," Roland said to Marcel.

"Okay, you're right, it could be anybody," Marcel agreed.

Mamie and Iva Lynn were too preoccupied watching the boys dash away to notice the car that pulled up and stopped facing theirs, the grilles nose to nose. Roy McNeil opened the door and grabbed Mamie's elbow. Before Mamie could muster a response, Vivian Taylor opened Iva Lynn's door and tried to pull the old lady out of the car. Mamie's shocked gaze caught that of Imogene Park, who sat facing her in the driver's seat of her car.

50 TO THE RIVER

May 20, 1945. Pine Bluff, Arkansas.

"I think Imogene is not my friend." Uwe said as he and Fredericka covered ground away from Connie's.

"The evidence does point that way." Frederica's steady yet disembodied voice came through the gloom.

"I'm done with her. She's not a good person." He breathed in short puffs as they moved along.

"Don't beat yourself up, Ulysses. It happens to the best of us."

Although Fredericka's words were comforting, the more Uwe thought about the day's sequence of events the harder it hit him that he had been played, and it had resulted in an enormous security breach. Blind, he had been blind and betrayed.

"Someone has been using her to get close to me, to find out about my work."

"Yes, I think so."

"Fredericka, we need to find this Dwight person before anyone else does. He lives in a boat on the river?"

"That is my understanding, but of course I've never seen him in my life, never heard his name before today. He is a cook for the munitions factory workers who live on the boat."

"I wonder if this boat is protected like a fortress?"

"Maybe. Maybe not. It is not on the Arsenal grounds."

"Ulysses, is a car following us?" Fredericka asked after looking behind her.

"Yes!"

"To the woods! Run to the woods!" Fredericka cried as she turned off the main highway and dashed into the sheltering trees.

"Another car has pulled off the road!" Uwe panted, running beside her.

They heard the sound of pounding footsteps on dirt and grass close behind them.

"Fredericka, stay close," Uwe whispered. "It's difficult to see you in this fog! Take my hand."

"I'm right here, Ulysses," Fredericka whispered as she reached out and grabbed his hand.

They stumbled on rocks as they tried to keep their footing in the dark. The ground tilted downwards and they tripped and tumbled over and over down an embankment. When they landed, they could discern but the faintest outlines of two figures standing on the hilltop looking down.

"Lay down and hide here. Don't come with me," Uwe murmured.

Fredericka watched as Uwe freed his knife from his pants pocket and crept up the embankment.

When Uwe reached the top, he circled behind the men and grabbed the nearest one around the shoulders, holding the knife blade to his throat. Both men froze. Uwe tightened his grip on his captive and pulled him back. "Move and I will slit his throat," he said to the other.

A dark form that was Fredericka burst out from behind Uwe. "No, no, no! That's my brother! She shrieked, "Please don't murder my brother! Please!" She had run up the embankment and now she flung her arms around Marcel and pushed Uwe's knife away.

"Your brother? This is your brother?" Uwe dropped the knife to his side with relief.

"Yes. They both are." Marcel gave Uwe an offended look and moved out of his reach to stand next to his brother.

"Marcel, Roland, this is my friend Ulysses Jones," Fredericka said. "Ulysses, these are two of my brothers, Marcel and Roland Lane." The boys nodded at Uwe but made no move to shake hands.

"Why are you being so polite? He just tried to kill me," Marcel yelled at Fredericka.

"Sometimes politeness helps smooth over touchy situations," she shrugged. "Mama says so anyhow."

"About the knife, I'm sorry," Uwe said.

As he struggled to see in the dark, Uwe realized how young Roland and Marcel were, about fifteen or sixteen years old. "How could you recognize them in the dark?" he asked Fredericka.

"I don't know exactly," she said, giving Marcel a strong hug. " It was the way this guy was standing, something about how he holds his head was very familiar. He's my brother, you know? Besides, I've been expecting somebody from home to track me down. It was only a matter of time before they caught up with us. I'm kind of relieved now, actually."

"What have you gotten yourself involved in?" Roland said, shaking his head in disapproval at Fredericka.

"Don't be put out with me. Boys, Ulysses only did what he did because he was trying to protect us," she said.

Giving Uwe a wide berth, the boys stepped forward to stand on either side of Fredericka. "Freddie, Mama says you're supposed to come home with us," Marcel said. "Miss Mamie Holt said she would wait over yonder in her car and carry us all home. Come on, let's go."

"I got the feeling from Miss Holt that you are in bigger trouble than she would let on, Fredericka. You need to go home," Roland said.

"I don't want to go home. You go home. I'm staying to see this out."

"Fredericka," Uwe interrupted. "I need to go. Maybe you should leave with them. This is getting dangerous and time is passing."

From her stubborn frown and the way she folded her arms over her chest, the boys knew it would be difficult to convince Fredericka to leave with them. An image of his mother's expression if he and Marcel arrived home without Fredericka came to Roland's mind. "Come on, Fredericka," he said. Roland and Marcel grabbed her arms and started to pull her back towards the road where they had jumped out of the car. At first she tried to yank her arms away from her brothers' iron grips, and then she stopped struggling. "All right, I'll go and speak to Miss Mamie. I bet she knows what's at stake here. Take me to her." She pulled away from them and pointed towards the road and they fell in together.

"I'm worried Miss Holt will call Colonel Edmund and he will arrest me," Uwe said to Fredericka. "Mr. Jake Holt may have told him about my medal. I don't know what the colonel will do when he finds out I haven't been completely open with him."

"Why don't you hold back and I will see what I think. If it looks bad you can run," Fredericka said. He nodded.

When they arrived at the dark stretch of highway where the boys had darted after Fredericka, Mamie's car was gone. An unfamiliar truck was parked down the road and a group of men was sweeping the ground with the beams of flashlights, searching for something or someone.

Roland, Marcel and Fredericka, with Uwe behind them, crouched in the brush and then crept away.

"They must be the other people who were following us," Uwe said.

"Where did Miss Mamie and Miss Iva Lynn go?" Roland breathed, worried. "What could have happened to them?"

"Do you think she got tired of waiting?" Marcel said.

"No," Roland answered. "That would be highly unlikely. I don't like the looks of what I saw back there."

Fredericka pulled her brothers along with her away from the strange men. "It's worrying, Roland, but Ulysses and me, we've got to find some people who we think are hiding out down on the river. It's probably all tied together. Maybe if we find these guys we'll find them too."

After having toured the neighborhood in Imogene's car, Fredericka and Uwe had a sense of the area's layout, and they made their way parallel to the highway in the general direction of the river. "I don't believe she would have gone off and left us when she said she'd wait," Marcel said.

"That doesn't sound like Miss Holt at all," Fredericka agreed.

Uwe thought Mamie's absence was ominous. He worried that she could be undergoing torture to disclose details of Project Stonehenge. He should contact Pete or Colonel Edmund with a telephone call, but he saw nothing but empty fields stretching in all directions.

The fog thickened, and when they reached the river road they walked four abreast, confident for the time being of having eluded their hunters.

"You think this guy name of Dwight knows where the boys are who robbed the Holt's house?" Marcel asked.

"Yes," Fredericka answered. She and Uwe had given Marcel and Roland a brief explanation of the reason for their trip but with some major omissions.

"And we'll have to be careful not to arouse suspicions on the boat or I am certain they will try to run. They may well fight," Uwe said.

"Boys, this is your chance to get out now," Fredericka said, taking his meaning.

"How could we ever tell Mama we left you?" Roland asked.

"And how about brother Frederick off fighting who knows where, how could I face him if I told him I left you alone in Pine Bluff and you got yourself killed? No, miss, we're staying with you." Marcel stopped talking because they had reached their destination.

The same array of quarter-boats that had dismayed Lazarus and Gabriel earlier in the evening lay in front of them. The moored boats made muted thumping sounds as they swayed in the mild current next to shore.

"Could someone make a phone call to North Little Rock and tell Miss Mamie's family she has gone missing?" Uwe said, spying the phone booth at the dock.

Marcel dug in his pocket for change. He slipped into the booth and emerged a minute later. "I made an anonymous call to the police department." Uwe's brow furrowed at the thought of more police heading to Pine Bluff, but he shrugged and kept going.

"Okay," Fredericka said, looking at the row of boats, "Mrs. Jackson said Dwight is on the third boat from the right. Let's hope she knew what she was talking about."

Fredericka and Uwe led the way, followed by Marcel and Roland. Fredericka's footsteps reverberated on the steel surface and she stopped to quiet the noise. Uwe and her brothers followed suit. Fredericka was midway down the gangplank, holding onto the railing as a guide, before she realized she had left land behind and there was only water below, so dense was the fog.

Daryl, from his camouflaged vantage point on the riverbank, watched Fredericka, Uwe, Marcel and Roland walking onto the gangplank. Heaving a sigh, he ground his cigar out with his shoe, pushed up off the grass and followed them.

"We owe this fog some thank you's on a number of fronts," Fredericka murmured.

"How's that?" Uwe said, following close behind.

"Well, for starters, I shouldn't be here because women aren't allowed in the men's quarters, and white people and people of color don't generally mix, so you are standing out. And too, you and me together, we stand out."

"Then I'm glad to have the fog." Uwe answered.

Fredericka spotted a directory mounted on the wall. She pointed to where the mess hall was located, on the lower level, and they made their way there.

"Fortunately, it looks like we're arriving during a work shift at the Arsenal, and most of the people here are probably either asleep or working," Fredericka whispered.

"Less people to notice us," Marcel agreed.

The mess hall was deserted when they arrived, but they heard voices in the back. Uwe motioned to the others to stay while he approached the kitchen door. He walked around the stainless steel serving tables that formed a barrier between the kitchen door and dining area.

Uwe peered into the back room and saw Lazarus, Gabriel and Dwight in the kitchen. He crept back to the others. "I think they're there, and we can surround them if we keep it a surprise," he reported.

Marcel pulled a knife from his pants pocket and shrugged when Roland made a questioning face at him. "He caught me by surprise," was all he said, in answer to Roland's unasked question as to why he hadn't pulled the knife on Uwe instead of the other way around.

Uwe made shushing noises.

"Keep your voices down, they might hear us," Fredericka said.

51 BOXED IN

May 20, 1945. Pine Bluff, Arkansas.

The light from the open kitchen doorway streamed into the darkened mess hall. A murmur of voices and the occasional outburst of easy laughter came through the door. Uwe stayed close to the edge of the room as he made his way back to the kitchen with Fredericka, Roland and Marcel following. Uwe was more optimistic than before that with help he could get his medal back.

Peeking into the kitchen, they saw Dwight, Lazarus and Gabriel sitting around the prep table between the large sink and an industrial sized stove. A half empty bottle of whiskey was making its way amongst them as Lazarus dealt cards.

Uwe motioned with his knife to Marcel and Roland to help him seize control, but Roland was staring at Lazarus and Gabriel. Catching Marcel's eye, the brothers exchanged a look. Keeping his knife visible but not brandishing it, Marcel walked into the room with Roland beside him. Dwight jumped up in alarm.

"Sorry to break up your party, Lazarus." Marcel said.

"Marcel? What are you doing here? Who are these people?" Lazarus' expression was one of complete shock.

Abandoning any effort at stealth, Uwe and Fredericka crowded into the room and closed the door behind them.

"A couple of good for nothin' nobodies, that's who you are!" Roland exclaimed at the pair, who were immobile in surprise. They rose to their feet.

"You know these people?" Fredericka asked her brothers.

"We, the three of us, are in the same class at Jones," Marcel said, gesturing at Lazarus and Gabriel.

"That's their high school," Fredericka told Uwe. Staring at Gabriel and Lazarus, she said, "How did these two end up hiding out here in a floating kitchen?" She waved her hands to usher the others to close in. Marcel, Uwe and Fredericka moved to hem Lazarus and Gabriel in the back of the kitchen as Roland reached over and removed the whiskey bottle.

"Please put away your knives," Gabriel said. "Marcel, I can explain."

"Did you break into the Holt's house today?" Fredericka asked.

Uwe stepped forward. "Did you take a small gold medal from a wooden box?"

Gabriel looked down at his feet and frowned.

"Did you take the medal?" Uwe repeated his question. "Do you have it now?"

Fredericka leaned in, waiting for the answer in the now silent room.

"I'm sorry, I guess we shouldn't have taken the job," Gabriel said.

"Where is the medal?" Uwe asked as he pulled out his knife.

"Hey, fella, we don't have it!" Lazarus exclaimed.

"Where is it?" Uwe put the knife to Gabriel's throat as the others in the room watched. "Did you give it to someone else?"

"Does he really have to threaten everybody in sight with that thing?" Marcel whispered to Fredericka.

"Don't worry, it's all show," she whispered back. "He does not have the heart of a killer. Anyway, somebody needs to make those boys straighten up. They've been very bad."

"Oh, mmm, maybe we threw them away?" Gabriel had started to talk.

Uwe's heart lurched. "Where?" he asked.

"On the street back home."

"Where exactly?"

"On Broadway!"

"I told you, you shouldn't have thrown them away!" Gabriel said to Lazarus. "That was not the right thing to do and now we are going to pay, pay, pay, just like I said we would. Don't you think this is payback time? It looks like payback time to me."

"All right. It's worry time," Lazarus retorted, unable to brush it off.

"Let's go now," Uwe told Fredericka. "Let's take them back there and make them show us where they dropped it, if that's what really happened."

She nodded. "Should we believe you?" she asked Gabriel.

"Yes. I swear it on a stack of Bibles. A tall one. Stack, I mean."

"Who hired you?" Fredericka pressed hard.

Relaxed by the whiskey, Gabriel and Lazarus talked louder, each trying to be heard over the other.

"It was Abe!"

"He 'proached us after school a few weeks ago."

"Abe? Abe Kenner?" Roland's eyes were grave.

"Yes."

"Why would somebody fine like Abe Kenner get involved in this kind of business? That doesn't make sense."

"He paid us big money."

"How much money?"

"Fifty dollars cash money."

"Aw, I don't believe it!" Someone in the room yelled. "Nobody would pay you that kind of money!"

Somebody chuckled, and then everyone except Uwe and Fredericka shouted out laughing. No one heard the kitchen door open, and therefore it was a full minute before Fredericka shushed the group and they turned, silenced, to see Imogene Park standing in the doorway.

"Hi there." Imogene blushed in the awkward moment. "Can I come in?" Not waiting for an answer, she walked in and closed the door behind her.

"Imogene?" Uwe said, trying to conceal his anxiety at her sudden appearance in the kitchen. He rewound the conversation Imogene had interrupted, trying to determine how much she had heard before they realized she was there. Her expression was unreadable.

"Hey, everybody. Ulysses, Fredericka, why did y'all run away from me? It took me like forever to find you." Fredericka thought Uwe's expression was almost as irritating as Imogene's words. He was backsliding. "Ulysses," she said in a warning tone. Uwe's expression was such that she pulled him over to her. "Stop. Do not play the fool," she instructed in a low voice. "Struttin' in here like a peacock." Observing him with an analytical eye, Fredericka noted with relief that she had pulled him back from the brink.

"Who are these people, Lazarus?" Dwight said. "Girls aren't allowed on the quarter-boats. It'll be my job if somebody finds out I'm harboring ladies here, and I need this job." He pulled Gabriel over. "That new girl?" he whispered. "She needs to leave."

"How did you find us here, Imogene?" Fredericka asked.

When Imogene answered, "I'll be straight with you," Fredericka's eyebrows rose up and the corners of her mouth turned down, but oblivious to her lack of credibility, Imogene continued, "Some friends of mine, really friends of friends, you know, want to talk to Ulysses and," she paused as she searched their faces before settling on Lazarus, Gabriel and Dwight, "you three. Fredericka can come too." Fredericka's eyebrows rose even higher but she didn't say anything.

"Who are these people you want us to meet?" Uwe asked.

"What do they want with me? I'm just a cook!" Dwight exclaimed.

"Why don't you let me take you to them?" Imogene flinched as the closed expressions of the others in the kitchen registered. Her hand sought the doorknob behind her. "We should go soon because they're waiting," she said.

"No, I don't think so, Imogene," Uwe said. Fredericka relaxed in relief. "We're going back to North Little Rock."

The eyes of everyone in the room bounced back and forth between Imogene and Uwe like they were watching an unusual high stakes poker game.

"Oh well, then, let me go with you," Imogene said, changing tack. "The only thing is my car is out of gas or I'd offer to drive. I had to leave it on the highway."

Roland and Marcel exchanged a significant glance.

"Yes, you should come with us," Uwe said, staring at Imogene and ignoring Fredericka's warning frown.

"All right then. How will we travel without a car?" Imogene asked.

"I suppose the same way we took to get here," Uwe said. "We'll have to determine the path as we go." He motioned to the others that it was time to leave.

Dwight stepped forward and shook hands with the twins, his expression worried. "I'll say goodbye now and then show y'all the quick way out."

Uwe looked at Lazarus and Gabriel and gestured towards the door. Marcel and Roland took positions on either side of the twins as they filed from the room with Dwight in the lead.

The procession made its way down the hallways to the gangplank. Since the yellow floodlights mounted on the walls did not penetrate far into the river fog, it was remarkable that Imogene saw anything at all. "Hit the floor!" she exclaimed as she crouched down. Roland followed suit as he pulled Marcel and Fredericka to the deck. The rest followed like dominos.

"Hide in the kitchen!" Imogene hissed while crawling away from the railing on all fours.

They retraced their steps as a unit, moving like spiders. Back in the relative safety of the kitchen, Fredericka stood nose to nose with Imogene. "What was that about?" she demanded.

"Didn't you see all the people waiting?" Imogene exclaimed.

"See who?"

"Those men on shore. I know it was foggy, but couldn't you see them?"

"I saw some shadows moving around the shoreline. I thought I recognized someone," Uwe said.

"Wait here and I'll go look," Fredericka said. She slipped back into the room five minutes later. "She's right," Fredericka said, nodding in Imogene's direction. "There are people out there. She shot a piercing look at the twins. "Is somebody after you?" she asked.

"All the way across Little Rock!" Lazarus burst out. "It's what led to our tick encounter!"

"Ooo, Creepy Man dogged us to the train," Gabriel said.

"It sounds like he followed you further than the train," Dwight frowned.

"They're right," Imogene said. "A local was on their trail, but there's more to it than that. There are people, tough people, who came up here from Dallas, but Dallas was just a waypoint. I think they came through the border at Juarez, funneling up from Mexico."

"Mexico?" Uwe repeated.

"Mexicans from Mexico?" Fredericka said.

"No, I don't think so." Imogene answered.

"If they're not Mexicans, what are they?" Fredericka asked.

"What do they want?" Uwe asked.

"The people want to talk to those two." Imogene pointed out Lazarus and Gabriel, who looked worried. "They're interested in Dwight too. They want to know why those boys came here to see him. And Ulysses and Fredericka. Especially Ulysses."

"Who are you mixed up with, Imogene?" Fredericka asked.

Imogene took a deep breath and then exhaled. "I don't know exactly, to be honest, but I do know this much, they aren't people to mess around with."

"What do they want with these boys?" Dwight said. "They're just kids."

"People think they know things."

"Why should we trust you?" Roland blurted out.

"Look, the best thing for us to do is try to sneak out of here," Imogene said, ignoring the question.

"Us?'

"Yes, 'cause if I don't deliver y'all I'll have to run too."

"Why not go ahead and 'deliver' us? What's changed?" Fredericka pushed. "I don't trust her," she said to the others in the room.

"It's, I don't know how to say it," Imogene said. "I guess it's my gut telling me to break it off with them and get out while I can." She tossed her long blonde hair back, adding, "Plus, really they're just a bunch of old people. Not as fun as I thought they would be. They offered me money to turn you over," she ended with an offended tone.

"You'd think they were Russian spies after us!" Fredericka said after a shocked silence.

When Imogene said, "Well, I wouldn't say no to that, Fredericka," Gabriel groaned.

"You mean there are Russian agents coming through Mexico all the way to Pine Bluff?" Lazarus said. "That's ridiculous. Nothing like that happens here."

Imogene's response was raised eyebrows.

"We should make a plan to get out," Uwe said. "There are so many of us. We'll have to find a way to change our appearances, but even then it won't be easy."

"Maybe you could lose yourselves during a shift change at the Arsenal," Dwight thought out loud, "but that wouldn't work for the girls. There aren't supposed to be any girls on this boat, and the twins stick out, plus it sounds like they have been identified and people are watching out for them."

"Do you think this a trap?" Fredericka asked Uwe. "This better not be a trap."

"I can't think of anything else to do, Fredericka," he shrugged. "We have to get out of here someway."

Dwight agreed completely.

52 THE LADIES DRIVE DOWN

May 20, 1945. Little Rock to Pine Bluff, Arkansas.

Nearing Pine Bluff, Gwen slowed the car. "Check out this fog!" she said.

"Look at you," Claudette observed. "You're unflappable. Aren't you the least bit nervous?"

"Nervous about what?" Gwen asked before adding, "Okay, I'm a little keyed up."

"Will you get in trouble for coming down here?" Claudette asked.

"Agent Jennings opted out of this assignment and gave it to me; his instructions were clear," Gwen answered as she stared at the road ahead of her. Unable to maintain a poker face, she chortled. "He said it was routine, clerical, and he was too busy to be bothered."

"Oooh, well, tracking some culprits to Pine Bluff gives clerical new meaning," Claudette said, starting to laugh, then she frowned. "Those two! I can't believe those boys broke into Jake Holt's house, stole and then sold his wedding ring! They've got a lot of nerve."

"It was a lucky break you were with me at the pawn shop and could recognize the ring and place it at the Holt's," Gwen remarked.

"I hope hauling all the way to Pine Bluff is not a wild goose chase. Wasted effort and gas, all that good stuff, you know," Claudette said. "Seems kind of far to go on the basis of a stolen ring. But I do like spending time with you, Gwen."

"Gil's description of the guy who loiters outside of his shop is a spot on match for Daryl Green. Since Daryl is an agency person of interest we're on target to go to Pine Bluff because that's his home territory. Plus, with your boss down here I can't help but think they're tied together. I'm sure there's more going on here than we can see."

"Do you think Daryl's dangerous?"

"Mmm, I doubt it, well, probably not too dangerous. He's a B-stringer. It's a shame you couldn't weasel more information out of Pete."

"Oh, my gosh, Gwen, we're lucky to get what we did," Claudette said. "The house on 8th Street is sealed up tight. Pete must be working security for it. Something's up. Colonel Edmund just said he was going to Pine Bluff on business when he called in. He didn't elaborate."

"I think those boys were after something more than your typical jewelry, and the ring was an add-on, if you know what I mean," Gwen said.

"Do you think there's something going on at the Arsenal?"

"I've got my eye on a fellow by the name of Roy McNeil who is a supervisor there," Gwen said as she pulled off the highway, having arrived to town. "This business with Daryl makes me think he and Roy are connected. My informant says Roy missed work today. I'm going to cruise by some of the off site Arsenal housing and then drive along the river road for a little look see."

"Gwen, don't you think we need a plan? I'm not sure how effective we'll be bumping around down here. Feels kind of aimless."

"My hunch says those boys are down here, and they're probably in trouble. I want a word with them."

"Look at those shacks," Claudette breathed. The road was lined with rough shanties and tents.

"They sprang up like mushrooms after a good rain when the Arsenal opened," Gwen remarked.

"Rough," Claudette commented, and Gwen nodded in agreement.

"Gwen, let me out."

"Why? Are you sick?" Gwen asked as she stopped the car on the shoulder.

"No. But this looks like a great hideout for a couple of kids on the run," Claudette said. She got out and walked over to tap on the door of a dilapidated shotgun house. A slovenly woman answered the door. Gwen could see the woman shaking her head at Claudette, who instead of returning to the car, went on to the next house.

"Claudette, get back in here!" Gwen called from the car.

Claudette waved and continued on. Gwen sighed and followed in the car, watching Claudette's yellow dress as she popped in and out of shacks in the seedy neighborhood. Gwen hit the brakes and reached over to fling open the front passenger door when Claudette came limping to the street with a scraped chin and bleeding knee. "What happened? Did somebody hurt you?" she asked.

Claudette sank onto the seat and accepted the handkerchief Gwen handed her. "Thanks," she said, using it to dab at her knee. "Nobody hurt me exactly. I tripped and fell flat when I was trying to get away from a horrible woman. She was running after me and throwing things. It knocked my breath away. I landed hard. The worst thing is I tore my stocking. Look, it's ruined."

"It's toast, but really, Claudette, it could have been a lot worse than a torn stocking. Are you okay? What happened?"

"I'll be fine, no big deal, but nobody wanted to tell me squat."

"You look too nice, of course nobody's going to talk to you." Gwen said. She passed Claudette a box of band-aids. "There should be a big one in here."

"The woman who chased me thought I wanted to bring her to the Lord," Claudette commented as she bandaged her gashed knee.

"She was not receptive?"

"She said she didn't want to hear about it."

"Honestly, you do kind of look like a preacher's wife. Give you a Bible and some tracts and you're good to go."

"Well, this is fertile ground. I kid you not, Gwen, you should get your entire office down here and clean it up. You could make massive numbers of arrests. I can't believe these people are helping the war effort. Gambling and prostitution, I guarantee."

"The Hamptons it's not," Gwen said, glancing around the neighborhood.

Gwen started the motor, but before she could pick up speed Claudette said, "Let me try over there." She pointed down the street. Gwen watched Claudette limp over and enter a large tent with a makeshift bar at one end. A few minutes later she emerged and hopped back in the car. "Bingo! Money talks," she said with satisfaction. "No news about the boys, but a dollar bought us Daryl's whereabouts."

"No kidding?"

"That was his lady friend in there. She said Daryl is working late over on the river, which is thataway," Claudette said, pointing in the general direction she had been told.

"Working late? Hmm, I wonder what that means. I doubt Daryl ever worked a legitimate job in his life."

53 THE LADIES STEP IN

May 20, 1945. Pine Bluff, Arkansas.

"I keep these on hand in the trunk just for such an occasion." Gwen passed Claudette a pair of overalls. She stuck a cap on her head and handed another one to Claudette. "Cover your hair with this, it'll help with camouflage in case this fog lifts and the moon comes out." Gwen pulled on a stout pair of hiking boots she kept in her trunk.

"Good deal." Claudette talked while she pulled the straps over her shoulder and snapped them to the bib. "Let's hope nobody asks us to drive a train."

"I wouldn't know where to start," Gwen agreed, laughing.

"I'm glad I wore these practical shoes today instead of my nice pumps." Claudette flexed her sore knee back and forth. "In case I have to make some quick moves," she said.

Gwen had parked on the dirt road on top of the levee not far from the quarter-boats. Walking towards the boats, Gwen stopped and pointed at the figure sitting on shore smoking and watching the boats. "That's him," she breathed, "Daryl Green."

Gwen and Claudette sank down on the damp grass to watch. From their vantage point they could see Daryl and one side of the quarter-boat he was watching. Through the fog they saw a shadowy group of people illuminated against the white wall of the boat before they disappeared.

"What's going on?" Gwen breathed as a car load of tough looking men drove up, parked on the dock lot, and walked over to talk with Daryl. One of the men took over for Daryl, who left and drove the car away.

"While I'm not sure what it should look like, this crowd level doesn't seem right, does it?" Claudette said. She squinted at the people who were fading in and out of the heavy fog. "The people seem odd. Some of them are kind of dressed up, and others look ready to rob a bank."

"I don't like the looks of this at all," Gwen said with a tone of great interest as she took in the scene before them. "If I'm not mistaken, the guy who took over for Daryl is Roy McNeil."

"Oh, oh, look back there." A sheriff's car had pulled up behind Gwen's car. The two men inside did not get out. "Something's going down. I hope your car will be all right."

"Claudette, you stay here and keep an eye on things and I'll go look around."

Gwen slid down the levee and approached the boats from a path along the shoreline. Thirty minutes later she surfaced behind Claudette, who jumped in alarm. "Where have you been?" she hissed. "I was about to go looking for your body."

"I eavesdropped on those guys who came in with Roy. They're real thugs. Our thieves are on the boat all right, and those men are planning to capture them."

"Could you figure out what they want with them?"

"It was hard to tell. Only that they are going to be taken away somewhere. There's a ski boat docked nearby that might come in handy tonight. The keys are in the ignition."

"Gwen! You can't possibly know who owns it."

"We may have to commandeer it," Gwen answered. "No telling how things will shake out here, and water access to the boats may come in handy.

As the evening wore on, Gwen and Claudette settled down in the wet grass to keep watch. "This is better than the picture show," Claudette said, "Except I'm hungry. Do you have anything to eat?"

Gwen passed her a crumpled sack. "Just these saltines."

54 ESCAPE

May 20, 1945. Pine Bluff, Arkansas.

"Listen up," Dwight said, motioning to the door. "We should move to the storage locker on the backside of this barge and hide while we figure things out. The breakfast shift will be in here before we know it."

Dwight led the way across the boat to the end and unlocked a door. "This room is unused," he said. They peered into the dark interior as he reached in and pulled the chain to turn on the bare bulb that illuminated a limited area and left the corners in shadows. A walk-in refrigerator was across from the door. The seven of them crowded inside and sat down on the corrugated floor.

"Let me tell you something straight off." Dwight looked around as though to challenge anyone who disagreed with him. "I'm staying here. It would be my job to take off without some kind of notice. Besides, I can't believe those people are after me. I haven't done anything wrong."

"Oh Dwight, you should think about that," Imogene answered. "These people aren't to be fooled with."

"My supervisor here will protect me. But the rest of you'd better move along."

"You have a lot of faith in your boss, is all I can say, Dwight," Imogene said.

"How are seven people, well, six if Dwight stays, going to get away without being noticed by the crowd out there?" Fredericka wondered aloud.

"According to Imogene there's a spotlight on the twins," Marcel remarked. "I'm not sure about Roland 'n me. Maybe we can pretend to be munitions workers and slip out with the crowd during the shift change, but my sister has a bull's eye on her back, and you put it there!" he said. He shot an accusing look at Uwe.

"Marcel, we have to try to extricate ourselves from this predicament and not place blame. You should know, I asked to come with Ulysses," Fredericka said.

"Still," Roland muttered, and Marcel nodded.

"I've said it before, there aren't supposed to be women on this boat," Dwight said. "They stand out. I don't know how to get them out, and we'll have to disguise the twins somehow."

"I have an idea about how to get the twins away and at the same time keep us from being discovered," Imogene said, looking at Fredericka, "but it won't be inconspicuous," and she outlined her plan.

"You know, it is a good idea, to escape in plain sight, and a diversionary tactic would give Fredericka, Imogene and me a chance to slip out," Uwe said.

Gabriel refused and Lazarus backed him up, "No way!"

"Why don't you girls do it? You're already dressed," Lazarus told Imogene.

"I think Fredericka and I would be recognized," Imogene said. "Besides, a man of color with a lady of different color on each arm would draw the wrong kind of attention. Attention we don't need. You know that. Plus, Fredericka is taller than both of you by quite a bit. I think she and I could pass as men in the dark. I will keep my cap down over my face and stick to the shadows until we get off the boat, then I can blend in with the workers."

"Look here, fellas," Dwight said. "Unless you make a change and do it soon, you'll be wearing prison stripes and chopping cotton down at Cummins with a rifle toting guard on horseback at the end of the row. How could I face your mama if the warden used his Telephone to make a call on one or both of you? How about a long distance call? Huh?"

The twins blanched at the thought of even a short local call, much less a long distance call.

"What is this Telephone?" Uwe had to ask.

"Ordinarily, I would not say this in mixed company, but the situation has become critical, so I'll tell you," and looking straight at his cousins, Dwight said, "they clamp one cable on your big toe and another on the most sensitive place."

Everyone present grimaced and Fredericka covered her eyes at the thought, but Dwight continued to drive his point home, "and a current run through it like you would jump a car battery, but it ain't a car battery, you know?"

"Torture," Uwe said.

"Yes, sir, it's torture, and I'm certain it would scramble the tadpoles. Do permanent damage," Dwight said.

"An appointment with Old Sparky would be better," Gabriel exclaimed.

"That's the electric chair," Imogene contributed.

"So, the plan is to have the twins and Dwight leave first," Uwe said, glad to have a viable escape plan at last. "The twins will be in disguise and accompanied by Dwight as far as the train. Marcel and Roland will follow and make sure the twins get on board. Imogene and Fredericka will go next and I will follow. Imogene, will you be able to identify the people who are after us?"

"Yes, I think so."

"I don't see another way out of this. Let's stop talking and get moving," Dwight stated.

"The Telephone probably is only used in extreme cases, Dwight," Lazarus said. "I think Gabriel and me could take our chances."

"The kind of trouble you boys are mixed up in? They might use it on you or you might not even make it to Cummins, you might get knocked off first." Dwight instructed the twins, "Follow the plan." Dwight stepped out and then reappeared a few minutes later with two sets of clean cotton pants, shirts and aprons he had lifted from the kitchen worker's supply closet. "Wear the aprons, they'll make you look more authentic," he advised.

Imogene and Fredericka slipped into the walk-in refrigerator and changed from their skirts and blouses into the kitchen help's clothes. Emerging from the refrigerator, they hid their hair in the crowns of the caps Dwight provided and tied the aprons strings behind their waists. Imogene had to roll her pants legs up so that she wouldn't trip, but Fredericka's were a good fit.

"It's a maybe," Dwight appraised them. "You'll pass as fellows only if somebody ain't lookin' too close. Best get out of here as soon as possible."

"Next." Imogene held the refrigerator door open and motioned for Lazarus and Gabriel to go in.

"What is taking so long?" Uwe said when they had been in there twice as long as Fredericka and Imogene.

"Dawdling." Fredericka said.

Uwe pounded on the refrigerator door. The boys emerged wearing the ladies clothes and sad expressions. Fredericka was pleased to see how well her red and white striped-shirt and skirt fit Gabriel. "I'll not be letting you see the rest of my wardrobe, buddy, else you'll be wanting more!" she said. Gabriel frowned.

Lazarus did not fare as well. "I can't fasten my skirt," he said. Dwight handed him his belt. The fitted blouse hung flat on Lazarus' top. Fredericka handed him two wads of tissue from her purse and nodded at him to pad the space. When he was done, she leaned back and assessed his appearance. "Go on, sit down," Fredericka said. She and Imogene had pooled the considerable amount of cosmetic supplies from their purses. Fredericka furrowed her brow in concentration while contemplating the art project in front of her. Imogene knelt beside her and started work. They leaned back on their heels to analyze the result when they were done.

Checking in from where he had been keeping watch, Dwight did a double take. "That looks good," he said, "the shoes are the only thing that don't look right, but they'll do, 'specially if it's not too light out."

As the finishing touch, Fredericka produced two scarves from her purse and tied them on each boy's head. "There," she said, reviewing her work, "you can't see their boy heads now." Imogene stepped back. "Fredericka, you are an artist," she said.

"Lucky day I had two scarves in my purse," Fredericka said in satisfaction.

"We will follow you onto the train and back to North Little Rock and you will take us to where you threw things away," Uwe told the twins, careful to say nothing in front of Imogene that she didn't already know.

"All right," Lazarus agreed after exchanging a glance with Gabriel.

"Roland and Marcel will go first," Uwe continued, outlining the plan. "Imogene and Fredericka will follow, and I will bring up the rear. Dwight will show you the correct train, then Imogene, Fredericka and I will jump on the same train and watch you all the way home."

"I don't like it," Roland told Fredericka. "I think it would be better if you, me and Marcel walk together and Ulysses and Imogene follow."

Fredericka shook her head. "If we get separated, Ulysses will need me to help him, and you will be able to get us help. In case something happens and we don't make the same train, we'll meet you at the fillin' station at the corner of Broadway and Maple. You should find Mama and tell her everything if we're not there after an hour or so. She will know what to do next."

Marcel didn't like the sound of the possible hitches in the plan, but he nodded in agreement. "Hear this," he said to Lazarus. "We are going to stick to you like ticks."

"Please. Use a different comparison," Lazarus shuddered.

Fredericka pulled her brothers into a firm embrace. "I love you," she whispered. She tightened her grip on their shoulders before releasing them.

The Arsenal shift change was underway and workers were trickling in. Dwight took Gabriel on one arm and Lazarus on the other. "Let's make this work," he said. "Remember, you're two gals out on the night." Lazarus looked at Gabriel and they shrugged, and then the two of them gave it all they had. Dwight walked down the gangplank with Gabriel and Lazarus sauntering along beside him. Marcel and Roland trailed about ten paces behind. When they approached a group of off duty workers, an adrenalin jolt hit Gabriel, not unlike that gotten when robbing a house, and he started to enjoy himself. The twins played their parts well, drawing whistles and catcalls from the returning workers, and somebody yelled, "Hey, Dwight, my man, share the wealth!"

As the catcalls grew in strength, several of the workers pressed in close to the boys, and one of them reached out to swat Lazarus on the bottom. He jumped as though shot and started to return the favor but stopped in time, heeding Dwight's warning iron grip. Instead, he leaned in as though for protection. "Back off! Leave my women alone!" Dwight yelled into the crowd.

Meanwhile, the fog had started to lift. Imogene, Uwe and Fredericka had a clear view of Dwight and the twins illuminated in the barge floodlights as they became the target of a circle of taunting men. Marcel and Roland blended in with the workers, ready to pounce and extricate the twins if need be. Uwe breathed easier when

Lazarus did not rise to the bait and the twins and Dwight were allowed to pass. The three continued towards the train yard with Marcel and Roland following at a discrete distance.

"Here's our chance," Uwe whispered. A bus from the munitions plant had pulled up while the first stage of escape was underway. As the off duty workers filed off, Imogene and Fredericka pulled their caps down to hide their faces and walked off the quarter-boat with Uwe bringing up the rear. They slipped through the crowd of men and followed the path taken by the others.

Once away from the barges, it became quiet and Dwight and the twins, followed by Marcel and Roland, walked unimpeded towards the rail yard. They could hear the familiar sounds of clanking machinery and train engines ahead of them. The sky above the yard was bright with train headlights and floodlights. Dwight made a show of hugging the twins good-bye in case they were being observed. "Good luck," he whispered to Lazarus and then Gabriel. "I'm sorry I can't go with y'all the whole way," he said before starting back to the quarter-boats.

Gabriel and Lazarus hurried to the trains, taking care to stay in the shadows of the brightly lit yard. They scrambled onto a car of the Missouri Pacific Line Dwight said would take them home. Imogene's skirt got caught on Lazarus' way up the stairs at the end of the boxcar, and he winced when he heard it tear. He glanced down and determined that the rip was not fatal to the integrity of the skirt and would probably make it home. He hoped Imogene didn't want it back. He considered himself lucky she wasn't there to see her nice outfit getting ruined. Going home. The thought made him wince for a different reason. How would he and Gabriel explain arriving in ladies clothes? How humiliating. At least it should be dark when they arrived.

Lazarus looked at Gabriel, who also had fought Fredericka's clothes on his way into the boxcar, cursing as his knees slid back under the skirt, causing him to fall onto the deck of the boxcar.

"Lazarus," Gabriel said after they had gotten comfortable, "I've been thinking about something." His eyes, owlish with the heavy mascara, eyeliner and dark blue shadow, were troubled in the dim light.

"Yeah?"

"We were disrespected back there by those men."

"Weren't we!" Lazarus responded. "They treated us like pork chops in the display case and I did not care for it one bit."

"I used to think that kind of thing was funny myself, but I don't anymore," Gabriel said.

"There's nothing funny about it."

"But you know, Mama was right about something."

"How so?"

"I guess we could say, after a fashion anyhow, that bad women did figure into this!"

Gabriel's remark broke the tension of the past day and the brothers howled with laughter. Relaxing, they leaned back against the metal side of the car.

"Shouldn't the others be here?" Gabriel wondered.

"Oh they'll be along, I'm sure. That was the plan."

From the shadowy corner in the boxcar, a hobo known only to his fellow travelers as Boll Weevil, his given name lost to the sands of time and another life, stared at Gabriel and Lazarus. Illuminated in the shafts of moonlight pouring through the open car door, they sat on the floor with their skirts pulled around their knees. Their skinny, hairy legs stuck out in front of them. Their scarves had shifted to reveal their short-cropped hair, but their make-up held.

The chocolate cake made by Mrs. Gilcrest of Redeemer Baptist Church, Sheriff Alvin Lemoyne's sister, had survived Uwe and Fredericka's tumultuous trek across town to the quarter-boats. Some of the cake wasn't squashed. Unaware that he was being observed, Gabriel unwrapped a generous slice, the wax paper wrapping making crinkling noises, and handed it to Lazarus.

Watching the boys laughing and enjoying their cake, Boll Weevil found himself swallowing hard and his bleary eyes starting to ooze tears. *I wish I had their nerve to live how they want to live. If I had, I might be in a better place today*, he thought.

55 HOLY WAR

May 20, 1945. Pine Bluff, Arkansas.

"We're almost there," Uwe whispered as the train came into sight.

"The inside of a dirty old boxcar sounds like heaven," Fredericka breathed as they walked faster.

"Oh, thank goodness, they made it!" Fredericka said when Marcel and Roland came into view. The boys stood side by side in the doorway of an open car watching for them.

"Hurry up, I'm afraid it's about to take off," Roland whispered as he hopped from foot to foot, mad with anxiety that the train would leave before Fredericka and Uwe could get on.

Fredericka ran ahead and hoisted herself into the opening. Roland leaned down and grabbed her under the arms and pulled hard to drag her on board. Imogene was next, and she struggled to get on, her feet slipping under the white canvas apron. "Help me, please," she panted as she dangled half on and half off the car. Uwe picked up her feet and pushed while Roland pulled on her arms. Imogene landed on the floor with a thud, winded but happy.

Uwe pulled himself over the side and rolled onto the floor alongside Fredericka and Imogene.

"Where are Lazarus and Gabriel?" Uwe asked Marcel.

"They're on this train a few cars up," he answered. "We ducked in here when we saw a railroad bull walking the line. We'll make our way up there once we're rolling."

"Looks like everyone made it," Fredericka said in relief.

"Shhh. I think I heard something. Did anybody else hear something?" Imogene asked. The mood in the car changed from relieved back to anxious as though a switch had been thrown as they strained to hear. No one had time to answer because two men somersaulted into the car from the roof to land like cats on the floor. "This must be them," one said to the other, and without waiting for a response he launched himself onto Marcel. His accomplice did the same to Roland. Caught off guard, it took Marcel and Roland a second to collect themselves before fighting back.

"They must have us confused with the twins!" Marcel exclaimed.

"White people can't tell us apart," Roland shouted as he dodged a fist.

Uwe fought as hard as he could when three men tried to pull him from the train. "Hey, buddy, some of us are on your side," a man whispered in his ear. Relieved, Uwe recognized Clyde Moore, from Christ the Redeemer, who leapt forward, seemingly from nowhere, to help. More and more people were entering the car.

"Ernest, glad to see you," Clyde yelled when Reverend Smith, pastor of the AME, jumped into the car, loosened his tie and fought beside him like a man possessed.

The scream of a familiar voice cut through the violence. There was a moment of shock and then dread when Uwe realized that Fredericka was no longer in the boxcar. He felt a lurch through his entire body when he heard the words, "I'm stuck." Fredericka's voice came from underneath the train.

"Go!" Ernest Smith roared at Uwe.

Uwe jumped off the car. "Fredericka?" he called into the darkness underneath the train, expecting the worst.

"Help. Ulysses, help me. My apron is stuck on the rail." He could hear the desperation in her voice. "I'm tied down."

Above them the floor of the boxcar echoed with thuds and bangs. Uwe fumbled towards the white glimmer of Fredericka's clothes. When he reached her, he discovered by feel that her apron strings had caught on the track bolts and pinioned her to the rail. She was tied like Joan of Arc waiting for the fire.

As the 3000 horsepower locomotive roared into life, they felt the heat from the engines blowing down. "Hurry. Please hurry," she said. Uwe sawed with his knife at the strings binding Fredericka to the track, trying not to cut her in the process. "Don't worry, Fredericka. We are making progress," he said, his voice a calm lifeline that kept her sane as he hacked through the twisted mess. "I've got one side cut, now I'll break the other one."

Fredericka whimpered when they realized the train was beginning to move. Uwe sawed harder. With a violent twist of her body, the final restraining tie severed and Fredericka rolled free. Together she and Uwe scrambled out from underneath the train. The steel wheels rolled over the apron, leaving behind tattered pieces of canvas. Neither of them looked back.

"How did you get caught there?" he asked.

"I was pushed under the train!" she exclaimed.

"The boys!" Fredericka cried as she watched her brothers, who were locked in combat with unknown assailants, roll away with the train. "Oh no, oh no," she moaned. "Let's try to catch it!" she called, running towards the train as it gained speed. She stopped when she realized they were surrounded by a group of menacing men. Like members of a pack under siege, she and Uwe stood back to back, walking in a small circle.

"Where's Imogene?" Fredericka asked in a low voice, her eyes scanning the crowd. "Is she on the train?"

"Maybe. I don't see her here."

"It figures."

Before anyone moved to break the standoff, rustling sounds came from the brush beside the path to their left. Dwight burst out pursued by two men. His face was set with determination as he tore through the circle of men surrounding Uwe and Fredericka. Clyde Moore, Reverend Smith and their friends emerged from the brush, chasing Dwight's assailants.

Seeing Uwe and Fredericka surrounded by the threatening mob, Clyde Moore stopped. "We'll hold them!" he shouted.

"We'll help Dwight!" Fredericka cried as she and Uwe took off, leaving the townspeople to fight in the darkness.

"They've got a jump start on us, but maybe we can catch up," Fredericka panted.

"He went towards the river," Uwe responded.

"Probably he's going to try to hide in the barges."

"He's running onto the boat on the right."

Fredericka and Uwe followed the sound of footsteps pounding on the metal floor of the abandoned supply barge. There was sudden silence and a pause and then they heard someone cry "Help." They ran towards the voice calling from the back of the barge, stumbling on the unlit walkways. "Back here." It was Dwight. Gripping the boat railing, Dwight dangled over the water. He was alone. "The guys chasin' me run off." Dwight said. "They thought I drowned."

Uwe leaned over to pull Dwight to safety. Dwight's sweaty grip loosened, then he regained traction and hung there before losing it again and dropping into the muddy river water with a splash and a despairing cry. Fredericka screamed.

Fredericka and Uwe watched in horror as Dwight fought the water. It was dark, but the lights from the neighboring boat shone down into the water between the barges. Dwight did not know how to swim. His legs were board stiff and his arms sawed at the water. He was failing to make any headway and beginning to sink. Uwe started to pull off his shoes, preparing to jump in.

They didn't hear the approaching footsteps because they were preoccupied with Dwight's predicament. Imogene Park appeared beside them.

"Imogene?" Uwe said in surprise.

"I'll explain later," she said, grabbing a life preserver hanging on the wall and throwing it up current from Dwight. The current carried it downstream as she calculated it would, but he missed it and started to sink.

Grabbing the second life preserver attached to a coil of rope, with shaking hands she tied the unattached end to her waist. Pushing the life preserver on the other end of the rope into Uwe's grip, Imogene jumped overboard. The water was cold, colder than the frigid source of Richland Creek, her favorite Ozark swimming hole, and nothing like those clear, tree-shaded waters. Imogene struggled to maintain her bearings with the shock from her plunge as she went underwater. The rough water was foreign, having traveled all the way from the great Rocky Mountains, and not recognizing Imogene, it tried to kill her.

Imogene kicked against the current as it pulled her deeper under. She surfaced and swam to Dwight despite the strong undertow. In a classic drowning person's move to reach safety, he grabbed at the nearest object, which was Imogene, and he clung to her head, pushing her underwater. She choked when she gulped a mouthful of river water on her way down.

Imogene recalled the life saving skills she had practiced often but not yet used in a real life situation, had in fact practiced only in a sanitary swimming pool. They had not been recommended for the currents of a major river. She had disregarded the cardinal rule of lifesaving, which was to save oneself first.

Spitting out muddy water, coughing and gasping, Imogene tucked her neck so she couldn't be strangled, grabbed Dwight in a hug and pulled him underwater with her, a place he didn't want to go. He released his hold as she knew he would, allowing her to swim away from his reach. She approached again but ducked underwater before he could grab her and pull her under, kicking with all her might to keep the current from carrying her into the swirling channel. She flipped Dwight onto his back, grabbed him in a cross-chest carry, pushed her hip up to support his body and signaled to Uwe to bring them in.

Uwe and Fredericka hauled Imogene and Dwight to the boat and dragged them to safety. The two lay on the deck streaming water and gasping for air before sitting up. Dwight clasped Imogene's hands in his and leaned over and pressed his forehead on them, expressing his gratitude to her for saving his life. "You saved me from death as surely as God pulled Jonah from the whale's belly," he said with a shuddering breath. Imogene looked pleased.

"That current will suck you under and ask questions later," Imogene said. She had known better than to mess with trying to swim in the river. It had been a gamble of her own life to try and save Dwight, but it had worked out after all.

"A whole lot of heart break was saved thanks to you, Imogene," Fredericka said as she wiped her eyes. "I could not have done what you just did. I don't know how to swim either."

Uncontrollable shaking overcame Imogene. Uwe removed his jacket and wrapped it around her. "This agitation is from the exertion to save Dwight," he said.

"My loyalty is not for sale. Just saying." Imogene leaned her head back as tears trickled down her cheeks and mingled with river water.

"What do I hear?" Uwe asked.

"It sounds like an outboard motor," Imogene said. They looked in the direction of the noise as a ski boat pulled up next to them and the motor was shut off. Before they could decide whether to stay or go, a voice spoke to them through the night, "G. Weintraub. FBI."

"FBI?" Did she say "Agent? I'm not sure I heard right. Is that a lady speaking? I've never heard of a lady FBI agent before." Fredericka said, but no one had an answer.

"Get on board this craft. The Sheriff's Department is engaged out front. We're going to pull you people off back here." Gwen spoke from her position behind the steering wheel.

56 DELIVERANCE

May 20, 1945. Pine Bluff, Arkansas.

"Better get on," Fredericka said. Unable to see a better alternative, Uwe agreed. They settled Dwight on the cushioned seats in the stern, Fredericka tucking a blanket around him that she had found in a compartment on the boat.

Imogene was leaning over to step down from the barge to join them when she was grabbed from behind. Imogene whirled around as she jerked free and found herself looking at Vivian Taylor.

"There is an extraction team waiting out front," Vivian hissed. "I can slip us by the police. Either run with me now or take your chances."

Imogene stared at Vivian.

"Talk to me," Vivian said.

"No." Imogene found her voice.

"This is your last chance, chicken head," Vivian said.

"What did you call me?" Imogene demanded.

"Chicken head," Vivian repeated. "I noticed you have one the first day we met at the pool, and you've got it again right now."

Incensed, Imogene slapped Vivian hard on the face. Vivian slapped her in return. They stood glaring at each other.

"Traitor," Imogene said.

"Weakling," Vivian responded, and she reached out to grab a handful of Imogene's long wet hair. "Per-ox-ide," she said, yanking hard and drawing the word out.

"LIAR!" Imogene turned her face to the sky and yelled, her words carrying over the water and broadcasting to the world.

"What's going on up there?" Gwen exclaimed from down in the motorboat.

But Imogene was through talking. She threw a punch at Vivian and they raged together, snarling and punching each other.

The motorboat swayed as Claudette pushed off the boat and jumped onto the barge. She ran a few steps and launched herself onto Vivian's back. Vivian twisted around trying to dislodge Claudette, who clung on and clawed at Vivian's face and neck. Vivian bucked so hard that Claudette fell off with a thump and rolled away in a somersault, but Imogene grabbed Vivian and brought her to the ground.

Fredericka and Uwe scrambled back onto the barge to help Imogene, although there was no need. Vivian lay face down on the barge floor, Imogene breathing hard but pinning her down with clamped legs well muscled from horseback riding. Imogene smiled in triumph. Claudette busied herself binding Vivian's hands and feet with rope she had found on the deck. "There," Claudette said. "She's trussed up like a Thanksgiving turkey."

"That was your last chance," Vivian said, tilting her head to look at Imogene. "There's a hit out on you now, chicken-hea-."

Her mouth a disapproving line, Claudette pulled a bandana from her pocket and tied a silencing gag around Vivian's mouth, keeping her from finishing the sentence and risk provoking Imogene further. Uwe, Fredericka, Imogene and Claudette hauled Vivian into the boat.

Gwen started the motor and steered the boat into the channel. "Sheriff Lemoyne is waiting for us at the dock," she said. "I want to get this cargo delivered ASAP." Gwen was pleased with her haul. The bound up fish in particular might lead to something big. *Not bad for a middle-aged rookie, not bad,* she thought as she piloted the boat towards shore.

Claudette, Gwen's bedraggled partner, was oozing blood from her scratches and a black eye was starting to sprout, her chin and knee scraped from the gypsy camp fall. Gwen was impressed with Claudette's aptitude for spy craft and foresaw a bright future for her. As for the others, the Fredericka girl would be turned over to the authorities for questioning, while her friend was destined for military interrogation. The half drowned man needed a good rest, but he would recover from his ordeal. Gwen considered the blonde's future. The girl was contradictory. There weren't many who could pull off a spectacular water rescue like she had done, but what was she doing mixed up there in the first place? At least everyone was safe and able to talk. She still had to make delivery. So far so good and they didn't have far to go.

As the boat picked up speed, Dwight plucked at Fredericka's sleeve. "Dwight, did you have something to say?" she leaned down close to him.

"I need to tell you," he said. "You know the fellows who chased away some of the men who jumped me on my way back from dropping Lazarus and Gabriel at the train?"

"Yes."

"They said your brothers were safe."

"Oh, Dwight, really?"

"They had those bad fellas dealt with before they jumped off the boxcar."

With the breeze from the river blowing over her face, Fredericka looked ahead and felt liberated knowing that Marcel and Roland were all right. The sky was clear and the moon and stars were out. "I'm so grateful to hear that. Thank you for telling me. Ulysses, did you hear?" She motioned to Uwe to lean in.

"But Dwight," Uwe said, "I don't understand who saved us on the train. I recognized Mr. Moore from my dinner, but who were the others?"

"I recognized some low type people from town in the circle around y'all," Dwight said, talking loud enough to be heard over the motor, "people who like to be mean and nasty, along with strangers I had never seen before, but nice people were there too, pitching in against them. That's how you got through."

"The Reverend Smith and some of his friends were there from the AME," Fredericka put in.

"I witnessed two miracles tonight," Dwight mused. "I've never seen so many different kinds of people, good people, pull together to do the right thing. Then Imogene saved me from drowning. I got a second chance at life. That's my own miracle."

With the wind blowing against their faces and the boat bumping up and down in the river, Uwe, Imogene and Fredericka thought about what Dwight said.

Uwe listened to Dwight with a furrowed brow, trying to make sense of the evening's events. He thought about the men from town who had surrounded Fredericka and him by the train and wondered if they were all connected to the spy web. That seemed unlikely. He should look for an opportunity to speak privately with Imogene and discover how much she knew. He should try to escape and make it back to North Little Rock on his own. Maybe the authorities could sort it out, but he was not optimistic about that.

Officers were waiting for them on the dock. When Gwen steered the boat up next to the pilings and stopped right in front of them, Sheriff Lemoyne caught the mooring line Uwe tossed him. "Hey, Gwennie, I can tell this ain't your first rodeo," he said as he wrapped the line around a post.

"Al," she called, "I've brought you some customers."

"Hmmm, so it's Gwennie and Al, now, is it?" Claudette whispered, chuckling at Gwen's satisfied expression in the dim light shining from the dock floodlight. "Quick work."

Sheriff Lemoyne motioned to his officers to step forward. Vivian was packed away into a waiting truck, but as Imogene stepped from the boat, shots rang out across the levee. The Sheriff and his men hit the ground and returned fire. Uwe grabbed Fredericka's hand and they hopped out of the boat and ran as fast as they could away from the dock.

"Was Imogene shot?" Fredericka gasped.

"I don't think so, but I can't be sure. I thought I saw her run for cover."

"Oh boy, Ulysses, this has been some kind of night," Fredericka said as they slowed to a fast walk, creating distance between themselves and the riverbank.

Uwe looked over his shoulder. "I can't tell if we are being followed. We should use this opportunity to find the spies ourselves and get my medal back."

"Do you see those guys?" Fredericka asked in a strained voice. "I thought I saw two men following us."

"Let's go in here," Uwe said when they reached the shacks lining Dollarway Road. Fredericka followed him as he ducked into the nearest bar.

"Sorry, we closed at midnight." A burly man with a forbidding expression stood in front of them. "There's a curfew on bars. Them's the rules," he said, waving them towards the door. They stood irresolute, afraid to leave.

"Hey, shug, you can come into my bar anytime." The booming voice came through an open door off to the side. "You can even bring your girlfriend. Aw, what a cute couple!" Lady Bess, the entertainment, the red sequins of her dress sparkling in makeshift stage lights, had seen them. She was singing and dancing and waving them inside. Her band joined in with a riff. The bouncer shrugged and moved aside to let Uwe and Fredericka in before locking the door behind them.

A late night party was roaring inside and the clientele, who didn't seem particular, pounded their beer bottles on the tables and shouted hello. Strangers pressed drinks into their hands. Relieved, Fredericka and Uwe dissolved into the crowd. Scattered here and there was a soldier in uniform, but most of the customers were off duty factory workers blowing off steam. Fredericka and Uwe stared at the buxom Lady Bess in her low cut dress. Fredericka's first thought was, *at least she's got clothes on*, but she knew Uwe was thinking something different. She brought Uwe back to reality with an urgent tug on his sleeve. "Sorry, buddy, we can't stay here forever," she whispered.

Noticing the back door, Fredericka pulled Uwe outside and then into the shotgun house next door. They ran through it from back door to front, the sleepy occupants staring at them as they went. They tore through the one next to it too for good measure.

"It's a good thing nobody had time to shoot at us," Fredericka said.

"Everybody seemed quite relaxed," Uwe agreed as they stood on the dirt path behind the houses. He looked around to get his bearings. "We should travel north to get back to town," he said.

"I'm done with the freights, Ulysses," Fredericka said. "We can either hitch a ride or wait for a bus, but I am not jumping onto a train."

"I guess that leaves the highway," he said.

The truck pulled out onto the northbound road. Uwe and Fredericka sat in the cab of the pickup trying to relax. They had waited in the dark on the roadside watching cars and trucks whizz by, their anxiety mounting with each failed opportunity. Not one bus came. Then an old pickup truck stopped on the shoulder of the highway.

"Fredericka, I'll go first in case of trouble," Uwe had said before opening the truck door.

The driver gave a brief wave of his hand that was around the shoulder of a girl who was about Fredericka's age. "Faber Mayhew," he said.

"I'm Jerry, and this is Carolyn," Uwe said. "I'm pleased to meet you, thank you for stopping." Fredericka caught herself before laughing out loud as she wondered how he came up with those names so fast. Ulysses was full of surprises.

Looking straight ahead at the road as he drove at high speed, Faber nodded. "Where y'all headin'?"

"North Little Rock," Uwe said.

"That's good, 'cause that's on our way," Faber said.

"I'm Jessie," the girl said. She squinted through the darkness at Uwe and Fredericka, and then her eyes widened and she averted her gaze so as not to get caught staring at the pair sitting next to her. She shot another look from the corner of her eye at Fredericka, absorbing the fact that a mixed race couple was in her truck and that the girl was dressed like a boy line cook.

"I'm driving like a crazy person 'cause if I don't get back to Fo't Leonard Wood by noon I'll be AWOL," Faber said with a laugh.

Fredericka could tell by his expression that Uwe was struggling to understand the conversation. She turned to him and mouthed, "Tell you later." Frowning, as he mouthed back, "What?" She shook her head at him and made a covert slicing motion with her hand to silence him.

"I runned away and he come after me," Jessie explained in a dreamy voice.

"She'd got to tha' other side a Vicksburg befo' I caught up with her," Faber put in. "I made a guess as to where she'd cross the riva'. Had to be either Natchez or Vicksburg, and I got lucky. She was goin' south o' course."

"I wuz hitch'n rides to go home to Mama," Jessie said. "Are y'all runnin' away too? You look like you might oughta go farther north than North Little Rock, 'ya know?"

Just then a fast driving car approached from behind and pulled up close, too close to the back bumper.

Faber looked in the rear view mirror. "Hey now!" he exclaimed. "What's that car doin' almost in my truck bed?"

Uwe and Fredericka sank down in the seat. Without further comment, Faber leaned over and pulled a sawed off shotgun out from under his seat.

"Baby, can you steer for me?" he asked Jessie. "And stay down, will 'ya?"

"You betcha," Jessie said, sinking down but not so far that she couldn't see over the steering wheel, which she took hold of with her left hand and kept the truck on the road while Faber rolled down his window.

"What! Did y'all get on the wrong side of somebody? Did you bring a fight into muh truck?" Faber shouted.

He stuck the shotgun muzzle out of the window and fired shots at the car. Instead of backing off, the car pulled up beside their pickup, driving into the oncoming traffic lane.

Enraged, Faber fired more shots at the car that was beside theirs, and they traveled down the roadway headed in the same direction on a two-lane road. Fredericka and Uwe slunk down further and held on as best they could.

One of Faber's shots had taken out a tire, and the chasing car careened off the road. Rolling up the window, Faber returned the shotgun to its hiding place under the seat and took back the wheel. "Thanks, baby," he said to Jessie, and she returned to leaning against him.

Uwe and Fredericka sat up and exchanged a relieved look.

"Anybody ridin' in muh truck gets automatic protection," Faber said.

When they reached Broadway, Fredericka pointed out where they wanted to stop, then she and Uwe climbed out. Uwe handed Faber three dollars and shook his hand. "Thank you, I don't know how to thank you, Faber."

"Pass it on, brother. Pass it on," Faber said as he stuffed the money into his pocket.

Uwe and Fredericka stood watching the taillights disappear down the road.

"I hope he gets to Fo't Leonard Wood in time," Uwe said in all seriousness.

57 LEAVING PINE BLUFF

Midnight, May 21, 1945. Pine Bluff, Arkansas.

"But Colonel, do you think you'll get the straight story?" Pete wasn't convinced.

"They've lost the war. It behooves them to cooperate," Edmond answered.

After going around once more with Kaspar Bauer and Walter Witte, Uwe's DAK buddies, Bill Edmund hit pay dirt. As he told Pete when he issued instructions for their transfer to Pine Bluff, "Those army pals of his should be able to predict Uwe Johannes' moves better than we can." When he mentioned medal, the men had exchanged a look. Edmund could be persuasive when he tried.

"Johannes' medal? He would return for it." Walter Witte sounded certain. Sitting next to Walter, Kaspar agreed, "He risked his life to keep it in Tunisia." They were in the confined space of the captain's office on a quarter-boat, their military escort doubling as a guard at the door.

Uwe Johannes, aka Ulysses Jones, was in the wind and time was wasting. Bill was deciding what to do next. He should find out who was responsible for the break in at the rock house, and a missing prisoner was a serious problem. By rights the FBI should be launching a manhunt. The situation was ticklish, given the fact that an FBI employee was sitting right around the corner waiting to talk to him. Bill knew she should report everything to her boss. Gwen Weintraub had been on the cusp of turning Johannes in to law enforcement when he slipped away under sniper fire. On the positive side, Bill thought neither Gwen nor Claudette knew about Project Stonehenge. He might still be able to keep a lid on things.

The sentry knocking on the door interrupted him. "What?" he asked in annoyance.

"Sir, I think you'll want to take this call. It's Peters in North Little Rock."

"Fredericka Lane and her brothers are here. Ditto the two kids. No trace of Johannes."

"Keep looking," he ordered, then disconnected the line and went to question Vivian Taylor.

Emerging from his session with Vivian, Bill Edmund shook his head in distaste. "Shameful woman," he said, "but she talked." Sheriff Alvin Lemoyne, Gwen Weintraub and Claudette Reynolds sat around the conference room table on the top floor of the quarter-boat waiting for final instructions.

Bill had managed to free Mamie and Iva Lynn from Daryl Green and three of his associates but not without cost. He eased himself into the chair at the head of the table, trying to avoid setting off spasms of pain from his various injuries. "I need to hit the road soon," he told them. "We're letting McNeil go on a technicality. From what we got out of Daryl Green and Vivian Taylor, Roy most likely will go to Little Rock. I plan to follow him and see what his next move is."

"The FBI has been watching McNeil," Gwen said.

"From what Miss Park, Miss Taylor and Mr. Green said, I think we'll be able to connect him to an arson sabotage plot at the Arsenal," Edmund said.

Gwen's eyes brightened at the news. Edmund stood up. "Which means I'd better get a move on and see if he leads us up the chain of command before we arrest him." He looked at Sheriff Lemoyne. "A team will be by in the morning to pick up Vivian Taylor and Daryl Green."

"Okay. Do you need help tracking McNeil?" Lemoyne asked. "I could spare some men."

"No thanks." Edmund answered. "I've an idea about where he's going and I've got good soldiers in place on the ground. Plus, I don't want him to suspect he's being followed." He stood up and turned at the door. "I'd appreciate it, though, if you could find someone to drive Miss Iva Lynn Jones and Miss Mamie Holt back home. They're okay but too shook up to drive."

"Done," Lemoyne said. "When you're ready to leave say 'when' and we'll give McNeil a wee bit of a head start." He walked out of the room to make the arrangements.

Despite his straightforward nature, Bill Edmund could follow someone to ground without his ever knowing about it. It was a talent he had and he used it that night on Roy McNeil. As soon as he was free, McNeil stopped to place a call from a gas station pay phone before heading north. From his vantage point in his car, Edmund figured McNeil was calling to report in.

Bill was curious about where he and Roy were heading as they neared Little Rock. He hoped they were going to a meet up with Roy's next in command, but he frowned when they drove down Broadway in North Little Rock. His frown deepened when Roy pulled into the train station parking lot. If Roy planned to jump on a train and leave town he would have to arrest him first. But there weren't any trains running that late. Roy was meeting some men outside the station.

58 THE LADIES LAMENT

Early hours of May 21, 1945. Highway 65 North outside of Pine Bluff, Arkansas.

"It could have gone worse, I guess," Claudette said.

"Much worse," Gwen agreed.

Colonel Edmund's expression when Claudette emerged from the boat looking like a prizefight contender was scary, and there was more explaining to be done, but it would wait until things settled down.

"Colonel Edmund looked offended," Claudette said. "I think his feelings were hurt when he found out I have been reporting to you. I feel bad about that."

"That's the way it is in this business, Claudette. Besides, I think he was worried about you."

"Worried? I think my overalls shocked him."

"For sure, but really, his secretary appearing at a Pine Bluff crime scene delivering a trussed up prisoner and three wanted persons? That had to be a surprise even if two of them got away. Plus, you haven't seen your face recently."

Imogene drove ahead of them in the turquoise car. Claudette and Gwen followed in Gwen's car. They were driving north on Highway 65 returning to North Little Rock.

"Don't you think this new assignment is kind of a let down?" Claudette asked.

"You mean we got a babysitting job?"

"Yes. Exactly. Because we're women."

"It was either that or go home," Gwen sighed. "Besides, we should be good soldiers, Claudette, and take our orders. We'll turn her over to Pete Peters when we get to town."

"The colonel thinks she might be able to draw our runaways out if they went back to North Little Rock," Claudette said. "If the runaways don't surface, at least we get her back home. I think he is giving Imogene a chance to redeem herself."

"He laid it out about as clear as he could," Gwen agreed. "Either toe the line or jail."

"Call her daddy is more like it," Claudette said.

"Yes, but maybe he wants to keep her available for awhile longer."

"Roy McNeil doesn't know she was captured." Claudette said.

"Right. So our job isn't strictly babysitting, and we sure don't want to lose track of her. Besides, Claudette, I see potential in Imogene. Raw material."

"Oh Gwen, give me a break. Potential trouble is what she is!"

"Do you think she used her feminine wiles and manipulated Colonel Edmund into letting her go?"

"No. Not even Imogene Park has that much sway, but I do think he off loaded her to us because he thought we were impervious to her charms."

"I guess we should take it as a compliment to our abilities," Gwen said.

59 THE A TEAM

Early May 21, 1945. North Little Rock, Arkansas.

"Well?" Fredericka whispered, not sure why she was whispering since at two am Broadway looked deserted. "Did you find the medals?"

"They're not here." Marcel shared the depressing news. "We've looked where they said they threw them away." He, Roland, Lazarus and Gabriel had materialized out of the night once Faber Mayhew's taillights disappeared down the street. They stood underneath the darkened red, white and blue DX sign of the service station at Broadway and Maple.

Fredericka had yanked both brothers into a bear hug when she saw them safe and whole. "Dwight said the Pine Bluff folk helped y'all out." She squeezed them hard and then walked over and hugged the twins too. "What happened to those guys who attacked you?" Fredericka asked Roland and Marcel. The boys shrugged and everybody laughed when Roland said, "They're kind of tied up, probably somewhere around Thebes or Cairo, Illinois right about now, on their way to Chicago."

A car driving down the road towards them diverted their attention away from worries about the medal. "Imogene!" Fredericka exclaimed, and she ran out in the road in front of the turquoise car waving her arms. Imogene pulled over and got out. Fredericka hugged her, crying, "I'm so glad to see you! I want to hug your neck!" Imogene grinned and hugged her back and then went over and shook hands with the twins and Fredericka's brothers.

"I see you've found boy clothes," Imogene said, appraising the twins.

"Yes, indeed," Gabriel said." Somebody livin' over yonder failed to bring the clothes off the line tonight."

"Lazy housekeepin'," Lazarus added.

"I'm sure you will return them freshly cleaned this week." Fredericka told him. "I'm going to follow up with you," she added, noting their noncommittal expressions.

"Where's Ulysses?" Imogene asked, looking around.

"Good question. He was right here," Fredericka answered.

60 LOST DOG

Early May 21, 1945. North Little Rock, Arkansas.

"Porter!" George called again, but there was no response. He was in a panic after looking for Porter alone and in the middle of the night. George had let Porter out when he whined, and when he hadn't returned after fifteen minutes, George went looking. An hour later, still no Porter. Never before had he disappeared without a trace, and it was unsettling. George continued calling into dark yards, whistling and clapping his hands, but there was no responsive bark and wriggling happy dog nuzzling up to him. There was only silence.

Afraid to look, George peered down streets hoping and praying not to see a motionless dark form. Porter struck by a car was an unbearable thought, but if that was his fate George would have to claim the body and give him a proper burial, not leave him like common road kill. He would have to face the horror of his beloved boy lying in the road, his fur ruffling in the breeze but no spark of life in his face.

George sat on an old carriage block to compose himself. A moment later he stood, determined to forge on. Maybe Porter had found the girlfriend George knew he wanted and they were running far with a pack in pursuit of an irresistible scent. In his heart, though, George knew that wasn't what had happened. A beagle might have been tempted, but Porter was a working dog. Porter would not have abandoned his post even for love. George decided to double check near his house before broadening his search. He went home and got his bicycle and installed the saddlebags in case he found Porter and needed to carry him.

George rode up and down streets, going all the way up to front doors and then bumping over lawns to check backyards and calling for Porter. Then, in a side yard he caught a glimpse of what he thought was a big rabbit in the moonlight. Trying to see in the dark, he realized with flooding relief that the ears were Porter's. It wasn't a rabbit at all. "Porter!" he cried. They were ecstatic to see each other. Porter was shivering. They sat a moment, Porter cuddling up closer and closer to George. "Why didn't you bark for me, boy?" George whispered as he scratched at the base of Porter's ears. "You were trying to come home, weren't you?"

Standing up to leave, George saw two men walking down the road. They were calling a dog. Porter pressed into George for protection. George picked Porter up and lugged him into the saddlebag. He rode away as fast as he could go in the opposite direction from the men. He knew why Porter hadn't barked. He was being hunted. George didn't know why Porter was being hunted, he only knew they couldn't go home.

When George looked back, he realized the men had seen them and were running towards him. At first he turned right, intending to go to the train station and take a train out of town, but after he rode onto the wide driveway at Broadway and Orange he turned around and pedaled in the opposite direction. He didn't like the looks of the men loitering at the entrance to the deserted station. He would try the Rock Island station on Hazel, or maybe he should make a beeline to the bakery on Main. It was closer and the baker might already be starting work and would let him hide in the kitchen.

George rode up Broadway. Looking back to see if he was being pursued, George didn't see the two figures who jumped out at him from the deep shadow of the DX gas station. He almost went head first over the handlebars when they grabbed the bike, but somebody caught him. "What do you want?" he said, his voice almost a squeak.

Nobody answered him, but another man pulled him off his bike and someone else grabbed the bike and took him and the bike around the far side of the closed garage. Porter jumped out of the bag and followed George.

"Is there any chance your dog is wearing a necklace?" Fredericka asked.

61 CHARLIE

Early May 21, 1945. North Little Rock, Arkansas.

Charlie Cartwright lay on the ground half in and half out of a flowerbed. His wheelchair had turned over on its side and the wheels spun in the air. Charlie was stranded. He couldn't believe his luck when he saw Pete Peters striding down the road under the streetlight. "Pete," he called out.

"Who's there?" Pete stopped and called.

"Charlie Cartwright," he answered. Pete ran in the direction of the voice. When Pete reached Charlie, he dragged him out to the sidewalk. He grabbed Charlie's wheelchair and righted it.

"What happened, Charlie?"

"George Blackburn is in some kind of big trouble, Pete. He and his dog."

"George? The paperboy?"

"Yes. I was keeping an eye on things when I saw two men watching George's house. George had let Porter out and the men went into the yard and grabbed him. I couldn't believe it. They just grabbed that dog."

"Okay, on the count of three," Pete said, and with his help Charlie got back in his chair. "It's a good thing you were there, Charlie. What happened next?"

"I'm not sure exactly how I did it, to be honest, Pete. I was mad as hell to see somebody taking advantage of a dog. I rolled over and fought like a wild man and got Porter away. He ran off. I ended up on the ground, but that's okay."

"Charlie, I've got some business to take care of tonight. Any chance you'd like to ride with me?"

"You bet, Pete."

Pete transferred Charlie to his car and tossed the wheelchair into the trunk. He got behind the wheel and started the engine.

"I didn't lose my legs at Anzio to watch somebody mistreat a little dog in my hometown," Charlie said through the darkness.

"I hear you," Pete responded.

62 BILL EDMUND GETS READ IN

Early May 21, 1945. North Little Rock, Arkansas.

"Pete?" Uwe whispered when Pete stepped forward in the darkness beside the rock house.

"It's been shut down temporarily, Johannes, and there's an arrest warrant out for you," Pete said. He figured he knew where Uwe would return unless he had decided to run, and he had checked at the house throughout the evening.

"I'm not running away, Pete. Can you take me to Colonel Edmund?"

"Sure can." Pete ushered Uwe to the car where Charlie waited.

"Where is the family?" Uwe asked Pete.

"They've been relocated."

Pete approached the train station so that he was behind the men gathered there and parked in a place hidden by the bridge. "We'll walk the rest of the way," he told Uwe.

When they reached Colonel Edmund's car, Pete nodded at Uwe to get in.

"Here I am, sir," he said, easing into the front passenger seat. Pete slid onto the backseat.

Later Bill reflected that it might have worked to his favor that he had to restrain himself or risk disclosing his location to the men at the train station, considering what Johannes had to say.

"You're telling me you brought with you the German scientific team's data, given to you by their director, Werner Heisenberg, on how to build a uranium bomb. You hid this information on a military medal and brought it into the United States and into this town and hid it in the Holt's living room, and yesterday it was stolen?"

"Yes, sir."

Edmund swore.

"Do you know who broke in?" Edmund asked Uwe.

"It was just some kids, sir, who took it," Uwe answered. "When we were in Pine Bluff, we discovered that a Russian agent had commissioned the job, but although I am not certain, it being a confusing sequence of events, the thieves who are waiting at the service station not far from here were unaware of the significance of the medal. They threw it away here. I therefore don't know if the agent responsible for the burglary fully understood what was at the Holt's. But the medals are gone."

"You mean they were chasing you because you were running?" Edmund said.

"Maybe."

Bill's face was serious as he tried to think of what to do next. The implications of what Johannes had told him were mindboggling. The director of the German military research program could have built the bomb. The information had surfaced within his jurisdiction and on his watch.

The three stared at the train station in front of them as the implications registered and they thought about the events of the past day. Through his connection up the Stonehenge command chain, Edmund knew that Werner Heisenberg had been arrested in Germany on May third and was being held in a secret location somewhere in England. He knew Heisenberg was the focus of an intense investigation into the German effort to build the bomb. He marveled that a piece of the puzzle had surfaced in his own backyard. With mounting anxiety, he realized he had to find the medal.

"While the information on it is old now, it could be useful to someone who is building their own device. It does still pose a risk," Uwe said.

"It could be anywhere, couldn't it?" Edmund said.

"I might know where it is," Pete said. "We need to find George Blackburn and Porter."

"Who?"

"The paperboy and his dog. I think the dog has it."

Bill groaned. "A boy and his dog have this information?"

"I think so," Pete said.

63 THE TURNABOUT

Early May 21, 1945. North Little Rock, Arkansas.

Sheltered by the roof over the gas pumps and out of sight of the train station, the group reached consensus. "Let's turn things around. No longer will we be the hunted," Uwe said, and everyone agreed. Uwe and Tom's medals were pinned side-by-side to the inside of Uwe's shirt pocket. The feeling of relief when Fredericka had handed them to him was indescribable. His thoughts became clear and decisive. Pete had relayed the news to Bill Edmund, who in turn had mobilized reinforcements.

"Porter. No bark," George whispered. "You cannot bark. Do you understand?" George repeated it for good measure, "No bark." George couldn't tell if Porter understood him, he looked like he did but that didn't always mean anything. Porter might understand but disagree, it had happened before, and if it happened now George didn't like to think about the consequences.

The others looked at George. He'd gotten over his fright from being chased and grabbed, right after Porter had almost been done in. Once George saw Mr. Peters join the strangers who had stopped him he felt better. Plus, Porter trusted him so he must be okay. And Charlie Cartwright and Pete Peters being such good friends counted for a lot.

Porter had identified the twins from the residual scent on the discarded ribbons. He was familiar with their scents after sniffing the ribbons the day before and wearing the medals around his neck ever since. Now George was ready to see if Porter recognized some of the men waiting at the train station as being those who had tried to kidnap him earlier that night. "We'll only go as far as the corner of the station and see if you and Porter recognize them," Pete said.

"I don't understand why we need Porter and George to go over there. It's too dangerous." Fredericka said, and the other ladies nodded in agreement. Gwen and Claudette had joined the group soon after Imogene arrived.

"If those guys aren't working for Roy McNeil, then giving them the note won't do us any good and could actually cause a big problem. I'm going with them," Pete said.

Fredericka, Gwen and Claudette allowed the plan to continue, especially after George got exasperated and told them it was his patriotic duty to go look, said he was going anyway.

"Porter and I say they're the same people." George, Porter and Pete returned from their reconnaissance mission. Porter had held his tongue, but George had something to say. "That kid over there? The shoeshine boy? I know him from school."

"What is a shoeshine boy doing out so late?" Charlie wondered.

"What do you bet he was working yesterday afternoon and saw the boys throw the medals away and then me pick them up out of the gutter and put them on Porter. He told those guys and that's why they tried to steal Porter?" George said.

"But why did they run after Lazarus and Gabriel to Pine Bluff?" Uwe asked.

"Probably he told them late, after they'd already chased off after them," George shrugged.

"He must be on their payroll," Marcel said.

"Where did this nice stationery come from?" Claudette wondered aloud as they consulted on the next phase of the plan. "Did somebody steal it? I hope not."

Suspecting the twins, Fredericka was glad to have somebody else hold the moral line with them for a change.

Gabriel and Lazarus were quiet. They had jimmied the lock to the store attached to the service station and removed notepaper, envelope and a pencil from the office. They'd freed up a flashlight also.

"The owner and I are friends. It'll be all right," Gwen remarked.

"You're sure this will appeal?" Gwen asked Imogene.

"While I have never spoken to him or laid eyes on him, yes I do. Vivian assured me that he is a lech," Imogene answered.

"All right then, let's get creative," Gwen said. She, Claudette, Fredericka and Imogene sorted through options, trying to strike the perfect tone.

"What you want." "I can give you what you want." "I want you." "Just you and me." "I'm waiting for you." "Run with me." "I'm ready."

Claudette read the finished product aloud. "Greetings to Goliath from Cupcake. I know what you want and I can give it to you. If you're interested, meet me on the big bridge at the Old Mill at 4 am. Come alone. I'll be waiting for you."

"That should do it," Pete said in approval.

They folded the paper and Imogene wrote "To Goliath" on the envelope and gave it to Marcel.

"It's a shot in the dark," Imogene said. "I don't know who or where Goliath is, but I think he lives in Little Rock."

Marcel rode off on George's bike to deliver the note.

"They're looking at it." He reported, returning by a back way.

A few minutes later Roland joined them. "Roy made a phone call."

"Okay, we have about an hour to get into place," Pete said.

"What if he doesn't show?" Uwe said.

"At least we'll get Roy and those thugs who tried to kidnap Porter, but I hope to hook a bigger fish," Pete said.

Fifteen minutes later they were in place in Old Mill Park. George proved to be an excellent guide. "I spend a lot of time here," he said. "I can show you all the best hiding places." Charlie stayed outside, hidden from view in the dense shrubbery lining the entrance.

Standing in the middle of the bridge overlooking the lake water exiting the mill, Imogene tried to read the luminescent dial of her watch. Three fifty a.m. Three fifty-five. Four a.m. No Goliath. Uwe looked at the sky, hoping Goliath would arrive before sunrise and avoid exposing their hiding places. Already the sky was starting to lighten.

Imogene was beginning to think Goliath was going to be a no-show when Charlie whistled a soft warning. A lone figure was walking down the stone steps into the park and onto the dirt path. He paused and then turned right towards the bridge. Shivers of fear ran through Imogene, but she squared her shoulders and tossed her head back. Uwe, Roland and Marcel were crouched out of sight, holding onto the outside of the bridge ready to catapult over. Pete was hidden in the crow's nest over the arched entrance to the bridge, poised to jump down on top of Goliath.

"Hi there," Imogene said, stepping forward.

"I'm pleased to finally meet you. You've done a lot of fine work for us."

"Thank you."

"So, you have something for me?" he said.

"Yes, do you have something for me?" Imogene responded.

He moved closer to her. Imogene started to unhook the medal from her pants waistband when shots rang out from behind the man. He collapsed on the ground shrieking and holding his arm as it pulsed spurts of blood.

At the first shot, Imogene hit the ground and started to crawl away, shots not being part of the plan, when she heard Charlie say, "Well done, sir. Well done."

Bill Edmund appeared at the entrance to the bridge gripping a woman by her arm. Edmund had wrested a pistol away from her. When she got closer, she looked at the man lying on the narrow floor of the bridge. Pete had jumped down from his hiding place and wrapped his handkerchief around the arm to staunch the bleeding.

Gripping his arm above the tourniquet, Max Manning met the woman's eye. "Why, Jean?" he gasped.

"Cupcake?" she said, her voice breaking.

64 MORALE WINS THE VICTORY

May 21. Old Mill Park. North Little Rock, Arkansas.

"Fredericka, let's run away, Uwe said. "Let's do it today." A train whistle sounded nearby. Dawn had arrived and the cream colored stonework in the park glowed golden in the morning light.

"Run away?" Fredericka repeated.

Uwe stared at his medal in his open palm. "Maybe it would be better if I did not wear any country's uniform," he said. "We could go far away, out west. California maybe. We could live in peace together. I could fix cars or something."

"Just you and me?" Fredericka said with a yearning in her voice.

"Maybe somewhere we could be married," he said.

Fredericka and Uwe looked up, distracted by wild barking. They watched Porter running circles around Charlie, who had further excited Porter by wheeling his chair after him. They were both thinking about how Charlie had lost his legs.

"It isn't over yet, is it?" he said.

"No it's not," Fredericka shook her head. "You have something to accomplish and so do I. I need to complete my college education. I want to become a teacher."

Uwe pulled Fredericka close for a long minute. She wiped her eyes but the tears kept coming. He patted her on the back but had to wipe his eyes too.

"You'll make an inspirational teacher, Fredericka."

"You're going to shake up the world, Ulysses."

The military police truck holding Roy, Max and Jean drove away. Bill Edmund and Pete were waiting. Edmund waved at Uwe. "Ready," he called.

Uwe paused a moment before walking towards Pete and Colonel Edmund.

"Ulysses?" Fredericka called.

He turned around.

Although Fredericka stood on the overlook, her back was to the view. "Maybe, when you're done doin' what you gotta do and I finish what I want to do, maybe things will be different," she said. "We could, you know, keep the door open, because when we're together I feel like…"

"Like we're in high cotton?" he asked, smiling and holding his arms out wide.

"Yes. That's it," she laughed.

"I will find you."

"I'll count on it."

Later that week Bill Edmund, Pete Peters and Uwe Johannes stood on the grass beside the tarmac at Little Rock's Adams Field. An airplane had taxied to a stop in front of them and a crew jumped forward to refuel. Meanwhile, the airplane door opened and a staircase unfolded. A tall, thin man stood at the entrance blinking in the bright sunlight. Although he wasn't old, his face was lined. He wore a dark suit, a white shirt and a black cord tie with a silver bolo. As he descended the stairs, his porkpie hat created a distinctive silhouette.

The man was traveling under the alias of Mr. Smith, but his real name was Robert Oppenheimer. He was traveling through from a quick trip to Washington, D.C. When Bill stepped forward to introduce himself, he was struck by the penetrating quality of the man's eyes. One look at them and it was clear that he was a person of deep intellect. Oppenheimer was en route to an obscure town in New Mexico near Santa Fe, and he had stopped to pick up a new colleague.

Uwe and Oppenheimer shook hands, unable to speak of anything beyond trivialities. Bill ushered them towards the airplane hanger's office. "I'm sorry we don't have more than this," Bill apologized as he passed around coffee poured from a thermos bottle.

Oppenheimer waved his hand, his mind far away. Smoke spiraled from his cigarette as he sipped the coffee.

The crew boss appeared in the doorway. "The plane's ready."

Uwe quickly shook hands with Colonel Edmund and Pete before boarding, the roar of the plane engines making conversation difficult. In fact, they had said their goodbyes at a little get together the night before.

Colonel Edmund and Pete watched the plane take off and disappear in the distance.

"Given our engineer's considerable ingenuity and perseverance," Edmund remarked, "I am confident a certain project just got a shot in the arm."

"And is the military decoration on the plane too? Pete asked.

"Oh, yes. I made sure of that."

"And I'm off the security detail!" Pete smiled.

"But you did it well, Peters."

They drove back to Camp Robinson, their thoughts turning to the future.

Uwe sat beside Oppenheimer on the fold down seat against the wall of the C-47.

"Welcome," Oppenheimer said. "Your work has been helpful. Heisenberg taught you well."

"Thank you, sir," Uwe said. "I'm looking forward to joining the effort."

Oppenheimer nodded before falling asleep as the plane took off and gained altitude.

Uwe looked down at the curving Arkansas River and the railroad bridges crossing it. The Holt's neighborhood was a speck. He thought what a relief it was not to be hunted by Russian spies and the US Army. The drone of the engines underscored the fact that he was still Ulysses the traveler, on the go again. How fitting that Cristobel had pulled his new name from the air that morning in the Holt's kitchen. It even flitted through his mind that she had been divinely inspired when she named him. He smiled to himself as he imagined Cristobel nodding her head at the idea. He thought about how far he had traveled and how much he had learned since those early days in the mountains with Heisenberg. This next step he was making seemed like a logical bookend to his work at the Kaiser Wilhelm Institute.

Observing Oppenheimer napping, Uwe thought the responsibility of the Manhattan Project must be exhausting. He looked forward to working collaboratively again, an impossibility for years, but he also knew what he was getting into. Leaning his head back against the wall of the plane, he thought about the numbers trickling in on the news reports, of millions of innocent people who had been mass murdered in concentration camps. Pushed deep down within him was the incompletely processed knowledge that his parents and sister Ursula were part of that large number. Now he was throwing himself into a plan that would create further mass casualties.

If the project were to be successful it would change the world in unimaginable ways, but he wanted to help end the war. He saw no other option but to go forward, and would give the project one hundred percent of his ability. It was something he felt he had to do. How to avoid getting in this position again, well, that would be the work of future statesmen and philosophers, their current course being charted. He thought about the question of future leaders. There would be no room for mistakes in selecting them because the consequences of failure would be too high. They would have to be people of the highest character.

The most lasting impression of his journey to date was the people he had met. Fredericka was never far from his thoughts. He remembered his near death experience at the Holy Ghost trial and his delivery from it. Uwe thought about Tom trying to save his brother and how that had led him to Project Stonehenge and now to the Manhattan Project. He thought about what Dwight had said about their witnessing miracles in Pine Bluff. Uwe had seen first hand the transformative power of the fair treatment of enemy soldiers, in spite of those soldiers' beliefs and values, in a prisoner of war camp. That had to have been a miracle. Maybe there was a chance that the sacrifices of so many would not have been in vain and that there was hope for a better world.

THE END

Notes
G. Weintraub
June 1, 1945

Kaspar Bauer: 30 yrs., Medical doctor. German POW Camp Rob.
Karl Becker: 25 yrs., Nazi agitator, German POW Camp Rob.
George Blackburn: 12 yrs., paperboy. Porter is Geo.'s dog.
Charlie Cartwright: 24 yrs. Wheelchair bound.
William "Bill" Edmund: 44 yrs. Col., State Dir. POW camps.
Ava Gilcrest: 40 yrs. Parishioner Christ the Redeemer Baptist Church, Pine Bluff, sister of Sheriff Alvin Lemoyne.
Daryl Green: 52 yrs. History of assault and battery, theft.
Werner Heisenberg: 44 yrs. German. Director Kaiser Wilhelm Institute. Berlin.
Holt Family: Jake, 69 yrs. Insurance agent. **Tina,** 60 yrs. Housewife.
 Mamie: 35 yrs. Lives with parents. Sec. Office Price Admin. Unmarried.
 Barkley: 33 yrs. Soldier. Deployed Europe. Married, one child.
 Tom: 31 yrs. Soldier. Deployed Pacific. Single.
 Luke: 25 yrs. Deployed Pacific. Surgeon. Single.
 Beryl Barkley: 58 yrs. T. Holt's sister. Teacher. Unmarried.
 Iva Lynn Jones: 90 yrs. Tina Holt's widowed aunt.
Pearl Jackson: 40 yrs. Parishioner Pine Bluff Mt. Zion AME.
 Guthrie: 16 yrs. Pearl's son.
Uwe Johannes: German POW. 28 yrs. Aka Ulysses Jones.
Marilyn Kenner: 35 yrs. Housewife.
 Abe: 15 yrs. Marilyn's son. Scipio Jones HS. Honor roll student.
Lionel King: 62 yrs. Blind. Broom salesman.
Lane Family: **Cristobel**. 40 yrs. Holt family housekeeper.
 Fredericka: 19 yrs. Student at Philander Smith College.
 Marcel: 16 yrs. Student Scipio Jones HS. Honor Roll.
 Roland: 15 yrs. Student Scipio Jones HS. Honor Roll.
Alvin Lemoyne: 41 yrs. Jefferson County Sheriff, Ava G's brother.
Roy McNeil: 43 yrs. Pine Bluff Arsenal employee.
Jean Manning: 51 yrs. Married to Max. M. Little Rock, prev. NYC.?
Maxwell Manning: 50 yrs. Little Rock, prev. NYC.?
Clyde Moore: 55 yrs. Choir dir. Christ the Redeemer Baptist Church, Pine Bluff.
Imogene Park: 18 yrs. Little Rock socialite.
Pete Peters: 25 yrs. Sergeant. Assist. Col. Edmund.
Claudette Reynolds: 23 yrs. Aka LaChar. Cousin to Holts. Sec. Col. Edmund.
Juanita Simmons: Teen. Victory Girl. Beebe, Ark.
Ernest Smith: 51 yrs. Pastor Pine Bluff Mt. Zion AME.
Vivian Taylor: 27 yrs. Little Rock socialite.
Walker Family: Opal, 30 yrs. Police record petty theft- NLR.
 Lazarus and **Gabriel**: Twins, 15 yrs. Student Scipio Jones HS-NLR.
Dwight Washington: 18 yrs.-cousin Laz. & Gab. Quarter-boat cook. Pine Bluff.
Walter Witte: 24 yrs. German POW Camp Rob.

Bibliography

The Unwomanly Face of War. An Oral History of Women in World War II. Alexievich, Svetlana. Random House. 2017.

American Prometheus, The Triumph and Tragedy of J. Robert Oppenheimer. Bird, Kai and Sherwin, Martin J. Alfred A. Knof. 2007.

We Were Each Other's Prisoners. An Oral History of World War II American and German Prisoners of War. Carlson, Lewis H. BasicBooks, A Division of HarperCollins Publishers. 1997.

Double Agent. The First Hero of World War II and how the FBI Outwitted and Destroyed a Nazi Spy Ring. Duffy, Peter. Scribner. 2014.

Dunger, JP, Gaines, Elizabeth. Personal communication. Arkansas Railroad Museum. March 10, 2018.1700 Port Rd, Pine Bluff, AR 71601.

No Time For Fear. Voices of American Military Nurses In World War II. Fessler, Diane Burke. Michigan State University Press. 1996.

Hays, Patrick. NLR AR. Mayor. Personal communication. 2017 and 2018.

Hitler's Last Soldier In America. Gaertner, Georg with Arnold Krammer. Stein and Day, 1985.

German POWs on the American Homefront. Garcia, J. Malcolm. Smithsonian.com. 2009.

Now It Can Be Told. The Story of the Manhattan Project. Groves, Leslie R. Harper & Row, Publishers. 1962.

Recollections of a life with Werner Heisenberg. Heisenberg, Elisabeth. Birkauser. 1984.

Across the Frontiers. 1990. Heisenberg, Werner. Ox Bow Press. 1990.

Douglas MacArthur. American Warrior. Herman, Arthur. Random House. 2016.

Physics and Beyond. Encounters and Conversations. Heisenberg, Werner. Volume Forty-Two of World Perspectives. Harper & Row, Publishers. 1971.

German POWs, Der Ruf, and the Genesis of Group 47. Horton, Aaron D. Fairleigh Dickinson University Press and Rowman & Littlefield. 2014.

Horton, Aaron D. Personal communication. 2016.

On Shipboard with German Prisoners. Humphrey, Yvonne. E. The American Journal of Nursing, Vol. 43, No. 9. Lippincott Wiliams & Wilkins. 1943.

Stark Decency. German Prisoners of War in a New England Village. Koop, Allen V. University Press of New England. 1988.

Nazi Prisoners of War in America. Krammer, Arnold. Scarborough House. 1996.

Krammer, Arnold. Personal communication. 2017.

The FBI-KGB War. A Special Agent's Story. Lamphere, Robert J. and Schachtman, Tom. Random House. 1986.

Reminiscences. General of the Army. MacArthur, Douglas. Time, Inc. McGraw-Hill Book Company. 1964.

The Deadly Brotherhood. The American Combat Soldier In World War II. MacManus, John C. Presidio Press 505. 1998.

Hildegard of Bingen, The Woman of Her Age. Maddocks, Fiona. Doubleday. 2001.

Arkansas's Reaction to the Men Who Said "No" to World War II. Morris, Cynthia Hastas. The Arkansas Historical Quarterly. Arkansas Historical Association. 1984.

The Alsos Mission. Pash, Boris T. Charter. 1969.

Judging Jehovah's Witnesses: religious persecution and the dawn of the rights revolution. Peters, Shawn Francis. The University Press of Kansas. 2000.

Prisoners of War at Camp Robinson-A Document. Volume 39. The Pulaski County Historical Review. 1991.

The Afrika Korps in Arkansas, 1943-1946. Pritchett, Merrill R. and Shea, William L. The Arkansas Historical Quarterly. Arkansas Historical Association. 1978.

A German Prisoner of War in the South: The Memoir of Edwin Pelz. Shea, William and Pelz, Edwin. The Arkansas Historical Quarterly. Arkansas Historical Association. 1985.

Bedpan Commando. The Story of a Combat Nurse during World War II. Wandrey, June. Elmore Publishing Company. 1980.

http://www.encyclopediaofarkansas.net..

http://www.macarthurmemorial.org.

ABOUT THE AUTHOR

Rachel A. Goss is a fifth generation Arkansan. She received an AB degree from Washington University in St. Louis, majoring in English Literature and Biology, and she has a Master of Science in Biology from Texas A&M University. Her interest in ethics, scientific research, local and world history intersect in *Driven by Conscience.*

Made in the USA
San Bernardino, CA
12 May 2020